THE MOST DANGEROUS OF OTHERS

I tried to find the words to speak, to tell Royce to stop, but all I could manage was a feeble cry when he took hold of my wrists, pulling my hands off his chest and pressing them to the wall. He said nothing, simply studied me while that gibbering terror romping through my mind didn't want to acknowledge that he hadn't hurt me yet. It only wanted to focus on the fact that I was pinned, he looked ravenous, I was the only human in sight, and his fangs were literally inches away from some all too vulnerable parts of my body. Places where the blood runs hot and fast and close to the surface of the skin.

Why was he doing this? What did he want from me? Panic clawed at my throat, and as he leaned in, his lips brushing against the side of my neck, I found my voice again, letting loose with a shriek as I twisted away. He was going to bite me!

"I'd never hurt you," he whispered, his voice low and soothing. He didn't touch me save for the velvet soft brush of his lips against my skin, followed by the brief rake of fangs. Hinting at penetration, but never quite sinking in. It was enough to drag a little cry from my lips, too breathy to properly be called a scream. I thought I might just die of fright right then, closing my eyes and trying to remember how to breathe as my heart tried to pound its way out of my chest.

"You could stay young and beautiful and strong forever," Royce whispered. "With me. Think about it . . ."

Books by Jess Haines

HUNTED BY THE OTHERS

TAKEN BY THE OTHERS

DECEIVED BY THE OTHERS*

Collections

NOCTURNAL
(with Jacquelyn Frank,
Kate Douglas, and Clare Willis)

Published by Kensington Publishing Corporation

*Coming soon

TAKEN BY THE OTHERS

JESS HAINES

ZEBRA BOOKS
KENSINGTON PUBLISHING CORP.
http://www.kensingtonbooks.com

ZEBRA BOOKS are published by

Kensington Publishing Corp.
119 West 40th Street
New York, NY 10018

All Kensington titles, imprints, and distributed lines are available at special quantity discounts for bulk purchases for sales promotion, premiums, fund-raising, educational, or institutional use.

Special book excerpts or customized printings can also be created to fit specific needs. For details, write or phone the office of the Kensington Special Sales Manager: Attn. Special Sales Department. Kensington Publishing Corp., 119 West 40th Street, New York, NY 10018. Phone: 1-800-221-2647.

Zebra and the Z logo Reg. U.S. Pat. & TM Off.

ISBN-13: 978-1-4201-1188-0
ISBN-10: 1-4201-1188-4

First Printing: January 2011
10 9 8 7 6 5 4 3 2 1

Printed in the United States of America

Chapter 1

I don't usually have people pointing guns in my face. Or in my direction at all, really. I'm a private detective, so I know some people have certainly *thought* about shooting me after I reported their illicit activities to my clients or the cops, but looking down the barrel of a .45 was a new experience for me.

"Jack, can we talk about this without the gun?"

Jack was precisely as I remembered him. Tall, slender, with close-cropped blond hair and the coldest blue eyes I'd ever seen. His long-sleeved flannel shirt was rolled up to just above his elbows and left unbuttoned for easy access to his shoulder holster. He's clean-cut, looks like the poster boy for some white bread good ol' boy magazine, and crazy as a loon. He belongs to a group of extremists and vigilante vampire hunters who call themselves the White Hats.

His thin lips quirked in a polite smile. No real emotion shone through the empty mask. I was praying he was just using some of his psycho scare tactics again. I deeply regretted leaving my own guns in my bedroom all the way across town. Fat lot of good they did me there. Maybe I should have our receptionist frisk the clients before letting them into my office from now on.

"Shiarra, I'm disappointed. I've left you a number of invitations to come work with us. Why didn't you get back to me? Did you succumb to Royce after the little fiasco this spring?"

That again. A few months ago I took a job I should've known to leave well enough alone. When your business is failing and someone offers you a lot of money, sometimes you do stupid things. For example, you accept a job trying to find some powerful magic artifact that a vampire was hiding from a bunch of magi. I suppose you could call accepting a proposition like that suicidal. These days, I just called it a bad business decision.

"No, I haven't gone to see Royce since the fight at his restaurant." One little white lie couldn't hurt. He'd come to see me, not the other way around. I'd stringently avoided Royce since the day I got home from the hospital, when he visited to apologize and thank me in his own way for pulling his ass out of the fire. "Listen, I don't deal in that shit anymore. Once was enough."

"You've taken on clients, done other jobs for supernaturals since your recovery. You have strong ties to two of the most powerful Were packs in the Five Boroughs. You're linked to the most influential vampire in the state. We need your expertise, and your connections."

The only reason the Moonwalker tribe had anything to do with me was because, like Royce, I had saved their butts from a crazy power-hungry sorcerer. They owed me. The only reason the Sunstriker tribe had anything to do with me was because the leader of the pack was my boyfriend. Aside from that, the occasional (nondangerous) case notwithstanding, I tried to keep my connections to anything furry or with fangs to a minimum.

I took a deep breath to steady myself while I thought about how to get Jack to get the hell out of my office, and take his gun with him. He'd tried this tactic before; I wondered why he'd never figured out that waving a weapon in someone's face was not a good way to get them to cooperate with you for any length of time. "You know I don't like vampires. I don't have much to do with Weres anymore either. I don't take jobs that have anything to do with the supernatural, no matter what the papers say about me."

"You have the equipment and connections to be a hunter." He frowned. "We need you. I won't have you going to them, taking their side."

"Whoa now, who said anything about that?"

His eyes narrowed, something passing through them I couldn't read. "There's a new player in the game. It'll be down to him or Royce. Or us."

I stared blankly. "Who?"

"Word on the street is that Max Carlyle is coming to town." He stared back, expectantly.

Silence. After a moment decidedly lacking any explanations, I urged him along. "And he is?"

"You really don't know?"

"Would I ask if I did?"

He grinned; the flash of white teeth against his pale skin was ominous. Predatory. Too much like the things he hunted—vampires.

"My, my. I hate to spoil the surprise." One hand reached up to rub his smooth-shaven jaw while he stared at me. After another long, drawn-out moment of silence, he raised the gun, thumbed on the safety, and tucked it away in its holster under his flannel shirt. "Ms. Waynest, again I must apologize for my methods. Unfortunately, your reputation leads me to worry about what needs to be done to ensure you're playing on the right side of the field."

Holding a knife to my throat in the dead of night after breaking into my bedroom didn't exactly give me warm fuzzies, and neither did holding a gun on me in broad daylight. I was hoping my expression was more neutral than pissed, but I wasn't holding my breath.

"Look, for the last time—I don't want anything to do with

Others. I don't talk to Royce, I don't give a shit what the White Hats are doing, and I'm not about to do the tango with things that could eat me for breakfast. I'm a private detective, and that's all. Someone go missing? Think your girlfriend is cheating on you? Great, I'll go look for them. But I will *not*," I stressed, leaning forward across the desk and pointing one admonishing finger in his direction, "be bullied into dealing with vampires and Weres again. Coming close to dying once was enough. You can't pay me enough to put my life on the line. Not again."

"Oh, don't worry, Ms. Waynest. They'll be coming to you soon enough. And once they do, you'll come running to us for help."

I stood, a thread of fear trailing down my spine, even as I finally boiled over. I pointed at the door. "Get the hell out of my office! Stay away from me!"

He swung the door open and sauntered out of the room, his cool, arrogant laughter trailing behind him. My glare stayed trained on him until his shadowed frame was no longer visible behind the frosted glass of the front door.

Jen twisted around in her chair to peer into my office, staring at me with wide brown eyes over the rims of her glasses. "Jeez, Shia, what was that all about?"

I shook my head. "Nothing. But if he comes back, or tries to make another appointment, I'm out of the office. No—out of the country."

She shrugged, muttered something, and turned back to her desk to work on the stack of papers in front of her. I glared at the frosted glass door with its gold leaf–inscribed H&W INVESTIGATIONS, even though Jack was long gone.

As much as he pissed me off, he scared me more. Or maybe him saying the Others would come looking for me scared me more. Hell, I think I was entitled to be a little un-settled considering I'd had a gun waved in my face. Irri-tated and upset, I twisted around, calling over my shoulder as I shut the door, "Hold my calls. If anyone asks, I've gone home for the day."

Some preventative measures needed to be taken about this Max Carlyle, I thought. I sat in the squeaky office chair, rolling it back so I could riffle through the back of the top drawer. After rummaging through a scattering of old Post-it notes, paper clips, pens, and papers, I finally found the leather-bound notebook I kept business cards filed in.

I flipped through the pages until I found the neat, professional card for A.D. Royce Industries. It had all the data I needed to contact Alec Royce, the vampire I'd been doing my best to avoid for the past several months. The one I'd ended up legally, contractually, bound to, and who'd been sending me invitations to nights on the town and, presumably, other things. All of which I'd carefully ignored up until now.

Daylight still shone through the window behind my desk, but I figured I could leave a message if he didn't pick up. I grabbed my cell, dug the card out of the little plastic holder, and dialed the handwritten number scrawled on the back.

Tucking the phone between my head and shoulder, I fixed my eyes on the framed photograph of Chaz and me on the corner of my desk. We were leaning back against the rail together at the end of the pier in Greenport and his arms were wrapped around me. I tried not to think about what Chaz would say about me calling the vamp, listened to the ringing, and finally, a click. "You've reached the desk of Alec Royce. I'm not in right now, but if you leave a message with your name and number, I'll get back to you."

That mild, friendly voice gave me the shivers, worse than anything that Jack had said or done. Did I really want to get back in touch with the vampire? After swallowing hard and hesitating a bit longer than I should have, I remembered I was supposed to be leaving a message and squeaked out a few words.

"Yeah, Mr. Royce, this—it's Shiarra Waynest. I'd like to ask you a couple of questions. I might need your help with something." I left him my cell number and was about to hang up, hesitated again, and added, "Thanks."

I hung up and set the phone down, wondering if I'd done the right thing. Damn it all to hell and back, I was putting myself back in the fire by contacting him again. Regardless, I needed to know who Max Carlyle was, and what sort of danger he represented. Since Jack specifically brought up Royce when talking about Max, I had to hope Royce would have some idea about what was going on. After all, he was an elder, influential vamp. He had all sorts of connections that informed him well ahead of time when somebody gunned for him or planned to do something that would affect him or his properties. I knew at least that much about him from prior experience.

Depending on what Royce told me, I might have to lie low and hide somewhere out of town for a few days. Or a few months. Whatever would keep my ass out of the fire.

Chapter 2

I stayed late in the office. Sara, my business partner, was out of town until Sunday. Jen had gone home hours ago. The office was dark, the only light a small lamp illuminating the pictures I had spread out across my desk. Since it was Friday, I'd made plans with my boyfriend, but for later, when I got off work. Chaz would pick up dinner and come to my place around eight. Until then, I wanted to keep busy rather than sit around worrying about what big bad monster was coming to town this time.

The photographs in front of me were arranged in a series, laid out carefully next to a detailed inventory of stock. An insurance agent had called me in to investigate one of her clients. Jeremy Pryce claimed his company warehouse, which had a large store of valuable designer clothes, had burned down in an accident. The fire department had closed its investigation into the cause, reporting that faulty electrical work set off sparks during a thunderstorm and sent the whole building up in flames.

The agent, Cheryl Benedict, was convinced that Pryce had rigged the fire somehow. I didn't know who tipped her off, but she was right. The pictures in front of me were the ones I'd taken over the last two weeks of Mr. Pryce giving gifts to different beautiful women—women who were definitely not his wife. Unsurprisingly, the gifts were clothes—designer ones, as a matter of fact. Many matching the exact descriptions in the inventory of everything that supposedly went up in flames two months ago.

"Gotcha." I grinned, carefully ticking off and noting everything claimed destroyed that appeared in the photographs.

When I was about halfway through my notations, my cell phone belted out Beethoven's Fifth. An unknown caller.

I picked it up, glancing at the window and noting the sun had nearly set. There were a few last rays turning everything a golden hue at the edges and leaving deep shadows between buildings.

"Hello?"

"Ms. Waynest," Royce's voice was smooth and cordial. "You do have the most fortuitous timing. I was beginning to think you were avoiding me."

I cringed. My, how perceptive. I bit my tongue to keep from saying that thought out loud. Wasn't it too early for him to be up and about? "I heard from a little bird today that someone of interest to both of us is coming to town. Know anything about that?"

He laughed softly, the sound at once delightful and dreadful. Something that evil shouldn't sound so good. "Someone told you about Max Carlyle, I take it?"

"Yeah. Who is he?"

"Not someone to discuss over the phone. I will tell you everything you need to know if you meet with me."

Uh-oh. "You know what, this was a mistake. Never mind, I'll figure it out myself."

Before he could say anything, I ended the call and turned the cell off. Vampires were manipulative bastards, Royce worst of all. He made no secret of his interest in me despite knowing I had a boyfriend. Even worse, Royce had blackmailed me into signing one of those contracts that made it legal for him to drink my blood, turn me into a vampire, or even murder me with no consequences. All fabulous reasons to keep him as far away from me as possible.

The only good thing about that contract was that, due to the way it was worded, I could also hurt or kill him if it came down to it. My partner Sara had helped see to that. The only problem was that I wasn't nearly confident enough that I could hurt or kill him without some help from outside sources. I suppose I shouldn't complain, though. Most contracts didn't offer that luxury, leaving the signed human stuck in the crappy position of facing death—or worse—at the hands of their host. If they tried to fight back when they decided they didn't want to play the part of midnight snack anymore, they could look forward to some jail time and a hefty fine.

Some people (read: anyone but me) would love to be in the position I'm in, seeing as how Alec Royce is one of the most high-profile vampires in the United States. He's got a power base that extends through most of New York, New Jersey, and Connecticut. Any vampire within his territory is required to get his permission to do so much as blow their nose. Okay, maybe not to that extent, but they were supposed to get his permission to hunt outside their territory, turn anyone else into a vampire, or do anything that might be construed as expanding their own power bases. He also oversaw all purchases or sales of buildings, land, or other valuable properties. Not to mention he owned a string of the hottest nightclubs and restaurants in the city. There were probably other businesses he dipped his fingers into, but publicly he was known for the clubs and eateries.

Royce even posted a calendar on his Web site of his scheduled appearances at his various establishments. Yes, a vampire celebrity with a Web site, what a novelty. When I first met him, I'd used that as a tool to figure out where to find him. These days, I also used it to figure out where *not* to be when I needed to check out the club scene in search of cheating lovers or shady business partners.

Some of the crazies like Jack the White Hat probably used it to find ways to corner or hurt him. The police have done more to protect the Others in the last few years, cracking down on the overzealous groups like the White Hats. In addition, Royce and a few other supernaturals had slapped lawsuits on those who discriminated against or attacked them, further curbing such delightful White Hat activities as burning down known Other establishments and hangouts, riots, beatings, even murder. That didn't stop all of them, of course, but things were starting to settle down and the anti-Other crowd was beginning to look worse than the creatures they hated so much.

Sometimes the Others gave the general human populace good reason to be afraid of them. Despite their nature, they had rights now, and could walk the street like anyone else, but having legal citizenship didn't do a thing to change the fact that Weres and vampires and even magi were monsters straight out of fairy tales. Weres could tear you apart bare-handed, even when they weren't shifted. Vampires survived by drinking blood. Magi could twist and bend reality to their whims.

None of those were human traits, and even when you did your best to put those things aside, they would always be dangerous and inhuman.

Six months earlier, I'd seen firsthand how horrifically inhuman they were. I would carry scars across my chest and stomach until the day I die thanks to fighting with a crazy sorcerer, his bitch of a vampire girlfriend, the leader of the Moonwalker tribe, and last but certainly not least, Alec Royce.

I did not want to deal with other supernaturals. It was more than the scars left behind from my last up-close and personal experience. These things are scary. Some of them enjoy eating people. You don't fool around with monsters like that voluntarily unless you know you'll come out on top. Even then, your judgment would be questionable, at least in my book.

With those thoughts in mind, it no longer felt like such a great idea to be in my office all by myself after hours. Deciding the rest of my work could wait until Monday, I scooped up the Pryce paperwork, tucked it all back in its file, and tossed it into my pending basket on the corner of my desk. There were other businesses in the building, but they were mostly marketing firms and dentist offices, and I doubted anyone else was here this late on a Friday.

Grabbing my purse, cell, and keys, I turned off all the lights, set the alarm, and headed down to my car. Once in the parking lot, huddling in my jacket against the chill autumn wind, I thought about Chaz. He was my boyfriend, yes, but he was also a Were. Did I really want to have a werewolf alone with me in my apartment after tonight?

Yes. Yes I did. Unlike a human, Chaz had kept me safe from some threats that were too much for a deadbolt or a burglar alarm to keep out. There were some perks to having a monster on your side.

Not that I'd ever call him a monster to his face.

No matter how well behaved he might be, I knew it was there. I'd seen it. Touched it. Rolled my fingers through the fur, felt the weight of that not-man, not-wolf body. Known that, if not for his control over the pack he led, I'd have been nothing more than food to the rest of them. I'd also watched him fight another shifted Were, one much bigger and scarier than he was, keeping it away from me long enough to save everyone's ass.

Chaz had also been useful in tracking down some of my clients' marks. After the showdown against David Borowsky and his band of enslaved Weres made the news, a whole bunch of Others contacted H&W seeking our services. Sara and I decided we'd take the work, as long as it didn't look too risky, unlike the majority of PI firms who won't touch anything Other-related. I don't have as much of an issue helping Weres and magi as I used to, though vampires still go to the back of the line. And for the most part, I don't socialize with Others, since I still consider the majority of them scarier than Michael Myers with a machete and a grudge.

Chaz is the exception to my "keep the hell away from anything with fur or fangs" policy. Since he'd saved my life, it was hard to think of him as a bad guy. And we'd dated before, until he revealed what he was after we'd been together four or five months, and I freaked out and dumped him. This was admittedly a stupid move on my part. I came to realize this when I finally saw past my own blind idiocy that he cared about me and was showing me he trusted me with knowing what he was. Of course, it took him rescuing me, and helping me save Sara from the clutches of a mad sorcerer, to bring me around, but hey, at least I saw past the fur. Right?

We weren't contracted. I refused to sign the papers that opened me up to being changed into a werewolf. It also meant we couldn't do the nasty, but that didn't bug me so much. Chaz hasn't been brave enough to bring the subject up again, and I was happy to put off making a decision that involved the possibility of me being turned into an Other for as long as possible.

Contracts were all that saved humans from indiscriminately being eaten or injured by Others. The laws governing the wording of the contracts also made it abundantly clear that no Other was to chance turning a human, accidentally or otherwise, into one of their own. Given the passions attendant to things like sex and feeding, it prevented any Other from getting intimate with a human until they had all their legal ducks in a row.

In other words, Chaz and I might hug or kiss each other, but if we were going to do the horizontal tango, it would require a far greater commitment to him than I was willing to give at the moment. Dating was one thing—the kind of courage it would take to put my life in his hands quite another.

After mulling all this over, I realized that Chaz might know something about this Max Carlyle guy. He didn't speak of it often but I knew he kept on top of the supernatural community's secret goings-on. I figured I'd ask him about it when he came by later that night.

The whole ride home, I wondered who this Max person was, and what he wanted with me. Also, why did Jack care so much about me? Even though my business would be a great front for the mostly illegal activities of the White Hats, it didn't explain why he kept pestering me or why he considered me such a threat. What connection did he have with Max Carlyle, if any? What was the connection between this newcomer and Alec Royce?

None of these questions could be answered easily, which didn't improve my mood. By the time I pulled into my parking space at home, I'd resolved that tonight was going to be a stress-free evening with my boyfriend and that I'd worry about it all tomorrow.

Chapter 3

By nine thirty, I was getting pissed. Chaz was supposed to have shown up hours ago. He wasn't picking up when I called. I'd turned my cell back on once I got home—no missed calls, voice mails, or text messages. Nothing on the answering machine at home. I even checked my e-mail—nothing but spam. That made two no-call-no-shows from him so far this month.

Where was he?

The last time it happened, he said it was pack business. Nothing to worry myself about. Something unavoidable. Something like when he called in his pack mates to help deal with David Borowsky, psychotic sorcerer extraordinaire, and his unwilling pack of lap-Weres. Nothing I wanted to get involved in, or know anything about.

After a while, annoyed and tired of waiting, I ordered Chinese from down the street and sat down in front of my computer. Curiosity getting the better of me, I did a Web search for any information about Max Carlyle. Nothing came up except hits that I was pretty sure had nothing to do with the person Jack had been talking about. A movie character? Surely not.

I leaned back in the chair and stared at the ceiling. Royce

knew something about this guy. Jack knew something about this guy. The idea of talking to either one of them wasn't appealing. Chaz might know something, but I was more than a little ticked off at his inability to pick up a phone to call me and say, "Sorry, honey, running late," or even a simple "An emergency came up, I won't be around." For his sake, his butt better be rotting in a gutter somewhere or I was seriously going to rip him a new one the next time I saw him.

Out of my three choices, Royce seemed the least offensive of the bunch. Chaz would hate that I'd called him. He'd hate it even more if I set up a meeting with him.

I reached for my cell.

"Well, this is decidedly unexpected," came the dryly amused response from the other end of the line.

"Yeah, I know. I'm sorry about what I said, and hanging up on you earlier."

"An apology?" he said, his quiet laughter making me grit my teeth. "I must admit, I did not anticipate this from you."

"Listen, I know I made a mistake. You don't have to rub it in. Are you still willing to meet with me or not?"

"Of course. We'll put that little faux pas behind us. I realize it may be a trifle late for you, but I would suggest we meet as soon as possible so you understand what you will be dealing with once Max gets into town. What would be convenient for you?"

I spoke without thinking. "You know where my apartment is. Why don't you just come over?"

"I need to wrap some things up at the office, but I can be there in about an hour."

"Okay. See you then."

After he hung up, I stared at the cell phone cradled in my hand. I'd just invited Alec Royce, the oldest and most powerful vampire in the United States, to come to my apartment.

Guess it beat waiting for Chaz to show up.

With that thought in mind, I got off my butt and started

tidying up the place. I shoved loose papers lying around on my desk into a drawer and turned off the computer monitor. I loaded the dishes piled in the sink into the dishwasher, then grabbed my shoes from by the door and my jacket off the arm of the couch and tossed them in the bedroom closet. I figured that would do well enough for the fastidious Royce.

Part of me even wanted to pass by the mirror to see how I looked. The rest of me knew it was stupid and that this was for unofficial business, not a client or even a friend. Besides, I didn't want to give Royce the wrong idea. As good as the vampire looked, he *was* a vampire. You know the sort. The typical tall, dark, and handsome man who also happens to be an evil, bloodsucking creature of the night. Not the type of guy you take home to Mom. Not like Chaz.

Figuring it wouldn't hurt to take some precautions, I dug into my dresser and pulled out one of my guns. I'd picked them up way back when I thought Royce was trying to kill me. Turned out at the time Royce just wanted to make me his living slave and it was someone else who was out to kill me. Funny how these things turn out.

While I was in the drawer, I ran my fingertips over the leather belt with three matching silver stakes in their sheaths. I could literally *feel* discontent radiating from the thing.

"Sorry," I said, feeling more apologetic toward the inanimate object than I was toward the vampire a few minutes ago. "Maybe after Royce is gone, I'll take you out. Not right now."

There was a brief sense of anger, but the bad vibes and discontent dissipated. Still, I could practically hear it grumbling. The spirit inhabiting the thing was not happy being cooped up in my drawer. Sometimes I took it out and wore it around the apartment when I was alone. The only way for it to experience life was through the one wearing it, and I was the first person to take any notice of what it wanted for

the last fifteen years or so. It had been a while since the
last time I took it out. I felt bad leaving it rotting with my
winter clothes, but I couldn't exactly walk around the city
with a bunch of deadly weapons wrapped around my waist.

Then again, this *was* New York.

Whatever. I'd worry about the belt's hurt feelings later,
after I was done dealing with Royce. Sliding the drawer
shut, I headed out to the living room and set the gun on an
end table. Just in case the vamp got any funny ideas. I
wasn't as good a shot without the belt, but I figured the visible threat would serve better than any words I could dish
out. Aside from which, if it got to the point where I needed
to use the gun to deal with Royce, I was royally screwed
anyway.

Next came perfume. I went into the bathroom and dug
around under the sink until I found one of the small glass
vials that held cinnamon- and clove-scented liquid. It
gleamed a pale golden hue in the harsh fluorescent light.
Dabbing a couple of drops onto my wrist, I rubbed it into
the skin and then applied some to my throat, right above the
pulse point.

The Amber Kiss perfume was a concoction made by
some alchemists centuries ago that keeps Others from
being able to pick up the wearer's scent and suppresses the
appetite of a vampire. It makes me smell less like food, ba-
sically. I liked the way the stuff smelled, though Chaz
didn't and complained that it made him sneeze. I didn't
need it to protect against him, of course, but I would wear
it if it worked on vamps and other, hungrier, Weres. Fortu-
nately for me, my encounters with such creatures were in-
frequent enough that I had a supply to last a few lifetimes.

Lastly, I adjusted the little black charm I was wearing so it
lay hidden under my blouse. According to Arnold, it kept magi
and vamps from using their mind-mojo on me.

Arnold, Sara's current beau, had given me all of the stuff I
used as protection against Others. He also happened to be

head of the security section for The Circle, the East Coast's premier coven of actively practicing magi.

Frankly, I wouldn't be alive right now if not for all the help Arnold had given me the last few months. It was with the help of his magic, his ideas, and his choice of weaponry that I made it out on top fighting against the Borowsky kid and his girlfriend. I was also glad Arnold and Sara had hooked up. They'd taken a much-needed vacation out to Sara's property in the Hamptons for the last two weeks and were due back on Sunday. I wouldn't pester him with questions until they were back. Hopefully Royce would be co-operative enough as to let me know exactly what was going on before I had to resort to bugging Arnold about it. Knowing the vampire, I wouldn't hold my breath.

I knew very well that Royce's modus operandi was essentially "manipulate first, ask questions later." He'd see my contacting him as an opportunity of some kind and use it to the hilt. The only question was how he intended to go about it. I'd have to be on my toes to make sure I didn't fall for any of his tricks or machinations.

Like it or not, we were still contractually bound. As far as I knew, we were not in any danger that might lead him to needing me or my skill set. However, there was a chance he might try to talk me into working for him. I had the feeling he was afraid of me, and that was why he was always trying to find a way to get me under his thumb. Better to control that which you fear than be ruled by it, right? Was I playing right into his clutches by inviting him over?

Well, yes.

However, unlike the first few times we'd met, this time I knew exactly what he was capable of and would be on guard. I'd been able to avoid his manipulations in the past, so with some ingenuity, a little luck, and by keeping alert for his tricks, I should be able to do it again.

While I rubbed the last little bit of the Amber Kiss into

my skin, I could hear my cell chiming from the other room.
A text message.

When I opened it up, I saw it was from Chaz. I glanced
at the time; it was already past eleven. Bastard.

**SORRY ABOUT 2NITE. PACK EMERG. WILL
CALL U LATER. RAIN CHECK 4 SAT? LOVE U.**

Disgusted, I tossed the phone back down on the table.
He was three hours late getting back to me. I'd answer him
when I was good and ready.

Muttering darkly, I huffed over to the couch and sat
down. I flicked on the TV but didn't focus on the screen
as I stared. I wasn't sure why I was so mad. I mean, things
came up at work all the time that made me late for our
dates. It wasn't entirely fair of me to be pissed at him for
putting his responsibility to his pack first—but I could not
let go of my anger.

About five minutes after I sat down, I heard a brisk
rapping. I remembered the Chinese food I'd ordered that
felt like a decade ago, and my stomach growled right
on cue.

"One sec, be right there!" I jumped up and hurried to
the door, snagging up my purse on the way to pay the delivery guy.

I pulled open the door, and was met by the glowing red
eyes and bared fangs of a very pissed-off-looking vampire.

Chapter 4

I screamed and backpedaled as the vamp reached out for me, tripping over my own feet and landing on my ass as he was blasted back by the shields Arnold had thoughtfully installed for me.

"Fuck!" the thing exclaimed, bringing singed, reddened fingers to its mouth to suck on.

I couldn't help but stare, open-mouthed, wondering where the hell this guy had come from. Supernatural power aside, he was built like a linebacker and looked like he could have snapped me in two without breaking a sweat while he was still alive. Trying to contemplate how strong he must be now with added vampiric strength was terrifying.

"Who the hell are you?"

He looked up from his injured hands to glare at me, his eyes still glowing that fierce red. I flinched when he raised a fist the size of my head to send a shockwave through the barrier as he punched it. "Come to me!" he demanded, staring right into my eyes.

I couldn't help but bark out a short laugh. "Are you crazy? I'm staying right here. Well, not right here." I struggled up to my feet with as much grace as I could muster, backing up a bit more from the door for good measure. I trusted Arnold's skills, but I wasn't sure how much physical force the barrier could withstand. This would be the first time it had been put to the test against forced entry, so I wanted to have some distance between us in case the thing gave out. "Get out of here! Leave me alone!"

His face twisted in confusion, some of the anger dwindling out of his eyes. "I said come here. Why aren't you obeying me?"

"Gee, I don't know. Maybe because I think you're a freaking lunatic?"

His shoulders slumped, his eyes turning a warm, chocolate brown, a slightly darker shade than his hair. His hair was short, but he ran his hands through it in a nervous gesture, like he was used to it being longer. "Well, that's never happened before. Uhm. Look at me! That's right, look right into my eyes. Now—come *here!*" he demanded again, this time with a touch of desperation.

It'd be sort of funny and corny if I hadn't realized he was trying to use a *very* illegal black enchant to get me to do his bidding. All praise for the good luck charms given to me courtesy of The Circle, bless their magic little hearts.

"No," I said flatly, regaining some of my confidence since both the shields and my charm looked to be holding up just fine. "Who are you? What do you want?"

He scratched the side of his head, looking puzzled. I started edging toward the table with my cell phone and the gun on it.

"Well, shoot. I really didn't want to do this. Thought this was just gonna be some quick smash-and-grab."

Exasperated, I repeated myself. "Hello? Who sent you? What do you want from me?"

"Max Carlyle wants you. I'm one of his assistants, Peter. He sent me to come get you." He brightened up some, sounding hopeful. "Don't suppose you'd come along willingly, would you?"

My God, this guy was dumber than a box of rocks.

"Not after that little show of temper," I said.

"Damn!"

"So, get the fuck out. Go away. If Max Carlyle wants to talk to me, tell him to just call my fucking office to arrange an appointment like everybody else," I said, grabbing my phone. "If you don't leave in the next ten seconds, I'm calling the cops."

"They can't do anything to me. No human is strong enough to take me on."

"Good for you," I muttered, shaking my head at his naïveté. He must be newly turned. Like within the last few days newly turned to be this stupid. Guess he hadn't heard that it was now standard issue for cops to carry crosses and holy water with the rest of their equipment.

I could practically picture a dim lightbulb buzzing to life above his head, his look suddenly going sly. His voice turned sickly sweet, cajoling. "You've got to come out of there sometime. Why don't you come along now and make this easier on everyone?"

Yeah, like he could possibly sweet-talk me after flashing fangs. "Give me a break. Look, fang-boy, I'm not interested. If you hadn't gone all vampire-y on me, maybe I would've listened to what you had to say. As it is, I'll be calling the police now." I started dialing, staring at him, free hand braced on my hip as I waited on hold for an operator to pick up. It didn't take long.

"Hi, I've got a vampire who's threatening me and trying to break into my apartment." The angry epithets and pounding sounds followed by pained howls must have sounded awfully funny to the operator on the other end of the line. "Could you guys get here quick? I could really use some help. Here's the address . . ."

I hung up while the operator was still sounding completely frazzled, telling me to "stay calm" and that "help was on its way." I was more interested in what Peter was up to. Tilting my head to the side, I examined the vampire, who was alternately cursing the pain in his hands and still trying to find a crack in the defenses around my door.

"Not the brightest crayon in the box, are you?"

He glared at me, a glimmer of red returning to his eyes. "Shut up! Max said you were a troublemaker, not a bitch."

"Guess he didn't hear I'm a New Yorker."

Peter was abruptly jerked backward off his feet, out of my line of sight. I shifted to peek into the hall and see what was going on.

"What is the meaning of this?" came Royce's smooth voice, warm with anger as he held the much-beefier-looking Peter by the back of the neck. He picked him up like he weighed as much as a housecat and flung him down the hallway. My brows rose to my hairline at that little display. I knew Royce was strong, but I'd never seen him use that strength so blatantly. Except when we were fighting to the death that one time—but I digress.

"You presume to touch my property without permission?" My eyes narrowed at that. Property, was I? "Go back to Max and tell him I want recompense for this grievance. *Immediately!*"

Peter growled out something I couldn't quite hear, then audibly lumbered off toward the stairs. Weird. Never heard a vampire that tromped around so loudly. Usually they were light on their feet, quiet and swift like cats. Like predators.

Royce, for example, could move with a speed and fluidity that defied physics and not make a single whisper of sound in the process. The one time I'd seen him do it, it scared the living hell out of me. That, coupled with the stupidity of Peter's actions, only reinforced my assumptions about him being newly turned.

Royce's gaze shifted to meet mine, and for just a second I thought I felt the same type of pull and compulsion to come to him that Peter had vainly and oh-so-obviously tried to use on me. I turned my gaze away with more effort than such a simple act should have taken.

"Thanks for getting rid of him."

He nodded and then turned his attention to my doorway. His thin lips quirked upward in a smirk as he ran a finger-tip along the frame, sending luminous ripples through the otherwise invisible shield that kept out all things Other aside from those I personally keyed to it. A tendril of whitish smoke curled from his fingertip as it reddened, much like Peter's hands had. "This is new."

"Yeah, well, some creatures of the night can't take a hint," I said, moving to take his wrist below the cuff of his elegantly tailored suit jacket and pull him past the barrier. Though he looked surprised at the touch, he didn't resist. The barrier clung to him like Saran Wrap, more grudging than it had been for Chaz the first time I tried this, not wanting to let the vampire pass. Guess it was smarter than I was, trying to keep the dangerous stuff out instead of inviting it in for a little chat.

Once he was past it and the tug of resistance faded, I immediately let him go, shut the door, and backed away to put some much-needed space between us. "You've got good timing. Want to tell me what that was all about?"

"That vampire you just met is the progeny of Max Carlyle. I assume he told you why he was here."

"Yes, but that's not what I meant. What's the big idea, calling me property?"

His smile could have melted the coldest of hearts. "Simply that. You and I are contractually bound rather than by blood or bond, but the old ways still apply. Long before these courts and contracts came about, any vampire binding a human was considered to have staked a claim that other vampires had to respect. It's simply not done to harm or feed upon a human claimed by another vampire without his permission. You would not take your neighbor's dog or housecat and do harm to it. You might play with it, but you

certainly wouldn't kill it or take it from its owner without
permission. Do you see?"

I'm pretty sure my face must have registered some in-
credulity. He was comparing human servants to the family
dog? He sighed at my speechless reaction and continued.

"I'm not saying that it is right or fair for humans to be
considered this way. It is simply how it has always been
done. To be bound to one of us is also considered an honor.
It means that person has the benefit of the protection of the
one who chose them and that they are being considered as
a candidate for being turned. Since we are bound by the
contract, you are 'taken territory,' so to speak. It puts you
off limits as food or sport by anyone else since you are, by
our laws, my property." He paused thoughtfully before
giving voice to a little laugh, amused by his own thoughts.
"Though in this case I suppose ownership goes both ways,
considering those little changes you made to the contract.
An interesting and novel concept, though I don't see how
you might take any advantage of it."

Great. Just great. Shaking my head, I stalked to the
couch and sat down, folding my arms over my knees as I
leaned forward to watch him. "Okay, you know, I'm not
going to debate the morality of the subject with you, but I
want to make one thing crystal clear. We have a working relationship. I will *never* be bound to you or anyone else by
anything more than paper. Understand?"

He regarded me thoughtfully for a time, head tilted
slightly to one side. That look from those black eyes was
intense enough that I wondered if he now saw me for who
I really was; not just another threat or conquest. He
nodded and approached, settling himself with that envi-
able, centuries-practiced grace on the other side of the
couch. "I understand."

Somewhat mollified, I eased back into the couch cushions. He was a lot of things, but not a liar. Since he seemed
to respect my stance on the matter, I trusted him to play

nice for the time being. "Good. So what can you tell me about Max Carlyle? Any idea why he sent a flunky out to play fetch?"

"He considers you responsible for the death of one of his latest creations. Through your actions, he also holds me accountable."

I stared blankly. Royce gestured at the gun I'd almost forgotten lying on the table. "Surely you remember Anastasia Alderov?"

"What?" Confusion assailed me. "You mean he made her a vampire? How could he hold me responsible for that when *you* were the one who threw her to the Weres? Completely aside from being batshit crazy, she betrayed him when she hooked up with David Borowsky. That's not my fault!"

He smiled thinly, though there was no humor there. "Yes, he made her a vampire. He may not know about her treachery. His information about what happened that night was probably limited to what was in the papers or on the Internet. Perhaps the police report. You should know that we are not allies by any stretch of the imagination. Since I was the only other vampire present and I can almost guarantee that no Were who was there that night would have divulged what happened, he couldn't possibly get a first-hand report. He probably assumed from the data at hand that you were the one who killed her. Particularly as it is public knowledge now that you are bound to me, and some of the pictures in the news showed you garbed as a hunter. He would have recognized the belt you were wearing at the time for what it was and thought you were fighting her under my orders. Also, as I said, I'm not entirely sure that he understands that Anastasia betrayed him. Even if he did know, I can tell you that he'd take any excuse to undermine my authority and reputation."

"Peachy keen. So why did he send rocks-for-brains to drag me off? I thought you said when a vampire claims a person, they're under their protection and others have to lay off?"

"Precisely so. The exception to this rule is when violence is committed between one vampire and another, whether or not it was justified. Since he thinks that you or I killed Anastasia, he wants recompense for the grievance and sees doing harm to you as that recompense. However, he went far out of line by trying to take you. You see, he has no solid proof that either of us were responsible for the loss of his progeny. All he can be sure of is that we were involved somehow. Due to that, he probably thought to take you so that he could use you as leverage in negotiations to get me to give him something he wants."

I rolled my eyes. "Sure, that makes all kinds of sense. Vampire politics are ridiculous, you know that?"

He laughed and leaned back in the couch. One hand brushed those shoulder-length raven tendrils out of his eyes so he could regard me fully, resting his other elbow against the back of the couch and knuckles under his jaw as humor sparkled in his eyes. He looked like he was posing for a photo shoot. If I didn't know any better, I'd say he was being flirtatious. "I can see where others might think so. We tend to stick to our ways since that's what has worked to keep the majority of us alive for so long."

I pursed my lips in thought, wondering why he was being so accommodating and what was in it for him. He was being far too casual and nice to me tonight. What did he expect to get from me?

"Are you the exception to the rule then?" I asked, hoping this was a safe topic. "You're the one who decided it was such a great idea to follow in Rohrik Donovan's footsteps and get people to see the warm, fuzzy-bunny side of vampires after all."

I'd always been curious why Royce had been the one to reveal the existence of vampires to the world. Rohrik Donovan, the leader of New York City's largest pack of werewolves, had been the first Other to openly declare himself as such. He and his pack, the Moonwalker tribe, helped search for survivors in the rubble of the Twin Towers after September 11, 2001. Shortly after, Royce pulled a similar stunt at a press conference and demonstrated that he was no pretender with caps from a dentist and too many role-playing games under his belt. He'd managed to prevent widespread panic by the charitable contributions of his coven and offers of aid to the families of those affected by the terrorist attacks.

Royce was one of a very few elder vampires who was open to being interviewed or approached. He was often found at charity auctions, theater and restaurant openings, political rallies, and other events that might attract media attention. It didn't make him any less dangerous, of course, but his actions seemed to help the overall public image of vampires. Yet considering what I knew of him, it was odd that he would put himself at such risk; being out in the open meant hunters like the White Hats could find him that much easier.

He opened his mouth to answer me, but there was a heavy pounding on the door that cut him off. "Police! Open up!"

I sighed. "Here we go."

Chapter 5

"It's okay, the bad guy is gone!" I shouted as I hopped to my feet and went to the door.

Two of New York's finest were waiting on the other side with hands on the butts of their guns, looking alert but relieved. They were probably thanking their lucky stars they wouldn't have to deal with a vamp attack.

"Everything okay here, ma'am?" one asked.

"Yeah. Thanks for coming, but you missed the action," I said. I noted that his eyes widened in surprise and looked back over my shoulder, starting slightly when I saw how close Royce was behind me. Jeez, he moved like a ghost. A *fast* ghost. Gave me the willies. Both officers instantly had their weapons out and pointed at him.

"Hands up! Get away from her *now!*"

"Move it!"

Not having anticipated that reaction, I quickly spread my arms out and tried to shout loudly enough over *their* shouting so they could hear me. "Wait, wait, wait! This isn't the vampire who attacked me! Hold on!"

Royce did what they ordered and lifted his hands, slowly backing away from me. He looked more amused than upset or frightened, which ticked me off. If he hadn't been acting

all creepy behind me, the police wouldn't be on the verge
of shooting him. His amusement with their reactions was
more irritating than anything. Did he ever take anything
seriously?

One of the two officers, D. BOWMAN by his name tag,
slid around me into the apartment and kept his gun trained
on Royce. He was a big guy, but he moved pretty well and
knew what he was doing. I stepped aside to give the other
officer more room, praying they weren't so jumpy that they
had itchy trigger fingers. "This isn't the same vampire, you
said? Wait a sec. You look familiar."

"No, it's not the same vampire," I said, some exasperation trickling out despite my better intentions. "This is Alec
Royce."

The other cop blinked and turned to look at me, his
weapon slowly lowering. "Did you say Alec Royce?"

"Yes," Royce put in, that same bemused smile curving
his lips. "That's me."

"Jesus, Derek, put down your gun," the first cop exclaimed as he quickly holstered his piece. "So sorry for the
mix-up, Mr. Royce. Is everything okay here?"

The other cop looked confused—and then recognition
dawned. His jaw dropped, and he had to try twice to get his
gun in the holster as he backed up. He was gaping at the
vampire while his partner was thinking fast and trying to
do a PR salvage of the situation.

Royce lowered his hands, patting the nearer officer on
the shoulder. Judging by how he flinched, the vamp might
as well have touched him with a hot iron. "Not to worry,
you're just doing your jobs. I'd be happy to give you a statement and cooperate in any way you deem necessary."

I watched this unfold, nonplussed. Royce had the NYPD
in his pocket, too? I knew he was influential and well
known, but this was crazy. You'd think they'd pulled a gun
on the mayor by the way the two were reacting, going from
bristling protectors of the damsel who wasn't exactly in

distress anymore to suave politicians trying to smooth any of the big bad vampire's potentially ruffled feathers.

"Excuse me, ma'am, but would you come this way so I can take your statement?" Officer Bowman asked with just a little too much strained politeness, stirring me out of my thoughts. When I nodded assent, he led me across the room. He pulled a pad of paper and a pen from his shirt pocket to take notes, speaking quietly. "Sorry about all this, we didn't realize that Mr. Royce would be here. Can I get your name, and what happened exactly?"

I glanced at the other officer, who was chatting with Royce like they were old buddies from high school or something. Rolling my eyes, I proceeded to tell Officer Bowman what happened. "My name is Shiarra Waynest. Another vampire showed up shortly before Royce did. When I opened the door, the other vamp tried to grab me, but I managed to keep away." Easier to explain it that way than to enlighten him about the intricacies of the metaphysical shields on my door. "He said his name was Peter and he was trying to take me to see someone named Max Carlyle."

"Max Carlyle? Any idea who that is or what he wants with you?"

"I wish I knew," I said, keeping as straight a face as I could. All I had right now was conjecture. I wasn't going to tell him anything about the little party I'd crashed or the details about Anastasia's death. What the police already knew was all that I, Royce, and the Weres who had been present were willing to give on the subject.

The cop stared at me for a sec, his gaze taking on that flinty, steely look that said, "I know you're lying to me." I stared right back, not giving an inch. I'd done this routine with the cops enough times in my line of work to know when to talk, and when to keep my mouth shut. Plus, I knew I didn't have any other information that would be useful to their investigation.

"You're sure there's nothing, no connection between you and this Carlyle guy?"

I shrugged, gesturing at Royce. "He's a vamp, maybe he knows something about it. I don't have a clue what Max Carlyle wants with me." That much was true, at least.

He took some more notes, more than what I'd said. I wondered idly what he was writing down, hiding a yawn with my hand. It was way past my bedtime.

"Okay. So what happened after he told you what he wanted?"

"That's about the time Royce arrived and scared him off."

Officer Bowman nodded, rubbing the five o'clock shadow on his chin before jotting down what I'd said on his notepad. I gave a description of Peter, answering the rest of his questions as accurately as I could, though there wasn't much more I knew beyond what I'd already said. He did ask a couple different ways for some hint of a connection to Max, but I didn't know what else to tell him. I'd never seen the guy, couldn't give a physical description, and had no idea where he was from or why he was trying to get his hands on me.

Royce had finished talking to the other officer by the time I wrapped up my statement. I walked the two policemen to the door.

"Thanks again, Officers. Hope you find that guy and get him off the streets."

The one who had been taking Royce's statement nodded, tipping his hat at me. "We'll put out an APB on the vamp. I'm going to arrange for a security detail to keep watch on your apartment for the next couple days in case he takes another go at you. Is your office building where you work secure, or will you need some assistance there as well?"

Huh. The officer was really going out of his way on this. There were not enough police in this city to cover something so inconsequential as watching out for my ass, even if it was only for a few days. "No, I think I'll be okay. You don't have to go to the trouble; I'll call again if I need help."

He smiled and shook his head, spreading his hands a bit. "Sorry, ma'am. If a vamp is after you, it'd be on my head if something bad happened because no one was around to prevent it. Being threatened with kidnapping is serious business. You're lucky Mr. Royce stopped by when he did." The officer and vamp shared a look that made me wonder what private joke I was missing.

I gave a frosty smile and brushed a stray curl out of my eyes. "Okay, whatever you think is best."

He apparently didn't get the hint since he smiled back and gave a cheery wave before heading off down the hall, Officer Bowman in tow. I shut the door behind them and stalked to the couch, dropping down with a muttered curse. Trying to do my job with a bunch of cops following my ass was going to be hell.

"So, you want to tell me why the cops were so happy to see you and so insistent on treating me like a Fort Knox shipment?"

Royce shrugged and resumed his comfortable lounging position. "Probably because I donated half a million dollars to their Police Association two weeks ago. I imagine they want to do what they can to ensure I remain so generous the next time they request donations."

I blinked. "Yeah, I can see where that would do it." No wonder they wanted to keep a tail on me. They wanted to be ingratiated with Royce, not protect me for the sake of it. Wonderful. Stifling another yawn, I rubbed at my eyes. "So what were you saying before?"

He studied me before speaking, looking hesitant. "It's late, and I can see that you're tired. I don't think Max will try anything else tonight, but it may be wise for you to stay elsewhere for a few days."

I shook my head, managing a wry grin. "The shields

here work beautifully. I think Arnold outdid himself on them. I'll be okay."

"If you insist. I have an idea that might handle this problem, but I don't think you'll like it."

"What's that?" This ought to be good.

He hesitated again, looking away before speaking. "While I completely understand and respect that you are averse to being bound to anyone, as you know, you are still contractually connected to me. Since you refuse to hide yourself, perhaps we can use the connection we already have to appease Max without any loss to either of us. If you go to him willingly, it may cool his anger enough to listen to reason and accept your explanation regarding Anastasia's death, where he did not listen to me."

"Oh, hell no!" I exclaimed, jerking back from him. Was he crazy? I paused, eyes narrowing. "Wait, you already talked to him? You didn't mention that!"

He smiled grimly. "No, I didn't. We've been speaking by phone for the last several months, negotiating a price for the loss of his agent. He isn't a forgiving sort, and our rivalries from past times have made him exceptionally bitter about Anastasia."

"So what is handing me over to him supposed to solve? What does he want me for?"

Royce's gaze was dead serious as he turned back to meet my eyes. I was almost too shocked by what he said to notice there wasn't a hint of compulsion behind it.

"He wants you to take her place."

Chapter 6

"You are out of your fucking mind if you think I'm going to give myself to him. *Especially* to be turned."

Royce shook his head, gesturing for me to calm down. "He won't rest until he's had some measure of vengeance. Taking you is probably the only thing he would consider adequate amends. However, if you went to him willingly, it would ruin any plans he might have of taking you by force. It would also make his claims for retribution look less valid in the eyes of those who enforce our laws. Or if he saw you as more trouble than you're worth, he may leave you alone and attempt some other means of getting to me. It is also entirely possible that you could use the tools The Circle gave you and kill him."

"I can't believe this." I was seething and not about to be placated so easily. I got up and stalked to the door, opening it and pointing to the hall. "Get. Out. *Now!*"

With a deep sigh, Royce rose to his feet. He moved closer, but rather than leave, he put one hand on my shoulder and tilted my chin up with the other. I was sorely tempted to jerk away, but stood still long enough to hear him out. However, I kept glaring spitefully into his eyes, making sure it was no secret that I was still pissed at him for even suggesting I deliver myself up to Max or, worse, fight him to the death.

"I do not want to see harm come to you. I only make the suggestion as I don't like the idea of leaving you to fend for yourself against Max, and I fear that he might hurt or kill you if he gets his hands on you by his own means. It's much preferable if we handle this on our terms rather than his."

I slowly pulled away from his touch, some of my anger cooling at his explanation. Despite his logic, I wasn't sure how much I believed him. I was sure he was saying he cared about me because he was trying to save his own ass and saw me as a means of protecting him. After all, I'd done it before.

"There has to be another way. Whatever that option is, I'm going to find it."

He let his hands drop to his sides, sliding them into the pockets of his slacks before leaning casually against the door frame. There was something about the look in his eyes I didn't like. A winsome smile curved his lips, one that would've been warm and inviting if not for the hint of extended fang that was all too visible. "You could always let me turn you. He'd likely lose interest if I did."

I immediately regretted having moved so far from my gun, stiffening and taking a few swift steps away from him until my back hit the wall. His gaze darkened, becoming all too predatory as he pushed off the door frame, closing in. Panic threaded through me, though I was clearheaded enough to wonder what brought this sudden hunger to the forefront. Particularly after he'd been taking such pains to be so carefully polite and cordial earlier; he only used this tactic with me when he saw no other way to force me to agree to something.

Before I could run, he reached out until his hands were pressed against the wall on either side of me, effectively trapping me between his arms. In return, I let out an involuntary squeak of fear, wondering how the hell this had turned so bad so fast. Maybe he just wanted to make a point again. Maybe he was pushing my buttons because he knew this would terrify me. Oh, God, please let him be trying to scare me and not really *do* anything to me.

I braced myself against the wall and put my hands against his chest, trying to push him back as he leaned toward me. I might as well have been trying to move a boulder.

He stopped of his own accord and stared down at me for a moment. His chest felt solid and cool, only the material of his shirt shifting under my hands. There was no sense of *life* to him, no heartbeat or shifting muscle or rise and fall of his chest to breathe. This close to me, I smelled mint and copper and, underneath that, the cool, musty, neck-ruffling scent of vampire.

I tried to find the words to speak, to tell him to stop, but all I could manage was a feeble cry when he took hold of my wrists, pulling my hands off his chest and pressing them to the wall. He said nothing, simply studied me while that gibbering terror romping through my mind didn't want to acknowledge that he hadn't hurt me yet. It only wanted to focus on the fact that I was pinned, he looked ravenous, I was the only human in sight, and his fangs were literally inches away from some all too vulnerable parts of my body. Places where the blood runs hot and fast and close to the surface of the skin.

Why was he doing this? What did he want from me? Panic clawed at my throat, and as he leaned in, his lips brushing against the side of my neck, I found my voice again, letting loose with a shriek as I twisted away. He was going to bite me! This couldn't be happening!

"I'd never hurt you," he whispered, his voice low and soothing. He didn't touch me save for the velvet soft brush of his lips against my skin, followed by the brief rake of fangs. Hinting at penetration, but never quite sinking in. It was enough to drag a little cry from my lips, too breathy to properly be called a scream. I thought I might just die of fright right then, closing my eyes and trying to remember how to breathe as my heart tried to pound its way out of my chest. "You could stay young and beautiful and strong forever. With me. Think about it."

With that, he was suddenly *gone*.

I stumbled away from the wall, making a hectic dash for my gun. The rational part of me knew he was long gone, that he'd used that uncanny speed of his to leave this place, but the rest of my frazzled brain was screaming to get the hell away from there as fast as I could. I grabbed up the re-assuringly heavy hunk of metal, aiming for the open doorway in case he decided to come back. It took quite a bit of effort, but I eventually talked myself into getting close enough to the door to slam it shut.

Once it was closed, I locked it and turned around to lean against it, shaking. He was gone. I was safe. He wouldn't touch me. Couldn't, not even if he'd crossed the threshold of my door. The barrier would keep him out, I hadn't keyed him to it, only given him a one-time pass. He *could not* touch me. He'd done all of this to scare me, that was all.

I closed my eyes and took deep, panting breaths as I tried to remind myself that hyperventilating wouldn't solve anything. Jesus H. Christ on a stick, I'd never come that close to being vamp chow before. It was one thing to face Royce in open battle, knowing we were going to kill each other if we could. Quite another to have him go from friendly and cordial to I'm-about-to-eat-your-face-pass-the-salt-please.

Fuck. I should've known better than to trust a vamp. I never should've called him. I never should've invited him into my home. Never, ever should have let my guard down.

Right at that moment, I wished more than anything that Chaz was with me so I could hide in the protection of his arms. His strength and courage were unquestionably greater than mine. He never hesitated in his loyalty or when he felt it was his duty to protect me. I'd feel safe for a while if he were here.

Besides, it was two weeks 'til the next full moon, so I wouldn't have any worries of him accidentally going furry on me. Not that it was that big of a deal when he did. As scary as he looked when shifted, as man or wolf, Chaz was nothing but a big teddy bear. Okay, a big teddy bear with fangs and claws that also happened to be strong enough to tear me in two, but unlike Royce, he'd never done anything to overtly threaten me with his nature as an Other.

My hand crept up to my throat, shaking fingers checking for any signs of blood or cuts. Nothing. He hadn't actually bitten or scratched me. Still, I'd felt his fangs *on my skin*. Not just anywhere but *on my neck*.

I couldn't imagine the level of self-control it must have taken for him to keep from carrying through and biting me. From what I'd heard, when it came to drinking blood, vampires were as driven by their instincts to feed as shifted Weres who were threatened in their own territory while under the influence of the full moon. Maybe even more than that. Then again, all I knew about that was what the tabloids told me, and they also said that shifted Weres ate babies and were nothing but slavering animals 24-7. Considering what I knew about Weres from my experiences with Chaz and the rest of the wolves from the Moonwalker and Sunstriker tribes, they were probably wrong about vamps, too. Still, I couldn't be totally sure.

Okay. Maybe Royce wasn't completely driven by a desire to feed every hour of the day. He caught me off guard, had me pinned without a weapon and easy access to my throat. So why didn't he go through with it? Thanks to the contract, I couldn't slap a suit on him or go whining to the cops. He wouldn't have to suffer any consequences for his actions other than my wrath (hah!). Did he want me cooperative while he sucked the life out of me or something? Not a chance of that.

He must have been trying to manipulate me somehow. The more I thought about it, the angrier I got. Was he trying to bully me into seeing him as the better alternative over Max Carlyle?

That had to be it. Why he wanted me was a mystery I wasn't going to dig into. Whatever it was, something had to be done about this. I didn't have the first clue how to find Max, but I *did* know how to find Jack the White Hat.

There was an alternative to going along with the vampires' machinations. The White Hats despise all things with fur and fangs. Though I didn't agree with their credo or methods, their membership included a bunch of crazies who were insane enough to hunt down and kill vampires, Weres, and the occasional mage. Since Jack was all too keen to have me join Psychos "R" Us, maybe I could use that to get him to help me do something about Max and Royce. Becoming a White Hat wasn't on my "Top Ten Things to Do Before I Die" list, but maybe if I agreed to help them now and again, they'd return the favor.

Despite my decision, I now had a new problem. I didn't have a phone number for Jack, so I'd have to go see him in person. The trouble with going to see Jack (completely aside from his tendency to wave guns and knives in my face) was that he worked at a black market weapons emporium downtown. I did *not* want the cops to see me go in there. Worse still, I did *not* want to have a bunch of pissed-off White Hats blaming me for the police raiding their place.

Unfortunately, the police were going to be keeping an eye on me for the next few days. They'd probably have a tail on me, at least during the night, in case Peter took another stab at snatching me. Since they knew I had ties to Royce, they'd take the duty very seriously, too. I cringed as I realized they'd probably stick around even longer once they pulled up my records and found out I was contractually bound to the vamp. That was guaranteed to pique their interest further.

I could contact one of my friends at the station, Officer Lerian, and ask him to get his buddies to lay off. Of course, he'd want to know why I needed the protection in the first place and would probably cheerfully proceed to tell me all the reasons I needed the NYPD to baby-sit me for the next couple of months. And he'd grill me about why Sara wasn't returning his calls, which was definitely not a can of worms I wanted to open.

Then another possibility occurred. Arnold was acquainted with Jack and he'd be back in town with Sara on Sunday afternoon. It was technically Saturday morning now. I could tough out one more night home alone. Chaz blowing me off suddenly didn't seem like such a crime. Inviting him to make up for missing tonight by offering to spend the night tomorrow seemed like a grand idea. I could also call Arnold once he got home and ask him to get in touch with Jack for me. Arnold could ask him to call me and I could take it from there.

Feeling a bit better for having a plan, I pushed off the door to get my cell phone from where I'd tossed it. Without going into what happened, I texted Chaz that coming by tomorrow was fine and I looked forward to seeing him. As much as I wanted to sob on somebody's shoulder right now, I didn't look forward to telling Chaz what I'd done. He'd be royally pissed I'd let Royce in past the shields on my door. Hell, I was royally pissed at myself for letting Royce in. That had been a spectacularly stupid move on my part. I'd trusted the vamp to be civil rather than remembering who I was dealing with—one of the most dangerous of the Others.

That wasn't a mistake I'd be making again anytime soon.

Though I was exhausted, my stomach growled and I wondered whatever happened to my Chinese food. Poor delivery guy probably saw Peter or Royce or the cops and went running in the other direction.

I went to the kitchen to fix myself something to eat, putting the gun on the counter in easy reach. Distantly I noted that my hands were shaking. I grabbed some leftover pasta from the fridge and tossed the container in the microwave. While I pulled out some dishes and silverware for myself, I mulled Royce's offer.

I'd never hurt you. You could stay young and beautiful and strong forever. With me. Think about it.

Creepy asshole.

Chapter 7

I spent the rest of the night huddled in bed, gun in my lap, and every light in the apartment burning. I couldn't fall asleep until after the sun came up. By then, I was completely exhausted.

I woke up after eleven, not feeling at all rested and still jumpy as anything. Showering helped, but I was still bleary-eyed when I headed down to my car so I could pick up some groceries. There was a black-and-white parked conspicuously in front of the building when I nudged my SUV out of the gated garage. One of the officers sat up straighter and I noticed they pulled out behind me when I merged into traffic. I sighed, wishing for the patience and fortitude to make it through my errands going exactly the speed limit for the rest of the day.

At first I was nervous, but after a while I stopped paying attention to the police cruiser riding my ass. Until I got to the grocery store, where they followed me into the parking lot and parked next to me, stepping out when I did.

"Good morning," I said, attempting civility. "Or good afternoon, whatever it is."

One of the two officers, a young kid, looked fresh out of the academy. The other was a grizzled old bear of a man who looked like he'd been there, done that, didn't like any of it, and didn't get the T-shirt. The kid kept a serious face until I greeted him, then cracked a goofy-looking grin that made me take about five years off his age. Were they recruiting fresh out of high school or something? "Good morning, Ms. Waynest. I'm Officer O'Donnell, and this here is Officer Grady. We're assigned to you until six tonight. Doing your groceries?"

He hooked a thumb at the store, and I nodded, feeling more tired than ever. "Yeah. You guys aren't following me in there, too, are you?"

"No, but we'll hang around by the exits until you come out."

Biting my tongue to avoid saying something caustic, I nodded again, hefted my purse strap up to my shoulder, and headed to the store. It was entirely too weird having people stare at me as I was flanked by a couple of uniforms. At least they were going to wait outside.

Since I'd be staying in tonight, I thought I should pick up dinner for Chaz and myself. I pulled out my phone to call him. Forcing the rickety shopping cart to stay on something resembling a straight line, I tilted my head to hold the phone to my ear as I perused the aisles in search of something promising for a romantic dinner for two.

"Hey, love, sorry about last night. What's up?"

It was a relief to hear his voice, and I couldn't stop myself from smiling despite all the worries plaguing me. "Hey, I wanted to check and see what you'd like for dinner tonight. Going to stay home and cook something since I can't go out right now."

"What? Why's that?"

"Err, I'll tell you about it when you come by. Just make it before dark, please."

A low, ominous growl rumbled in his throat. "Vampires bothering you?"

"Something like that. Listen, don't get all upset about

it right now, I've got it under control. Come over tonight and let's relax, and take advantage of the time to ourselves, okay? I'll put out some candles, make some pasta, pour the Chianti, and make with the cheesy Italian love songs. It'll be just us, promise."

"Okay," he grudgingly agreed after a long we'll-be-talking-more-about-this-later pause. "Try not to get into any more trouble today, all right?"

"All right," I promised. "Love you."

"Love you, too. See you later."

Feeling much better, I called Arnold. When he picked up, I jumped right in. "Hey, it's Shia. I've got a favor to ask."

"What's up?"

I cringed, knowing what his response was going to be. "When you get back in town tomorrow, can you get in touch with Jack and ask him to call me?"

"Jack?" He didn't sound like he knew the name, then recognition dawned. "Oh, shit! You're not talking about the guy at the weapons dealership, are you? That guy is bad news, you should stay away from him."

"I know, but this is important. I'm not going to go into it, but I *have* to get in touch with him. There are cops following me everywhere I go, so I can't meet him in person."

"Why are there cops following you?" I could dimly hear Sara's voice in the background. *What the hell is going on?*

"Look, I'm okay. Your shields work perfectly, so you don't have to worry. There are cops following me around keeping me totally safe and completely paranoid about my driving skills. I just need to get in touch with him to see if I can sic some White Hats on this new vamp in town."

A woman across the aisle looked up at me sharply. I ignored her and kept going until I got to the canned soups. Hmm, chicken noodle or beef stew for lunch tomorrow?

Arnold laughed incredulously, and I could hear Sara demanding to know what was happening. "You are crazy,

Shia. Absolutely, completely nuts. I'll see what I can do for you. Hold on, Sara's going to tear my arm out of the socket if I don't hand her the phone."

I grinned at that, waiting for her imperious voice to come on the line.

"What the hell are you doing over there? Do you need us?"

"No, no, no. I didn't call to spoil your vacation, enjoy what's left of it. I just needed help getting in touch with someone Arnold knows."

Sara harrumphed. "Oh yeah? So what's this about the cops following you around?"

"I'll tell you all the dirty details when you get into town. The short story is, someone's sent a vampire after me, and I called the cops when the vamp kept trying to get past the barrier Arnold put on the door. I'm fine."

Dead silence. Then, "I'm coming home. Right now."

"No, you're not! For God's sake, enjoy the rest of your trip and help me deal with it tomorrow. It's daytime, no vampire is going to assault me right now, and I'll be back behind the shields long before any of them are up and about." I maneuvered around a guy's shopping cart. He'd stopped in the middle of the aisle to stare at me open-mouthed. I growled a curse under my breath and reminded myself to talk more softly in public when mentioning the Others. "Don't worry about me, Chaz is coming by before dark. Everything will be fine."

"You better be right about that. If something happens to you before I get back, I will beat you myself."

I laughed. "Trust me, you've got nothing to worry about. Besides, I'd whip you in a fight and you know it."

Her own laughter sounded a bit less strained, and I was relieved she wasn't going to go ballistic and come charging back to town to "save" me or something. "Okay, okay. It does sound like you've got things under control. Seriously, though, call me if you need me. Don't wait until you're in up to your neck to ask for help, all right?"

"I won't. That's why I invited Chaz over, remember? He'll keep me safe."

"Yeah, I got it. What's the name of the vamp?" she asked. "I'll stop by the office and run a background check."

"Max Carlyle. I did a brief search, didn't come up with anything solid. If you want to dig deeper, you're welcome to—*tomorrow*."

"I plan on it. I'm coming over as soon as I get back."

"Okay, sounds good," I said, making a mental note to pick up more snacks if I was going to have everyone camp out at my place all day tomorrow. Hmm, maybe some movies, too. "See you then."

"Later," she said.

The call went over better than I'd expected, mostly because I hadn't told her I'd let Royce into my home. Oh well, I'd tell her when I saw her tomorrow.

I continued stuffing my shopping cart, then got in line at the check stand. A couple waiting two stands down kept looking in my direction and whispering to each other. Had they overheard me talking about White Hats and vampires in the tea and coffee aisle?

Shrugging it off, I glanced at the headlines of the magazines and silly news rags. A special edition newspaper caught my eye. One of the headlines made my jaw drop, and explained why so many people had been staring at me—completely aside from my tendency to talk too loudly on my cell phone.

Right there, under yet another story about a crooked politician, was: VAMPIRE ROYCE SAVES DAMSEL IN DISTRESS! There was a ridiculous, obviously computer-altered picture of a vampire that looked vaguely like Peter looming in a doorway. Royce stood nearby with his arms around . . . was that *me*? I snatched the thing up, trying to figure out how in the hell the newshounds could've heard about it, let alone gotten close enough to snap pictures.

IS NEW YORK'S NEWEST HERO A VAMPIRE?
by Jim Pradiz

TERRACE HEIGHTS (Sept. 21)—Calls made to the police requesting assistance in a vampire attack last night were answered by Alec Royce. Royce chased away the vampire who assaulted local private investigator Shiarra Waynest shortly before police arrived on the scene at her apartment.

Sgt. Daniel Vega, the officer in charge of the investigation, made a statement regarding the attempted assault on a human and Alec Royce's involvement. "Right now, this attack is under intense scrutiny. We will find the Other responsible and bring him to justice. Vampires are not exempt from the law. That girl was very lucky that Alec Royce was there to save her."

Waynest fell into the vampire's arms after the timely rescue (see photos next page). Neighbors and friends say that Royce and Waynest have known each other for a long time, but some sources stated that Waynest was seeing someone else.

There is speculation that, despite any other men in her life, she will be accompanying Royce to the joint NYPD/NYFD Charity Ball to be held next month at the Metropolitan Opera House. Alec Royce was named New York's most eligible unliving bachelor earlier this year after ending a tumultuous long-term relationship with runway model and environmental activist Dawn Hartley.

Per public records, Waynest was contractually bound to Royce on March 13 of this year. It is not known if they are officially dating or if Royce has plans to turn her into a vampire. Messages left for comment with Royce's publicist and H&W Investigations have not been returned.

The story was almost as ridiculous, and parts of it as obviously fabricated, as the doctored picture. I cringed at the photo spread inside featuring the very real, very unaltered, shot of me pinned in Royce's arms as he leaned down to bite my neck. Even worse were the implications that we were dating and that I was being a ho-bag. The writer, Jim Pradiz, had managed to dig up the information on who I was and that Royce and I were contracted. But who the hell had said we were dating? The speculation that I was going to be Royce's honey for the next millennium or so gave me the dry heaves.

The photographer must have been following Royce. The picture of my attacker looked like someone had taken a badly cut photo from a cheesy eighties B-movie, blurred it to make the face indistinct, then inserted the vamp in the appropriate spot in what was supposed to be my living room. They'd used another of me from when I'd given statements to the press after an incident at the Embassy Suites, and what I thought might be a stock headshot of Royce. But the pic of Royce about to bite me was genuine.

What was the point of this story other than to give me heartburn and a bad case of the heebie-jeebies? Was Royce behind it? Max Carlyle? Someone else entirely?

I tossed the paper on top of my groceries on the counter, feeling ill and shocked as I waited to be checked out. I felt like I was being railroaded toward some unknown destination and that each of the events of the last few days were tied into it. But untangling how it came together was beyond me right then.

Once everything was paid for and loaded back into my cart, I trudged to my car. I'd almost forgotten about Officers O'Donnell and Grady. They fell in step on either side of me once I emerged, drawing yet more unneeded attention. Sigh.

Officer O'Donnell piped up, his serious-cop-face on. "Ma'am, can we escort you home? We heard on the radio that there are an unusual number of paparazzi at the station asking about you. It might be best to get you back to the privacy of your home."

"Ugh, thanks for telling me. Yeah, let's go." I paused. "Actually, do you guys want to come up for coffee or anything once we get back? I've got enough food here to feed a herd of elephants."

Officer Grady finally cracked a smile, looking like a grumpy old bear who'd just been given a pot of honey instead of one woken from hibernation. His voice was surprisingly mellow, and didn't match the gruff exterior. "Thanks, miss, but we should probably stay posted at our vehicle and keep watch outside."

I shrugged and nodded, pulling open my trunk as I got to the car. As I dumped the groceries in the back, I thought about what to do next. The rest of my errands could wait. I could watch movies or fart around on the Internet until I needed to start cooking dinner. My answering machine was probably overloaded if paparazzi were asking about me at the police station. I could while away some time by returning a few calls and threatening to bring a suit if they didn't retract the ridiculous stories about me.

Hopefully none of my friends or family had seen the stupid article.

Chapter 8

Though it was a little chilly, I put the windows down while I drove to help wake myself up. The cold air was nothing compared to the chill I was feeling wondering what would happen if Chaz or my parents stumbled across that article before I had a chance to explain.

The cops were once again in tow. At any other time it would've been funny how everyone around me all of a sudden found it vitally important to slow their pace to a crawl, but I was not in the mood for a laugh. The mix of good music and fresh air was helping my sour frame of mind. It's hard to stay mad when you've got the wind in your hair with rock 'n' roll blasting out of the speakers.

I was only a few blocks away from home when a black sports car with tinted windows screeched around a corner and zoomed past us. It scraped a good chunk of paint off the cop car behind me and clipped my side mirror on its way, making me yelp in surprise. Jeez, the guy must've been going ninety in a residential area. Blue and red lights flashed to life, followed by the wail of sirens as my escort slid around my car to give chase.

"Stay put!" Officer O'Donnell shouted out the passenger window as they pulled away. I watched as they zipped out of sight, shaken and hardly able to believe some idiot would pull a stunt like that right in front of the cops.

I was so close to home that it would be stupid to let my groceries spoil while the officers were off chasing the speed demon. I started to take my foot off the brake when another black car pulled up at a slant in front of me, blocking any attempt to pull into traffic and forcing me to slam on my brakes again. I saw through my rearview that a similar car had pulled the same move right behind me. Now I couldn't back up either.

Shit.

I put the car in park, rolled up the windows, and locked all the doors, watching with narrowed eyes as two men stepped out of the car in front of me. They looked like feds with their matching black suits and reflective shades. One of them walked up to the driver's side door and unnecessarily rapped on my window with his knuckles. This close, he looked more like a bodyguard than a government official. Eyeing him nervously, I turned off the radio, but didn't roll down the window.

"Ms. Waynest? Shiarra Waynest?"

His voice was muffled by the glass, but I heard him well enough. "Yes?" I gestured at the car in front of me, blocking my path. Other cars were forced to maneuver around and people were honking irritably at the hold up. "Do you mind?"

"Don't worry about that. Could you step out of the car? We have a few questions."

Something wasn't right about this. If they were official and it was that much of an emergency, they would've met me at my house or had my cop escorts pull me over. As they showed up right after my cops left me to chase a highly unusual distraction, their appearance was extremely suspicious.

"Let's see some ID first."

The two men shared a look. As I suspected, no ID was

forthcoming, so I stayed put. They stepped away from the car and spoke to each other for a moment, too quietly for me to make out. After a short debate, the other man came forward. He was short, skinny, and didn't fill out the suit very well. His eyes kept darting around, not focusing on anything in particular. Despite his slight frame, something about him scared me more than the other guy. He radiated *wrongness* on some fundamental level, in a far more subtle way than his failure to fill out his suit properly. Whatever it was about him, I couldn't quite put my finger on it.

He was smiling absently at nothing, and I watched nervously as he placed his hand against my door, fingers splayed directly above the handle. I couldn't tell what he was doing, though I pressed against the glass to try to see. His lips moved, and there was a brief flash of bluish light from his palm that left me blinking spots out of my eyes.

Right after the flash, my car died. What the hell?

Another flash of light and the doors unlocked of their own accord. Oh crap. A mage!

The bigger guy stepped in, reaching out to open the door. Cursing under my breath, I slapped at the lock to keep the crazies out. At the same time, I reached for my purse on the passenger seat, scrambling for mace or my cell or something I could use against them.

Too late. I missed the lock on the first try, my fingers scraping the handle as he yanked the door open. Instead of Mr. Muscles reaching for me, it was the creepy guy pressing clammy fingers to the side of my face. "Sorry, lady. You should've come quietly."

In response, I kicked at him, satisfied with his wheezed "oof" as he was driven back. It wasn't a hard blow. The angle was awkward since I was still in the seat, but he was surprised and in enough pain that he staggered back a step. I had just enough time to grab my purse and undo the seat belt before the buff guy reached for me.

He grabbed my arm and yanked me out of the car. As

my feet hit the ground, I steadied myself and used all the momentum I could muster to swing my purse up and around to whack the side of his head. He cried out and staggered to the side, letting me go so he could clutch at his bleeding cheek. The cute little buckle on my bag must have caught his skin. Poor baby.

I whipped around, shocked, as a gunshot went off and pedestrians screamed and scattered. Another crazy guy had stepped out of the other car and shot a round into the air from what appeared to be a Desert Eagle. Color me impressed—and scared shitless. Guns meant that Very Bad Things were bound to happen.

The small, creepy guy took advantage of my surprise to make a grab at me.

Without much thought, I drove my elbow back into his sternum, once again knocking him away from me. Gasping like a landed fish, he staggered toward the black car in front of mine while I was still trying to figure out what was going on and what the hell to do about it.

One of the benefits of having used the hunter's belt given to me by The Circle was that the fighting skills of all previous users were retained by it and then shared with the next person to wear it. I knew I didn't remember everything about fighting, nor had I retained all the skills I would have had with it on, but it still made me a far more formidable opponent than I used to be. Though I wasn't as effective without it, I'd also started taking self-defense classes, and I'd kept enough knowledge from the belt to hold my ground against human attackers. For the most part. If they all came at me at once, I was screwed.

The guy who'd shot into the air leveled the gun at me. "Stop fighting us! Put your hands up!"

I told myself that if he'd meant to shoot me, he would've done it already. And that they weren't out to hurt me too badly or the mage would've blown up my car instead of killing the engine. I still couldn't ignore the gun, though.

Especially when Mr. Muscles and another beefy guy from the second car came after me, hands out for another shot at grabbing my arms. They were going for subduing, not killing. I hoped.

Rather than stick around to be grabbed, I ducked across the car, weaved past their outstretched arms, and ran down the street. My apartment was only a couple of blocks from where I'd stopped, but my keys were still in the ignition. Maybe I could scream for help at the manager's door.

One of the black cars roared to life and started after me while the men pounded the pavement behind me. I quickly veered onto the sidewalk, dodging pedestrians left and right. I was in shape, but I was more of a slow and steady marathon runner than a sprinter. At least one of the guys was catching up.

Breathing hard, I glanced over my shoulder to see how close. He was *way* too close for comfort. It was the guy I'd decked with my purse, the right side of his face now twisted into a hateful mask of blood.

I still had the purse with me. What worked once should work again. I stopped abruptly and pivoted, swinging my purse up to bash him on top of the head.

This time he blocked, swinging an arm up to deflect the blow. Shit. I backpedaled as he barreled right into me, taking me down to the concrete in an incredibly painful tackle. My turn to have the air knocked out of me and little stars in my vision.

Though I wasn't in the right position for it, I tried shoving him off me. He was growling curses and highly uncomplimentary remarks as he grabbed at my hands, forcing them down to the pavement on either side of me. So I did the next best thing and rammed my knee up as hard as I could into his crotch.

His eyes bugged out so much I could see the whites behind his sunglasses, which had somehow managed to stay on his face during the fight. Unfortunately, my tactic didn't work as well as I'd hoped. He didn't let up his grip on me, the other two guys ran up, and as some of the stars cleared from my peripheral vision, I could see the two black cars double-parked and idling beside where I was pinned to the pavement.

Each of the suits grabbed an arm, hefting me to my feet as the guy with the bloodied face slowly levered himself up to stand. I kicked at kneecaps and bit at the hands on my shoulders and arms, but they had me pretty well pinned. It was hard to keep fighting after the first guy jabbed a harsh punch into my stomach, once again driving the air painfully out of my lungs. I prayed he hadn't hit me hard enough to crack any ribs.

"You're under arrest for attempted murder," the bloody-faced guy said loudly in a wheezy, slightly higher-pitched voice than before. I imagine that was due to my kneeing him right in the 'nads. Lots of people were staring at us, watching open-mouthed from apartment windows, out of their cars as they passed by, or peeking from storefronts. "You have the right to remain silent. Anything you say can and will be used against you."

Gasping back some air, I spat at him. "You lying sack of shit! Somebody call the police, these aren't cops!" I cried out louder, hoping someone in the crowd would believe me. "Help, they're kidnapping me!"

Nobody moved. Goddamn useless rubberneckers!

The two guys holding my arms wrestled my hands together at the small of my back so that bloody-face could whip out some handcuffs from a back pocket and snap them around my wrists. I struggled and screamed again, trying to twist out of the cuffs even though I knew it wasn't doing much more than bruising my wrists.

"Shut up," he growled into my ear as he leaned in at my back, soft enough that only the guys holding my arms and I could hear. "Nobody in this crowd believes you, and I'm pissed off enough right now to punch your face into the back of your skull. Nicolas is a good enough mage to make you feel like I did that and more a few times over without leaving a mark, and I *will* give him the green light if you keep this up. So shut . . . up."

I did as I was told, panting slightly as I tried to think of a way out of this. The men at my side used their grip on my upper arms to practically lift me off the pavement, dragging me to one of the cars. The other guy picked up my purse and trailed behind us. Once I saw that creepy little mage glaring at me from the back seat of the car they were dragging me toward, I started struggling again.

I did *not* want him anywhere near me! Thanks to Arnold, I knew a bit about what magi were capable of and was not interested in being within touching distance of one again. God only knew what the jerk was trying to cast on me earlier. Whatever it was happened to be nasty enough to require a physical touch. I'd seen enough magic, and had enough discussions with Arnold, to know that only the strongest, nastiest, most illegal sorts of spells were cast by that method.

The two men shoved me into the back seat, right up next to Nicolas, Creepy Mage Extraordinaire. The guy in charge slid in next to me on the other side and shut the door, trapping me between them. The driver twisted around in his seat, brows raised. "Jesus, Logan, looks like she did a number on you."

"Shut the fuck up," Mr. Muscles—better known as Logan—said, his voice a girlish squeak. "Let's get the hell out of here."

The driver shook his head and turned his attention back to the road. Logan reached into the pocket of the passenger seat and pulled out a small med kit. I had a moment of feeling proud of myself for having done so much damage before I felt those cold, sweaty fingers on my temple again.

"Can I hurt her?"

I twisted away, scared out of my mind by the venom in

Nicolas's voice. The move left me pressed up against Logan, but hey, anything to get me away from a pissed-off Other. Worse, one who was pissed off specifically at me.

"Not yet. Remember what the boss said. He wants to question her," Logan said, shoving me back toward Nicolas with an elbow. He started dabbing at the cut on his temple with his other hand, cleaning some of the blood off his face with a medicated pad. "Put her out, though. I'm tired of dealing with her shit."

Nicolas nodded, reaching out to take my face into his hands, fingers digging into my temples as I wrenched away from his touch. He was grinning at me, an odd light in his eyes. Was that fae energy or simple insanity? After a few seconds, searing pain blasted through my skull, so abrupt and painful I couldn't remember how to breathe.

Then there was darkness.

Chapter 9

I woke up on my stomach on a thickly carpeted floor, my hands still cuffed at the small of my back. I had no idea how much time had passed, or even what time of day it was since there wasn't a window in the room. Judging by the slightly damp feel to the air and the musty scent, I thought I might be underground, possibly in a converted basement. The only illumination came from a few candelabra on large brass stands.

Despite the clammy feel to the air, the place was lovely and spacious. The carpeting was a pale cream color, and the molding and oaken furniture had gilded scrollwork, the gold reflecting dim candlelight. A large walk-in closet with mirrored sliding doors was left open, revealing more ball gowns and ladies' dress shoes than a bridal depot at the mall.

Whoever dragged me in here hadn't thought to dump me on the thick, comfortable-looking bed done in crimson and cream, and I groaned as I twisted onto my side and struggled to sit up. At least I was left to sleep off whatever Nicolas had done to me on carpet instead of hardwood. And hey, I was still alive. My ribs ached, but the pain wasn't so sharp as to make me think they'd been broken. That much was a blessing.

However, I had no idea where I was or what my captors wanted with me. I was alone in the room, and when I awkwardly tried opening the single door with my cuffed hands, it was locked.

I spotted my purse on top of a dresser. With a little ingenuity, I unzipped it and spilled out the contents on the floor. My cell phone and mace were still there, mixed in with my makeup and breath mints. Once the screen of the cell was illuminated, I saw that it was well past nightfall, almost nine. Thankfully it was still Saturday. I hadn't lost an entire day to unconsciousness, so I figured they must be planning to do something with me on a relatively immediate basis. Joy of joys.

It took some shifting and twisting and struggling, but eventually I slid my arms under my butt and got my hands in front instead of behind me. I quickly texted Sara, Arnold, and Chaz a message:

KIDNAPPED! SEND HELP! THINK IT IS MAX CARLYLE, CALL COPS OR ROYCE OR JACK/WHITE HATS. DON'T KNOW WHERE I AM. CAREFUL, HE HAS MAGE ON HIS SIDE. (NICOLAS?)

I frantically jabbed at the send button as I heard a key in the lock and the handle of the door jiggling. The phone slid across the top of the dresser and fell off as I scrambled for the mace, backing up as far from the door as I could get. There weren't any good hiding places, and with my hands bound, I felt more than a little vulnerable.

Worse, Peter was the first person through the door. He grinned nastily when he spotted me, baring fangs and stalking closer. I found myself abruptly backed into the farthest corner, looking around frantically for something more useful than mace to attack him with. Since he was a vampire, I couldn't be sure it would work on him. Maybe I could use one of the candelabras to hit him or set him on fire?

Nicolas trailed into the room next, followed by a man I didn't know. My big worry was the vampire right in front of me, so I didn't pay a whole lot of attention to them just yet. One bad guy at a time.

Peter moved human-slow. He didn't have that deadly speed and grace that Royce commanded. That didn't stop him from being fast enough to cut off my attempt to escape as he grabbed my arms. He lifted me up and shoved me back, cracking the back of my head against the wall painfully enough for my vision to blur and the little canister to drop out of my bound hands.

"That's enough. Put her down," said the man I didn't know. Peter might've obeyed if I hadn't kicked him as hard as I could before he had the chance.

Peter staggered back, wincing. More evidence that he hadn't been turned very long; he still felt some modicum of pain at a blow from a human. However, it wasn't enough to get him to drop me. Rather, his fingers tightened punishingly around my biceps, making me gasp. After a moment taken to recover, he glared and pulled me away from the wall, shoving me back in the direction of the mage and the guy who I was guessing was Max Carlyle.

The guy caught me before I could fall to my knees. His grip was tight, but not painful. He carefully set me back on my feet, making sure I could stand before he let me go. I glared at him as I straightened, not in the least bit grateful for his help.

"What the fuck do you want me for? Let me go!"

He smiled, amused with my reaction. I noted that his features were similar to Royce's in that he had a strong jaw and swarthy skin. However, his hair was dark brown, cropped short but still showing hints of curls almost as riotous as my own. His eyes were an odd shade of dark gray, crinkling at the corners when he smiled, and he was a bit shorter and stockier in build. His taste in clothes was impeccable; he looked sleekly sophisticated in a dark business suit. He didn't *look* like evil incarnate, but he obviously had something sinister in mind since he shook his head at my request, politely refusing to let me out of this place.

"You'll have to excuse the drastic methods I took to have your company. I couldn't be sure Alec wouldn't spirit you away before I had the opportunity to speak with you."

I growled at him. "Max Carlyle, right?" He nodded, and I ground out, "Did Peter neglect to relay my message for you to just pick up a fucking phone and call me like a normal person? Or is the lack of consideration on your part a delightful little personality trait?"

He laughed and shook his head, reaching out a hand to lightly brush his fingers through my hair. I jerked back from the touch. "Yes, he gave me your message. A phone call wouldn't suffice for this. I want to know what happened the night Anastasia died. You were there. Tell me."

I shifted my weight uncomfortably and looked away. "She betrayed you. When she came back to New York, she joined up with a guy named David. He was a sorcerer."

He said nothing, simply stood quiet and motionless, waiting for me to continue. I wasn't entirely sure I wanted to, but since the silence was getting awkward, I felt obligated to say something. "He made a thing to control the local Weres and vamps. I think it was called a *Dominari* Focus."

"The *Dominari* Focus? Go on."

"David's plan was to use it to set up shop and settle down for a nice long eternity with Anastasia, using Royce's fortune to live out their little twisted fantasy and the local Weres as bully-boys to make sure they stayed on the top of the food chain. With some help, I destroyed the focus, and Royce and the Weres got rid of Anastasia and David."

"I see. They killed her?"

"Yes," I said, wondering how deep of a hole I was digging for myself and for Royce by admitting as much.

He voiced a soft "hmph" and stood there looking puzzled, one hand rubbing at his clean-shaven chin. Those unnerving gray eyes shifted back to focus on mine, and I quickly shifted my gaze away to avoid them. More out of habit than necessity when I was wearing the charm, but something told me it was a good idea not to take chances and avoid eye contact. "Was she under the influence of the focus at the time? Could you tell?"

"No, she wasn't. She and David were in on it together. They loved each other."

Apparently, that was the wrong thing to say. He reached out with that same impossible speed that Royce commanded to grab my shirt collar. He dragged me close enough to see the little pinpoints of red in his eyes and exactly how long his fangs were as his lips pulled back in a snarl. Petrified, I froze, unable to keep myself from staring into his eyes as he hissed at me. "She was *mine*. She loved *me*, not that talentless little spark."

Hoo boy. This could get ugly fast if I didn't do something. "I—I'm sure you're right—"

"Of course I am!" He shoved me back, sending me sprawling on the bed as he started pacing back and forth. I twisted up to a sitting position as fast as I could, wondering what the heck I could do to placate the pissed-off vamp. "She loved *me*, and Alec took her away."

For a second, I had this hysterical thought that I was stuck in a bad movie. Come on, was he seriously spouting lines like that?

Those hellish red eyes were once again suddenly, terrifyingly focused on me, frightening enough to kill even my perpetual sense of humor. "He values you. It doesn't matter why, but since he does, I'm taking you for my own."

"What?! No!" I rolled off the bed and to my feet. Peter was there to stop me from running before I had my footing. He shoved me against the bed, a hand on either shoulder and one leg leaning heavily against both of mine to keep me from kicking him again. I used my clenched fists to pound at his broad chest instead, but it didn't seem to be doing much to hurt or deter him.

Max was seething, fists clenching and unclenching at his sides as he stared at me. After a few moments taken to collect himself, the angry glow in his eyes faded to pinpoint sparks and he turned to the vamp whose grip I was still vainly struggling to escape. "Peter, you can have her for now."

The look on Peter's face was terrifying. "Yes, master."

Max growled a low warning. "Keep her alive and unharmed enough to speak. I need to make some calls, and I may have more questions later. Nicolas, guard the door. If she tries to escape, you know what to do."

I didn't see Max or Nicolas go, only heard the door closing behind them. My attention was too wrapped up in trying to wriggle and twist out of Peter's grip. "Let me go, damn it!"

"No." He laughed at me, thick fingers twining in my hair and yanking my head so hard, my back was forced to arch so he wouldn't break my neck. Involuntary tears of pain sprung to my eyes, and I tried raking my nails across his face. He caught the chain between my wrists with his free hand before I could do any damage, forcing them down.

"You don't seem like such a tough little bitch now. What, no begging?"

I gritted my teeth and closed my eyes, trying desperately to think of something to say, something to do, *anything* that would get me out of his hands.

"No one here to stop me this time," he whispered. I

could feel his fangs brushing along my collarbone, trailing up to my neck. He paused over my jugular, and for that moment I forgot how to breathe, feeling tense enough to snap. He pulled back, eagerness and triumph lacing his voice. "Royce is going to hate that Max gave you to me. How many times has he bitten you, huh?"

I didn't know how to answer him. My scalp was tingling from his grip on my hair, my back was starting to develop a twinge, and my ribs were screaming a silent protest from being held in such an uncomfortable position. Hot tears stung my eyes, and I couldn't bring myself to look at him.

"What, no smart remarks this time? Not that it matters."

As he leaned in close again, I screamed, though I knew it wouldn't help anything. God, oh God, he was going to *bite* me, he was going to *kill* me—

He let go of my wrists and clamped his hand over my mouth to stifle my screams as his fangs dug deep into my throat.

Chapter 10

You know, I've heard all kinds of conflicting stories on what it's supposed to feel like when a vamp bites you. It's been said it can feel like anything from the most orgasmic experience in your life to the most unbelievably painful. It's definitely one of the most terrifying. It's hard to explain, but while any of those descriptions fit, neither describing it as pleasurable or painful does it justice.

At first, it felt like exactly what it was—someone was jabbing sharp, pointy objects in my skin. It *hurt*. Before long, it changed, becoming something else. Something better, yet infinitely worse. Like fire in your veins and lightning down your spine, you can't move, think, or breathe around the shock of it. It seemed to go on forever.

When Peter reluctantly pulled away from my throat, I was left gasping for air, lying limply on the bed. Sometime during the course of feeding on me he'd let go of my hair. He backed up from me, wiping thin trickles of blood from his lips with the back of his hand. My blood. I thought I just might throw up.

"No wonder Royce wants you. You taste good," he said rather breathlessly, licking his fangs clean of their faint crimson sheen. I shut my eyes and took deep breaths, trying to stop crying and keep from being sick. I wasn't being too successful at either of those things. My hands shook, rattling the chain between them as I lifted them to prod gingerly at my neck. "Too bad you're such a pain in the ass."

I couldn't move, and my hands were shaking too much to tell how badly I'd been hurt. Threads of mixed revulsion and pleasure were making it hard to concentrate. I had to be stronger than this. I needed to stop crying and think of a fucking solution, not lie back and sit here doing nothing. The blood making my fingers slick was proof enough that I desperately needed to do something about this. I just couldn't find the strength to get up on my feet, and despite the deep breaths I was taking, I felt extremely short of air.

Peter studied me for a time, not moving. "You haven't been bitten before, have you?"

I had to breathe deeper yet to keep from sobbing. I'd done enough breaking down. Telling myself that wasn't helping much. I didn't want to answer him, but he was shifting like he was going to touch me again. Before he could, I choked out an answer, though I couldn't speak in much more than a whisper. My voice still cracked as badly as a twelve-year-old hitting puberty.

"No, I haven't."

He frowned, mulling something over. I could practically hear the boulders rolling around in that thick skull of his.

"Don't stand up too fast. You'll feel dizzy for a while. It'll pass."

Without saying anything else, he prepared to leave. Pausing in the doorway, he looked back at me. If I didn't know any better, I might have called the look in those brown eyes regret. Made me wonder if there was some part of him that remembered what it was like to be human, to be afraid of monsters like him.

Without another word, he walked out and shut the door quietly behind him.

I twisted onto my side and gripped the covers of the bed tightly, trying to get my footing and stand up. In the process, I noticed a few drops of my blood had stained the covers. Retching, I turned away, standing up way too fast.

My legs didn't want to hold me. I went down on my knees and stayed there for a few minutes, gasping for breath while I tried not to pass out. My vision was blurred with more than tears. I hadn't had any idea you felt this sick after being bitten by a vamp. After this little escapade, I'd never leave the house without my body armor ever again. If I ever saw my apartment again.

I spotted my cell lying about five miles away across the room.

Desperate to call for help before one of my captors came back, I crawled across the floor as swiftly as my numbed limbs would take me. Maybe Chaz would know what to do. He had connections in the supernatural community, so maybe he could find me. It wasn't until I started dialing for help that I distantly noted I was badly shivering. Shock? Or cold from the blood loss?

His phone went straight to voice mail. Shit, shit, *shit*!

Who else could help me? Though I hated the idea of doing it, there was only one other person, Other, whatever, that I could think of who might have any idea where Max had taken me. I desperately wanted to call Royce and offer him anything, anything at all, to get me out of here. I never wanted to feel this way again. His phone number was still in memory.

After a few rings, Royce picked up. "Shiarra?"

Huzzah for caller ID. As much as it hurt my pride to ask for his help, I didn't know what else to do at that point. Voice thick with tears, trying to keep quiet so Nicolas wouldn't hear and investigate, I did something I never thought I'd be desperate enough to stoop to.

"Please help me . . . Please, Royce, get me out of here, I'll do anything, just get me out of here . . ."

"Where are you? Did Max take you?" Cold anger radiated through the line. The only other time I'd heard him sound anything like this was right before he threw Peter like a football down the hallway at my apartment.

I looked around again, trying to spot something, anything that might be of use. "Yes, but I don't know where they took me. I'm in some kind of basement room, there aren't any windows so I can't see where I am."

"Okay, don't panic," he soothed, some of the anger trickling out of his voice. "Do you know how many other vampires he has with him?"

"No. The only other vampire I saw was Peter. He sent some men after me during the day. He's got a mage guarding the door. I haven't seen anyone else since I woke up in here."

"A mage?" There was some surprise there. Magi and vampires aren't known for getting along with each other. Nicolas didn't strike me as the sort to play well with anybody, so maybe he was an exception. Hell, anybody might work for an Other if the price is right. I was living proof of that. "All right. Stay put, and try not to provoke them. I'll see what I can do."

"Royce . . ."

"Yes?"

I hesitated. What could I say?

He broke the increasingly awkward silence before I could think of something to tell him. "What else did they do to you?"

For some reason it bugged me that he could read me well enough to know that I was scared and upset about more than just being kidnapped. "Peter bit me." It took some courage to say it out loud. Even then, I couldn't quite bring myself to speak over a whisper.

"He bit you, did he? We'll have to do something about that."

The flat, disenchanted tone of Royce's voice was scarier than anything else that'd happened to me today, including being bitten. That should tell you something.

What was I getting myself into? Hadn't Royce stopped just shy of biting me himself last night? Maybe calling him for help wasn't the fabulous idea I had thought it was. It stung when I realized that his little ploy to make me see him as the lesser evil in comparison to Max was working so well.

Worse yet, Max walked in just then, Peter at his heels. His eyes narrowed when he saw the phone in my hand.

I tried to get to my feet, to back away, but my limbs were flat out refusing to work the way I wanted them to. Max yanked it out of my hands with little effort, and he studied the screen briefly before putting the phone to his ear. A smile slowly curved his lips, one that would've been charming if it hadn't been so evil.

"Alec Royce. What a surprise."

Since I'm no Other with hypersensitive hearing, I couldn't determine what Royce's response was. He must've talked for a bit, because Max simply stood there, staring down at me with the occasional "mmhm" or "mm-mm" punctuating his end of the conversation.

After a few failed attempts, I gave up attempting to stand. My legs were too rubbery and weak to hold me.

Suddenly, Max started talking, his voice abrupt and harsh. It was unexpected enough to make me flinch. What had Royce said to him? "No. I know you had a hand in Anastasia's death. For that, you pay the price. Your little toy will suffer because of your mistake. Remember what happened with Helen of Volos? Think long and hard on it, Alec. This is as much for her as it is for Anastasia."

He passed the phone to Peter, then reached down and

plucked me off the floor by my shirt collar. I almost passed out again, actually kind of wished that I had.

"Scream loud enough for him to hear you, lovely," he said. "Wouldn't want to disappoint my old friend."

I couldn't help but oblige him as he yanked me up against his chest and I was bitten for the second time that day.

Chapter 11

I must have passed out again. Whether from the shock of being bitten or the blood loss, it didn't really matter. I panicked for a second when I woke up, not knowing where I was. I was tucked into a warm, comfy bed with dark red covers and matching pillows. Lovely oak furniture matched the bedstead. A few candles flickered from tall brass stands and candelabra scattered throughout the room, illuminating it just enough to cast deep shadows in the corners and give a softer edge to everything.

At the sight of the bloodstains on the bedspread, it all came back. I considered panicking some more, but felt too sick, tired, and hopeless to make the effort.

Someone had thoughtfully taken off my sneakers and thrown the blanket over me. Could it have been Peter having an attack of conscience?

I was cold, short of breath, and a tad wobbly when I sat up. Though Peter's bite had hurt at first, and badly, Max's hadn't. My dim recollection of the attack before blacking out included a hazy memory of clinging to him, wanting more. That sent a chill down my spine, doing more to frighten me than my capture and confinement.

The difficulty breathing and sickness roiling my stomach

intensified on spotting the dried flecks of blood on the covers down near my feet, the ones from when Peter bit me the first time. Now I felt·like puking, too. Not a pleasant combination.

Max's voice broke the silence, and my attention whipped to one of the shadowed corners where he'd been quietly lurking. "Good to see you're awake."

The nausea made me take a number of deep, steadying breaths. Even though I was sitting down, I was intensely dizzy. Mental note: do not move head that fast after being bitten by a vampire. Wow.

"The sickness will pass. Don't move around so much."

I managed to scrape up a semblance of courage and gave him as thorough a glare as I could muster. My throat felt dry, my voice coming out raspy, sandpaper rough. "Why am I still alive?"

"It's not time for you to die just yet. I still need you for a few things." He smiled benignly, not showing any sign of fangs. Sometime while I was unconscious, he'd taken off his jacket. He adjusted one of the cuffs of the button-down shirt he was wearing and met my eyes, making my breath catch in my throat and my heart seize up in renewed terror. He walked to the bed and sat down beside me, folding his hands over one of his knees as he turned to face me. I pressed back against the headboard as hard as I could, my grip on the sheets making my knuckles go white. "Why, would you prefer I end it now?"

The casual way he asked if I'd rather die now or later made it a bit difficult to find my voice to answer him. "No. Not really."

"Good." He studied me with those cold gray eyes. It was unnerving as hell.

Some tension filtered out of his expression as he picked up a glass of water from a small dresser next to the bed. Someone must have brought the drink in while I was passed out. He helped me hold the glass since my hands were shaking so badly I would've sloshed most of it all over myself before getting it halfway to my mouth. His touch did not make it any easier to get my shivering under control.

Though I wasn't sure why he was doing this, I was grudgingly grateful for his help. Once I'd swallowed enough to soothe my parched throat, he put the glass back and returned his gaze to mine. At least he wasn't glaring at me now. However, I was finding this gentlemanly behavior almost as disturbing as when he was pissed off. What was with the sudden "nice guy" act?

"I do want you to know that none of this is personal."

Oh, that was rich. "Then why are you doing it? Just let me go."

He smiled again, the look an adult might give a child for doing something stupid but cute or amusing. I hated it. "You're the first chance I've had at revenge on Alec in centuries. I'm not going to waste the opportunity."

"Why me? What do I have to do with it?"

He closed his eyes and lowered his head, his features hardening. "We were both sired by the same vampire. Did you know that?"

I shook my head, wondering what that had to do with what I'd asked. He smirked, the expression bitter and cold. "Alec has not been very forthcoming with you, has he?"

"No offense or anything," I said, hoping this wouldn't piss him off further, "but he's a vamp. I never really expected him to be."

The smile he gave me was more genuine this time. "Wise of you to know our nature so well. It's unfortunate that we could not have met under better circumstances."

God, he sounded apologetic that he was going to kill me. A tinge of hysteria was creeping up on me despite my attempts at keeping my panic under control. What could I say to make him change his mind? "You don't have to do this. I don't even *like* Royce. We do business, that's all."

"He wouldn't bind himself by contract to someone he planned to use and discard. I know Alec. He only plays by the rules when it suits him."

"So what about you?" I asked him, regaining some confidence now that I might have something to use against him. "We aren't contracted. I'm not contracted to Peter. What's to stop me from slapping a suit on either of you once this is over? Or Royce from filing a grievance complaint against you for touching me? When the cops find out you two bit me outside a contract, that's an automatic death sentence for both of you."

His laughter was so condescending, I had to grit my teeth to keep from slapping him. Not that I'd dare, but it was a nice, soul-warming thought to keep the creeping terror momentarily at bay. "You really think I plan on leaving either of you alive?"

After some silence, I realized he expected me to answer him. I ground out a faint, "No."

"Very good. Like I was saying earlier, this isn't personal between us. I want you to understand what kind of monster Alec is. Only then will you be able to grasp my motivations. Do you see?"

I didn't see, but I nodded anyway. When he was talking, he wasn't hurting me. That was good. In that case, he could talk all night. He wanted me to have some insight on why he was doing this, after all. Guess he hadn't seen enough James Bond movies to know better than to tell me his Evil Master Plan. I don't think he believed that I understood where he was going, but he continued anyway.

"We are from a very different time. It was expected that we find ways to best each other, to show our strengths and find new ways to please our sire. She loved—"

"Wait a sec. 'She'? I thought you were talking about your sire."

His lips twitched in amusement at my question. "Among vampires, the term is used to refer to the ones who make us what we are. Whether they are male or female is of no consequence."

Ah. I nodded.

"As I was saying. She loved us both deeply, but we were constantly competing against each other to be seen as the greater in her eyes. We both worked toward this end for many years. Until I met Helen of Volos."

He quieted, head bowed again, seemingly lost in thought. I was too afraid to disturb him.

Eventually, he picked up his train of thought. His voice was low and flat, and I thought I detected the tiniest edge of frustration. "Rha—Alec had started out as a farmer, his family and abilities completely unremarkable. I was a *basileus*—one of the leaders of my city—before I was turned. Our sire came to the town I ruled and decided she wanted me for herself. Despite my better judgment, I agreed to leave my mortal life behind in return for what I thought would be an eternity of godhood at her side.

"We traveled much after that, which was how she met Alec. He'd been indentured into the army to aid Alexander, and we happened upon the encampment of his regiment. Our sire was taken with him and his skills at fighting and warfare. She found his stories of murder and pillage more to her liking than my tales of politics and intrigue, so she turned him into one of us, and he usurped my place as her favorite."

I knew I was staring, but I couldn't help it. The guy thought vampirism would equate him to the status of a god? I'd heard of megalomania, had heard it joked about, but this was my first brush with the real deal.

He was apparently oblivious of my reaction, lost in his own thoughts as he recited these events like he was reading off a grocery list. As if it had happened to someone else.

"It was difficult for me to stay enamored of her when her attentions were so fickle, you understand. When our travels brought us to Volos, it was only natural that I might find love in another. Helen didn't know what I was, and I did not want to tell her. I kept our relationship secret, and continued to play petty games with Alec to keep suspicion from what I was doing in the small hours before dawn."

Royce had been part of Alexander's army? Alexander the Great? I didn't remember ancient history well enough to know what time period that was, but I was starting to get an idea. I'd never heard of Volos, but the mention of Alexander might mean they were ancient Greeks. Or was that ancient Macedonians? Something like that. I knew Royce was an elder vampire, but had he lived *that* long? After seeing him prancing about dressed like a Goth in his nightclub, The Underground, it was hard for me to picture him in a toga with a wreath of laurels on his head.

Despite myself, I found this fascinating. None of the newsrags ever talked about Royce's past this candidly. "I take it they found out about you and Helen?"

"Alec did. At first it was just another contest between us. He saw her as no more than food. But once he spent some time with her, attempting to seduce her away from me, he found himself in love with her, too. It wasn't long before we were both competing for Helen's affections." He sighed, lifting a hand to rub at his eyes. Vampires do not age physically, but he seemed older to me now in some intangible way I couldn't really describe. It was as if telling me this story was making him grow older in spirit and mind, if not in body. "When he saw that she did not care for him, he revealed his true nature. And mine. While she was still reeling from the shock, he drove his sword into me, leaving me pinned against a wall, unable to reach her. He killed her, drained her while I watched, helpless and unable to do anything to save her." He looked up at me; the haunted cast to his eyes an odd counter to that bittersweet smile. "If he couldn't have her, no one could."

My eyes widened, mouth gaping in shock. *Royce* did

that? *The* Alec Royce, darling of the media and New York's high society, a cold-blooded murderer?

A kind of incoherent "uh?" was all I could manage in response to this revelation.

He reached out, and for the first time I didn't flinch at his touch. As much as I wanted to be afraid of him, in that moment I felt nothing but pity. His fingers trailed lightly along my temple, down to my jaw, tipping my chin up as he looked into my eyes.

"So, you see, now I have a chance to make him feel that same pain. I've waited for centuries for him to find love again. To take it from him, so he could know what it is to feel such loss and betrayal." His voice became soft, almost loving, and that chill started creeping back.

What was I thinking, leaning into his touch? I pulled away, his hand falling back to the bed.

"While your suffering will be much more than hers before you die, I hope that now you understand the reason for it."

Thoughts were whirling in my head, but it was hard to come up with a logical plan or something to say that might make him change his mind. All I could think was that I was going to die.

"Please," I stuttered, trying to beat down the panic rising in my breast. "You don't have to do this. There is no *way* he loves me. We hardly know each other!"

His smile could have charmed the angels from the heavens. That sad, soft voice almost made me believe him. Almost. "I know what he offered you. He hasn't turned a woman in close to four hundred years."

I stared. Was he joking? It couldn't be. It just couldn't be. How could Royce love me? I'd seen his thoughts six months ago when I held the focus in my hands, right before I destroyed it, and love sure as hell wasn't on his mind.

Max lightly rested his palm against my cheek, searching my face as he spoke. What did he expect to see? Agreement?

Please. "You know there is no other way. It's a pity that it has to be you, but Alec is the one to blame for that. More's the pity you don't love him in return—but I'm sure you can see why I need to take advantage of the situation."

Maybe if I played dumb, he'd change his mind. It was the one notion I could focus on considering the only thought running through my head was that he was going to kill me. "No. I really don't."

He leaned forward to place a cold kiss on my brow, and it was all I could do to hold back the scream that threatened to escape me at his touch. "Don't worry. You will."

With that, he rose slowly from the bed, sliding his hands down his slacks to smooth out any creases. He didn't look back as he walked out the door. Nicolas peered in at me before closing it behind Max, leaving me alone in my gilded prison once more.

I was so dead.

Chapter 12

Once Max left, I tried to think, through the fuzz in my brain, about how to get out of this nightmare. All of my stuff was still on the dresser except for my cell phone. I sat there for a while, trying to come up with a plan, to remember if I had anything that I could use to fight back. My mind didn't seem to want to function correctly. All I could focus on was that I was trapped and was going to die here.

Well. If I was going to die, I wouldn't do it lying down. Though I did briefly consider closing my eyes for just a few more minutes to rest and regain some strength, it wouldn't do me any good if I was flat on my ass when one of the bad guys came back into the room. While I didn't understand Max's reasoning as to why he hadn't finished me off yet, I was pretty sure he wanted to use me as a lure to trap Royce. For a fish that big, you had to have live bait. I guess I was lucky that I was worth more to Max alive than dead just then.

Pulling the covers aside, I gingerly slid my legs over the side of the bed, shivering in the sudden cold. The room hadn't felt *that* cold when I first got here, but it felt like an icebox to me now. I was only wearing jeans and a long-sleeved T-shirt, nothing very well insulated, but I suspected feeling so chilled had a lot to do with the loss of blood.

Taking stock of the room, I figured my best bet would be to use one of the standing candelabras for a weapon. The brass stand would be heavy and awkward, but they were the best things I had to keep the vamps at a distance.

Something made the furniture rattle, a low, resounding boom that echoed through the building.

I didn't want to stand up too fast and pass out again but a sudden urgency drove me to move. There was a muffled sound, like gunfire, beyond my door. I could hear distant shouts and running feet, and every few seconds it sounded like there was a new explosion, scream, or gunshot, each burst of violent noise coming progressively closer. At one point, a low *whumph* preceded an explosion followed by a network of hairline cracks appearing across the ceiling. What the heck was this, World War III?

Though I managed to get upright, I couldn't walk just yet, having to clutch the bed to keep from sliding right down to the floor again. There was a harsh battle cry that abruptly turned into a pained scream right outside the room I was stuck in. Closing my eyes, I took deep breaths to fight the dizziness, praying for the strength to face whatever new hell was waiting beyond that door.

Resolved not to sit and wait to be vamp chow again, I moved as fast as I could, without falling on my face, to the nearest brass candle stand. I blew out the candles and tossed them to the floor, then hefted the stand up so I could carry it closer to the door. The thing came up to my shoulder and was heavier than I expected. Keeping my balance carrying the heavy hunk of metal was not easy with my hands cuffed and feeling so out of it.

With a great deal of effort, I brought my makeshift weapon closer to the door. I looked up at my crap on top of the chest of drawers, and decided that the only thing I didn't want to leave behind was my wallet. I grabbed it and shoved it into my pocket just as someone kicked the door open.

I grabbed up the brass stand and lifted, taking a wide stance to help my balance. A man I didn't know stepped in just past the door, holding a gun in each hand and rapidly scanning the room. His hazel eyes locked on mine, and I was surprised to see relief flood into them. He tucked one of the guns into the waistline of his cargo pants and held out his freed up hand to me.

"Shiarra, right? Come on, we're here to rescue you."

Rescue? My wits didn't want to wrap around that statement right away. I stared rather dumbly for a second, slowly lowering the brass stand I'd been brandishing at him, unable to find my voice or an intelligent course of action to take. When he saw my hesitation, his gaze slid to my throat. I saw little crow's feet appear around his eyes as they crinkled in concern.

"Shit, sorry we didn't get here in time," he said, glancing back over his shoulder before gesturing again for me to come to him. "Come with me, we'll get you out of here."

Part of me was worried he was here to use me the way Max and Royce intended. Still, this was the closest thing to a shot at freedom I'd had so far and I wasn't about to turn it away. Maybe Royce was the one who sent him. I dropped the candelabra and shuffled to him as fast as I could, fighting back tears as I took his hand. If he turned out to be another bad guy, I didn't know what I'd do.

He didn't say anything about the handcuffs, barely took note of them, in fact. Instead, he smiled warmly at me, taking my hand and nodding encouragement before heading toward the door. I clasped his hand tightly with both of my own, noticing absently as he was turning away that there was a tiny pin of a white cowboy hat on the collar of his auburn bomber jacket. No way would White Hats work with Royce. Did Arnold somehow get in touch with Jack already? Was Jack the one who sent him to rescue me?

I was infinitely relieved to see Nicolas slumped against the wall in the dimly lit hallway, his eyes closed and blood streaming from a wound on his scalp. There were a couple of other White Hats, most of them holding guns at the ready, some of them kicking in doors and checking the other rooms.

The guy who'd taken my hand called out to the others. "Found her!"

"Great, let's get the hell out of here. There's too fuckin' many of them," a vaguely familiar voice rumbled out from down the hall. I started when the speaker stepped through one of the busted doors; the huge dark-skinned man who had broken into my apartment with Jack a lifetime or so ago. He came to save me?

He hefted a shotgun and jerked his head to indicate the direction for the others to go. He grinned at my shock as the guy in the bomber jacket pulled me past him. "Good to see you again."

"Guard the rear, Tiny?" the guy holding my hand asked. The larger man—wow, did he call that moving mountain Tiny?—grinned and gestured for us to keep going.

I hadn't yet found my voice. This was something of a record for me.

A group of us rushed headlong through the place, taking a flight of stairs and running down another hall. There were signs of the White Hats' handiwork all over the place. The acrid smell of gun smoke lingered in the halls. Even in the dim light of candles and gas lamps (didn't this place have electricity?), I could see bullet holes and bodies scattered on the ground, all vamps, fangs bared in rictus. While many showed signs of having been shot, every one we passed was also staked. One had a metal spike shoved in so deep that it held his limp body a foot off the floor. Projectile stakes?

A vampire suddenly dashed out of one of the rooms ahead of us, grabbing the White Hat in the lead and shoving him up against the wall. I gasped and recoiled as it savagely bit into the arm the White Hat raised in defense, worrying at it like a vicious animal. The guy leading me stopped in his tracks, sighted down the handgun he was holding in his free hand, and carefully squeezed off a round.

Part of the back of the vamp's skull suddenly turned into a fine pink mist. It screamed and staggered back, blood trickling from its mouth, its reddened eyes wide with shock and pain. The guy it was attacking quickly followed up with a stake he pulled from his stake-lined vest. The vamp clawed at the air weakly as it tumbled back to the floor and presumably died. For real this time.

Nobody was very shaken up by the incident. The guy who'd been attacked barely took the time to wrap some cloth around his arm before moving again. Everyone hurried along, my rescuer jerking me off my feet. I had to step carefully around shards of broken glass and pools of blood, since we rushed out of my prison before I could put my sneakers back on.

At the end of the hall we came into a sprawling foyer. There was a delicate crystal chandelier illuminating the badly singed Persian carpets, blackened marble floors, and somewhat charred carved oak stairway. The splintered remains of the doors were scattered across the floor, and white marble statuary that must have been lovely at some point lay shattered into a thousand pieces.

Through the gaping hole where the front door used to be, I could see a pack of thirty or forty vampires standing on the lawn, Royce in the lead.

He looked pretty surprised. The other vamps were milling around muttering to each other. I could tell they were vamps right off since most of them had their fangs out, eyes glittering with that strange reddish light they get when excited or pissed off. I was disturbed to note that they were mostly men, lending some credence to what Max had said earlier. Or maybe Royce was bi? Whoa. Not going there. *Really* not going there.

The whole pack of them went on the alert as the hunters stepped forward, brandishing their weapons. Twelve White Hats against three times that many vampires? Hoo boy. This wasn't good.

"Let's rock!" one of the White Hats shouted, lifting a sawed-off shotgun to his shoulder. The pack of vampires surged forward, Royce's eyes narrowing as he made a gesture to direct them at the guys with the guns first.

"No! Stop!" I cried, shrinking at the looks I was getting from the White Hats and even some of the vampires. It worked, though, since all of them paused, looking at me expectantly. I added a little more in the hopes it would stop them from shooting or clawing each other up. "We're all on the same side, sort of."

The guy with the shotgun couldn't have looked more surprised if I'd sprouted horns and a tail.

"Let go of her, boy," Royce demanded, staring hard at the man in the bomber jacket. His hand immediately slid from mine. Was Royce using mind tricks on him? The other vampires started forward again, some of them growling and baring their fangs. To their credit, none of the White Hats flinched or stepped back.

Royce turned to me, his anger fading into concern. "Shiarra, come with me."

Looking back and forth between the White Hats bristling with weapons and the dozens of vampires surrounding Royce, I realized for the first time why the White Hats did what they did. How scary it must be to them, standing there, expecting to die. Kind of like me.

"No."

Royce was at a loss, particularly since I took the hunter's hand again. The guy looked at me with brows arched in surprise at my touch. There was some comfort in feeling that human warmth, and I drew strength from it. We'd survive this.

Frowning, Royce started in again, sounding all too reasonable. "Shiarra, I came here to save you. I can keep Max away, something they can't promise you."

"They're doing just fine so far. They saved me, Royce. I'm going with them."

He growled softly in frustration, gesturing for the other vampires to back up. Most of them did, one or two staying at his side. I recognized the one on the left as his lieutenant, John, who didn't look very happy. His gaze slid from me to the interior of the house, and I looked back to make sure there weren't any baddies sneaking up. The room behind us was empty. My paranoia wasn't appeased, however—I still had a bunch of trigger-happy fanatics on one side of me and a crowd of pissed off, hungry-looking vampires on the other.

Royce stared at me for quite a while, his black gaze as piercing as, and more unnerving than, Max's. Somehow I managed not to waver, meeting his eyes and keeping my expression as neutral as possible. Hard to think of him as a monster, looking so human in jeans and a casual-but-tailored shirt, hair swept out of his face by the wind rustling through the trees surrounding the house. Unlike the other vamps, he wasn't outwardly ruffled, showing no hint of his fangs and no trace of red in his eyes. It was hard to tell what he was thinking. He was studying me with such a bland expression that we might as well have been discussing the weather over coffee. But I still couldn't meet his eyes; it was obvious by his gaze alone that he was still intensely scrutinizing me, maybe gauging what I felt about him after talking to Max. Or maybe he was trying too hard not to show interest in the damage to my neck.

It was hard to see the man in front of me as the murderous beast Max had described, the same one who'd come within a hairsbreadth of drinking my blood less than twenty-four hours ago. He was here to save me. All these vamps at his back weren't here to kill me. They were here to help him get me free. Well, more likely to help him tear Max and his cronies into itty-bitty pieces.

What had he intended to do once he got me out? If he had gotten to me before the White Hats, would he have tried turning me? Somehow I couldn't picture him giving me a lift home and dropping me off with simple admonitions to watch my back.

Eventually he relaxed a trifle, waving a dismissing hand. "Fine. For the time being, go with them. I do want a chance to speak with you about this. I'll be calling you later, as soon as I'm done here."

Oh, whatever. He sounded like a jealous boyfriend. I frowned at him in disapproval. "Max took my cell phone."

"I see. I'll be in touch, then."

How? I shook my head, not wanting to think about it any longer, tugging lightly on my savior's hand to lead him and the rest of the White Hats past the vamps. None of the vampires or hunters looked very happy about it. Royce's followers watched us go with naked hunger in their eyes. If Royce hadn't kept them in check, I had no doubt they would've fallen on us like a pack of ravenous dogs the instant we came into view in that doorway.

Once the last hunter was clear of the shattered doors, the vampires spilled in with Royce in the lead, disappearing into the house using that unearthly speed of theirs. The hunters kept their weapons trained on the vamps, staying close to each other. Obviously they didn't trust that one or more of those monsters might not decide to grab a snack before battling Max's minions. Honestly, I didn't totally trust that they wouldn't try something like that either.

I shuddered once the last of them was out of sight. The guy at my side gave my hand a reassuring squeeze, his words punctuated with soft, shaky laughter. "That was really something. For a second there I thought we were toast."

"For some reason, Royce has a soft spot for me," I said, my laughter wavering more than his. "It'd be a shitty way to stay in my good graces if he went and killed all the people who saved me just because they got here first."

He nodded, his nervousness fading as he gave me a lop-sided smile. "The name's Devon, by the way."

"Shiarra," I replied, letting go of his hand and taking in the surroundings. We were in the woods. The big house—more of a mansion really—stood by itself in the forest, a whole crapload of cars parked every which way on the grassy lawn and scattered over the dirt road winding through the trees. I could see the moon peeking out between naked branches, illuminating cars in the clearing that varied from jeeps and SUVs to unassuming compacts to high-end sports cars. Where the heck did all these people come from?

"Jack told us you needed help. He's been . . . uh . . ."

"Tailing me?" I guessed. Devon looked sheepish, but still nodded. Guess not all White Hats are equally crazy or use the same methods. "I figured. That's how you guys found me so fast, huh?"

He nodded again, clearly relieved that I wasn't pissed. "Yeah."

The big guy with mahogany skin, who had come along with Jack to bully me into joining the White Hat cause a long time ago, fell into step beside us. "Jack wanted us to give you a message. He said to tell you the offer is still open, if you know what side you're on now."

I thought about it. Really thought about it. As crazy as their methods might be, the White Hats knew what they were doing. I had watched them take out a vamp with my own eyes. They had experience, access to all kinds of weapons, and were willing to save my ass if an Other decided to get too up close and personal.

"I don't know yet," I said as we stopped beside a beat-up jeep, its dark paint covered with scratches and dents.

Chapter 13

The drive took forever; Devon was concentrating on driving and Tiny didn't seem to be in a talkative mood. I didn't recognize the area we were in, and the back roads that cut through the woods surrounding the vamp house were mostly without signs of human habitation. I didn't see any telephone poles or power lines, so I presumed the house was extremely old, off the grid, abandoned and forgotten. Which would also explain why the only illumination in the place was from candlelight and gas lamps.

The other White Hats were following us in four beat-up jeeps and SUVs. When we finally pulled onto a paved road, we only had to go a few blocks to get onto an expressway but I still didn't know where we were. Then, after a long time, we pulled onto the 87, a road I recognized.

I must have been out like a light for hours for the bad guys to drag me this far away from Queens. No wonder it took so long for Royce and the White Hats to get to me. We were way out, upstate, in the ass-end of nowhere.

It gave me a chill to think of what might have happened if Jack hadn't kept a tail on me. Would Max have used me as bait for Royce? Turned me into a vampire? Somehow I didn't think he planned to keep me around for an eternity.

I pondered where we were going once we got to the George Washington Bridge. The steel beams and cables were lit by glittering bluish lights running along their length, brighter white lights illuminating the two towers that supported the massive structure and cars trickling along both levels. Traffic on it was crawling, as usual, even at this time of night. At the peak of the graceful arch of the bridge, I studied the skyline shining with lights like stars fallen to earth, scattered all along the waterfront. With the moon hanging high in the sky and the mixed lights from the bridge and city far across the span of concrete and steel reflecting off the water below us, a deep sense of relief and calm overtook me.

I was home.

It took a while for us to make it into the city, and I took careful note of the streets when we exited somewhere in the Bronx. We were headed more toward the East Bronx than South, but to my surprise, we ended up on City Island, crossing a tiny three-lane bridge over Long Island Sound.

The minuscule island held a quaint town like you'd see on a picture-perfect New England postcard. The streets were lined with shops selling high-end antiques or boating and sailing goods. Seafood restaurants abounded. Due to the hour, most, if not all, of the shops were closed. There was no traffic, and it didn't take long until we were cruising down a back road, passing homes out of a Victorian fairy tale.

Soon we pulled up in front of a charmingly rustic house with a gorgeous view of Eastchester Bay. The faintest scent of wood smoke was in the air, mixing with the cool, salty ocean breeze. Lights gleamed from the wide windows across the front of the house. The White Hats who had been following our lead found their own parking spots, scattered here and there along the quiet street.

As we stepped out of the car, parked under the protectively outstretched limb of an enormous oak, someone opened the front door and stepped out on the porch to meet us. With the light from inside the house shining behind him, I couldn't make out his features clearly, but from the slender frame and blond hair I could tell it was Jack. Clearly he'd been waiting up, expecting us.

Jack was the last person I would have expected to live in a place like this. For one thing, his (very illegal) gun shop was in downtown Manhattan, a hell of a commute. The affluent neighborhood didn't strike me as his thing either. Did he make enough money to afford digs like this? What *was* the sort of place I expected to see him living in? A spartan apartment with minimal furnishings and guns and weapons scattered around the empty floors maybe. Not a sprawling, pastoral house with wind chimes hanging from the eaves of the porch and a ship's anchor leaning against a wooden barrel filled with sand and seashells, propped in place by a thick coil of rope.

A wave of dizziness swept me when I stepped out of the car, and I had to clutch at the door to keep from going to my knees. Silly as it sounds, I'd forgotten how weak I was from the blood loss and wasn't expecting the abrupt wave of nausea and vertigo that hit me. Tiny, who'd already started walking toward the house, turned back at the little cry I gave. He and Devon were soon on either side of me, supporting me so I could walk. Embarrassing, but without their help I never would've made it to the front door.

"Being bitten takes a lot out of you," one of the other White Hats commented on our way up the walk. His gruff voice was sympathetic; it occurred to me that some of these hunters might not be as crazy as I'd thought. "Once you get some fluids and protein, maybe a little rest, you'll start feeling better. Do you know your blood type?"

I had to think hard for a second to dredge up the answer. "O-positive."

Tiny said, "Jack, do we have any on ice?"

"I think so." He held the door for us as the guys practically carried me through. They took me into a spacious living room, setting me down on one of the plush couches. I was grateful to be off my feet; sitting down helped the dizziness pass. Even better, they put me in the spot closest to the stone fireplace, which was radiating blessedly welcome warmth from a brightly burning stack of logs.

The other White Hats filed in, taking seats or disappearing deeper into the house. Jack stood across from me, a low coffee table between us. He was eyeing me speculatively, disapproval written all over his features. Knowing Jack, I'd bet dollars to donuts he thought I'd wanted to be bitten. "We'll get you something to eat and drink in a moment. Did Max make you drink any of his blood?"

The thought alone made me gag. Making a face, I shakily sat up a bit more in the thick cushions. One of the other White Hats sidled closer, taking my arm. I was a little slow on the uptake, not thinking to pull away before he jabbed me with a needle and took some blood. Like I hadn't lost enough of that already. I glared ineffectually after him as he disappeared around a corner.

Jack cleared his throat, bringing my attention back to him. "Well? Did he?"

I growled out my response. "No. Of course not, that's disgusting."

Tension I hadn't noticed at first suddenly left him relaxed and smiling. He wasn't glaring at me anymore. Huzzah.

"You're right, it is disgusting. It's also how a vampire bonds a still-living human to them, and part of the process of turning you into one of them. You're sure?"

I had to swallow back bile at the thought. "I'm sure."

"Excellent. Our facilities aren't the best, but we have a makeshift hospital set up in the basement here. Dr. Morrow will give you a transfusion once he's prepared the equipment.

I'll let you get some rest, but in the morning I'd like to get the details on what happened."

"Sure."

He nodded sharply and backed away, settling into an empty seat and falling into quiet discussion with Tiny about the events of the evening. I found myself looking around curiously.

It seemed Jack had a thing for the beach. There were shells and miniature sailboats lining the mantel, and on the whitewashed wall, a gorgeous oil painting of a harbor with hundreds of boats lining the beach. The floors were honey-eyed pine varnished and waxed to a pale golden glow, and the furniture was upholstered in dark blue with treated wooden accents slightly darker than the floors. There were bookshelves with books on sailing and the sea, more little boats, some large pieces of frosty sea glass, and even a tall jar with sand and brightly colored seashells inside. All in all, a cozy, lovely place. It completely skewed my impression of him and his hunting buddies.

Said hunting buddies did look out of place in that bright, cheerful sailing enthusiast's haven, what with all the leather, fatigues, and combat boots. Not to mention the weapons bristling from every pocket, peeking out from under jackets or casually propped up beside chairs. They all looked tired and drained. A couple guys appeared to have fallen asleep in their seats.

Devon, who had disappeared into one of the other rooms after helping me to the couch, reappeared carrying a tray. A tall, slender woman dressed in hunter's garb accompanied him. She introduced herself as Nikki. They offered me sandwiches, which I didn't feel much like eating, but the hot tea with honey and lemon that Devon pressed into my hands was welcome.

"Drink that, then I'll help you downstairs," he said.

I did as I was told, closing my eyes as I sipped at the tea.

There was a faint medicinal undertone to it that made me wonder what he'd laced it with.

A few minutes later, Tiny was nudging my shoulder. The soft murmur of conversations between the other hunters in the background—or whatever was in the tea—had lulled me to the edge of sleep. "You still awake?"

"Ugh. Yeah." Opening my eyes was phenomenally difficult.

He grinned down at me, holding out a hand. "Let's go see Dr. Morrow. Then you can sleep as long as you want."

I nodded wearily, taking his outstretched hand in both of mine. He engulfed my fingers with his, bringing me up to my feet. I stumbled along with Jack, Devon, Tiny, and the hunter woman hovering over me. They helped me down the wide wooden staircase into the basement, which had been converted into a tiny hospital complete with beds, IV drips, and even lab equipment. Squinting against the harsh fluorescent track lighting, I spotted two other "patients." They were swaddled up in clean sheets and warm blankets, both fast asleep. I could see that the leg of one was in traction. The left forearm of the other was sprawled across his chest, showing bloodstains seeping through white gauze wrapped around it. It was the guy who had been bitten in the hallway while we were escaping.

Tiny lifted me up, despite some protest on my part, and laid me out on one of the empty gurneys. A short, bookish-looking Asian man with thick glasses, who reminded me a great deal of Arnold, came to the bedside. He was pushing an IV drip with saline solution and packaged blood already hooked up.

"Shiarra Waynest, right? I'm Dr. Morrow."

I tried to keep my eyes open as I returned his warm smile. "Hi."

"I don't know if you remember me. I treated you for shock after that fight you had at the Embassy Suites."

"You did?" I blinked, trying to recall. Everything, from

my thoughts to my vision, was hazy. Whatever they put in the tea was working fast.

"Mm-hmm. Just lie back, relax, and I'll start the transfusion."

His voice was soothing enough that I did what he said without protest. A pinprick in my arm made me wince, but that was all. I was incredibly tired, but somehow managed to stay awake and listen to Jack and Dr. Morrow talk about me like I wasn't there.

"Any idea how much blood she lost?"

"No," the doctor said, sounding concerned. "It must have been a lot to cause such a severe reaction. She's lucky we had some of her type on ice."

Jack sighed. "How long before she's on her feet, do you think?"

"She should have at least four or five days of bed rest. I want to keep an eye on her for a few days in case there are any complications. Don't push her, Jack. I know what you're thinking, and she's not ready for it. Not by a long shot."

"We've had other hunters bitten and up on their feet the next day."

"Leave it alone. A quick bite is a lot easier to treat and recover from than being drained from a prolonged feeding like this." Dr. Morrow sounded irritated. It was too hard to open my eyes to see, so I just listened. I could picture the little frown lines appearing between his eyebrows, and found the idea of the smaller man glaring at Jack comical. "A bit more and they might have killed her. Don't you find it odd that she's still having a hard time finding her balance even though it's been hours already? That she practically needed to be carried down the stairs? Trust me on this. She's not ready for what you want."

Jack cursed, and I heard the sound of a few pairs of feet tromping away. Devon's voice surprised me; I would have thought he'd left with the others. "Will she be okay?"

"Yes," Dr. Morrow said, more tired than annoyed now. "She should be fine given some rest and time to recuperate. I'm just afraid Jack won't wait that long."

Devon's voice followed me into the blessed dark of unconsciousness. "I don't think any of us can wait that long. We need her."

Chapter 14

"For the last time, I need to go home!" I shouted, struggling to sit up on the gurney. "People are looking for me!"

"And for the last time, you are staying put! Doctor's orders!"

Devon was laughing at my efforts to sit up, easily pushing me back down thanks to how weak and shaky I was. I'd swear his eyes were positively twinkling with laughter. The patient with the busted leg was also chuckling, not helping my bruised ego any. The guy who'd had his arm bitten was back on his feet and upstairs with the other hunters, so it was just the three of us down here in the basement.

With a low growl of irritation, I sank back, too exhausted to keep fighting. It was great that someone sawed the chain apart while I was asleep, but I found myself rubbing impatiently at the cuffs locked on my wrists. Feeling the stupid things chafing my skin made me feel trapped, like my brush with death had only been temporarily delayed.

It didn't help that I felt cut off from my friends and family in this makeshift hospital. Without my cell phone,

I didn't have any phone numbers with me. I was starting to regret not keeping them memorized. I could wait for Jen to get in the office tomorrow morning or somehow get to my computer. There should be an e-mail somewhere with Arnold's phone number. Sara and Arnold both had Chaz's number. I should call Officer Lerian, too; the police were undoubtedly looking for me, especially with Royce's encouragement.

"Look, if you need something that badly, one of us can go pick it up for you."

I shook my head, making the tape holding gauze over the bite marks crinkle. No way was I going to give anyone connected to the White Hats the passwords to unlock my computer. Even Sara, who is the sister I never had, doesn't get access to my e-mails.

"What will you tell the police if they're staking the place out and see you trying to break in? 'Hi, Officers, just trying to pick up some stuff for the lady who was kidnapped yesterday. Nope, can't take you back to the White Hat super-secret hideout, where she's recovering from an unreported vampire assault. So sorry.'"

Bo, the guy who had his leg in traction, was laughing heartily. "Admit it, Devon, she's right. Even you couldn't charm the cops with that one."

A lopsided grin curved Devon's lips while he rubbed the back of his neck. "Okay, okay, I get the point. I guess I can take you there. Dr. Morrow won't be happy about it, though. Neither will Jack."

"Jack can kiss my ass."

"Not a very nice thing to say, missy," Bo said. "If he hadn't been keeping an eye on you, there's a good chance you might be dead right now."

I shrugged uncomfortably, pulling at a loose string on the button-down shirt I had to borrow from Jack since my T-shirt got trashed with blood stains. "Royce showed up shortly after you guys did. He would've gotten me out of there."

Devon tilted his head to one side, curious. "How is it that you came to be a hunter but still deal with Alec Royce? He's practically king of the vampires. I'm surprised he lets you live."

"I'm not a hunter. It's a long story; I don't really want to go into it."

"I'd like to hear that story sometime. How about over coffee next Saturday?"

Well, that was unexpected. Under the circumstances, it was an odd place to be propositioned for a date. Still, it was flattering, and I gave Devon a wry smile, flipping off Bo when he let loose a raucous wolf whistle. "Sorry, Dev, not unless my boyfriend comes with us. He's the jealous type."

Bo snickered and threw a minimuffin from his breakfast tray to bounce off the top of Devon's head. "Ha! Told you she wouldn't be single. You owe me five bucks!"

Devon sighed and shook his head, shoulders slumped in disappointment obviously feigned to be greater than it was. "Knew you were too good looking to be single."

I grinned and leaned forward to pick a hunk of banana nut muffin out of his gelled, dark brown spikes. He really was a charmer. Probably a player too, seeing as he wasted little time trying to win me over. "Keep your distance, mister. I'll let you know if something changes."

He chuckled and brushed his fingers through his hair. "That's all I ask. I'd still like to hear that story of yours. Maybe you can tell me the Cliff Notes version in the car."

"Sure," I said, accepting his offered hand. Once I stood up, dizziness made me stop for a second to get my balance, but it wasn't anything like it had been last night. The transfusion and a good night's sleep, followed by a hearty breakfast with lots of protein, had helped quite a bit. Any lingering feeling of sickness was mild enough that I was no longer worried I might toss my cookies every time I turned my head. The cold from the linoleum tile seeped through my socks, and I hustled as best I could to the stairs.

Bo called out plaintively after us, "Can you at least send Nikki down so I have another pretty lady to talk to? You're leaving me all by my lonesome."

Devon held out a supporting arm as we reached the stairs, grinning back at Bo. "Tough it out, you wuss."

I punched Devon lightly in the arm, smiling. "Don't worry, Bo, I'll bring you back some movies and books. We can watch *Beaches* together when I get back!"

Devon and I cracked up at the horrified look that crossed Bo's face.

When we got upstairs, most of the other hunters were gone. Nikki, the tall blond who had helped get me downstairs last night, ran into us in the hallway. She looked surprised to see me on my feet. "Hey, good morning. I take it you're feeling better?"

I smiled, spreading my arms and taking a breath deep enough for my ribs to twinge. "Good as new."

She returned the smile and followed us to the front door. Judging by his pace, I was guessing Devon wanted to sneak out before either the doc or Jack knew we were leaving. Devon talked to her as we walked.

"Can you let Jack know we're just going to pick up some of her stuff? Shouldn't be gone more than a couple hours," Devon said.

"Sure. Watch your ass, though, you know he won't like it."

"Don't worry, I can handle it," he said, grabbing his auburn bomber jacket off the coat rack and stepping out into the cool shade of the porch. Jack was sitting on a wooden bench against the wall, casual in jeans and a T-shirt, one leg comfortably thrown over the other. He took a deep drag on a cig, his gaze neutral and tone noncommittal once he addressed us.

"Going somewhere?"

I opened my mouth to speak, but Devon cut me off. "We're going to get some clothes and shoes and stuff from her apartment. We won't be long."

Jack closed his eyes, tilting his head back and blowing a smoke ring. "I wouldn't go down there if I were you."

"Why not?" I asked, frowning.

"There are cops and reporters crawling all over it. I'd think you'd want to lay low after last night's escapades."

"What? I can understand the cops, but why reporters?"

He didn't bother to open his eyes. "Don't you watch the news, Ms. Waynest? The press loves anything to do with the Others. You've recently been attacked by a rogue vampire, saved and apparently wooed by Alec Royce. They found your car abandoned in the street. It's all over the police bands that you were kidnapped by men impersonating plain-clothes officers. You're a hot story—I'm sure they're just dying to reach you. Or find your body. Whatever creates the most sensationalism."

Yikes.

"I wouldn't worry about it too much," Devon was quick to reassure me. "I doubt there are many reporters hanging around with no story to report. They're probably down at the local station bugging the cops or listening in on the radio bands for any hints. As for the police, well, you're okay. They can stop looking for you."

Jack opened his eyes, a single platinum brow perking up as those cold blue eyes regarded the other hunter. "They'll want her statement. Probably want to take her into protective custody."

"I think I can handle the cops. I've dealt with them plenty of times before."

"Are you sure?" Devon asked, looking a trifle uncertain. "I mean, I don't want to end up getting you in even deeper trouble by taking you back there."

"I couldn't possibly be in any deeper trouble than I'm in now. Don't worry about it, let's just go."

"Don't tell the police anything about us," Jack warned as Devon and I started toward the car. "Tell them you escaped when Royce showed up, and stayed with a friend last night."

Rolling my eyes, I gave him a sarcastic salute. "Aye, aye, Cap'n."

Devon coughed into his fist to hide his laughter, but the bemused curve of his lips gave him away. Jack just looked annoyed.

"I'm not joking. If you tell them anything that even hints at the involvement of White Hats in this mess, Alec Royce and Max Carlyle will be the least of your worries."

Devon shook his head, his smile fading. "Stop scaring the poor girl. She's had a rough night, and I'm sure she knows what she's doing. Right?"

"I'm a PI, of course, I know how to deal with the police."

Without any more delays, we continued to his jeep. While Devon was settling himself in, I fastened my belt and took a look around.

It was absolutely gorgeous out, only a few puffball clouds in the sky and the crisp salt breeze carrying seagulls out over the bay. The water shone a lovely deep blue, spotted here and there with sailboats and yachts. The house was even prettier during the day. The white trim and dark brown paint made it look like a rustic, homey shack overlooking the beach, though its size would probably qualify the place as a mansion.

Most of the other houses on the street were the same— large, comfortable, picturesque Victorians. Definitely not a neighborhood I would have pegged as a White Hat haven.

This would be a great place for a vacation, but I couldn't afford to linger. I had to get in touch with Chaz, Sara, Arnold, and as much as I dreaded it, the police. Jack did say they found my car, so I'd have to get it out of impound. Thank goodness it hadn't been stolen.

The thing I dreaded most of all was calling Royce. After all, he did come to save me last night. I didn't want to alienate him, so I needed to express some gratitude. Chances were high that, until Max was out of the picture, I'd need his help again.

As Devon started the car, I considered how to handle the situation with Max. If he was still alive after last night, I would need to lie low for a good long while. If I went to Royce, he'd probably start that crazy talk about turning me again. Hiding with the White Hats might work for a while, but I had a business to run. Max obviously wasn't beyond playing dirty and might go after my family or friends next. After the story he'd told me about Helen of Volos, it was clear he wouldn't stop until Royce and I were dead. Max had the patience of an immortal, and intelligence enough to wait until I was off my guard to make my death work to his advantage. Unless I found some way to prevent it, he could strike at any time.

Since I couldn't hide forever and wasn't interested in crawling to Royce for safety, there was only one answer to (almost) all of my current problems.

I had to kill Max Carlyle.

Chapter 15

Once we hit the road, Devon started prying about how I met Royce and how I came to be a hunter. He didn't appear to notice my newfound resolve to become a murderer. Maybe I could ask him for tips later, hunter to hunter.

"What did you do after you signed the contract?"

"I promised Royce I'd save his ass. Which I did. That's probably the only reason he even talks to me."

"Jeez. No wonder Jack's been trying to get you to work with us. What changed your mind?"

I shrugged uncomfortably, staring at the road ahead. We were a couple blocks away from my apartment building, and I was grateful I wouldn't have to keep talking much longer. Though Devon was easy to get along with, I was uncomfortable discussing that crazy period of my life. Arnold and Sara knew better than to bring it up, Chaz liked to pretend it didn't happen, and Royce wasn't around enough to act as a painful reminder. I may have irrevocably involved myself with the hidden, darker underside of the Others, but that didn't mean I couldn't make a healthy attempt at wallowing in denial. Until they butted their way into my life and I had no choice but to deal with them, that is.

"Turn right here."

He glanced at me briefly, though I had the feeling he'd have tried to hold my gaze if he didn't have to keep his attention on the road. "Really, what was it?"

His voice was gentle, understanding, and that was my undoing. Only Chaz and Royce had any insight into exactly how much vampires scared me. This was the first time someone human, like me, seemed to have any idea what I was going through. I had to swallow back the lump that formed in my throat.

"I've never felt as helpless in my life as I did last night. I don't ever want to feel that way again."

As we turned the corner and pulled into a convenient parking space a block down from my building, the flickering of red and blue lights caught my eye. I squinted against the glare of the sun to see what was going on. There was a crowd gathered on the sidewalk, blocking any view of what was happening.

Devon turned in the seat to look at me, really look at me, and I couldn't hold his gaze. "You don't have to feel that way again. You've got us at your back now."

I nodded as I opened the door, quickly stepping out on the sidewalk to avoid answering him. I started walking, not waiting for him to catch up, focusing on the lights flashing up ahead. What was going on?

Zipping up his jacket to hide his shoulder holster and guns, he jogged to my side just before I reached the fringe of the gathering in front of my building. I was very surprised to see a bunch of cops pushing the crowd back from the front door, shouting for everyone to move back and keep clear. A few reporters strained to get closer. The civvies were more conservative, watching from across the street or back a little ways from the yellow caution tape, hands in pockets. Two uniforms had their guns out, covering the front door. Another one was leaning against the wall, clutching his chest, taking deep, gasping breaths while two others hovered over him. Someone else was shouting orders into a walkie-talkie, screaming for backup and an ambulance. What the hell was going on?

One of the officers looked in our direction, glancing at me and Devon briefly before doing a double take. A grin lit his face and he waved, ducking under the tape and ushering the reporters back.

"Ms. Waynest!" the rookie kid, Officer O'Donnell, shouted in relief. "You're alive!"

The reporters jumped on his statement like a pack of Rottweilers on a fresh T-bone.

Both Devon and I abruptly backpedaled, seeking escape from the stampede of reporters hurling questions like javelins. Someone made a crack about Royce that brought a blush to my cheeks. Horror struck when I spotted cameras and video recorders aimed at me—and there I was, in my borrowed, oversized shirt, walking around in socks with telltale bandages on my throat. Let us not forget that I had a strange guy, who was decidedly not a vampire *or* my boyfriend, escorting me back to my apartment. This was not something I wanted splashed across the ten o'clock news.

"Ms. Waynest! Ms. Waynest, there were reports you were kidnapped yesterday, are those true?"

"Were you really pulled out of your car by a vampire?"

"Is Alec Royce the vampire who bit you? Are you going to be turned into one?"

I couldn't hide from the cameras, but I did shoot one of the more brazen of the bunch a dirty look when she asked if I wanted to comment on Royce's skills in the bedroom. The other reporters quieted, waiting eagerly for my answer.

What the hell did they take me for?

Devon was practically cowering behind me, looking as alarmed as I felt. Officer O'Donnell elbowed his way past the crowd, taking my arm and hurrying me to a black-and-white. He threw an apologetic glance my way, realizing the extent of his error as he tripped over one of the trailing cables from a reporter's mic being shoved in my face.

It wasn't much of an improvement in the car. I scrambled into the front passenger seat while O'Donnell shoved the White Hat in the back. Maybe since I wasn't obliging them with details about my kidnapping or love life, a bunch of the paparazzi were now asking who Devon was and what his connection was to me. The three of us tried to pretend that there wasn't a flock of rabid reporters knocking on the windows and pressing mics and recorders at us, and slumped low in our seats. O'Donnell broke first, rubbing the back of his neck.

"Sorry about that."

I quelled my urge to growl out some epithets at Officer O'Donnell, covered my eyes, and leaned back against the door, banging my head lightly against the window. He was a kid. A rookie kid in uniform. He didn't know any better. Telling myself that did not make it any easier to get a handle on my temper. Deep breaths, Shiarra. Breathe.

"What the hell is going on here? Why are there police and reporters crawling all over my apartment building?"

He looked sheepish, glancing to where the other cops were gathering. The ones who weren't attending to the guy hyperventilating at the side of the building were watching us. From what I could see around the crowd of reporters, none of them looked happy.

"A Were let himself into your apartment shortly before you got here. There were a couple of techs in there doing another sweep, trying to pick up fingerprints or something to figure out who took you. When he asked what was going on and they told him they were investigating your disappearance, he went crazy. Shifted right there in the room, chased the techs out. He drove off the first unit who got here. The rest of us have just been waiting for S.W.A.T. to arrive and keeping the civvies out of harm's way."

Damn. Chaz was here? I'd texted him what happened.

How could he not have known I was missing? How could he shift outside of a full moon, right in front of the cops?

"I've got to go in there."

"What?! No!"

"No way!" Devon said, putting a hand on my shoulder. "Are you kidding? You're in no shape to fight a Were. Shit, even I wouldn't go up against one without some backup."

I scowled at them, pushing Devon's hand away. O'Donnell eyed Devon suspiciously until my next words. "He's my boyfriend—it's not my fault he's freaked out. Somebody handled it pretty badly if he went so far as to shift outside of the moon cycle."

The two men couldn't have looked more shocked if I'd slapped them. I reached across the seats to shut O'Donnell's gaping mouth, not bothering to hide my irritation. "Stop staring at me like that."

Devon slumped back in the seat, his hazel eyes wide and confused. "You—you're dating a Were?"

"Yes, not that it's any of your business," I snapped before turning to O'Donnell. "Can I go now? I can keep him from trying to tear the place apart. You can call off the rest of the cops."

The young cop didn't seem to know what to do. He didn't move for a long moment, looking at me like I'd grown a second head, his mouth silently working as he tried and failed to find words to answer me. Annoyed, I shoved open the door, stepping out into the media frenzy. They didn't touch me, but they followed me closely, and with so many shouted questions, they were drowning each other out. It was unnerving. Devon was trying to figure out how to open his door, but he was in the back of a police car—someone would have to let him out. I wasn't worried about leaving him behind. I didn't want anyone, least of all a trigger-happy White Hat or some rookie cop, following me upstairs to face a panicked Were.

When I ducked under the caution tape, the nearest cop snagged my arm. "Stay back! This is police business."

I paused in my tracks, glaring at the guy. I knew he wasn't responsible for the mess going on in my life, least of all for Chaz having a panic attack, but I was too pissed off to keep my temper in check. The world was out to make my life miserable, what with Max attacking me and Royce trying to turn me. Ugh, and was that *gum* stuck to the bottom of my sock?

I let the cop have it.

"Let me the *fuck* go, right the *fuck* now! You call this mess 'police business'? I'm going to sue you assholes for gross negligence, unlawful entry, and deliberately aggravating my boyfriend into shifting outside the full moon! It's *your* fault he's shifted, not his! I'm going in there to clean up the mess *you* idiots made, so get your fucking hands off me!"

He didn't seem to know what to say. The moment I said "sue," he withdrew, letting go of my arm. A girl's got to know what buttons to push to get her way, I always say.

One of the cops tending to the guy having a panic attack looked at me, surprise mixed with disgust. "Are you shitting me? You're dating that furball?"

"He's not a furball, he's a *man*. It's not his fault he grows fur during the full moon, so leave him the hell alone. Let me pass so I can calm him down."

"Lady, you've got to be kidding. He'll kill you. Tear you to shreds."

I shook my head, raising my hand up to cover my eyes again. A headache started pulsing right between my eyes. It didn't help when I noticed how quiet it had gotten. The people gathered at the edge of the caution tape were hanging on our every word, microphones and cameras pointed at us, catching it all on film. Perfect.

Through the haze of my anger, a wild thought crossed my mind. Maybe I could use this disaster to my advantage.

I stood up straight and forced myself to appear as calm and rational as I didn't feel, after a couple of deep breaths to steady my nerves.

"Look, he's only shifted because he's upset. He thinks I'm dead or kidnapped or whatever. Once he sees me, he'll calm down. Even when shifted, most Weres have enough of their human intellect left to keep from doing anyone harm unless they're deliberately provoked. Right now, I'd say he's about as upset as he could possibly be. Shooting him won't solve anything. Follow me up there if you want, but if he doesn't get some reassurance, he's not going to shift back anytime soon. Besides, why not avoid a potential bloodbath when the S.W.A.T. team gets here? I don't think anyone wants that."

O'Donnell put a hand on my shoulder to show his support. He was ashen pale, but determined. "I'll go up there with her. I'll take the heat if Sergeant Vega has a problem with it. He won't be here for another twenty minutes. This can't wait that long."

The other cop shook his head. "You know I can't let you do that. You can't go in there."

"Watch me," I said, sidestepping around him and rushing up to the front door.

I ignored their commands to come back, and heard O'Donnell reassuring the other cops, following rapidly in my footsteps. He could get in a lot of trouble for this. So could I, for that matter.

Either way, I sorely hoped what I'd said outside was true. Chaz was the leader of a werewolf pack. That meant he was bigger, faster, and most importantly, smarter than the average shifted Were. He might be hotheaded, but he shouldn't be so out of control that he wouldn't recognize me. If he didn't, Officer O'Donnell and I would be mincemeat.

Chapter 16

The rookie was braver than I gave him credit for. His voice was firm and confident, but his hand was trembling as it hovered over his piece. "Are you sure he won't attack us?"

I kept the lead, taking the stairs up to my floor slowly, more because I was tired and didn't feel so hot than because I was worried.

"Pretty sure. If he didn't kill or attack anyone right off, chances are he's 'himself' enough to keep from hurting us."

"Okay," he said, quieting for a minute. We were almost to my floor when he blurted out another question. "Why are you dating a Were?"

A perfectly valid question. Pity he had to sound so disgusted and horrified when he asked it.

"He's good looking, makes good money, a perfect gentleman, and saved my butt more times than I can count. He's not a bad guy. Just is what he is."

The officer nodded, not seeming completely satisfied, but at least he stopped asking questions. Guess he was one of the "Weres are okay to work with, not okay to sleep with" crowd. Go figure.

When I pushed open the door on the landing, the first thing I spotted were pieces of splintered furniture lying against the wall a few yards away. Light was spilling into the dim hall from my apartment. I hoped those splintered wood shards weren't part of the door. Explaining the property damage to my landlord wasn't an appealing prospect.

Suppressing my fear was difficult with O'Donnell's rapid breathing punctuating the unnatural quiet. There should've been a radio or TV blasting from one of the other apartments at this time of day. Had the police gotten everyone out? Were they in hiding? Or had Chaz given in to his baser instincts and hunted my neighbors down?

"Chaz?" I called out quietly, knowing he must have heard us on the stairs. He should've had enough time to get himself under control and shift back to human, but I wasn't going to take any chances of startling him if he was still shifted. That could be deadly.

A low, plaintive whine drifted into the hall. Way too deep to be a dog.

I started forward, not rapidly, but not wasting any time either. When O'Donnell hissed at me to wait, to slow down, I ignored him.

I didn't have time to be pissed off about the bullet holes in the wall or the splintered door frame. A gasp was startled out of me at the sight of the monstrous, hulking form lying battered and bleeding in the corner. Chaz was curled up near the couch, blood streaming down the gray fur of his shoulder. Massive claws dug deep furrows into the carpet, flexing with each spasm of pain.

Ice blue eyes met mine when the great, shaggy head lifted, another whine drifting from his throat. I slowed, hands at my sides, fingers splayed and palms out to avoid triggering any fighting instincts. Chaz's ears flattened, showing his fangs in a silent snarl when O'Donnell appeared in the doorway behind me. The cop's hand was plastered to his gun, his knees shaking so badly I could hear them rattling. This must be the first time he'd seen a Were in their half-man, half-animal form. O'Donnell's fear could mean an itchy trigger finger or might provoke Chaz into attacking. Not good.

I spoke quietly, trying to pull Chaz's attention off the terrified kid. "Chaz, what happened?"

A growl escaped him, setting the hairs on the back of my neck to attention. My fear dissipated as Chaz lowered his head and stopped showing his teeth, a gruff, less irritated sound escaping him. With little cries of pain, he levered up to four paws, limping closer to me. Right now, we were nearly eye level. When he stood up on his hind legs, he'd have to stoop so he wouldn't bump his head on the ceiling.

The cop took a step back, gun clearing the holster as I reached out a hand to Chaz. I hissed at him to put the weapon away while I got down on one knee, examining wounds mostly hidden behind fur and blood. One of the rounds hadn't gone very deep, and I could see the hint of the metal shining through the mask of blood. It was difficult to tell how bad it was with his muscles rippling in an involuntary effort to dislodge the bullet.

"Chaz, come to the kitchen so I can get more light."

The kid rapidly backed out of the way. It was painful to watch Chaz limp, making little pained sounds with every step, the few feet from my living room to the kitchen. I watched just long enough to see him settle to the ground and then ran straight to my bathroom. I tore open the medicine cabinet and raced back with a pair of tweezers.

"For God's sake, don't just stand there. Help me!" I snapped at O'Donnell as I passed him the second time.

He came out of his frightened trance, skittishly following me to the kitchen. He was staring at Chaz like he was afraid the Were was going to turn around and bite him.

"Get some warm water and towels from under the sink. Chaz, don't move. Sorry, this is going to hurt."

Chaz whimpered like an injured puppy—a very large injured puppy—but stayed as still as he could while I prodded at the wound. The bullet was lodged in muscle, not very deep. He was lucky the rest of the shots had gone wild. I should be able to get it out. Lucky me, I'd get to pull them out of the plaster next.

His muscles twitched and jumped under my fingers while I worked. Careful as I was, with the way his body was reacting, it wasn't easy to find an opportunity to pluck the metal out. When he let loose with a deafening howl of protest, Officer O'Donnell jumped so badly I thought he'd smack his head on the ceiling. Okay, okay, I jumped, too. The sound *was* pretty unnerving.

I whispered soothing nonsense things while I worked, trying to focus on pulling the stupid hunk of metal out. I also tried to ignore the cracking of the kitchen tile as claws repeatedly flexed while I dug around, trying to get a good grip on the slug. After a few more hair-raising howls, a bit of pulling, and a few unfortunate slips of the tweezers, I finally dug the bullet out.

O'Donnell pressed the warm, wet cloth to Chaz's shoulder as he lay panting on the linoleum. I was thankful the policeman didn't seem squeamish about Were blood. Some people still thought you could catch lycanthropy just by touching infected blood, though that theory had been disproven long ago. The virus is passed through fluids, yes, but it has to work its way into your bloodstream through a bite or an injection of tainted blood.

I stared at the bullet. Hard to tell. I went to the sink to get the blood off my hands and the piece of metal. I had to be sure.

A rinse revealed the unmistakable gleam of silver shot. No wonder his body hadn't expelled it or started healing yet. Cops were supposed to carry regular rounds and switch to silver *after* it was confirmed they were dealing with lycanthropes. From what I understood, they didn't carry anti-Were equipment unless they'd been tipped beforehand. Too expensive to do otherwise.

How did this happen? How could they have known to be prepared with silver shot?

I turned back to the two, eyes narrowed. I was too angry to appreciate the irony of how scared O'Donnell looked. He was leaning to put pressure on the wound and at the same time holding as much of himself as far away from Chaz as he could. Like he was afraid he'd catch something if he got too close. "Chaz, can you shift back?"

He slowly lifted his head from his paws and shook it, unnerving O'Donnell even more.

"Too badly hurt?"

A nod this time.

"Jesus. He understands us?"

Chaz turned back to just look at him. O'Donnell backed up a step, putting his hands up. "Okay, I get it."

I moved to take his place putting pressure on the wound, worry settling in since it was still bleeding. I'd seen him take much worse damage fighting other Weres, but nothing hurt a lycanthrope like silver. Made me wonder who knew enough about me and my personal life to set up something like this.

That thought in mind, I turned my attention to the windows. The shades were up, sun shining merrily in the sky, oblivious of the little drama that had played itself out. Somehow, someone had been able to get pictures of the inside of my apartment. I was willing to bet there was a camera set up in the building across from mine. Someone was watching me.

I dragged O'Donnell by the wrist so he'd take over holding the cloth to Chaz's shoulder. Once I was sure he wasn't going to move again, I stalked over to each of the windows in every room, pulling down the shades, making sure the blinds were all closed. Once that was done, I dragged a duffel down from the top shelf of my bedroom closet, then proceeded to pull out the things I would need.

Guns. Amber Kiss perfume. Cross. Armor. Belt with

stakes. Enough fresh clothes for a couple days, ass-kicking boots, trench coat. Officer O'Donnell appeared in the doorway as I was putting on some sneakers. "I need to call in the guys downstairs. You okay?"

"Yeah," I said, standing up and brushing my hands down my pant legs. I'd caught a glimpse of myself in the mirror when I was grabbing some stuff in the bathroom, and wondered why the hell Devon had tried hitting on me today. I looked like I'd been on a three-day bender, then left forgotten in the rain to sleep it off in the mud next to the stoop. My hair needed a wash so badly it had lost some of its natural curl. There were bags under my eyes deep enough to carry luggage, and my skin was so pale I looked like a ghost. There was a bloody handprint on my stomach, probably left by me when I was tending to Chaz and wasn't paying attention.

O'Donnell didn't look much better than me. There was blood streaked on his nice blue uniform and on his hands. I only noticed since he gestured at the duffel on the bed. "What are you doing?"

"Getting ready to leave. I need to call someone, then I have to go."

He put on his cop face. It isn't as impressive when you look like you're on the verge of having hysterics. "You can't just walk out of here. There's going to be questions; nobody knows what happened to you last night. Besides, don't you want to get your car out of the impound? One of the meter maids found it on the street yesterday and had it towed. Grady and I caught ten kinds of hell for leaving you to go chase that speeder."

I groaned, slapping my forehead and making the short length of chain on the cuff jingle. Silly me, I'd forgotten about my car. "Crud, yeah. Okay, I'll stick around long enough to answer questions. I'll have to pick up the car later."

Some of the immediate panic left his face. His relief

would have been comical if I wasn't so pissed off right now. "It may be better if you wait with the wolf."

I nodded and picked up the duffel, walking out into the living room. Chaz was huddled where we'd left him in the kitchen. His head was on his paws, and half-lidded eyes were watching the doorway to my bedroom; a hulking mass of muscle and fur strong enough to tear through the walls to find me if he had a mind for it. His ears perked up but otherwise he didn't move.

I tossed the bag next to the shattered door and sat down on the kitchen tile, leaning against Chaz's uninjured side. He gave a rumbling sound of contentment when I rubbed the soft fur between his ears. He used to scare the hell out of me when he was shifted. After all the time we'd spent together, not to mention his saving my life, it was easier to be tolerant.

O'Donnell stayed in the bedroom, using his walkie-talkie to let the other officers know it was safe to come up and to put their weapons away. I wondered darkly which one of them had shot my boyfriend. My threat of a lawsuit earlier wasn't idle. I'd make it a point to note down their names and badge numbers for use later.

"Don't get up when the rest of the cops come in. One of them shot you, right?"

Chaz lifted his head just enough to nod, then twisted slightly to look at me. It was a pain in the butt he couldn't talk.

"I have a question. This is important. Did the guy who shot you already have silver bullets or did he switch out his ammo after you shifted? Did he come prepared?"

Chaz blinked those bright, luminous eyes at me before nodding again. Well, that answered that question. Conspiracy theory time.

"Okay. Try not to scare them when they come up here. Do you want to press assault charges?"

He growled. I took that as a yes.

Patting him lightly on his good shoulder, I levered back up to my feet and started making some coffee. Before long, a bevy of uniforms trickled in, all of them watching Chaz nervously. A couple kept their hands on the butts of their guns, but none of them had their weapons out. O'Donnell gestured for them to come away from the kitchen so he could speak to them in quiet, hushed tones. One of them looked mighty pissed. That one kept gesturing angrily in our direction, talking in a harsh whisper. Likely none of them realized Chaz could hear and understand everything they were saying.

I had a few mugs poured before they were finished talking. "Anybody need cream or sugar?"

I fixed the drinks and passed them around to the officers. They quieted once I brought the coffee around, shifting uncomfortably in the living room and looking unsure where to start. On the bright side, Chaz was being good, staying down like a gigantic, sleepy wolf. He didn't look quite so threatening that way. The occasional flash of his teeth was the only outward sign of his efforts to restrain his temper, ruining the image of a rather large but mostly harmless guard dog. He settled down after I gave him a nudge with my foot on the way to the kitchen.

I picked the bullet up off the counter as I grabbed the last mug, my own, and took a seat on the couch. The officers were huddling on the far side of the room, as far as they could get from Chaz without looking too conspicuous. None of them but O'Donnell were willing to come anywhere near the kitchen.

"I guess you guys must have some questions for me. Before we go into that, can I ask one of my own?"

O'Donnell answered me. "Sure. Shoot."

I leaned forward and carefully set the bullet down on the coffee table. Right in the middle where nobody could mistake the gleam of silver. "Who told you guys to be prepared to deal with a shifter?"

One of the cops rubbed his chin, looking nervously at Chaz. His badge said D. VEGA—the infamous Sergeant Vega perhaps? Was he the same one mentioned in that newspaper article about Royce saving my butt? I was willing to bet so. He was reluctant, but answered me soon enough.

"An assistant to Mr. Royce called last night and said there was possible lycanthrope involvement in your kidnapping. Since we had that complaint from you about the break-in the night prior, the captain advised us to load up silver shot before coming down here."

Huh. Royce said jump and the police asked how high. Why would he say Weres were involved in this mess when he knew as well as I did that Max was behind everything? Was he trying to get my boyfriend out of the way because Royce thought I wouldn't touch him as long as I was committed to somebody else? If that was the case, he needed a serious reality adjustment. There were a heck of a lot more convincing reasons I wasn't interested in socializing with the vampire. I'd worry about it later.

"Whatever's going on, it has nothing to do with Weres," I said, balancing my coffee mug on my knee. "The guy who tried to break in and the one who kidnapped me are vampires. Some yahoo named Max Carlyle is orchestrating the whole thing."

Chaz gave voice to a thunderous growl that caused everyone in the room, including me, to jump nervously.

I hushed him while Sergeant Vega, carefully ignoring the angry werewolf huffing a few feet away, said, "Ma'am, we're going to have to take you down to the station for questioning."

"You've got to be kidding me! I just got home, feel like shit, haven't showered in two days, probably need a doctor, and you want me to come down to the station? My life is stressful enough as it is. You can ask me whatever you need to know right here."

O'Donnell hid a smile behind his coffee mug. The rest of the cops were rolling their eyes; a couple were smirking. Seems a few of them were glad to see Vega taken down a notch. For his part, the sergeant looked like he'd just bitten into a particularly sour lemon.

"We need to know what happened so we can figure out what to do about it," Vega said. "If there's some psychotic vampire out there kidnapping women, we can't leave him on the streets. We have databases and files, sketch artists who can draw up the perp so we know who to look for. None of that is here."

"I understand that. Trust me, I agree with you. He's a monster and needs to be stopped. However, Alec Royce knows way more about him than I do. Hell, I was so out of it after this . . ." I pointed to the bandages on my neck that everyone had studiously been avoiding mentioning or looking at. Uneasy gazes flickered to the bandages and away again. Wusses. "I doubt I could tell you more than the general part of the state I was in, let alone the name of the town or address. Royce has some history with the guy behind it; he can tell you more about Max than I could. Give me time to rest and think about it, and maybe I'll remember some details that would be of use to you."

One of the cops was watching Chaz over his shoulder. "Would he know anything about that leech?"

I followed his gaze, questioningly meeting those gleaming husky eyes. Chaz shook his head slightly, fur ruffling up around his shoulders. He didn't know anything and wasn't happy about it.

The cop was surprised Chaz responded to his question. "He understands us?"

"Of course. He's furry, not stupid."

"Can he talk?" another cop asked.

"No," I responded, mildly amused. "Look at his muzzle. He can't form words with that. Wait 'til he shifts back, then we can go to the station and answer whatever questions you want."

Sergeant Vega turned back to me, scowling. "We need you down there to answer questions now, not tomorrow. We can't put the investigation on hold for this. It's willful obstruction."

"Tough shit," I grumbled, not sympathetic at all. "I told you. We're not doing this now."

"Yes, we *are*."

Yeah, this was going to take a while.

reminder that both Chaz and I were considering pressing charges, Sergeant Vega finally agreed. Technically, it wasn't Officer Lerian's jurisdiction, but the other officers didn't seem to mind so much that someone else would be dealing with me and Chaz.

Plus, they had no idea how to transport an injured thirteen-foot-something Were and were not up to answering my questions about what the hell they'd been doing in my apartment. I'd been kidnapped on the street. They had no business hunting around my stuff, particularly since they could've gotten the information about my whereabouts and kidnapper from Royce. The officer who interviewed Royce had established the vampire knew something about Max Carlyle. They could've lifted prints from my car or gotten physical descriptions from witnesses to the kidnapping on the street. Whatever their reasons for being here, I was willing to bet they were being so accommodating because of the stink I was making over the illegal search and the damage done to my apartment.

As for Chaz's injuries? We'd talk about that once he was back to his human self, seeing as he couldn't discuss much of anything as he was now. He'd need to heal a bit more and rest for a while before he'd be in good enough shape to shift back. Sadly, the laws governing Others mandated that any inhuman creatures unable to speak due to their shift, and anyone involved with them, could only file formal complaints when all concerned were in human guise (thus no immediate danger to other parties involved). That meant we weren't allowed to press charges until Chaz had a chance to talk about what happened and give his side of the story.

Whatever else was going on, I was convinced that the police search of my home was a setup of some kind, designed to either trap or kill Chaz. After all, what reason did the cops have to be here if not for the direction from Royce? Since it was one of Royce's lieutenants who made the call to the cops, he must be trying to get Chaz out of the way. It made me worry which of my friends Max or Royce might go after next. Why were they trying to get rid of him?

I also had to consider the possibility they were trying to find something of mine. If they were agents of either vampire, they might have been trying in a roundabout way to get their hands on the hunter's belt. No doubt, the cops would confiscate such a weapon and check if it was related to my kidnapping or something worse. If the belt was taken out of my hands, obviously I couldn't use it against Royce or protect myself if he decided to take a more forceful approach to turn me.

"It's going to get dark in a couple hours," Devon said, interrupting my thoughts. "We should get moving."

Chaz lifted his head from his paws, tilting his head slightly to one side. I got up with a groan, heading to my computer. "Give me a sec to make a couple calls, then we can leave." I paused in my tracks, looking down at myself. "Actually, let me make those calls, grab a fast shower, *then* we can leave."

He nodded with a wry grin, and I settled into the chair in front of my computer. I booted up and tapped out some passwords. After a quick search, I found Arnold's e-mail from what felt like a million years ago.

TO: S. Waynest
FROM: ArnieGoblinSlayer20
SUBJECT: V. W. and the belt

Hi Shiarra, hope this makes it past your spam filters. I am e-mailing you from home, I just saw the news. If you haven't already, pick up the paper or check the local news on the net, you'll see.

I figure by now you're probably in a tough spot. I might be able to help.

Start wearing the belt at night, no matter what.
Don't leave home without the necklace or perfume
on. You might be in danger during the day too,
call my cell as soon as you get this (212-555-9035).

Arnold

After Veronica Wright—former VP Acquisitions of The
Circle, and my employer during a brief attempt to locate a
dangerous artifact in the hands of Alec Royce—was murdered, I had to watch my ass a lot more closely than
before. Arnold had advised wearing the hunter's belt his
coven had given me so I could protect myself against
rogue vamps and Weres. Hopefully the belt would serve
me as well against Max Carlyle and his band of merry
men as it had against crazed sorcerer David Borowsky and
his psychotic vamp of a girlfriend, Anastasia Alderov.
Those cheering thoughts in mind, I snagged up the cordless phone on my desk.

"Hello?"

"Arnold, it's Shia."

"Holy crap! Are you okay? We came home as soon as
we got your message."

"Yeah, I'm fine. Shaken up, but I'll live. Listen, you and
Sara should hide out somewhere for a bit. Maybe with
Sara's sister, Janine? Chaz is hurt, and I'm afraid whoever
is behind it might go after you guys next."

He quieted for a second. He must have been talking to
Sara, since I heard some muffled noises in the background.
Abruptly, her voice was on the line. "Shia? What hap-
pened, where are you?"

"I'm okay, don't worry. I'm at home right now, but I'm
leaving in a few minutes. My cell is gone, so you're going
to have to reach me via Chaz for the time being. I need to
hide out for a bit. I told Arnold you two should as well.

Chaz got hurt, so I get the feeling Royce or Max are going after my friends next."

"Is he going to be okay?"

"I think so. Get this—the cops came to my place to investigate my kidnapping, right? Well, someone from Royce's office told them to be prepared with silver shot."

"What?!"

"Yeah. Watch your back."

"Christ. Okay. Where are you going to hide out?"

I glanced at Devon thoughtfully before responding. "Not totally sure yet, but I'll call you when I get there."

After I hung up, I turned back to my computer and searched for one of the old messages from Royce. There was an e-mail in there with his company contact info, including a phone number. Scooting the rolling chair to the window, I peered between the blinds and checked the angle of the sun. Not too high in the sky, but not quite close to sunset either. Was it late enough in the day for Royce to be awake? He'd called me before when the sun was up. If worst came to worst, I'd leave a message.

"A.D. Royce Industries. How may I direct your call?" chirruped the saccharine voice of the receptionist.

"I'm calling for Mr. Royce. This is Shiarra Waynest."

"Shiarra Waynest, gotcha. Hold for just one moment please."

I waited for quite a bit longer than one moment, thinking about what I wanted to say. If the bastard was out to get Chaz, I'd pay him a daytime visit and introduce him to Mr. Sun. After a close approximation of eternity, that irritatingly cheerful voice came back on the line. "I'm very sorry, but Mr. Royce is unavailable. May I take a message?"

Crap. "Sure. Tell him I want to know if Max is still in the picture. I'm available for the next fifteen minutes or so at this number . . ." And I gave her my home phone, waiting for her to repeat it back to me. "Right."

"Thanks for calling. Have a great day!"

"You, too." After hanging up, I wondered why the heck a vampire had Rebecca of Sunnybrook Farm answering the phones. Shouldn't she be more, I don't know, coolly professional or something? Maybe she was too new to be jaded yet. Or maybe I was just a grouchy cynic. Yeah, that sounded about right.

I turned away from the computer and tossed the cordless to Devon. "I'm taking a shower. If he calls back, ask him to hold on. I won't be long."

He set the phone on the table and took a seat, still watching Chaz like a hawk. Chaz was way too hurt and tired to be much of a threat to anyone, but Devon would never believe as much. Ah, paranoia—got to love it.

I grabbed some fresh clothes and ducked into the bathroom, looking forward to a hot shower. It took some effort to ignore how beat up I looked in the mirror once I shed my clothes. Working fast, I got the worst of the grime off my skin and washed my hair. For the first time, I was unnerved at how much it looked like blood when the long, wet strands lay plastered against my skin. That thought helped hurry me along.

Stepping out of the shower, I didn't take any time to primp. All I did was wrap myself in a big towel and run a brush through the wet tangles, throwing in some hair gel to keep it from getting too out of line. My frizz was probably a hopeless cause anyway.

As much as I didn't want to, I needed to take a look at the bites on my neck to see how bad the damage was. Nobody had given me a mirror at Jack's before the bandages were put in place. I used the towel to wipe some of the condensation off the mirror, then gingerly tugged at the medical tape holding the gauze in place. A hiss escaped me at the pull on my sore, bruised skin.

The fang marks weren't as bad as the bruising. In fact, they were just two pairs of dainty nicks, each one right over my jugular. I had to lean forward over the sink just to see them in my reflection.

I brushed my fingertips along the slight discoloration. I'd expected the hickeys from hell, and while there were definitely some marks, it wasn't nearly as bad as I'd feared. From all the horror stories and bad movies of my youth, I'd expected to see two pairs of gigantic, scabby holes in my neck. These little marks wouldn't even scar. Was this why no one had ever spotted vamp victims before the leeches announced themselves to the world?

Judging by the bites, it was hard to believe I'd even been fed on. There was some weakness from the blood loss, to be sure, even with the transfusion. If not for that, you might have overlooked that anything was wrong with me. The thing that bothered me most was that it felt *good* when they did it. The experience was made all the more frightening for that. Something so bad for you shouldn't feel that good and make you want more.

I abruptly recalled the harsh memories of bloodstained youths straining against their handcuffs at the police station as they wept and screamed for their dead master. Their cries were so heart-wrenching, their despair so deep, their raw pain so obvious on their pallid faces, it had been enough to thoroughly frighten me. That anyone could feel so deeply for a monster who had to feed on you in order to survive had been sufficient repellant to keep me away from vamps entirely. Until that unfortunate little incident with the *Dominari* Focus, that is.

A chill swept over me as I suddenly understood how the people bound to vamps could feel such loss—like an addict would despair at having their fix taken away. I gripped the edge of the sink so hard my knuckles turned white. I leaned forward to stare into the reflection of my eyes as I tried to remember what made the vampires monsters. Dangerous. Why I had to destroy Max Carlyle.

Why I had to stay away from Royce at all costs.

Swiftly turning away, I tossed on jeans and yanked a light turtleneck over my head to hide the marks. I would *not* think about this anymore. Not now. I told myself that, over and over, avoiding the mirrors as I hurried to dress and get out of the unbearably claustrophobic bathroom.

When I padded out of the bedroom, Devon shook his head. Royce hadn't called. Irritated and jittery, I sat across from the hunter.

"That's not like him. Usually he gets back to me right away."

Devon nudged one of the mugs left by the officers to one side. "Maybe he's ticked that you brushed him off last night."

"Maybe. I don't know." I leaned back, fingers drumming on the tabletop. "He wanted to talk to me back in the woods. Remember? Said he'd be in touch."

"Yeah, I remember."

I got up again, pacing briefly, and stopped to pick up the shredded remains of Chaz's clothes on the floor. His keys, wallet, and cell phone were in the pockets of his jeans, so I brought them to my duffel and tossed them inside before throwing out the remains of his ruined clothes.

"We can't leave Chaz here. He has to come with us."

"What!" Devon was so alarmed, you'd think I'd told him they were going to have to bunk together. "No, he can't come with us! There's no way I can take him back to Jack's. The other hunters would kill him."

I laughed, collecting a few of the empty mugs and bringing them to the kitchen. "I didn't tell you to take him to Jack's place. I just said he has to come with us."

Chaz moved when I nudged him with my foot, inching over to lie on the carpet instead of the kitchen tile. Devon surreptitiously scooted his chair back when the big Were moved closer. I ignored them both and dumped the mugs into the sink, then started digging around in the drawers.

"I'm taking you back when we're done here," he said,

scowling. "The last thing I need is Jack riding my ass for not following orders again."

Again? Hmm, wonder what he did the first time around.

"Don't worry, I'll go back with you. I just can't leave him here like this." My extra set of keys was in the back of the drawer, hidden under a pile of expired coupons. "Can you pull the car up to the front? I don't want to take him too far like this."

He eyed Chaz dubiously. Chaz flattened his ears, but otherwise didn't move. Muttering a low curse, the hunter rose to his feet.

"Come down in about ten minutes. I'll put the seats down so he can fit."

"Great, thanks."

Devon headed into the hall. I knelt next to Chaz to check his shoulder. After removing the towel that had been acting as a compress, I could see the bleeding had stopped. He made a grumbling noise when I tossed the towel onto the counter.

"Oh, hush, you. It's looking better already. We'll have to drop you off somewhere on the way. I can't take you to a White Hat haven."

His head immediately lifted, hackles rising and a deep, threatening growl rumbling in his throat. I backed up, raising my hands. "Whoa, whoa, I get it. We'll talk about it more in the car."

He gradually settled back with another low rumble. Yeesh. Touchy Were.

The phone rang. I made a little growl of my own and rushed to the table. Took the vamp long enough.

"Royce?"

"No, actually," came an unfamiliar voice. "This is John, his assistant. He's in a meeting, but I know he's been looking for a way to get in touch with you."

Oh. Great. So he has a lackey get back to me now? "Uhm. Look, I'm going to be out on the road in a sec. I really need to talk to him now. My cell phone is gone, so I won't have a way of reaching him after I go."

"I see. Can I arrange a meeting? He's got a slot available at ten tonight."

Crud. Considering he was under suspicion for planning the murder of my boyfriend and had evil designs on my body, meeting with Royce didn't sound like the greatest idea. "I don't have my car, so I can't commit to meeting him someplace. I'll call back later when I can get to another phone."

I didn't wait for a response and hung up on him. Rude, I know, but I was in a hurry. I grabbed a Post-it and went back to my e-mail, jotting down the numbers for Royce's office and for Arnold's cell before shoving the paper in my jeans pocket.

Scooping up my duffel, I gestured for Chaz to follow and headed out the door. It took him two tries to get up; he hadn't thought to favor the injured limb at first. He slid past me on all fours, not moving very fast, keeping the weight off one leg. I used my extra keys to lock the door behind us, swearing at the way it stuck in the busted frame. My eyes narrowed as I watched Chaz limp painfully down the hall toward the stairwell.

If Royce was the one behind Chaz's injuries, he was going to pay for it. Big time.

Chapter 18

The reporters surprised the hell out of me once we got outside. I'd done my best to put them out of my mind. I would've thought they'd have left by now. Instead, a bunch of them surrounded us, keeping a respectful distance, asking their questions from a few yards off. The few other mingling onlookers hightailed it, disappearing back into their homes at the sight of Chaz.

"Ms. Waynest! Ms. Waynest, who is this?"

"How'd the Were get hurt? Does it have anything to do with the police here earlier?"

"What's your connection? Are you a member of his pack?"

I hunched my shoulders and ducked my head, hurrying to Devon's car idling at the curb. The reporters followed, a worrying flock of sound in the background. Chaz snapped at a photographer sidling in to take a close-up, making the poor guy shriek and stumble back. And no, of course, he didn't bite the cameraman. As I mentioned to the cops earlier, he was furry, not stupid. His actions were calculated. The bared teeth and silent, vicious snarl were a sufficient deterrent to keep everyone else out of our path. It didn't stop the hurled questions, but the rest of the reporters took the hint and gave us more breathing room.

Devon, waiting in the driver's seat, watched us with interest. I slung my duffel into the front seat, then rushed to open up the back of the jeep. Even with the back seats down, it was a tight fit for a Were. Judging from the pained noises Chaz made as he climbed inside, it wasn't particularly comfy either. Devon twisted around at the sound of ripping fabric.

"For God's sake, can you not destroy my car while you're in here? I'm trying to do you a favor."

Chaz huffed and loosened his grip. I shook my head and shoved his tail in so I could close the door. Some of the reporters dashed to their cars and news vans parked on the street, obviously intending to follow us. A few hung around taking pictures. It was all I could do not to flip them off. As the stragglers sprinted to their cars, I made do with slumping in the seat, staring at the horizon turning the deep orange hue of sunset. There was very little daylight left.

Devon turned to me questioningly, hooking a thumb at the back seat. "Where do you want me to take him?"

"I don't know," I mumbled, giving in to suddenly overwhelming fatigue. The stress combined with lack of sleep was catching up with me. "Wherever."

I could feel his eyes on me, the unspoken concern radiating from him making me uncomfortable, but I was too tired and worn out to think of a better answer. He put the car in gear and started driving.

An irritating buzzing sound was coming from the bag at my feet. I cracked open my eyes and leaned down to open up the duffel. Someone was calling Chaz's phone from a restricted number. Since he wasn't in any condition to take the call, I answered it for him.

"Hello, this is Chaz's phone."

There was talking in the background, like a restaurant, punctuated by a whisper of breathing lingering on the line. A click, and the call was lost. Weird. Shrugging it off, I twisted in the seat to look at Chaz. "Do you mind if I use it?"

He gave a noncommittal sound which I took for affirmative. I scrolled through the contacts until I found Sara.

"Chaz?"

"No, it's me," I said. "Hey, do you have a safe place we can drop him off while he's furry?"

"He's furry? Hell if I know." She went quiet, considering, then apparently registered what I said. "Wait a sec. 'We'? Who's 'we'?"

"A new friend."

"Great. A vamp? Or a Were?"

"Neither."

"A mage?"

"Nope."

"Will you stop fooling around?" she complained, impatience lacing her voice. I couldn't help but grin. "Who the heck is helping you with Chaz when he's shifted?"

"You wouldn't believe me if I told you. You'll meet him soon; just tell me where we can go that isn't your place, my place, or the office."

"Janine would have a heart attack if she saw him. Your parents' place is out of the picture. Which reminds me, I think your mom called me looking for you. I missed it while I was driving. Let me ask Arnold if we can hide out at his place. I doubt anyone will come looking for us there."

That sounded like the best idea I'd heard all day. No doubt, both the vampires would have people searching for me. Royce might make a go for Sara since he knew she was my business partner and closest friend. One of us always knew where the other was. "Go for it, let me know what he says. Call me back on Chaz's cell."

"Got it. I'll call back in five."

"Oh, hey, before you go, can you also ask him if I can crash if I need to?"

"Sure."

I stuck the phone in the coffee holder and dug around in my pockets, looking for the Post-it with Royce's number. I didn't want to talk to him, but I also did not want to start the business week tomorrow with worries of a crazy vampire sending his daytime agents to my office to kill or kidnap me. The last thing I wanted was to have our office building go up in magefire. Sara would kill me herself.

Hiding out tonight sounded great in theory, but I knew if I ignored the problem and tried to avoid Max, he'd figure out some way to find me again. Quite possibly in person, seeing how his lackeys did such a shitty job of convincing me to play nice. Plus, Royce might decide he liked the idea of using his not inconsiderable resources or powers of persuasion to force me into playing his way instead of leaving me to choose my own path.

I dug the piece of paper out and dialed Royce's office. The cheerful receptionist greeted me.

"Hi, this is Shiarra Waynest again. Is Mr. Royce available, or is he still in that meeting?"

"I'll check," she said, far too chipper for my taste. "Hold on just a sec for me."

Once again, "just a sec" translated into "for-freaking-ever." My wait was rewarded with that familiar, smooth voice, though I had to fight not to cringe when he spoke. Far too tantalizing to the senses, unspoken promises behind the words making me squirm uncomfortably in my seat.

"Shiarra, I'm glad you called. There are things we must discuss, preferably not over the phone."

What was so bloody important that he always needed to see me in person instead of telling me over the phone?

"I didn't call to set up a meeting. I called to find out if Max is still alive."

"Yes. That's part of what we need to talk about."

"I'll say," I muttered, forcing myself to put my free hand back down in my lap once I realized I was unconsciously rubbing the bite marks on my throat. "Can't the meeting wait? I called to find out if you know where Max might be lying low. I need to find the bastard."

A long, incredulous pause stretched over the line. Glad I've got it in me to shock a vamp who's been around since before Christ was born. "I wouldn't advise that," he said after a long pause, his words spoken very carefully. "I am worried someone may be following you—an agent of his. Before you bring them back to your friends, it may be best if you come to one of my offices. I can provide a measure of protection."

"A lot of people are following me just now. There are reporters from every newspaper, magazine, and TV station from here to Jersey on my ass."

He went quiet again. Gee, I was rendering people speechless a lot these days. Rapid tapping on a keyboard was followed by amused laughter. "I see. All the better. Come to The Underground. Security will keep the press at bay, and we can speak in my office."

"No freaking way."

"Oh, come now," he said, lightly cajoling. "You know you could not ask for better protection than for the leading vampire of New York to take you under his wing."

"Who will protect me from you?" I shot back before I could rethink the words coming out of my mouth.

"I suppose my actions have been more forthright than usual."

"*Forthright* is not exactly the term I would have used. I'd say you were being a pushy bastard who needs to stay the fuck away from me and all of my friends. Why'd you sic the cops on Chaz?"

"You have good reason to be wary of me, but I don't know what you're referring to about your boyfriend. What happened?"

I was not appeased by how easily he agreed with me or

the apparent puzzlement and dumb act he was playing. "Fine, you want to play that game? I won't meet with you until I know it's safe. Oh, wait, that's never."

"You do make things difficult." I bristled at his laughter, knowing he found me trying to keep my ass out of the fire amusing. "All right, how about this. Why don't you choose the place we meet? Would that make you feel safer?"

"Barely."

"Where?"

I hesitated. "I don't know yet. Let me call you back."

"I'll be away from my office for a bit. You can ask for John if I'm not back by the time you call. Or you can use my cell phone."

I bit back on the temptation to ask him where he was going to be and just wrote down the number to the cell as he recited it. Would he be plotting more ways to get Chaz out of the picture? Meeting with his friends at the police station?

Feeding on someone?

"Are you still there?"

"Yeah," I answered shakily, not sure why. "Fine. I'll ask for you first, but if you're not there, I'll call John. Do you have the number I'm calling from on your caller ID?"

"Yes."

"That's Chaz's cell phone. I'll have it with me for now. You can call me if something comes up."

"Good. Don't wait too long to call, there is a lot to discuss and more that we will need to do tonight."

"What? Okay, whatever. I'll talk to you in a bit."

I stared at the phone after I hung up. Devon was studiously avoiding looking at me. "What happened to going back to Jack's?" he asked.

For no reason I could readily put my finger on, I was annoyed. Guess it was better than being scared of a voice on the phone. "We're still going back to Jack's. We're just going to have to take two side trips, is all."

"Two? Look, I don't—"

He was interrupted by an unladylike yelp startled out of me when the phone started vibrating. Even Chaz made an amused sound. I glared at them before picking up the call from Sara.

"Arnold's okay with Chaz coming over. He said to warn him ahead of time as he needs to wait in the hall until Arnold can escort him past the shields."

"Great, we'll be there in a bit."

After I hung up, we continued on in silence. I didn't want to talk, Chaz couldn't, and Devon was focused on driving. Every now and again I gave some directions, but that was all. Devon didn't find his voice again until we'd made our way to Greenwich Village.

"Can I ask you something?"

"Sure."

"Why aren't you afraid of Royce? Why do you work with him?"

That brought my gaze to focus solidly on him instead of the passing streets. He was concentrating intently on the road, not sneaking glances at me like before. It took a minute to think up an answer he would accept. Or one I would accept, for that matter. "If you think I'm not scared of him, you haven't been paying attention. He terrifies me. I work with him because I don't have a choice. Or rather, the choice of working with him is better than the alternative."

"Better than working with the White Hats?"

I was surprised at how bitter he sounded. "I'm working with him *and* the White Hats. Why, what's wrong with that?"

"Aside from the fact that he's our number one target, nothing, I suppose."

Ah. "Look, I'm not going to betray you guys to him. I'm unofficially one of you right now. Jack's the one who wanted me on the team, so all of them, including you, are going to have to accept that I deal with the Others. I mean, come on. I'm dating a Were. There's no way Jack didn't know that before he started trying to recruit me. It's not like it's a big secret or something. And dealing with Royce? He's known about that, too. I also have mage friends at The Circle—so just relax and try not to get too worked up about it."

He lapsed back into silence, not answering me. I didn't feel the need to continue explaining myself to him either. Aside from directions, I kept my mouth shut.

After a bit, he spoke up again. "I still see a bunch of reporters behind us. Are you sure you want to lead them to wherever we're going?"

Grumbling irritably under my breath, I glanced in the side mirror and cursed when I saw all the news vans behind us. I'd for the most part successfully forgotten about them, having hoped they'd lose interest and leave us alone. We couldn't lead them back to Arnold's or Jack's. Where could we go?

I gritted my teeth and looked down at the phone in my hand, once more finding myself considering turning to Royce for help. God, I hated how much it felt like he was herding me. Once again, manipulating me indirectly into doing exactly what he wanted. He was right in that he could keep the press away if we went to one of the clubs. Arnold and Jack couldn't promise the same and didn't need trouble like this showing up on their doorstep. If my location continued to be broadcast on the news, Max would find me in no time.

On the other hand, Royce could be planning something bad to do to me and quite possibly had a hand in the damage done to Chaz. If we showed up at The Underground, I couldn't leave Chaz behind and wouldn't be able to return to the White Hats. Chaz was in no shape to protect himself. Royce's reaction to Devon wasn't going to be friendly either. The vampire would never be so crass as to make an attempt on their lives where I would see it, but that didn't mean we'd be totally safe with him. I'd have to stay until Chaz was well enough to leave. God only knew how long that would take. Hilarious as the thought might be, if we went to The Underground, I'd have to be Chaz's bodyguard against Royce.

Resigned, I turned to Devon. "I know this isn't the greatest idea, but Royce offered to meet me at one of his clubs. Maybe we can do that and wait there until Chaz recovers enough to shift back. The reporters should be gone by then."

Chaz growled, low and threatening. He didn't like the idea. Devon looked as happy about it as I felt. "No way. We just saved you from a vamp last night, I can't just hand you back to them. Jack would kill me. Besides, didn't you say it was one of his people who tipped off the cops?"

I slumped lower in the seat, staring straight ahead. "Don't put words in my mouth. I just said I'd meet with him, which is something I have to do regardless."

"Why?" Devon demanded, sounding angrier than Chaz.

Their anger was spurring my own. "Because he's the only one who knows how to find Max Carlyle. I'm not going to sit around and wait for Max or one of his flunkies to come after me again. I'm going to find the bastard and stop him before he hurts me or someone else. I don't want him to show up at my office, or go after Sara or my parents or brothers next. Trust me, I like the idea of meeting with Royce again about as much as you do. However, if you've got another idea on how to lose those reporters on our tail *and* find Max before the end of the night, I'm more than willing to hear it."

Their silence was telling.

Chaz gave a low whine, and I twisted in the seat to look

at him, reaching out to rub the side of his jaw. Inhuman as that gaze was, concern was clearly reflected in the icy depths of his eyes.

"I wish I had a better plan," I said. "For right now, it's the only chance I've got."

Chapter 19

I felt stupid calling Royce back so soon, but didn't have much choice. I used his cell this time so I wouldn't have to listen to that gratingly cheerful receptionist or sit on hold for another half hour.

"We'll meet you at The Underground. I've got Chaz with me."

"Chaz?"

"Yeah, my boyfriend. Turns furry at the full moon? The guy you warned the cops about so they'd keep silver bullets on hand when he showed up to look for me?"

"I had nothing to do with whatever happened to him." I flinched at the harsh, calculated antagonism in his voice, knowing it was directed at me. Even over the phone, his anger was terrifying. "I would not abuse my ties to the police on something so trivial as to remove such a minor rival. I'd appreciate it if you'd at least make an attempt at being grateful for the help I am extending you rather than constantly treating me as an enemy or some terrible thing simply to be endured."

For a long time, I couldn't find my voice. He was completely right. I'd taken every offer he'd ever given me and thrown them back in his face, then grudgingly come back to him for help when I saw no other alternatives. He was nothing but a last resort to me. As much as I hated it and as little as I wanted to admit to it, I treated him like shit and felt guilty about it now that he'd pointed it out. Scary though he was, if it was true that he hadn't had anything to do with the police being involved in Chaz's injuries, he definitely didn't deserve to be treated that way.

Devon's sneaking glances and Chaz's gaze locked on me just made me feel worse. I closed my eyes and tried to pretend they weren't there so I could think of something to say that would salvage the situation.

"You're right," I said. "I've been callous and unthinking."

He didn't reply. I wondered what he thought about my confession. Hard to know or guess without the normal sounds of breathing to gauge, no expression to see, no words or tone of voice to go by. I plunged ahead.

"You have been trying to help me, and I brushed you off. I am sorry for that. However, try to see things from my perspective. I didn't ask to be hunted down by Max or to be bonded or turned by you. I've had more people trying to hurt, bind, or turn me the last couple days than I've had in my entire life. Your offer the other night didn't help my peace of mind any, it just made it worse. Someone's dragging my friends into this because Chaz is badly hurt, and it's somehow connected to whatever it is we have going on with Max. If I'm acting a little bitchy, it's mostly because I've been scared out of my mind and didn't know what else to do."

When he spoke up this time, it was more weary than angry. Thank God for that. "I suppose I should apologize as well. My actions were uncalled for. It's been a long time since I let my hungers cloud my judgment so badly. I won't let it happen again."

Well, maybe he could be civil after all.

"Does that mean you'll keep your fangs to yourself now?"

"Yes," he said, followed by a brief fit of laughter. Real

laughter, not the polite sounds you hide other, more human emotions behind. "Really, you don't have to worry about that. I won't touch you unless you want me to."

There was a world of heat and unspoken promise behind those words. I very carefully ignored them, and the implications behind them. "Good. Thank you."

"What time can I expect you at the club? You should come through the employees' entrance in the back. I'll inform security to escort you inside."

"Maybe around eight o'clock? Warn them ahead of time that we've got a shifted Were with us so they don't freak out."

"My. His injuries are that severe?"

"Yes, they are. I told you, someone from your office informed the cops to watch for Were when they came to scope my apartment. They came with silver shot preloaded in their guns. They were expecting him."

He made a thoughtful sound, barely heard over the sounds of traffic and background noise. "Did they say who from my office?"

"No, I don't think the officers knew. If you didn't tell them to do it, why would one of your people make that call?"

"As I said earlier, I do believe that someone is following you. The loyalties of some of my coterie are in question."

I opened my eyes and stared out the car window, rubbing at the deepening furrows between my brows as my frustration and puzzlement grew. "What does that mean exactly?"

"It means," he stated flatly, in far too neutral a tone for such a statement, "there is a good possibility that some of the vampires and possibly even humans who work for me are also working for Max Carlyle. It means you should be very, very careful where you go and what you do, because one or more of my own are using my resources to keep track of you. Not that it is particularly difficult with that trail of media you are leaving in your wake, but more than that, I fear they may be using my own resources against the two of us. Perhaps against others as well. That Chaz was attacked, but not your other friends or family, lends more weight to my suspicions that Max is using someone inside my own organization to find ways to hurt the people present the night Anastasia died."

I had to swallow back the bit of my heart that lodged in my throat at this news. How in the world could Max be using some of Royce's people like that? If he had access to Royce's resources, he might use the connection to find Sara, Arnold, and possibly my family. There were also dozens of werewolves involved in Anastasia and David's deaths. Did this mean they were in trouble, too?

Maybe I needed to get in touch with Rohrik Donovan and call in that favor the Moonwalker tribe owed me. At the very least I should warn them a vampire might be out to get them. I sure knew I'd appreciate a heads-up if some psycho vampire was coming after me.

"That's just peachy keen. Are you sure it's such a good idea for us to come to one of your clubs?"

"Yes. I can't give you the details about it just now, but I believe there is a way for me to get you and your friends out of the public eye and somewhere safe. I didn't survive this long by being easy to find."

My turn to laugh. "Could've fooled me. Why do you advertise your whereabouts on your Web site then?"

"Publicity has its benefits, as well as its drawbacks. These days, any move made against me publicly is more likely to raise an outcry and bad press against the ones who attack than against me. It doesn't seem to matter if it's the police, your White Hat friends, or some other equally brazen group of hunters. It also makes me a much harder target to approach due to the number of witnesses and potential casualties."

"Yeesh, I never thought of it that way." I'd never taken much interest in the politics or intrigue behind how the Others came to be accepted in society. Before I'd been involved in any of this supernatural hooplah, they were just . . . there. Not worth my time and attention, surely, other than to know that they were something to avoid at all costs. Not until my continued existence depended on thinking about it. "Do all vampires have the same world-view as you?"

"Few do," he said. "Most of my brethren don't view being in the public eye as beneficial. They see our new status in society as more of a nuisance than anything. Some of them find it dangerous. I've had to work almost as hard to convince them of the benefits as I have in speaking with government officials and committees to view us as something other than a menace."

By "us" I knew he meant vampires, not all Others. Elves, fairies, Weres, magi, and all the other many varieties of supernatural beings were more readily accepted in society than the vamps. Oh, don't get me wrong. There were still occasions where that wasn't the case, where hatred or fear or some other uglier emotions led up to dead bodies on the ground, not all of them human. Regardless, few Others were hated quite so much as vampires, who were seen as the unholiest and most dangerous of all supernaturals. Even I was guilty of looking at them that way—but that was probably because it was true.

Come to think of it, there weren't many vampires with celebrity status other than Royce. Aside from the ones involved in sensational headline-making crimes, there were only one or two who were so brazen as to publicly announce their scheduled appearances at charity functions or parties ahead of time. The one in Los Angeles, Clyde Seabreeze, was the only vampire other than Royce who made himself available for interviews or photo sessions by the general public.

"Okay, I would love to pick your brain about this some-time later, after all this is over. For now, I'm using up

Chaz's minutes, and I need to give directions. I'll see you at the club."

"Until then."

Chaz and Devon were staring at me, giving me weird looks. Well, Chaz's look was weirder than normal for a shifted Were. "What?"

"Nothing," Devon answered, turning his attention back to the road.

Chaz made a huffing noise and looked away. He started twisting around onto his back, rubbing his shoulders on the rough carpeting in the back of the jeep. The car swerved as Devon cringed to avoid the clawed paw peeking out between the seats as Chaz stretched.

"Jesus!"

"Watch the road!" I screeched, clinging to the oh-shit handle.

I slapped at Chaz's big, hairy arm as Devon got us back on a straight line to the accompaniment of honks and shouted curses. He'd gone rigid in his seat, carefully not looking at the thick black talons curled limply in the air a few meager inches away.

"Chaz! Stop scaring him."

He made a grumbly sound and withdrew that hairy, clawed arm. I twisted in the seat again so I could get a look at his shoulder.

The skin around the bullet wound had closed into a pinkish, puckered blemish. Since the wound was made with silver, it would remain a scar for the rest of his life. If he'd been hit with a lead slug, it would have healed hours ago, the flesh reformed as though he'd never been injured. The only reason he'd healed at all was because I'd pulled out the bullet. Even so, it was incredibly fast. It never ceased to amaze me how quickly a lycanthrope recovered. They couldn't heal back a severed limb, and damage caused by a silver weapon didn't heal quite as quickly, but damn, it would be nice if everybody's bodies fixed up so quickly and neatly.

If the bullet had stayed in much longer, he would've healed human-slow. Luckily no fragments must have lodged in the muscle since the wound was fully closed. Anyone who didn't know any better would have said the scar was from weeks, not hours, ago.

I leaned over the seat to run my fingers along his shoulder and was rewarded with a pained whine. It must have still been tender, the muscle not yet whole.

"I can't see out the rearview."

Whoops. "Sorry, Dev." Settling back, I gestured at the road before us. "You know how to get to The Underground from here?"

"Yeah," he said, hunching lower in his seat. "Are you sure about this?"

"Sure about what? Meeting with Royce?"

"Yeah."

There was a great deal of unhappiness lacing his voice, piquing my curiosity. "Why don't you want to go?"

"What makes you think I don't want to go?" he said, glancing askance at me.

"This is the first time I've seen you this jumpy and nervous."

"Am I that easy to read?"

"Yup. Spill it."

Devon looked up into the rearview at Chaz before focusing very hard on driving. A sheen of nervous sweat had broken out on his brow. "I'm afraid Royce will recognize me. The last time I saw him, not counting that night we came to save you, we didn't part friends."

"Shit, you tried to hunt him before, didn't you?"

He nodded, not looking at me, the muscle in his jaw twitching. I turned to watch the road, too, unsure what to think about that. How would Royce react to me bringing a hunter who'd previously attempted to kill him into his den?

After a minute of tense silence, I couldn't help it anymore. I started laughing.

"What's so funny?" Devon demanded, a mixture of worry and irritation on his features.

"It's just"—I had to gasp for air between words, rubbing away the tears forming in my eyes—"Oh, God, it just can't get any more complicated than this. My life. I'm dating a Were, I've got a crazy vampire trying to kill me, another one who wants to jump my bones, and I'm about to bring him a visitor who's tried to kill him before. How can it get any worse than this?"

Devon's lips cracked into a reluctant smile. "You're the only person I know who's got a crazier, more messed up life than I do. You make me seem positively normal in comparison."

This from a White Hat. It only made me laugh harder.

Chapter 20

My laughter was under control by the time we reached The Underground. It was far too early in the evening for anyone but the staff to be around. They hadn't yet opened the adjoining parking lot or set out the velvet ropes to control the inevitable crowd of revelers.

Devon pulled into an alley behind the building. Several news vans followed us, not helping my peace of mind. There was a loading dock and a handful of parking spaces for employees, every spot taken but one—soon occupied by Devon's jeep. The press would have a bitch of a time getting out of here or following us once they realized there were NO PARKING signs plastered all over the alley.

A heavily muscled guy jogged over when we pulled up into the last of the reserved spots for employees. His black T-shirt had SECURITY written in huge white letters; he was some new guy I hadn't seen before. He called out as I opened the door, his voice faltering when he spotted the Were in the back.

"You're Shiarra, right?"

"The one and only." I yanked the duffel out of the front seat and grinned at him before hurrying to the back of the jeep. Some of the news vans were parking despite the signs. Great.

The security guy nodded, reaching out to help me with my bag while Devon and I waited for Chaz to slink out of the back. Once he got out of the way, Devon growled a curse as he spotted the claw marks left on the upholstery. I sympathized, I really did, but we didn't have time for it and I slammed the door shut, urging everyone to hurry up and get inside. I was willing to bet we were being photographed as we stood there. Was Jim Pradiz, that lying sack of crap who wrote the article I spotted in the supermarket, somewhere in the mix?

The bouncer gaped at the wolf-man following in our wake. He wasn't struck dumb with terror, which was a plus. Up on his hind legs, Chaz's long, slow strides were smooth and predatory, fluid instead of a pained limp. It was good to see him back to himself. Aside from meaning the pain had lessened, it indicated he'd be able to shift back soon.

He still favored his injured shoulder, occasionally rubbing it with the pads on his hands—paws—whatever you want to call them. He was forced to crouch low to walk through the door. We all rushed inside as the first reporter came sprinting our way, having ignored the parking signs to get in a last couple questions before we were behind the safety of a locked door. I liked the security guard better for slamming the door in the reporter's face. Pushy bastards.

"Well, something finally went smoothly," I said, hefting the bag higher on my shoulder. Devon nodded, too nervous to smile or speak.

The security guard stared curiously at Chaz, who was returning the look in kind. "Mr. Royce said you could wait in his office upstairs. He's on his way and should be here in the next fifteen minutes or so. If you'll leave me your keys, I can move your car to the other lot so he has a place to park."

Devon reluctantly handed them over. Considering giving away his keys meant our means of escape from this vamp-infested club was gone, I couldn't totally blame the hunter for his hesitation.

After taking the keys, the security guard brought us deeper into the echoingly quiet club. It was stark with all the lights on, eerily empty without bodies packing the dance floor or music pounding so loud my bones vibrated with it. The only people aside from us were a janitor pushing around a mop and a handful of employees stocking the bars as we came through. Most of them stared open-mouthed. A couple shrank back when Chaz passed them. Funny that they had no problem working for a vamp but were scared of a shifted Were.

At the elevator, it became obvious that Chaz wasn't going to fit in the confined space. The guard scratched his head, then shrugged and moved down the hall. He unlocked a door that blended so well into the black walls, I'd never noticed it before.

We took the secret stairwell up, and by the second floor, I was panting. Just a bit, but it was a painful reminder of how weak I felt after being bitten by Peter and Max. By the time we reached the top floor, Chaz was holding one of those gigantic hands out as if he needed to be ready to catch me. It wasn't like I was about to pass out. Maybe I should've been worried, but there were too many other pressing matters on my mind to think about it for long.

The place was just like I remembered it. We came out closer to the fountain bubbling on the end table than we would have if we'd taken the elevator. It was quiet, peaceful, and looked nothing like you would expect to see on the inside of a Goth club. The guard showed us into Royce's office, then hurried off to move Devon's car.

The office had changed since the last time I was here. The décor was the same. English hunting scenes done in vivid oil hanging on stark white walls, framed by enough ivies and ferns to make the room smell fresh and earthy. There was a computer on the slick black desk now, and several posters of varying sizes and pictures advertising the club laid out on the end table, some marked up with notes. Similar posters and a number of invoices were on the desk, a few papers scattered on the floor. He must have left here in a hurry; Royce was usually more fastidious than this.

Despite this being a vampire's territory, I felt safe. Max Carlyle was unlikely to look for me here. I took a seat on one of the black leather couches, tilting my head back and closing my eyes. I pulled the duffel into my lap, resting my hands on it. I felt rather than saw Devon taking a seat next to me, and Chaz lying down by my feet. Quite the cozy little scene.

Devon broke the comfortable silence. "Jack is going to be so pissed off."

I cracked open one eye and arched a brow. "So?"

"You don't care what he thinks, do you?"

That earned a deep, rumbling sound that could've passed for a laugh out of Chaz. I nudged him with my foot. "Hush, you. No, I don't."

He must have been more nervous than he let on that Royce was coming. His hand kept creeping down to touch his gun, then jerking away like he'd been caught doing something bad. Rinse, repeat. When he figured out I wasn't about to say more, he kept talking.

"I still don't understand how you got on the good side of the monsters. Why you keep working with them. Doesn't it bother you? I mean, yesterday I would've shot him"—he gestured to Chaz absently—"on sight. Now we're working together. I feel like my whole world just turned upside down."

"Join the club," I said, sounding more wry than sympathetic. "It does bother me, but I am not about to let a little squeamishness get in the way of my survival. That comes first."

He leaned forward, his gaze narrowed to focus with intense scrutiny on Chaz. I wasn't sure he heard me. "Look at this. He's perfectly content to lie there like some gigantic puppy. I've never seen a shifted Were who wasn't in the middle of trying to kill me or someone else. I didn't know it was possible for them to be this still, this calm."

I shrugged, pushing the duffel to the side and riffling through the clothes I'd packed. "Then you haven't given them a chance to be themselves. They're not unthinking beasts unless they're really afraid or pissed off. Then, instinct kicks in and they can't help themselves until the threat is gone."

"That doesn't make any sense to me. Knowing they can be rational goes against everything I've ever seen or been told."

"Then, like I said, you haven't given the ones you've met a real chance. Come on, you've just driven for an hour with him in your back seat. He didn't do anything but tear up the carpet."

Devon scowled, and Chaz lowered his ears, hiding his head under his paws.

"What about vampires, then?" he asked, reluctantly turning his gaze off the embarrassed Were. "Are you saying they're like this, too?"

I glanced up from the bag, meeting his gaze. "No. Weres are a lot more easygoing about turning prospective pack members. Also, when a Were is going to hurt somebody, most of the time it's because they've been badly provoked. Not to justify it, but vampires go about things a lot differently. They prey on people, so they do what they can to appear harmless and friendly, then use that to get close enough to get what they want out of the people they hunt."

His look was very pointed. "Isn't that what Royce is doing with you?"

I smiled. His frown deepened. "I'm sure it is."

"And that doesn't bother you?"

"Probably not as much as it should. He is what he is. I won't hold his nature against him."

"I'm glad to hear that," Royce said, amused with my admittedly condescending statement. He had been leaning against the door frame, hands pocketed in his slacks while he listened to us. When he moved into the room, the fine hairs on the back of my neck and arms rose as if the air was crackling with static electricity. I rubbed my hands up and down my arms, noting that Devon was doing the same. Chaz didn't move but his hackles were raised, fur standing on end. He'd never liked Royce much. Not that I could blame him.

Royce moved with more outright menace than I'd ever seen. Hunger glinted in his eyes and every step was placed with slow and deliberate care. He wasn't even trying to play up a false front of humanity. He settled with an odd, liquid grace in an empty seat next to me. The creepy-crawly sensation grew with his proximity—some strange vampire power, then. What was he trying to accomplish?

Those midnight black eyes focused intently on the hunter, and I figured out fast enough that he was doing it to spook Devon. He was shaking, eyes wide, and sweat beading on his upper lip. His hand was plastered to his gun; still holstered, for now.

"Could you tone it down?" I asked Royce, annoyed. "We're all on the same side here."

I jerked back when the vampire shifted his gaze to mine. A sudden, unexplainable, gut-wrenching sense of terror swept through me when I met his eyes. Part of me needed to scream, to flee, to cower away. Another part knew if I moved, if I did any of those things, he'd pounce on me in the space of a breath and everything would be over. His hunger was waiting for me to slip, to twitch, to give it a reason—any reason—to swoop down and steal away every last drop of life my body contained. This was primal *knowingness*, not some vague conjecture or bad feeling. In that moment, I knew I was staring death right in the eye, and even the smallest movement would bring it right to my side to say hello.

I could literally feel myself vibrating with unspoken terror.

Royce blinked slowly, the hardened cast of his features fading and that screaming feeling of danger receding. It was like an invisible hand released its grip on my insides, leaving me gasping, coming close to folding double as I sucked in air around the steel bands of dread that closed my throat. Chaz was on his feet, growling low, deep in his throat. It wasn't helping my frame of mind. He took a stiff step closer to Royce, who ignored him.

His voice, when it came, was soft, warm, and pleasant, giving absolutely no hint to the beast that had been peeking out of the depths of those black eyes. "My apologies."

I took several deep breaths, closing my eyes and wrapping my arms around myself to get my shaking under control. For the umpteenth time, I had to remind myself what I was dealing with; this was a monster, an Other, inhuman. No person should be able to do that to another person. I bit back a shriek when he lightly touched my arm, jerking away from him. Chaz snapped at him and Devon shrank farther back into the couch cushions.

Royce looked utterly crestfallen at my reaction, and wasn't in the least intimidated by Chaz's display. "I am sorry, it wasn't my intention to frighten you both. When I saw the hunter, I thought that . . . well. I doubted your loyalties for a moment." With a faint sigh, he raised up a hand to hide his eyes, shaking his head. "Forgive me, I have tamped down on my abilities for so long, sometimes I forget how powerful the effects can be."

I wondered why the hell the charm around my neck

hadn't protected me from *that*. He was using mind-mojo, so shouldn't it have kept me safe? Devon was watching him like one might regard a poisonous snake. I had the feeling my expression matched his.

It took a couple of silently repeated reminders to myself that, despite this little temper tantrum, the vampire was on our side. Some more primitive part of me was still having the screaming meemies that I'd brushed with death and wasn't running the fuck away from it as far and as fast as I could. When I finally found my voice, it was shaking.

"Don't do it again. Chaz, sit down, he's not about to jump us. Right?" I'd meant that last to come out more like a statement and less like a frightened question. Oh well.

He nodded, his expression tightening when he looked at Devon. "Would you mind explaining why you've brought a hunter into my office? Specifically, one who has repeatedly made attempts to kill me?"

"He and the other White Hats helped save me last night, remember? Devon took me back to my place to go get my stuff earlier today. He's my ride while my car is in the impound."

Royce arched a brow at my explanation. He turned an incredulous look at Devon, who was rapidly regaining his calm exterior. It took the vampire a moment to collect himself and speak in an approximation of civility, though he didn't bother to hide his distaste.

"For the time being," Royce said, "I will set aside any animosity toward you until the situation with Max is addressed. Can I expect the same courtesy?"

Yeah, that was Royce. Good ol' Mr. Wheeler-'n'-Dealer.

Devon nodded curtly, remaining silent. He hadn't quite stopped shaking, but had schooled his features to hide whatever he was thinking. I was glad he'd agreed, though. Having the vampire and White Hat at each other's throats all night wasn't conducive to solving the Max problem.

The vampire watched him closely, sounding put out. "You should never have seen so much of my holdings. Is it too much to ask that as part of this truce, you swear not to reveal anything you see here to the other hunters or use the information against me later?"

Devon rubbed the back of his neck, considering. This was a once in a lifetime opportunity for him. If Royce's secret methods of getting around got back to the other hunters, the vamp could be in big trouble later. Not to mention that the layout of the building and some of his internal security measures had been revealed.

I felt guilty for bringing trouble to his doorstep, but there wasn't a whole heck of a lot I could do about it. We'd both have to hope that Devon would keep his word if he agreed to keep his mouth shut. God only knew what Royce would do to him if he didn't. Or to me, for that matter. I'd led Devon here, after all. What an ancient vampire could think up for revenge if given reason enough didn't bear dwelling on.

"Okay. I promise whatever I see while I'm here won't make it back to the other hunters." He took a breath, eyes narrowing slightly. "However, I won't promise that I won't use the information myself—just me—later."

Royce stared at him a bit longer. I'm not sure he believed him.

"I swear," Devon repeated.

"I sincerely hope you are telling me the truth," he said, black eyes glittering with malice. For Devon's sake, I hoped so, too. This time I kept my knee-jerk reaction under control when Royce turned back to me. "We can leave when your friend is back to himself."

I gladly shifted my attention to Chaz, avoiding looking at Royce. "Are you going to be able to shift soon?"

He nodded that great, shaggy head, lip lifting silently from his teeth. Not once did he take his gaze off the vamp. The fur of Chaz's scruff was standing on end like he'd been rolling on the carpet and was suffering from a bad case of static electricity. If not for the seriousness of the situation, his natural reaction to the proximity of a vampire would've looked funny.

As it was, I felt the same way.

Chapter 21

Royce didn't complain, but I could tell by his expression and tone of voice he wasn't thrilled when I asked for a place to change into my hunting gear. He showed me to one of the empty offices down the hall. I hoped the boys wouldn't end up killing each other while I was gone.

This office was quite a bit smaller than his own, but just as tastefully appointed. Framed photos were scattered here and there on the desk, peeking past a phone blinking with messages and papers stacked half a mile high. In the pictures, a man, a woman, and a towheaded girl were all smiling, holding each other, and generally looking like a normal, happy family. Some of the photos were taken at the beach or the park, and all three of them were standing in the sunlight.

I did what I could not to think about the pictures, not to wonder what would make someone so *normal* want to work for vampires. It bugged me, and the thoughts stuck with me while I shucked off my jeans and sweater and switched them out for the matte black armor. Next I pulled on my boots and put on the silver cross, but hesitated before putting on the finishing touch—the sentient hunter's belt, complete with three enchanted silver stakes.

It lay coiled, untouched in the bag. My hands weren't anywhere near it, but I could feel eagerness radiating from it. The dead hunter's spirit inhabiting the belt wasn't stupid. It knew I would take it on a road trip for only one reason.

When I ran a fingertip along the dark leather, the draw to put it on grew stronger. It was projecting that impatience, making me want it, yet I hesitated.

The last time I had worn this thing with the intent to fight Others, almost a year ago, I very nearly died. The belt was a thing of magic, and while it would make me stronger, faster, harder to kill, the artifact would also whisper its desire to destroy vampires. As soon as I put the belt on, it would adhere to me until daybreak. If I was going to be around Royce all night, this might not be a great idea. The spirit housed in the runes branded into the leather was eager, so eager, to see the stakes used to draw blood and to kill.

I was stronger than it. I knew that. I'd beaten back the urges it breathed to life in me before. I could do it again if I had to. I'd just never felt it like this, projecting those desires so strongly *before* putting it on.

Steeling myself against the inevitable mental intrusion, I reluctantly lifted it out of the duffel and settled it around my waist. The trio of stakes rode at my left hip. Extra ammo would go on the right. As soon as I slid the tongue through the buckle, the leather adhered to itself, and it was too late to wonder if I'd made the right decision by putting this piece of magework on.

'You're afraid of what I'll make you do. You've never been afraid of me before, not like this.' I'd been expecting a freight train, not a gentle breeze to whisper through my mind. While not as obnoxious as it could have been, it still gave me the shivers. Having something know you so intimately and see into your thoughts clearly enough to perceive what you were thinking was unnatural. It never made

mention of any previous owners, but I was sure it never forgot what it saw in those hunters' heads—or in mine.

"I don't want to hurt my friends. I wasn't sure you'd be able to see the difference between them and the real enemy."

God, I would never get over having conversations with a person who wasn't there. To anyone else it would look like I was talking to myself. It knew my thoughts, but I wasn't used to communicating to it without speaking.

'I know enough to restrain myself. No need to worry about that. I'm simply looking forward to the inevitable battle ahead.' Quiet laughter echoed in my skull.

"Great. Just fantastic." Even the belt knew I'd be fighting for my life later tonight. Then again, it knew what I knew, saw what I saw, heard what I heard when it was worn, so I shouldn't have been surprised. On the bright side, it wouldn't make me go postal on Chaz and Royce. I felt a twinge thinking about them, but that was all.

It stayed quiet, radiating muted excitement as I put on the holsters and guns, and clipped the extra ammo to it. I shook the wrinkles out of my trench coat to hide the weaponry from casual inspection. The soft hiss and creak of worn leather was more comforting to me than the weapons. Something about leather and guns just screamed "badass"—an image I would gladly uphold if it meant Max and his cronies would leave me alone.

Tossing my other clothes and sneakers into the bag, I left the room and approached Royce's office. The door was open and a vaguely familiar voice drifted into the hall.

". . . toward the properties on Staten Island, and I just received a report that the Endless Night was also taken. The rest of the clubs and restaurants haven't been touched. Angus called and said that one of his staffers found out that Max moved somewhere into the heart of the city. Other than that, no word."

The speaker was Royce's assistant, John. He blocked the door as he stood there riffling through a pile of papers on a clipboard. I tapped him lightly on the shoulder to get him to move.

He twisted around inhumanly fast, dropping the clipboard. His dark brown eyes were wide, wider than they should have been, and darkened perceptibly when he saw me. Fear? Or something else?

"How did you sneak up on me?"

Ah. I'd hurt his male—err, his vampire pride. Granted, it was strange he hadn't been able to detect my heartbeat or breathing or something, but I figured it was the belt's influence.

"Just talented, I guess." I peered past him to the others. They watched with a mixture of wariness and amusement as John collected his scattered papers.

Chaz had shifted while I was out of the room. His blond hair was now on the shaggy side; scruffy hints of a beard giving him a dangerous, feral look. Someone had thoughtfully loaned him a pair of jeans that looked to be a couple sizes too big. Where had those come from? Wait. On second thought, I didn't want to know.

"You guys ready to go?" I asked.

Devon nodded and rose up from the couch, eager to get out of here. He brushed past John, who was staring at me with a strangely wary expression.

Chaz followed closely in Devon's wake, giving Royce a dark look. What did they say to each other while I was changing? Nothing civil, judging by the tension in the air. Royce followed at the rear, his expression pleasant, but empty. He put a hand on John's shoulder as he moved up to the lead, discussing something to do with some of the other night clubs and restaurants. It took me a second to figure out he was talking about hostile takeovers by Max's men, and not of the corporate kind. Some of Royce's people had turned on him, and his properties were now being used as a resource by Max. What good a couple of eateries might do in this rivalry was beyond me, but John was pretty agitated about it.

We took the stairs all the way down to the basement, someplace I'd never been. This part of the club was storage, never meant to be seen by the public.

Most of it was open space, dotted with stacked pallets and crates of wine, beer, water, and soda. There was an employee kitchen/lounge, a couple of bathrooms, and prop, costume, and dressing rooms for the entertainment. For the moment, it was deserted. Around nine or ten, it would be buzzing with activity; people getting ready for the first acts of the night and running supplies upstairs.

Royce led us to a janitor's closet adjoined to the employee lounge. He had to use a key to open what looked like an unnecessarily heavy-duty deadbolt. Once the door swung open, its purpose was clear.

The walls on either side of the door were stacked neatly with mops, brooms, and other cleaning supplies, but there was a second door propped open in the back of the closet. It led to a cement tunnel that angled down somewhere below basement level. A secret passage? Cool!

"Remember, I expect all of you to keep this secret," Royce warned. His gaze lingered on Devon. The hunter gave back nothing in return but a sly smile. I could see why Royce would be worried; if the rest of the White Hats heard about this, they would use it to the hilt.

Royce led the way. John locked up behind us and brought up the rear. The passage was well lit and clear of debris, but the stone walls were damp and the unpleasant scent of mildew was in the air. Chaz's nose was wrinkled in disgust; he liked it less than I did.

There was no trash, no rats, and no roaches. Just halogen lamps set into the walls at intervals, lighting the way to some unknown destination. Guess even vampires can't see in perfect darkness. Or maybe Royce used this tunnel system to secretly move humans around for

God alone knew what reasons. That was a topic I did not want to explore. Suppressing a shiver, I shoved all thoughts of potential human trafficking to the back of my mind. Ick.

There were places where the passage broke off in other directions, branching outward. We stayed in a straight line, and I tried to figure out where we were. There were times when we must have come very close to some of the train stations or tunnels. The ground occasionally vibrated under my feet like when you're walking on the platforms and a subway train grinds to a halt before you. We walked for what felt like an eternity, though mainly I think it felt that way due to the scenery not changing and the unpleasant whispers in the back of my mind about human victims being spirited away.

Royce veered down one of the branches. I'd been following so closely I almost plowed into him when he halted before a recessed door. I'd stopped so abruptly Devon put a hand on my shoulder to steady himself.

My cheeks felt like they were on fire. The elder vamp grinned at me, a glint of humor in his eyes. "We'll be out of here before long."

I rolled my eyes at him to cover my nervousness. Royce pulled a key ring out from one of his pockets, flicking through them until he found the one he was looking for. This time we stepped out into a storage closet with boxes piled practically to the ceiling. Royce led the way to the other side, helping us negotiate a way around the obstacles and into another basement.

It was dark, and Devon's fingers dug into my shoulder again. "I can't see shit."

I looked around, seeing the dim outline of crates and boxes. I couldn't make out any details about the place, but it wasn't *that* dark.

Then I remembered I had improved night vision with the belt. Whoops. He was the only one with the poor night vision here; John, Chaz, Royce, and myself weren't having a problem because we could see in the dark in a way that Devon never would. Not without metaphysical assistance anyway.

"How much longer 'til we're out of here?" I asked, since I knew Devon was too afraid to say anything. I could feel his nervousness in the tension of his fingers, how tightly he held on to me.

"The service elevator is just ahead," John said.

I made it a point to watch my step, keeping clear of anything Devon might trip on in the dark. My vision must not have been as good as I thought. I didn't see the door that led to the service elevator until Royce opened it, leaving me momentarily light-blinded.

Shielding my eyes, I squinted into the room. It was a grungy open space with filthy linoleum floors and plain, whitewashed walls. The service elevator was pretty big, designed to carry crates and furniture, so there would be no difficulty fitting the whole party into it.

We were on the third and lowest level of the basement. Royce hit the buttons for the first-level basement and the eighth floor before turning his attention to John.

"I'm going to take them somewhere safe. Can you round up whoever isn't on duty and have them meet me back here in two hours?"

John nodded, and I put a staying hand on Royce's arm. "Wait a second, are you planning to face off against Max without me?"

"Yes."

My grip tightened until I saw little crow's feet appear around those black eyes. With my enhanced strength from the belt, it must have hurt, but his only reaction was the slightest hardening of his expression. I didn't let up the pressure, giving in to the silent, gleeful urgings of the belt.

"No way, Royce. This is my fight, too." It shouldn't have

been so hard to keep my voice under control. That last came out more like a hiss than I'd intended.

"The rest of the White Hats will want to come and help," Devon said. "I know I wouldn't want to miss this fight."

"I can't speak for the rest of the Sunstrikers, but I'm not interested in letting this guy get away either," Chaz added.

Royce kept his gaze locked on mine, making no attempt to pull out of my grasp. It was getting to me that he wasn't reacting to this little bit of violence I allowed myself, driving my nails into the muscle of his forearm and wrinkling his nice suit.

"If you wish this," he said, his voice as pleasant and level as though we were discussing stock trends over coffee, "you need to be prepared for what you will face. None of you have ever fought a vampire as old and powerful as Max Carlyle."

I released him as the elevator "pinged" for the first level of the basement. John stayed in the elevator as the rest of us filed out into a room much like the last one. If anything, the floor was even dirtier. The vampire lackey watched with avid interest right up until the doors slid shut behind us.

"That's not entirely true. I fought you before," I said, following Royce through some double doors and into a much cleaner hallway.

He shook his head, raven hair spilling forward to hide his features. "I held myself in check as much as I could. At the time, it was the only measure of defiance I could muster against the holder of the focus. I tempered the use of most of the powers available to me."

"So you're saying that wasn't really fighting? You were holding back so you wouldn't hurt me too badly?"

A chill took me at his grim nod. Every time we fought, I'd come away battered and bruised. The belt was supposed to make the wearer tougher, stronger, and he still did a number on me like I hadn't had any protection at all. It was even worse when I fought him and the Were, Rohrik Donovan, together. The doctors told me repeatedly after I'd gotten out of surgery that I was lucky to be alive. I would still be in the hospital if not for Arnold's magic speeding up the healing process.

Chaz slid up behind me, both of his hands coming to rest on my shoulders. I was grateful for his touch; it helped keep a sudden case of the willies at bay. "I've fought your kind before. You're not as tough as you think you are."

Anyone else probably would've been offended. Royce found Chaz's statement humorous. He laughed in a way that hinted he was hiding some wicked thoughts behind it. "You've never truly tangled with an elder, wolf. You're still alive."

"Yeah," Devon said, his agreement with Royce surprising me. "Vampires are scary as hell when they hit a certain peak in their power. We should call in the other White Hats. Jack has access to some heavy-duty firepower, and people with a lot of experience."

"You hunters have engendered enough public outrage against us. I don't want my name associated with a sudden drop in your population."

Talk about creepy. Devon paled and turned away, not pushing the issue.

"Aside from strength and speed, what could Max do? Something like whatever it was you did back in the office?" I asked Royce.

"That and more," he replied, rather nonchalant under the circumstances. "My lack of control was completely accidental. I stopped as soon as I realized what I was doing."

Nothing was completely accidental with Alec Royce. I carefully didn't say that thought out loud, but the belt gave me an awareness of its agreement. It also started speaking to me, and I quickly lost track of the conversation the others were having around the voice in my thoughts.

'You won't know an elder vampire's powers until he chooses to reveal them. That one is right—they are able to do a lot more than put a little scare into you. You'll be protected against most of the things they can do to manipulate your thoughts as long as you wear me and the charm. However, I wasn't designed to withstand the strength of leeches as ancient as Alec Royce. Even with my assistance, you will not stay alive if you rely on nothing but physical force. As much as I can boost your strength, it is not enough to grapple head-on with vampires who have had over two thousand years to hone their powers.'

Once the belt quieted, I noticed everyone was staring at me expectantly. "What?"

"Did you hear anything we just said?" Devon asked.

"No. Sorry, the belt was talking to me."

Chaz and Devon gave me funny looks.

Royce spoke up, just a touch of exasperation filtering through his otherwise placid expression. "I asked if you would submit to a demonstration so that you might better understand what Max may do in the heat of battle. You shouldn't insist on following me without first having a better grasp of what you will be dealing with. I promise I will not do any lasting harm to any of you. With your permission?"

I glanced at the other two boys. "What do you guys think?"

Chaz shrugged, but Devon was worried.

"I don't know. Maybe he's right. You should know what you're getting into before diving straight into it."

I silently asked the belt what it thought. It gave me the mental equivalent of a shrug. *'Do what you feel is right.'*

With that helpful little piece of advice, I frowned and gave Royce his answer. "Okay. If you think it's for the best, let's see it."

He took a deep breath, one I knew he didn't need. As he

tilted his head back, I felt a prickle of energy creep along my skin, raising all the hairs on my body. It didn't seem too bad.

Except the tingling turned into an abrupt, tidal force.

The sting of it crashed into me like a physical wall, driving me back a step as I threw my hands up to ward off the ethereal power. Chaz staggered back as well, using his jacket to protect his eyes. Devon fell to his knees and wrapped his arms over his head. It was like being bitten by hundreds of invisible flies while some unseen force simultaneously drove you back from the vampire. Even closing my eyes didn't make the sensation stop, like the invisible bugs had crawled beneath my eyelids and were digging under my skin. Screaming was impossible—the pain closed my throat too tightly to squeak out a sound.

As abruptly as it started, it stopped. The three of us were left panting for breath, trembling as Royce's voice cut through the newfound quiet of the hall. "That is but a taste. He may also try to bespell you, like so."

Devon was on his feet and reaching for the vampire's outstretched hand. Royce must have chosen Devon deliberately because the hunter was so frightened of him. Royce knew all the telltales: scent, a quickness of breath, a change in heartbeat, all the little things that tell the difference between who is predator and who is prey.

Devon's fear shifted to eagerness as he reached for Royce. I watched, not sure if I should do something to intervene. When I tried to move closer to them, I found I couldn't. My legs didn't want to cooperate. Chaz was also struggling, his hands pressed against the nearest wall to push himself away—but his feet stayed flat on the floor. The belt didn't answer my silent question as to what the vampire was doing. I didn't know how to break the unseen chains holding me in place. Terror drove through me as I turned my attention back to Royce, but the vampire wasn't looking at me.

His gaze focused on Devon. The hunter took his hand like a trusting child, soon enfolded in Royce's arms. Horror dawned as the two men leaned into each other, one of the vampire's hands creeping up to tilt Devon's head aside, leaving his neck a long, vulnerable line.

A scream lodged in my throat as Royce's lips curled back from his fangs, focusing on me with those black, black eyes as he bent over Devon's exposed throat.

Chapter 22

"So you see," Royce said, his eyes locked on mine as his fangs brushed Devon's neck, "an elder never fights on fair terms."

As the last words trailed into a sibilant whisper, Devon stiffened and started struggling. Royce must have released him from the charm. The vampire had no trouble keeping Devon's frantic squirming to a minimum.

"Fuck! Let me go!"

An arrogant, pleased smile curved Royce's lips as he released Devon, watching with hungry eyes while the hunter rapidly backpedaled, putting distance between them. I didn't realize Royce had let me and Chaz go until my back came up against the wall.

"Do you all get the point? Max would not stop. If you provoke him, he may do far worse than what I have shown you here."

Chaz was growling again, the deep, rumbling bass normally reserved for when he was shifted. "Don't do it again, you bastard."

The look the vampire shot him immediately made Chaz quiet, cutting him off in mid-growl. "I will remind you that I did ask your permission beforehand. I promised I would not bring permanent harm to you and I kept to my word. Don't play righteous with me."

Chaz's wordless rumble started up again, going deeper yet. My bones were vibrating in response. I put a steadying hand on his arm in a silent plea for him to stop.

He cut off again, reaching out to take me in a sudden, fierce hug. Though it was hard to breathe around his embrace, I was quick to return the gesture in the hope it would calm him down. He was so on edge, he might end up accidentally shifting on us.

The belt was amused by this, its low laughter bouncing through my skull. *'You have to admit your reaction was funny. You're a rookie! A hunter rookie!'*

"Shut up," I muttered to it, then speaking louder and much more clearly for Royce's benefit. "You've made your point—but it doesn't change anything. Max needs to be stopped. If he's that powerful, I'd think you'd want all the help you can get."

Royce nodded and stood up straighter. Some tension I hadn't detected earlier filtered out of his frame.

"As long as you have an understanding of what you will be fighting, I will not stop you. I would not have it on my head that you faced him without foreknowledge of the danger he represents."

"As much as I hate it, Shiarra's right," Devon said. He was rubbing his hands up and down his arms in a nervous gesture. He wouldn't be forgetting what Royce had done anytime soon. "We can't just ignore the problem or leave someone else to deal with it."

Chaz loosened his grip, peering down at me with concern and gently rubbing my arm. "Are you sure you want to do this?"

"I don't *want* to do this. I *have* to."

I closed my eyes and leaned into him. His body radiated warmth the way it did when he was close to shifting. I burrowed into it like I could take that warmth into myself and use it as my shield against the bad things waiting to swallow me up. He bowed his head to kiss the top of my own before turning his attention back to Royce.

"Do you know where we can find this guy?"

"Only a rough idea. We will have to draw him out somehow. My original plan was to find out who had turned against me and see if the connection could be followed back to the source."

"You were thinking of using Shia to get him to come out of hiding, weren't you?"

Royce's eyes slowly shifted to Chaz, who neither flinched nor stepped back from that piercing gaze. Royce's voice was flat, completely devoid of emotion. "The thought had occurred to me."

"Great, thanks for consulting me on that," I snarked. Chaz's tightening grip around my waist was bordering on painful.

Royce rolled his eyes before turning around and continuing down the hall. "It was not my only plan, but it might be the most reliable way to track him down. If one of his people took you again, we could follow you back to wherever he is laired. Much like your White Hat friends did last night."

"You followed us while we followed her kidnappers?"

Devon was clearly peeved at the idea. Royce didn't say anything, only glanced back with a sly, secretive smile.

We continued on in silence until we reached a pair of double doors that led to an adjoining parking lot. Royce showed us to a car parked nearby; it was an unassuming sedan that I never would have connected with the vampire. For one thing, it was a silver four-door. I never pictured him in anything but limos and sports cars.

Royce held the passenger side open for me while Chaz and Devon slid in the back. I watched the vampire, frowning as I breathed in the scent of leather. This was yet another facet of Royce's personality and mannerisms that didn't match what I thought I knew about him. He didn't bother to question my puzzled looks until he started the car.

"Not exactly what you were expecting, I take it?"

"No," I admitted.

He put his attention on driving, his tone blasé as we headed toward the parking structure's exit. "It helps to have a means of getting around that won't attract the attention of paparazzi or hunters."

I kept my mouth shut, hoping that wasn't meant as a dig at Devon, who was still pissed.

"No wonder we haven't been able to corner you. You'd sneak right out from under our noses in this thing and with those tunnels of yours."

Royce didn't respond, but the hint of a smile had his lips twitching. When we crept out into traffic, I groaned and sank lower in my seat. A couple of news vans were parked in front of what I now recognized as Royce's office building midtown. We'd walked pretty far in those tunnels to go all the way from The Underground to his corporate office. It made me curious what other offices and clubs were connected, but I quelled my curiosity and kept my mouth shut. It was doubtful Royce would answer any questions about his security around Devon or Chaz anyway.

None of the reporters noticed or followed us. Royce was right; they must not know all his means of transportation. I couldn't get over the understated brilliance of having such a car. It wasn't fair for a vampire to be rich, good looking, and smart, too. Two out of three wasn't bad; three for three was just plain unfair.

"I have faced Max before," Royce stated quietly, the sudden shift in mood and topic bringing me to stare at him. "I would appreciate it if the rest of you let me deal with him directly. He will have many servants there to protect him, so there will be others for you to fight. Leave Max to me."

"I can't let you do that," I said. "You're not the only one with a grudge against him."

Chaz growled, sticking his head between the seats. "I won't let anything happen to Shia. If she's fighting him, so am I."

"The other hunters wouldn't be willing to sit back and let you guys handle him alone," Devon said. "There should be enough of us to deal with the remaining vamps, but anyone who came to Shia's rescue last night will want a piece of Max. Including me."

Chaz's cell phone went off. He'd taken it off vibrate while I was changing, and answered the incessant jingle with a low, "Hello?" I peered back as he listened to the other end, a cheerful smile replacing his angry scowl. "Of course. Tell Arnold he doesn't get to sit on the sidelines this time. Can you meet us?"

After a brief pause, he tapped Royce lightly on the shoulder. "Where are we going? Sara and Arnold will meet us."

Royce didn't look very pleased with this news. "To the home of an acquaintance of mine. A neutral third party, if you will. I was intending on leaving you there, but it will serve as a meeting place for your friends just as well." He gave the address and some simple directions to a home on—surprise, surprise—City Island. Devon was the most astonished at this news.

Chaz relayed the directions to Sara. "Great. We'll see you there." A moment later, he hung up, tucking the phone back in his pocket. "Sara says she and Arnold will be on their way right after he finishes casting something. They'll take an hour, maybe an hour and a half, to meet us."

"Okay," I said, wondering privately what kind of magic Arnold was whipping up for the occasion. It was likely that Sara would expect to fight tonight. While that was worrisome, Arnold wouldn't let her out of his sight until he'd had a chance to shield her to the best of his considerable ability. Those thoughts in mind, I turned back to Royce. "I know you won't like this but we do need to let the White

Hats in on this sometime. Maybe you should let Devon and me meet with them before we go to your friend's place."

"If you must insist on bringing them, then, yes, it may be wise to go see them in person rather than calling to let them know who you are with."

Meaning, let them know ahead of time about the vampire and Were on our side so they wouldn't freak out and hunt down or kill their allies when they found out. Or at least keep the inevitable explosion somewhere out of Royce's immediate vicinity.

"Fine. I'll tell them."

Devon put a hand on my arm. "Why don't you let me do it? They're more likely to listen to me without instantly condemning the idea of working with these two."

Chaz coughed into his fist. "Arnold, Shia. Don't forget Arnold."

I groaned and brought a hand up to slap my forehead. "Oh, yeah. We're going to have to tell them we have a mage on our side, too."

"A mage?" Devon was quite surprised.

"Yeah," Chaz answered. "Arnold works for The Circle. I'll be calling around the pack and asking for help from that end, too."

"I'll be bringing those of my number who have not turned against me," Royce added.

"How do you know who is on your side?" I asked, unable to quell my suspicion. "How can you tell for sure, especially if some of them have turned on you already?"

Royce glanced at me, the flash of passing streetlights reflecting oddly in his eyes. Like pieces of black glass instead of the eyes of a thinking, rational being.

"I have ways."

Shuddering, I looked away, unable to meet that gaze for long.

"Okay," Devon said, cutting the uneasy silence. "City

Island is small, so you can probably drop us off at Jack's and we can walk to your friend's place from there."

"I'll call Chaz before we leave Jack's," I said.

"I'd rather go with you," Chaz muttered. "I don't like the idea of you walking around without one of us with you."

"I'll be with her." Devon scowled at Chaz, who flashed him an annoyed look.

"I meant someone strong enough to actually protect her."

I had to laugh. The hunter looked like he was on the verge of exploding. Their tough-guy macho bull was more funny to me than anything else. I don't think either of them realized exactly what I was capable of now that I was wearing the belt. Chaz should know better. He'd seen me in action.

"Guys, I've got enough weapons on me to make Rambo proud. Don't worry, I can handle myself if we run into trouble."

The belt gave me smug concurrence, even as I felt the waves of disagreement radiating from everyone else. The rumbling in Chaz's chest started up again.

"I don't want you going by yourself."

"Hello?" Devon sounded even more irritated than before, if that was possible. "I said I'd be with her. She won't be alone."

Royce kept the amusement in his voice to a minimum. "I believe he means he does not want her without an Other on her arm, protecting her. Isn't that right, wolf?"

"His name is Chaz, not wolf." I shifted my position so I could look at my grumpy boyfriend huffing in the back seat. "Is he right? Are you worried I won't be able to handle a bunch of White Hats without you protecting me?"

Chaz glowered at me, one hand lifting to brush fingertips against my cheek. I cradled his hand with mine, even while returning his disapproving look in kind. "Of course he's right. I don't want to see you get hurt, not even by accident."

It was hard to be mad or feel stifled by his overprotectiveness with those sad blue eyes looking into mine. Puppy dog eyes. I had to steel myself against them.

"Well, I feel the same way about you. Trust me, as soon as those hunters find out what you are, their first reaction will be to shoot to kill. It's best if you stay and wait with Royce."

I carefully didn't mention that I was also worried that, thanks to his being hyped up and on edge from his recent run-in with the cops, he might lose it and shift if Jack acted up around me. We had to give the hunters a chance to let the idea of working with the enemy, this one time, sink in. I sorely hoped Devon could get them to see reason and get the rest of the White Hats willing to temporarily work with Weres, magi, and vampires. I had some slim hope, thanks to Jack and Devon's attitudes toward me, that we might be able to talk some of the others into helping stop Max.

"Fine." Chaz snarled and pulled back from me, folding his arms across his chest as he glared out the window. "I'll stay. But if you don't call or come back within an hour, I'm coming to get you."

"Okay," I said, wondering why I felt so bad about this.

'You don't want to leave him behind,' the belt said in answer to my unspoken question. *'You want him to play knight in shining armor for you, that's why. You don't want to take your turn being the knight.'*

"Nobody asked you," I hissed under my breath. Resuming what I hoped was a normal tone, I asked Royce, "Where are we going after this?"

He glanced at me with a grin, and I had to suppress a chill at the sight of his extended fangs. He must be more agitated than his demeanor let on. "To hunt for Max, of course."

"Of course," I echoed back hollowly. Of course.

Chapter 23

Royce had pens and paper in the glove compartment. I wrote down Chaz's cell phone number and the address where we were to meet before Royce dropped us at Jack's house. Chaz and Royce would pool their resources while Devon and I convinced the rest of the White Hats to join our cause.

All the lights were burning in Jack's windows, but deep shadows managed to hide any occupants on the wrap-around porch from prying human eyes. The benches and barrels and plants were probably no more than dim outlines against the dark brown paint of the house to Devon, but I could make out the details perfectly clearly. Having night vision was odd, but useful in its way.

Devon took the lead. I trailed slowly behind, unable to tear my eyes off the sedan's tail lights until they disappeared around a corner. The salt breeze wasn't doing anything to clear my head or steady my nerves, and I wondered dismally if an hour would be enough time to convince the White Hats that Alec Royce could, at least temporarily, be their ally.

Devon rapped lightly on the front door before walking in. Jack was seated in the living room along with Tiny and

Nikki. They'd been in the middle of a conversation that died out as soon as we entered the room.

"Good to see you back. We were worried," Tiny said, smiling at me from his seat by the fireplace. He eyed the stakes on my belt appreciatively. "Decided which team you're on, huh?"

Devon seated himself on a chair as far from the others as possible. I sat on the opposite end of the couch from where Jack was settled. He spoke, one pale brow arching in question.

"How'd you keep the police and the newshounds off your tail? By the time I heard the reports and sent someone to check, you were gone."

Nice to know he was keeping such close tabs on me. I kept my gaze firmly focused on my clenched hands in my lap—a precaution against glaring at the arrogant prick. After all, I want him on my side tonight. I think.

"We ran into some trouble, but got away with some help."

"Help?" Nikki said, the skeptical note in her voice bordering on derisive. "What sort of help?"

Jack shot her a warning look. I didn't want to appear guilty for this part, especially considering to whom I was talking. Despite wanting to ignore Nikki's flinty look, and to stay in keeping with my image of badass, I met her gaze squarely and spoke as lightly as I could.

"The kind of help only Alec Royce can give."

The quiet that descended on the room was deafening, the silence punctuated by crackles and pops from the fireplace. I waited, taut as a bowstring, for one of them to respond. Devon broke the tension, his own voice quiet and composed as he stared moodily into the flames.

"We'll need him tonight. There's going to be a hunt, one we don't want to miss."

Jack's voice was empty, flat, more frightening for the lack of emotion. "We don't work with vampires."

"This time, we should."

There was a teeny, tiny part of me that was relieved Devon was fielding this argument. I kept as still and quiet as possible in the hope I would be overlooked or forgotten by the others as they hashed out the details.

"That doesn't sound like a very good idea," Tiny said, masking his distaste with puzzlement. "Why should we turn our backs on everything we've ever stood for?"

"I know you don't like it. I don't particularly care for the idea much either."

"So why do it?" asked Tiny.

"The vampire we're going up against is just as old and just as strong as Alec Royce. The same one we rescued Shiarra from. He doesn't play by the rules, not like Royce. Personally, just for this fight, I'd rather have one of them on our side instead of two against us."

"You're out of your mind," Nikki said. She rose, folding her arms and glaring down at Devon's calm visage. "We've never needed to work with vamps before. Why start now? We're supposed to be hunting these things, not kowtowing to them."

"Who said we were going to kowtow? All we'd do is work together to take down a threat. It's just a temporary alliance."

Jack leaned back in the couch, holding out a hand to forestall further argument. He was looking at me when he spoke, though his words were directed to Devon.

"What if we don't go? What if we decide not to fight this thing, to let the vampires kill each other off?"

Looks like it was my turn to speak up. I met Jack's gaze squarely, not giving him the satisfaction of showing him how riled I was. Instead, I drew on the strength and certainty the belt was radiating to temper my response and keep myself composed. It was sure that, if I said the right things, these hunters would be just as eager as it was to hunt down Max.

"You know as well as I do that Max Carlyle is after me. You wanted me for something, and if we don't help Royce stop him, Max might succeed in killing me before you get what you want out of me. Or he might just end up taking over the city, leaving an even bigger threat than Alec Royce in charge of the darkest Others in New York. That's why you're going to agree to this and help us tonight."

Jack's thin lips curved in a passable imitation of Devon's mischievous smirk. "Tiny had a good point. How can I agree to such a thing when it would go against all that we stand for? Regardless of who wins, both vampires are nothing more than our prey. Not our friends, not our allies, not even *human*. We've come very close to ridding this world of that parasite, Royce. It would suit us just fine if they killed each other off, or left only one of them standing so there's less work for us later."

"Because," I answered, somewhat unnerved by his cheerfully stated desire for Max and Royce to destroy each other, "you want Max Carlyle dead almost as badly as you want Alec Royce dead. Despite your best efforts, you haven't succeeded in getting rid of either one yet. This will give you a chance to feel out exactly what Royce is capable of when he fights Max. You'll be able to see if you can find a way to destroy him later."

"Sugar, I've been killing vampires since you were nothing but a gleam in your daddy's eye." Tiny grinned, a flash of white against dark skin. He lightly patted the gun he had tucked into the waistband of his jeans. The Smith and Wesson 500, one of a very few guns I recognized on sight, looked comparatively small in relation to his big hands and girth. "This is all we need to take down even a mofo as tough as Royce."

Devon laughed. "Stop showing off, Tiny. You know Royce is an elder. You'd never take him down with a peashooter like that."

Tiny fixed a glare on Devon that would've had a lesser

man quaking in his boots. Devon pointedly ignored the look, turning back to Jack with a touch more irritation coming to the surface.

"Shia and I are going on the hunt tonight. We could use help, but if you're going to be assholes about it, we'll take our chances with the Others and do this without you."

Hoo boy. Now that the gauntlet was thrown, Jack was getting pissed off, too. Nikki had placed her hand not-so-subtly on the hunting knife at her hip.

"Don't forget you're the new kid in town, Devon. We didn't have to take you in. Maybe you worked with leeches in Los Angeles, but you're in New York now. We don't truck with that sort, no matter the cause. We work as a team without outside help, or we don't go in on this thing at all."

Enough was enough. I rose from my seat and stalked to the door. The bickering stopped as the others looked at me in confusion.

"Where are you going?" Tiny asked, getting to his feet.

"To take my chances with the monsters. I think I'm more likely to survive that way." I was pretty sure I hadn't made myself any new friends with that statement, but Jack's and Nikki's narrow-mindedness made it clear this would never work. I didn't have the time or patience to deal with their mule-headed bigotry.

Someone grabbed my arm. Without thought, I twisted around, shoving my free hand up under his jaw and pinning him against the wall.

It was Devon. I immediately released him, mortified at my violent reaction. He rubbed at the forming red spots on his neck, looking at me with a mixture of fear and defiance.

"I'm going with you."

Too embarrassed to speak, I nodded, turning around to continue out the door.

Jack came up beside us, staring down at Devon with an unreadable expression before addressing me.

"Shiarra, please wait. You must understand our position

on this. We're White Hats, not police. What we stand for is completely against anything supernatural. We want things to go back to normal, to take these beasts and monsters out of our lives and put them back into the fairy tales where they belong. Not working beside us. Not hunting with us. They're just animals, vicious animals. Can't you see that?"

I stopped at the door and returned his cold look. "I can see I made the wrong choice in deciding to work with you. That's not what I stand for. Sure, I can see taking justice into our own hands in cases like Max. But there are plenty of Others out there who have never hurt anybody, who are innocent, decent people, just like us. You're lumping all of them together and I won't be a part of a group who can't tell the difference."

His eyes were blue fire, suppressing a deep rage as he fought not to say what was on his mind. I watched the muscle jumping in his cheek subside as he regained control of his temper. As much as I wanted to push his buttons, seeing his bigotry in all its glory, I didn't think it would be a wise move on my part. Surprisingly, the belt agreed with me.

'Don't do anything more to stir him up. If you aren't careful, he might start seeing you as one of the monsters, too.'

I hadn't thought of that. Rather than speak out loud, I concentrated mentally to let it know I agreed with it. Holding Jack's gaze as I was, I didn't think it would be a smart idea to start talking to myself. Explaining the mechanics of the belt around my waist to a White Hat didn't appeal to me either. It might be just the excuse he needed to put me in the "Other" category, enough excuse to kill me, now that the belt had so thoughtfully pointed this out. I was sure the only thing holding him back was that whatever plans he had for me would be ruined if I was dead. Or undead, for that matter. I was lucky they didn't think of me as a willing donor now that I carried bite marks from Peter and Max. If they changed their minds, I'd be only a marginal step up from an Other and have to duck for cover as much as Chaz or Royce would when faced with them in the future.

Jack's cool demeanor resurfaced. He slowly turned away from me, breaking the stare-down and gesturing for Tiny and Nikki to go back to their seats.

"Don't bother coming back, Devon. You're not welcome here anymore."

Devon stiffened beside me, his anger a palpable thing, tasted on the air. He reached up to his collar and ripped off the tiny white cowboy hat pinned there, placing it with deliberate finality on an end table. "When push comes to shove, Jack, you're going to regret not taking this opportunity when it came."

I arched a brow at that, turning to look at Devon. His eyes were focused on Jack, and he was obviously pissed off. There was something more to what he was saying than what was on the surface. He'd mentioned not following Jack's orders before. Perhaps that had something to do with why Jack was being so recalcitrant about helping us.

Rather than worry about it further, I snagged Devon's arm and pulled him out the door with me. He resisted at first, muscles tensing under the jacket before he turned to follow me, slamming the door behind him.

We walked down the street without speaking. I had my hands shoved deep in my pockets, shivering slightly in the bitter winds coming in off the bay. Devon was staring straight ahead, not saying anything. After a couple blocks, I couldn't take it anymore and broke the silence.

"That went over better than I expected."

He looked at me askance, too surprised to stay mad. "Did it?"

"Yeah, it did. I had him pegged to go on a rampage rather than just yell at us and kick us out." I grinned at him, reaching up to brush some stray curls out of my face. He gave a shaky laugh, kicking a few early autumn leaves out of his way.

"He's such an ass sometimes. I don't know why I came to work here. Things were going okay with the hunters I was with before. I guess I just thought it was time to move on. Jack never liked my methods. Thought I was too progressive, too willing to work with the monsters instead of against them."

I shrugged, the leather jacket rustling with the movement. "That makes two of us."

The silence between us wasn't so strained anymore. Maybe it was the nearby sound of surf or the wind whistling through the trees that made it easier to bear. Maybe it was the newfound shared understanding between two misunderstood hunters. Whatever it was, I was glad for it.

However, when a voice boomed out behind us, I was startled into giving a little "eep" of surprise.

"Make that three."

Devon and I turned back, shocked to see that Tiny had joined us. He clapped those huge hands on either of our shoulders, falling into step between us. "I'm not about to miss the fight of the century, no matter what Jack says."

I somehow managed to get my heart started again and smiled up at him. "Thanks, Tiny. You're the best."

He winked down at me. "You know it, girl."

Great. Two more human hunters might just make the difference in the fight against Max Carlyle. I had to hope Chaz was having better luck getting his wolves to agree to participate in tonight's showdown.

Chapter 24

Like most of the other houses on this tiny island, Royce's friend's address led us to a sprawling Victorian. It was painted the warm shade of summer skies, with darker blue trim. There was a wraparound porch lined with wicker furniture and a hanging seat for two, its thin chains creaking in the stiff ocean breeze. The landscaping was exquisite; a lovely mix of bluebells and white daffodils outlining the path to the front door, with sprigs of jasmine and ivies lining the edges of the porch.

Considering it was getting on into late September, daffodils were definitely out of season. I didn't know about the rest, but somehow the landscaping on this house seemed more alive than any of its neighbors. What sort of "neutral third party" owned this place?

I had my answer soon enough. A breathtakingly beautiful woman answered my tentative knock. She was tall, thin, statuesque. Bright green eyes set in a triangular face studied us. Her features were obscured in shadow as she was lit from behind, but she soon stepped back to give us room to come inside. Auburn highlights shone on richly dark hair and revealed the sharp planes of finely sculpted features. It didn't take long for me to dredge up her name. Hartley.

Dawn Hartley, the runway model, sometime actress, and environmental activist. I'd seen something in the tabloids that said Royce had dated her sometime last year.

"Hi," she greeted us, a warm, welcoming smile on her lips. Not the sort of smile you give three strangers standing on your porch in the middle of the night. "You're here with Alec, right? Come on in."

I shook her offered hand as we filed inside. "Thank you. I'm Shiarra Waynest, and this is Devon and Tiny."

The two men lost their ability to speak when they laid eyes on her. I suppose I couldn't blame them. I had to elbow Devon to remind him to shut his mouth and stop staring, which he did with no small effort. Tiny couldn't tear his eyes off her.

Jeez, she was pretty, but their reaction was a little much.

She led us to a sitting room that had couches and chairs arranged to look out across the water through wide bay windows. Fog was rolling in with the surf, blanketing the deep water in pale grayish-white mist. It was beautiful, but something about that fog gave me the shivers.

Chaz and Royce were both on their cell phones. Chaz was standing by one of the windows, staring out at the water. He gave me a smile before shifting his attention back to his phone and the waves outside. Royce was seated on the chair farthest from Chaz, a hand lifted to cover his eyes as he slumped deeper into the cushions. Neither one of them looked very happy.

"Can I get you anything? Coffee, tea, maybe some water?"

Tiny shook his head, tearing his eyes off Dawn and staring intently at Royce. It must have taken some effort for him to resist using his gun. I saw his hand hesitating over the weapon. Figuring it would be better to stop it indirectly rather than stir the hunter up further, I stepped in his line of sight to Royce and gestured toward what I thought was the kitchen. That seemed impetus enough for Tiny to resume staring at Dawn. "Coffee would be great. Do you need any help in the kitchen?"

"Oh, no," she said, the dazzling smile I'd seen on the cover of magazines as genuine as the cheerful exuberance she exuded. Though I hadn't given much thought to meeting celebrities before, I never imagined they'd be as nice and accommodating as she was turning out to be. I imagined she must have had plenty of practice playing the attentive hostess in her line of work. "Just have a seat, hon, I'll take care of everything. How about you?"

Devon blushed when she turned the full force of that killer smile on him. He was too stunned to speak, settling on a jerky nod in reply. I rolled my eyes as I wandered to Chaz's side and hugged his waist. He put his arm around me but was wrapped up in listening to the voice yapping away on the other end of his cell phone.

"I'll take coffee, too. Thank you very much," Tiny stuttered out. He and Devon watched her go, eyes plastered to the gentle swaying of that slender frame until she moved out of sight. It was amazing to me that she was so comfortable with it, completely ignoring the attention.

Shrugging it off, I lay my head against Chaz's chest and listened to the steady sound of his heartbeat, offset by the dim echo of the surf pounding on rock and sand beyond the glass. After a moment, he started talking, and I pulled back to watch his face. "No, that's not why I called. You know I wouldn't ask for your help like this unless it was important."

He went back to listening. He closed his eyes and grimaced at whatever the response was. "No. If you don't want to do it, I won't make you. I'm asking as your friend, not your leader."

He shook his head and hung up the phone without saying good-bye, scowling down at the hunk of plastic before shoving it in his pocket. "Hey, love."

"Hey. What was all that about?"

"There aren't too many willing to work with us tonight." He rested his chin on top of my head, tightening his grip around my waist at my bitter sigh. "I can't make them do it either. This isn't technically pack business."

I frowned, considering as I watched the silent fog outside creep closer.

"How about Rohrik Donovan? I could call in the favor the Moonwalkers owe me."

"No, don't involve them in this. I don't think he'd appreciate the gesture if he had to put his wolves' lives on the line when mine are nowhere in sight."

"There's no need for you to worry," Royce interjected, making me jump. Chaz tightened his hold on me just enough to be comforting. "The majority of my coterie are on alert. Not as many as I feared turned to Max. A number of my loyal flock will be with us."

When I glanced at Royce, he was watching us with those flat black eyes, giving no hint as to what he was thinking. Despite his words and lack of reaction, I was sure he was hiding something that was bothering him. What emotions was he keeping veiled behind that carefully serene mask?

"Sounds like good news to me, then. Why aren't you happier about it?"

"Oh, I am pleased, make no mistake." He dredged up a smile, faint though it was, as Dawn returned with a tray. She set it lightly on a coffee table before the couch, placing one of the mugs in my hands, one in Chaz's, one in Devon's, one in Tiny's, and surprisingly, one in Royce's. I hadn't thought vampires could drink anything other than the obvious. Shows what I know. "It will make him easier to handle since your hunter friends destroyed the bulk of his invading force."

"Well, that's good news," I said, not entirely convinced that he was telling the truth.

The coffee smelled divine, and I moved closer to the tray to add some cream and sugar to my caffeine fix. I breathed in the scent with a pleased sigh, loving that warm mix teasing at my senses before taking the first, soul-warming sip.

Dawn took a drink of her own coffee before adding her thoughts to the mix, placing her free hand lightly on Royce's shoulder.

"You'd be better off tracking him down and converging on his hiding place instead of trying to lure him out," she said. "I'm sure he must know you're looking for him tonight. He's old, so he'll be wary, careful of where he goes and what he does. He may be moving from place to place to keep from being found, too, so your best bet is to use someone on the inside."

I looked at her with new respect. Royce must have filled her in on the details of why we were here. Seems she had a crafty mind to match that pretty face. I watched Royce's reaction as he answered her, curious of what he thought of her. They'd been an item once, yet he pursued me like he was interested in prying me away from Chaz. Why go after me when such a beautiful, smart woman obviously liked him? I didn't understand it, and wasn't entirely sure I wanted to. The warmth behind the look he gave her made me wonder if they were still an item, damn whatever the tabloids said.

"True, but if he thinks he's cornered, he'll lash out. I don't want that to happen until I have him in a position where the damage he can cause is minimal. John tells me he found out Max is holed up in one of my clubs. There are too many innocent people in the way for us to come at him directly, so we have no choice but to lure him out."

She nodded, thoughtful, those mint green eyes focusing on me with an intensity that had me take an involuntary step back. The intelligence and force behind that gaze were amazing—not mind tricks, just powerfully compelling. No wonder she was so successful and got along so well with the vampire.

"He took you once," she said, her voice a throaty purr. Forget modeling. The woman could make a fortune as a 900-number operator. "He wants you for something. You could play bait, get him to come out."

"No way! I'm not going through that again." I scowled at her.

She tilted her head, regarding me thoughtfully. With a few strides she was at my side, fingers running lightly along my hair. I blinked in surprise, pulling back from that invasive touch. Her attitude toward me now was bordering on sexual, like a strong, unwelcome come-on from a guy I didn't know.

"So brave," she breathed, and I shot a dirty look at Royce. He did nothing but watch, both hands used to cradle his coffee mug as he held it to his lips. It wasn't my imagination—the bastard was hiding a smile behind the cup. "You taste of power. You have the strength to face him, if you have the will for it. You could last long enough for the others to come to your aid."

Once again, I found myself blinking in surprise. I set the coffee mug down and with great care, very gently and very deliberately put my hands on her shoulders to force her to put more breathing room between us. She tensed against it at first, then gave in to the pressure and stepped away. Judging by the brief resistance and taking into account the augmented strength from the belt, she was stronger than she should be. Not human.

"Dawn, please don't take this the wrong way, but stay away from me. You're creeping me out."

She kept moving until my hands fell away, those lovely eyes reflecting hurt and puzzlement. The more I thought on it, the more I was sure I'd never seen eyes so perfectly, flawlessly green. Eyes the gentle color of verdant moss in the spring. There was something off about them aside from their more than perfect coloration, but I couldn't put my finger on it.

Soon the lines between her brows cleared and the frown turned into a charming smile, one that made me want to smile in return despite that she had given me the willies just a second ago.

"I am sorry. I didn't mean to offend you. It's been a while since I've been around someone touched by fae."

"What?" The response was startled out of me. I hated when people talked about stuff I didn't know anything about. Seriously hated it. She looked at Royce, once again puzzled by my reaction. He shrugged at her, his gaze never wavering from me.

After a moment of consideration, she took another step toward me, and then hesitated. "May I?"

"Um. Sure, I guess." I wasn't totally certain what I was giving her permission to do, but she was a friend and ally of Royce's. He wouldn't let her do something to hurt me. I hoped.

She came closer, one of her hands drifting over the contours of my body. Not touching, but an inch or two away, starting at my face and working her way down the front of my chest, all the way down to my boots. She hesitated at the belt but didn't stop. Once she finished, she nodded to herself and rose, stepping back.

"You are wearing things made by magi. The strength you carry is fae-borne. Forgive me, considering the company you keep, I assumed you were Other."

Strange that she'd be able to sense that. Was she a mage? I'd never heard any mention of power like that in the tabloids. On concentrating on her features, that lovely visage suddenly wavered in my vision. My unspoken question as to what I was looking at was answered by an unlikely source.

'*She's of elven blood,*' the belt said, radiating impatience, but no sense of alarm. '*She's been using glamour to make herself seem friendlier, more attractive and desirable. Not that she needs it. The charm you're wearing is letting you see through the mask she's wearing for the sake of the men in the room.*'

I couldn't hide my shock. I'd never met an elf before. Wow, if that's what she looked like without glamour, I was almost afraid of what Devon, Tiny, Chaz, and Royce must be seeing. On closer inspection, I now recognized what seemed off about her eyes. Her pupils weren't like a human's. They were rounded slits, catlike, and watching me with a great deal of puzzlement. Maybe a dash of wariness, too, since I was looking at her like she'd grown two heads.

I'd wondered why Devon and Tiny were so affected by her when Royce and Chaz showed no signs of being drawn into her glamour. Maybe Royce wasn't because he was an elder vampire and a master at mind games. As the pack leader of a werewolf tribe, Chaz was stronger than the average Other. That might have given him some measure of immunity to her charms. I tried thinking more questions at the belt, but my internal dialogue was cut off by the outside world.

"Why are you so surprised, Shiarra?"

That was from Royce. He was enjoying my shock. I pushed some stray red curls out of my face before slumping into an empty chair. I needed to sit down for this. How many people knew what she was? What was Royce's interest in the fae? How dangerous was she, now that I knew her secret? Obviously not very, or Royce wouldn't be prompting me to say it aloud. What was his purpose in making me give her away?

Too many questions, not enough answers. I decided to

oblige the vampire, glaring at him to let him know I wasn't fooled by his innocent act.

"I've never met one of the fair folk before. Now that I see it, I'm wondering why I didn't notice it before."

Devon and Tiny were just as surprised at the revelation as I was.

"You're an elf?" Devon asked.

Dawn ignored Devon and pouted at me, her hands going to her hips. "How did you know? Who told you?"

"No one told me." I hoped I'd get away with the little white lie. After all, it was the belt—not a person—who told me. "Just looking at you, I'm surprised no one ever figured it out before. You're too perfect for a human."

I smiled to soften any criticism implied with the remark. She didn't seem appeased by my efforts, turning away in a huff. Now that I saw her in profile, the flawless line of her jaw and thin bone structure made it clearer than before what she was. Easy to pass, yet now that I knew, so hard to believe I ever thought of her as human. The only thing she was missing were the pointy ears.

"I should've held myself in check. It's just been so long since I've felt power like that." She turned back to me, that same lustful look in her eyes as she focused on the belt around my waist. I couldn't for the life of me figure out what was so attractive about it.

There was a knock on the front door. Dawn took a deep breath to compose herself. There was a tingling sense of something rushing over my skin before she went to answer. Elves could be as creepy and scary as vampires apparently. Devon and Tiny watched her saunter off like she was the last glass of water in the desert. It would've been funny if the effects of her glamour on the unprotected weren't so frightening. Would I have acted that way without the charm around my neck? The belt thought so.

Chaz and Royce obviously had immunity to her charms

or acclimated themselves somehow since they weren't watching her that way. Or maybe they hid their interest better.

Unsettled, I snagged my coffee and returned to the shelter of Chaz's arms, waiting for Sara and Arnold to join us.

Chapter 25

I was glad to see Sara and Arnold, even though Sara kept shooting me looks like she wanted to throttle me between furtive, fascinated glances at Dawn. Arnold didn't appear to be affected in the least by the elf's glamour. His smile wasn't worried or distracted, and he greeted me casually when they came into the room. He strode easily beside Sara, the two of them arm in arm.

"Hey, Shia."

I gave him a weak smile, relieved to see that Dawn wasn't pawing at him. "Hi, guys. How was the trip?"

"Great, tha—"

Arnold was cut off by Sara. "We'll talk about that later. What can you tell us about the guy that's after you?"

She obviously wasn't pleased. I wasn't happy about what we had to do tonight either, and wasn't about to give her a hard time for being upset.

"Come sit down and get some coffee. It's a long story."

Sara gave me a withering look for putting off my explanation, but did as I asked. All of us found empty seats to have our discussion. I settled back into the cushions of the chair and tried to explain as succinctly as I could.

"There's an elder vamp, Max Carlyle, who came to town

looking for revenge. You remember David Borowsky and Anastasia Alderov? Anastasia was one of Max's people, so he's pissed that she's dead. He blames Royce, so he thought he could get to him by taking me. Now he's messing with Royce's businesses and vamps, and he's still looking for me. We have to get rid of him before he manages to establish a foothold in the city."

Sara and Arnold nodded thoughtfully, taking in my explanation. Arnold spoke up next. "I thought vampire law forbids them from encroaching on one another's territory like this? Or from killing each other?"

"He thinks he can kill us both for wronging him," Royce answered, "and that he can escape punishment by claiming that we attacked his people first. If he is questioned by Others later, he will hide behind our laws of redress."

"What about the police?" Sara asked, her voice gone breathy. My attention centered on her, and I frowned at the sight of her bright blue eyes gone wide, lips parted as she stared at Royce. Arnold had his arm proprietarily around her shoulders and was glaring at the vampire. What was Royce doing? Whatever it was, while it may have drawn Sara's interest, she retained enough of her wits to ask pertinent questions. "Shiarra's contracted to you, not Max. What makes him think he can get away with hurting her without having to answer for his actions?"

"The police only hold as much power over us as we let them. There are few vampires as old as I am who agree it was a good idea to integrate ourselves into your society. Max is one of the dissenters; he comes from a time when we simply took what we wanted. He knows how to hide his dealings from or manipulate your police and judicial systems to escape punishment. Consider it a survival mechanism. If we did not know how to do these things, he and I would not have survived this long."

Though it was diversionary, my curiosity was piqued.

"Does that mean you could find ways to make people disappear, too?"

He looked at me, eyes narrowed with anger. Must have hit a sore point there. "Theoretically, yes, I could. Unlike Max, my conscience would not allow for me to stoop to such a level."

Royce had a conscience? That was news to me.

He must not have liked what he saw in my face. Or maybe one of his vampire powers was to read minds. His expression was bitter enough to choke on and I felt a momentary pang of remorse for having thought so little of him. At every turn I somehow managed to think the worst of him, his motives, and his actions. I felt like I should offer a comforting touch, say something to let him know I didn't think he was such a bad guy. I needed to apologize, though I wasn't totally sure what for.

The belt cut in before I could speak. *'Stop meeting his eyes like an amateur. You should know better by now. Draw on my strength and on the charm you wear, or you'll lose yourself to him the way the elf has.'*

I took a deep breath and did what the belt ordered, averting my gaze and focusing on calming down. Looking away took the edge off the shame. My reaction was unnaturally strong, like a kernel of real emotion had been fanned into an all-out conflagration, meant to override any other thoughts or feelings. How very odd that Royce could manipulate emotions like that. Fear and lust I could understand— but pity and guilt? That didn't seem his style.

Dawn broke the uncomfortable silence. "It's late. If you're planning a confrontation tonight, I would hurry or there will not be time for your vampires to seek shelter from the sun before this is over."

By my reckoning, it was only a little past midnight. I thought we had plenty of time, but then, I'd never fought a battle like this before, and Royce hadn't made us privy to his battle plans.

The vampire slowly rose to his feet. I felt a momentary pang as Sara pressed against Arnold's side, her fingers tightening on his jacket. Royce's gaze swept over the room, lingering on Sara before settling on me. Averting my eyes, I felt a pull of something, though exactly what emotion he was projecting or what he was willing me to do or think wasn't clear. The combination of my wariness and the belt and charm's assistance was halting Royce's mind games admirably. He closed the distance between us, extending a hand to help me up.

"Shall we go?" he asked.

Chaz made a grumbling sound under his breath when I slid my hand into the vampire's.

"Sure. I'll be riding with Arnold and Sara, by the way."

We hadn't discussed it, but there was no way I was going to ride with the vampire while he was projecting those weird moods. If I didn't know any better, I'd say he was having trouble deciding whether he was disappointed or happy about what was going on and was wavering somewhere in between. He didn't argue, which was a blessing, but he didn't let me go once I'd gotten to my feet either. Instead, he lifted my hand up and cradled it between both of his own. I couldn't pull away without expending more effort than it was worth. I'd never seen him act this way before.

"Are you entirely sure you want to take part in this fight? It is not too late for you and your friends to go."

Ah. The concern he radiated was so sincere, I couldn't help but smile and lose some of the tension that had threaded through me when he didn't let go of my hand. "No, I'm not about to run and hide. This isn't your fight—it's ours."

He returned my smile, his expression shifting to something dark and wicked and oh so bad for you. "So be it."

With that, he brushed a chaste, gallant kiss on the back of my hand, his lips grazing my knuckles before he released me. Oddly enough, it didn't bother me in the least. He was just being, well . . . Royce. Chaz didn't take it nearly so well, rumbling a low warning.

"Keep your hands off her," he spat, sliding an arm possessively around my waist. Royce barely glanced at him, a satisfied smirk curving his lips.

I just sighed.

Everyone else got up to file out the front door. Chaz refused to take his arm from around me until we got close to the car. Arnold's ostentatious sports car did not look so out of place among the convertibles and other high-end vehicles parked on the street and in the driveways around us.

Dawn surprised me again by wanting to come along for the fight. I wasn't sure what help she could be, but Royce didn't argue. Sara agreed to give up shotgun to Chaz so the couples could ride together in Arnold's car. Devon and Tiny had no complaints about riding in the silver sedan with the most dangerous supernatural New York had to offer. Then again, that might be because Dawn didn't seem to mind sitting between the two men in the back while Royce chauffeured them to our destination. Go figure.

Sara and I did the necessary contortionist acts to squeeze into the back seat of the convertible so we could have our own private discussion while Arnold, Chaz, and Royce discussed our destination outside.

"What gives, Shia?" Sara whispered, not wanting the Others to overhear. "How come you're working with Royce? I thought you swore off ever having anything to do with him again."

I didn't have any graceful way of avoiding her eyes while crammed into the tiny back seat. Hard as it was, I met the concern and fury in those blue eyes. This was worse than confessing to Mom—nobody could throw your own words back at you like your best friend.

"I did," I admitted. "I had to make an exception for this."

She twisted in the seat, putting one knee up so she could rest her elbow on it. She twined her enviably straight blond hair around her fingers in a nervous gesture that made her look uncannily like her neurotic sister, Janine.

"You don't go into this shit lightly. What changed your mind? Why now, months later? Don't tell me it's just because of this Max guy."

"I thought having an ancient vampire after my ass was sufficient excuse to call for backup."

"Bullshit," she said, looking pointedly at the belt wrapped around my waist. I huffed and drew the trench coat shut to hide it from view. "You could have called me or Arnold or even Chaz and hidden from this. Instead, you're playing Lone Ranger and riding in to save the day or whatever. I don't believe for a second you weren't thinking of running from this until *he* got involved."

"Sara! I don't always run from my problems."

Her wry grin wore away the immediate edge of my anger from her "accusations." Before long, I found myself grinning back.

"Okay, okay. I was pissed at Chaz because he broke off another date with me on Friday night. I thought it would get under his skin if I invited Royce to come to my place. At the time, I needed to know who Max was, so it was a convenient excuse to invite him over."

Her feigned shock was spoiled by the knowing grin splitting her face. "Ha! I knew it!"

"Oh, shut up," I said, unsuccessfully smothering a smile. "Anyway, Max backed me into a corner when he kidnapped me. He means business, and I don't want this to escalate to the point where he hurts my friends and family. Hence our little coup tonight."

"So how does Chaz feel about you and Royce making nice?" she asked me, her suggestive brow waggle completely ruining the innocent look on her face.

"Oh my God, Sara!"

I gasped in a mix of mock and true horror at the unspoken implications, making her burst into laughter. It was tough to be mad at her when she was laughing so hard. My face felt so hot, I was sure it must have turned as red as my hair. Despite my indignation, before long, the idea had me in giggle fits, too.

Chaz and Arnold opened their doors to join us in the car. They looked a bit surprised at our mirth, which was understandably out of place considering we were about to go into battle against an elder vampire. Their puzzled looks deepened as Sara hid her face behind her hands, trying to control the tears of laughter spilling down her cheeks.

"What's so funny, girls?" Arnold asked, sliding in and peering at us through the rearview as he started up the car. Once seated, Chaz craned his neck to peer at us in mystery.

It just made us laugh harder.

Chapter 26

An hour later, standing in the parking lot of Twisted Temptations (arguably the most risqué of Royce's many establishments), surrounded by a bunch of vampires and a handful of Weres, I didn't feel like laughing anymore. It was bitterly cold. The parking lot of the warehouse-like night club was packed full, so we'd parked a few blocks away. The armor and trench coat weren't protecting me well from the icy wind blowing through the streets as we hustled to meet the other vamps and Weres. Even the warmth radiating from Chaz's arm wrapped around my shoulders didn't help.

From the information John had scraped together, Max had moved into the club early in the evening and replaced all of the regular staffers with his own men. A runner was sent to fetch something from one of the offices here and reported a sign on the door saying the club was closed for a private party. After that, they didn't hear from him again. To the few hundred people who'd come for some dancing and drinking at the Goth fetish club, being turned away at the door would've been disappointing, but normal. Business as usual.

Meanwhile, anyone who was stuck inside when Max took

over may not have noticed anything out of the ordinary. Not until it was too late. Vampires and their contracted toys were no doubt still going up on stage, singing, dancing, even stripping or doing some BDSM crap for the amusement of the crowds. The only difference being that none of them answered to Royce.

I couldn't figure out Max's reasoning behind taking over a night club. I mean, it was Royce's property, right? Max couldn't get his hands on the titles or deeds to the business. Was it meant as a personal affront to Royce? More likely he knew something about the tunnel system that would give him access to the other businesses, and wanted to use this location to stage attacks.

Only three other Weres had showed up to help Chaz. He hadn't forced the issue, but it was interesting to see how few of the sixty-odd werewolves of the Sunstriker pack were willing to back up their pack leader against vampires without being directly ordered to do so. Of the Weres who did come to our rescue, Simon and Dillon had showed up with Chaz right before Sara got kidnapped earlier this year, and Vincent had come with us a few times when we got together for somebody's birthday, the debut of the latest action movie, things like that. None of them struck me as being particularly brave or loyal before now. Kudos to them.

More vampires had showed up to help Royce than had been present when he came to rescue me. It made me nervous as hell, and the belt kept interjecting little (and sometimes not so little) hints that it really, *really* wanted to take some of them down. Considering the thing had the purpose of ridding the world of vamps, I couldn't say I blamed it. I just wished it would shut up now and then so I could concentrate.

Simon and Dillon went with a few of the vampires to guard the back doors and make sure none of Max's vamps escaped. The rest of us just went straight for the front door—Chaz and Vincent at either side of me, with Arnold, Sara, Tiny, and Devon at our backs. I don't know what Dawn hoped to accomplish in a knock-down-drag-out fight, but she was somewhere in the mix of vampires, too.

We could all hear the music pounding from inside, some heavy metal with a lot of bone-shaking bass. There should have been bouncers guarding the front and some last-minute stragglers trying to get in, but the street was oddly deserted. Royce led the way; he didn't look happy no one was there to greet us. Though there were a few vampires between us, I saw him turn to John with a frown when he tried the front doors. Locked.

John unlocked the bolt so we could get in. The vampires around us didn't tense up so much as go deathly still in anticipation. I felt the tightening of muscles under my fingers on Chaz's arm, even through the jacket he was wearing against the bitter chill in the air. We all surged inside as soon as the double doors swung open, Royce in the lead.

The smell of blood was heavy on the air. If I hadn't had heightened senses from the belt, I might not have noticed, but the acrid, sticky reek was too strong to ignore. I couldn't ask what anybody else thought of it since the pounding music made conversation impossible.

I pulled a stake from the belt, running my thumb nervously along the leather grip to remind myself I had a weapon, that I could handle this, and it would all be over soon.

As a group, we moved forward cautiously, everyone else's pace slowing when Royce's did. When we passed through the hallway and reached the first room in the club, there was nothing much to see. There was no one behind the bar; the plush couches lining the walls were empty, as were the raised stage and two metal cages for dancers in the middle of the room.

If the situation hadn't been so serious and we weren't in the middle of looking for Max, I would have made some snarky comments about the décor to Royce. The neon whips and silver chains decorating the black walls were a bit much, even for one of his clubs.

Either way, there was nothing to see here. The room wasn't very big. Directly ahead was a stairwell. There was another hallway to our left, and a screen of thin silver chains to the right obscured the way into the largest dance floor. There were strobe lights flickering through the chains, but I couldn't see much more than a big, black, empty space beyond. The smell of blood and thicker things had become positively overpowering, so much so that I couldn't rightly say which direction it came from.

We separated into three groups to investigate. Royce and the majority of his people went into the main dance hall. Arnold, Sara, and Dawn followed him. We'd discussed this tactic earlier over a hastily sketched map of the club's layout. Max's main target was Royce. Arnold specialized in intelligence gathering and defensive spellcasting, so it made the most sense for him to stay close to Royce to help buffer up the vamp's abilities when Max struck. Sara wouldn't leave Arnold's side, and he didn't want her out of his sight, so she stayed with them.

A handful of other vampires separated off and went down the opposite hallway. Six vampires I didn't know, and one vampire I did—John—came with me, Chaz, Devon, and Tiny to check out the upstairs.

This club was a lot smaller than The Underground. There were two upper floors, both open to the public. Below was a basement connected to the webwork Royce's people used to get around his businesses without chancing police, reporters, or daylight. John, knowing the layout better than the rest of us, took the lead.

The top of the stairs opened directly onto a smallish dance floor. There was different music playing here, just as obnoxious as what was pounding out of the sound system downstairs. Actually, I think it was worse, seeing as the singer couldn't coherently scream his lyrics. Yeesh.

The creepiest thing about the place was that there were no *people*. Why all the cars in the lot below, but nobody manning the bars, no one dancing to the music, and not a soul reclining on any of the numerous plush couches and chairs scattered around the place? The people had to have gone somewhere. It was freaking me out that we hadn't come across a single one yet. Where were they being held? Where was the smell of blood coming from?

My heart had worked its way from my throat back down to my chest by the third empty room. It didn't make any sense. Everyone else looked just as grim and just as puzzled as I felt. I was starting to think this whole thing was a bust and that Max and his people must have gone through the tunnels or left by some other means, when we came upon the largest dance floor on this level.

There were bodies sprawled everywhere on the floor, many piled on top of each other. Skin pale, so pale, unnaturally so. Some of them flashed scarlet at the neck, on the wrist, or maybe the bend of an elbow, vivid against bloodless skin. Glazed eyes stared sightlessly up at the weaving spotlights on the ceiling. Images of macabre scenes, graveyards, twining bodies, and empty eyes shifted on the screen above the stage on the other side of the room, flowing to the beat of the music. It was twistedly apropos of the piles of dead sprawled atop one another, covering the dance floor like a grisly blanket.

I tried to stay detached. I tried very hard to think analytically about what I was seeing so I would not run screaming from the room. The floor wasn't literally covered—there were twenty or so bodies here; not nearly enough to account for all the cars in the lot below. There had to be more bodies around here somewhere. Maybe there were clues here as to where Max had gone.

The closest corpse was only a few feet away from where

I'd stopped—an Asian woman with hair dyed an appalling shade of purple. She was wearing a top that barely covered her breasts, and a chain ran from her belt to a studded collar around her neck. More chains extended from the collar to matching bracelets at her wrists and ankles.

The cuff on the left had been torn away, fingers limply curled up to expose the inside of her wrist. There was a bite there, two jagged tears far more visible than the neat marks on my neck. Fangs had been used to slash that otherwise flawless skin, not just to pierce. I quickly shifted my gaze to her face; those glazed brown eyes seemed to stare accusingly at me. We were too late to save her, save all these people, from the kind of death that had haunted my nightmares ever since I found out that vampires existed outside storybooks and bad horror movies.

I looked down at my feet, collecting myself before examining what was on the dance floor more closely. The shallow breaths I was taking made the smell of blood and dead meat chokingly thick on my tongue. That's when I noticed the ground was glistening. As if in a dream or trance, I slowly knelt down to touch it.

It wasn't the material of the floor making it shiny. It was slick with blood.

Twisting away, I staggered back to my feet. Chaz had to catch my arm and help me so I could throw up in the room behind us instead of on the bodies. He looked as green as I felt. Even the vampires looked disturbed by this much bloodshed, some of them wiping at their mouths, backing out of the room. Devon and Tiny were the only ones unfazed by the sight. In fact, they waded right into the mess, pulling gloves out of their pockets before touching anything. I noted with a detached sort of horror that each step they took kicked up droplets of blood.

They examined some of the closest remains. Devon shouted something, but I couldn't make it out over the heavy bass of the music. John shook his head and Devon shouted again. This time I heard him.

". . . got here in time! They've all been drained by vampires, no other injuries on any of them I can see. Why just leave all these bodies here? Why kill all these people that way, waste all this blood?"

"I don't know. Maybe Mr. Royce will have some ideas."

John looked frustrated and frazzled, running a hand raggedly through his short reddish-brown hair. The gesture didn't help his image. He may have been around since the Boston Tea Party, but dressed down in jeans and a plain blue button-down shirt, he looked too much the over-earnest intern to be taken seriously as Royce's second-in-command.

"Let's go find him," I said, lacing my arm through Chaz's so I wouldn't fall on my face. I'd disgraced myself enough by being the only person to toss my cookies. With the way my knees were shaking, I wasn't sure my legs would hold up on the stairs yet. At that point, I would have done anything to get us as far away from this room as possible, even if Chaz had to carry me to do it.

"I'm going to stay here and check for more clues," Tiny rumbled, barely heard against the deeper bass of the music. Devon went with him, the two crouching down to check the bodies more thoroughly. One of the vampires walked with them, an expression of severe distaste curling his lip as the hunters blithely rummaged through the macabre remains.

With me hanging on Chaz's arm, the rest of the vampires hurried after us a trifle faster than strictly necessary. I guess even vamps aren't always hardened to murder. Mass murder anyway. What's a single victim here or there?

I knew Max was a Bad Guy, with a capital B, capital G. However, I hadn't counted on him being quite this psychotic. Even after having been thrown so casually to Peter and then bitten by Max, too, I hadn't thought he was capable of this level of violence, bloodshed, and waste.

The belt forced calm on me, clearing my head so I could focus and think. Alien thoughts threaded through my mind, calculating the whys and wherefores of this massacre.

It was out of character for vampires to do something so openly destructive, particularly an elder, who knew his survival was dependent upon blending in with and hiding from mortals. If people were too afraid, it became harder to hunt, harder to seduce, harder to make them love you and let you feed on them. This number of dead humans was guaranteed to make headlines. There would be no possible way to hide this many deaths from the authorities or the media. It would cause trouble for vampires everywhere. He must be intending to use it somehow. But how?

Chaz yanked me back from the bottom of the stairwell, one hand tugging me up against his chest, the other arm blocking the way for everyone else. Only then did I realize something was different. The music down here was off. The only song still playing came from the second floor, muffled here in the stairwell. My eardrums weren't functioning right, still semideafened, so I wasn't sure why he'd stopped us. After prying his fingers off my stomach, I leaned forward to peer into the main room of the first floor.

Brows lowered in a scowl, Royce was staring in the direction of the room with the chains hiding it from view, three police officers holding guns and crosses on him and the vampires crowded around him. There were far too many of them for the cops to hold, but Royce was a law-abiding vampire. He wasn't the type to use trickery or force to avoid the police.

There was a fourth officer tossing his cookies in the corner, much like I had been a few minutes ago. The others looked green around the gills, too. I guess the rest of the bodies weren't far away.

One of the cops was giving some rushed orders into his radio, calling in for backup and as many people as the coroner's office could spare. The presence of law enforcement officials so close on our heels meant someone had been keeping tabs on us. This must be more of Max's plan to screw things up as thoroughly as possible for the rest of us. What else would Max do while Royce and I were cooling our heels at the station?

Seething, I pulled back into the shadows of the stairwell. This was just great. An intelligent, calculating, completely psychotic elder leech, who was perfectly willing to murder people and turn the police against us, was succeeding at putting the blame for his crimes squarely on an innocent—well, innocent of this crime—vampire's shoulders.

Just the kind of guy you want as an enemy.

Chapter 27

The police hadn't spotted me yet. We had some time and we needed to get out of here to find Max before he could take advantage of Royce being tied up in legal red tape. I gestured for the others to go back up the stairs. They hesitated, but at my insistent signals to be quiet and *move*, they made their way back up.

I explained as briefly as I could once our voices were safely drowned out by the music. "Someone tipped off the cops! They're holding the others downstairs. John, do you know any alternate ways out of here?"

"Yes," he replied, more distressed than before, "but I think it would be best if we didn't go in a big group. We might be spotted. There are a couple of alternate exits so we can split up and meet back at corporate later." He turned to two of the other vampires, pointing toward the room where Devon, Tiny, and the other guy were examining the bodies. "Derek, Rick, can you go warn the others and get them out of here through the fire escape?"

Derek nodded and the two rushed off. John turned to another pair of the vampires. "You two take the Weres out through the lift. Go out the back door, and get the people guarding it out of here, too."

"Wait, I'm not going without Shia," Chaz protested.

I opened my mouth to argue, too, but John lifted a hand to cut me off. "We have wards keyed against Weres in the passage she needs to go through to escape this building. She doesn't have the strength or constitution to jump rooftops like we can. Max must have planned for this somehow. Mr. Royce might need her help making a statement so the police don't hold him, and I don't want to chance her getting lost or hurt before she can do that."

Chaz didn't like it, his voice lowering and his eyes taking on a subtle amber glow as his anger started to get the better of him. "If something happens to her, I'm holding you personally responsible."

"I swear on my honor I will keep her safe." John stated curtly, meeting Chaz's heated gaze without flinching.

Chaz turned one last, anguished look to me. I gave him a smile to let him know I'd be okay, but I don't think it was very convincing. Chaz, Vincent, and the two vamps rushed off without another word.

That left me with John and a vamp I didn't know. The latter turned to me, gesturing to a hallway we hadn't checked earlier.

"This way."

We ran like our lives depended on it. I think I surprised both of them that I kept up with their pace. With the hunter's belt, I could run faster than this, but they were moving at a reasonable speed they thought I could manage. Some niggling sense of caution made me consider it might be better to keep the perks of the belt under wraps. I didn't try to outdo them, just kept up.

Down a dimly lit corridor, we came to a locked door that faded into the walls. Everything, from the hinges down to the doorknob, was painted the same flat black as the wall. Guess it kept people from snooping, though John was having some technical difficulties finding the key that fit the lock. Even with the enhanced night vision vamps are graced with, trying to find the right key in this hallway had to be difficult.

Just as he unlocked the door, an officer came rushing at us from the stairwell, his hand on the butt of his gun. The music was too loud to hear what he was shouting, but I'm pretty sure it wasn't anything encouraging.

The three of us ducked inside, scrambling to get out of the way before the cop could shoot or reach us. John slammed the door behind us and stabbed at the button for a service elevator. Guess this was how the employees trucked the booze up to this level. I wasn't tired, but I leaned against the wall while we waited, listening to the pounding of the policeman's fist against the door when he realized it was locked.

"That was close."

The other vamp grinned at me nervously, flashing fangs. "Yeah. Don't worry, we'll be out of here soon."

Shuddering, I turned away to avoid looking into the hazel irises of the strange vamp flickering to the red of agitation. John was rubbing his face in an uneasy gesture, occasionally throwing furtive glances in my direction. Me? I was busy worrying about the consequences of running, and sorely hoped that I hadn't left behind enough evidence for the police to figure out I'd been there. Had I left any fingerprints? Oh, shit. I'd thrown up. If they had any DNA of mine on file, they'd know.

Maybe running from the cops hadn't been the brightest thing to do, but being trapped in a police station wouldn't help anything. No doubt I would be stuck there for hours and lose any advantage or lead on Max if I got dragged down to the station tonight.

Where did Max flee to? Why had he set up Royce like this? It wouldn't take *that* long for the police to do the DNA tests, or to take measurements of the marks on the corpses against the bite radius of Royce's vamps to figure out they weren't involved. There were undoubtedly security cameras in or outside the building that must have caught the real culprits on tape, too.

Guaranteed, even with the lawyers on his bankroll, it would still take a while to sort out this mess and get Royce cleared of any charges. Was Max trying to temporarily get us out of the way, or was this meant as a smear campaign against Royce? The press would be on top of this in short order. No one, not even the feds, could hide a slaughter of this magnitude for long. The paparazzi would have a field day with this. No doubt the general public would be terrified of all things Other for a good long while.

That led me to wonder. Did Max have something more sinister in mind for this scene, or was he just trying to get us off his back long enough to do something even worse? Maybe he wanted time to entrench himself somewhere else, move to another haven. Maybe he wanted to make Royce's life an (un)living hell for the next few years. Let's face it: even the best lawyers and marketing people money can buy wouldn't fully remove the taint this would put on Royce's rep. But why would Max do that if he intended to kill Royce, as he'd said to me back at that house in the woods?

Maybe Max had meant to make people afraid of vampires again, stop seeing them as people, and view them all as a menace or a threat. Royce had mentioned Max didn't agree with vampires going public. Maybe that meant he didn't want vampires to be legal citizens anymore.

Or maybe I was just reading too much into it and he only did it to make things harder on Royce. I just couldn't be sure.

Damn it, I needed fewer questions and more answers.

John took us down to the basement and opened up another hidden escape tunnel below ground. Useful, but creepy.

'I thought tonight was about the hunt,' the belt whined at me as we ran, halogen lights flashing by. It was impossi-

ble to tell how many we'd passed or how far we were going.
*'I was looking forward to killing vampires again. Couldn't
you take down one of these? You don't need them for anything now.'*

I am so *not debating this with you right now,* I thought
as hard as I could at it.

'You're no fun,' it sulked, quieting again. Thank God.

John veered off down a narrower and not quite so well-
lit tunnel. Some of the lamps were out. Guess this one
wasn't used as often.

After a while, we reached a door for which he produced—
you guessed it—another key. He gestured for me to go
first, very gentlemanly.

Thus, I wasn't expecting to be faced with a smiling Max
Carlyle as soon as I emerged into a basement. I froze at the
sight of him, wide eyes taking in the crowd of vampires at
his back. There were almost as many vamps here as Royce
had brought with him to Twisted Temptations.

No. Not all vampires. I recognized some of Max's
human flunkies who'd helped kidnap me, as well as Peter
and Nicolas. The mage had a huge white bandage taped to
his forehead and temple, and was glaring daggers at me.
Crap, the White Hats hadn't killed him; they'd only
knocked him out when they came to rescue me.

My heart seized up on me, my shock leading me to
falter. The vampire beside John grabbed my arms, wrest-
ing them to the small of my back while John shut the door,
cutting off any hope of escape. There wasn't time to feel
betrayed; everything was moving too fast for that.

The vamp who grabbed me must not have known about
the belt. He wasn't holding me too tightly. In a panic, I took
advantage of his weak grip by twisting to the side, the
terror and surge of adrenalin making me willing to do absolutely anything to break free. God, I did not want to be
back in the hands of Max Carlyle. Not again—not after
what I'd just seen.

*'There's too many! Don't fight so hard. You'll give your-
self away and won't get another chance to escape.'*

Panting with terror, I did as the belt advised and stopped
pulling quite so hard. The vamp holding me was still
cursing and struggling with effort. Another set of hands
tightened on one of my arms. The first vampire shifted his
grip so he and John each held me pinned between them. I
made a little sound of pain when John's fingers dug in,
crushing my bicep through the thick layers of leather
trench coat and armor.

I could've kicked at them, and possibly succeeded at
cracking shins and breaking kneecaps with these heavy
boots, but the belt was right. It was too soon to give myself
away. For the moment, I'd play hurt and scared little
human.

"Good to see you again, Shiarra," Max purred.

He came closer and tipped up my face, though I tried
vainly to pull back from his touch. Panic threatened to take
me again, and it was all I could do to keep from throwing
my full weight back to avoid contact. Max's gray eyes were
calm, collected, nothing like they should be after he caused
the deaths of so many people.

I'm pretty sure mine reflected that I was scared shitless.

"I hadn't taken you for the sort to use such a hands-on
method at revenge. I'm glad you came with Alec to investigate the club; it makes things ever so much easier."

"So glad I could be of service," I snarled sarcastically,
falling back on bravado. There had to be something I could
do to escape. When his fingers tightened, tilting my head
back, I lost it. In my haste to keep from being put in a position to be bitten again, I lashed out at him and kicked his
knee. The belt interceded, preventing me from putting the
full force of my augmented strength and speed behind it.

Despite the belt dampening my efforts, it was still like
striking a solid block of granite. I winced in pain as Max
stumbled back, eyes widening as he reached down to clutch

at his leg. Damn it, I must have hit him too hard. John snarled and twisted my hair up in his fist, yanking my head back so hard, I'm surprised my neck didn't snap.

"No. Let go, John," Max ordered. He sounded rather breathless, his composure lost in an instant to interest, not fear or pain. John reluctantly disentangled his fingers from my hair, once again gripping my upper arm with both hands. "My, my. Not what I was expecting at all."

Damn it, damn it, *damn* it! I'd meant to make Max back off, not become more intrigued with me.

He slid closer again, the movement smooth and graceful. Either I hadn't injured him as much as I'd hoped, or he was very good at rapid healing. Probably both. I tried swallowing past the fear closing my throat, to think of some witty one-liner to deflect the turn of his thoughts, but nothing was coming to mind beyond gibbering terror.

"I suppose it wouldn't change anything to tip my hand now," he said, more to himself than anyone else. He put his hand under my chin again, but this time it was to force me to stare directly into his gaze. I couldn't look away. "Don't do that again, hmm?"

There was nothing for me but his eyes, his voice in my universe. I willed myself to fight, to strike him again, to lash out somehow, but my body didn't want to cooperate. Something was dreadfully wrong here.

"Behave yourself. I'll take care of you."

His voice wrapped around me like a security blanket. Safe, warm, comforting. Had I done something wrong? Maybe I shouldn't have tried to hurt him. I should apologize for kicking him, shouldn't I? Then I could bathe in that warmth, fall into the safety of his arms.

What was wrong with me? With a low growl, I closed my eyes, summoning as much strength of will as I could. This was a vampire, a murderous vampire who had killed too many people for me to count. I'd seen the evidence of it with my own eyes not an hour ago. Why did I feel such a strong draw to him, to do what he said?

Help me, I pleaded inwardly, mentally grasping at the only straw I had. I had the charm; he wasn't supposed to be able to do this to me. Why weren't the belt and the charm keeping him out of my mind? I tried to reason with the belt, pleading the only way I knew how without giving myself away to Max.

Please, do something, help me stop this. It's not supposed to be this way!

Distantly, very distantly, the belt whispered an answer. I'd never heard it sound so quiet and afraid before. *'This isn't something I can help you fight. The charm won't protect you from this. You're bound to him.'*

"No! Oh, God, no!" I cried, my voice gone thin and reedy with shock and fear. I hadn't meant to say those words aloud but I couldn't help it. *Bound?* I wasn't supposed to be bound to anybody! That meant he could bend me to his will, use me like those people I'd seen at the police station so many months ago, straining against the handcuffs binding them to their chairs as they cried and screamed for their dead vampire master.

Those soft hands caressed my face, thumbs lightly brushing along my cheeks to wipe away my tears.

"Hush," he said, that pleasant voice teasing at my senses. "Open your eyes, Shiarra. Look at me."

I tried to fight it. I didn't want to open my eyes.

But I had to.

I practically melted at the sight of his soft smile, seeing he wasn't angry. He cared for and loved me. Why was I supposed to be fighting this? He backed away a few steps, and I surged toward him, crying out as those cruel hands tightened on my arms, keeping us apart.

Some tiny voice in the back of my mind was screaming, but it was easy to ignore.

"You won't hurt me again, will you, pet?"

I shook my head, not trusting my voice. Was he angry with me for hurting him? It was accidental, like his hurting me before was accidental. I never should have touched him, not like that. He never meant to hurt me before. I was sure of it. That smile—I'd give anything just to see that smile of his one more time.

"Your scent is different. Muted somehow. Underneath it, it's like you're healthy," he murmured, regarding me with some wariness. "Humans don't heal that quickly. Explain."

"I have this perfume. A mage gave it to me. He says it's supposed to make me smell less like food to vampires." I rushed the words out, wanting to please him. He needed to know I wouldn't use it to hurt him. Not now. At his thoughtful nod, I continued. "The hunters who came to save me gave me a transfusion to help me get better faster from when . . . from before."

I faltered, not wanting to talk about being bitten. The thought still frightened me, even with the haze of adoration I had for him.

"Come to me."

As soon as John and the other vampire released me, I flung myself into Max's open arms. He'd keep me safe. He'd make the others stay away and leave me alone. Tears of joy sprang to my eyes when he wrapped his arms around me. He wasn't so mad at me after all. One hand lightly brushed through my hair, the other cradling me to his chest as he whispered so soft and endearing into my ear.

"You're mine now."

Chapter 28

I'm not sure where we were once we reached the end of the tunnel. Truthfully, at the time, I didn't care. Leaving the building was something of a blur. I don't have any recollection of the interior except for the basement. I didn't take note of my surroundings until much later, when I sat in the back of a car with John at the wheel and Max's arm around my shoulder. I'd never felt so safe, so loved, or so *needed* before.

A part of me—a very small part of me—knew I had to do something about my friends. A bit more knew I'd have to visit some revenge on John for his betrayal. Soon, but not now. For the moment, I was safe and happy where I was. The idea of leaving Max's side was about as appealing as stepping barefoot on a slug.

I thought about what was happening and what I was feeling. My analytical capabilities were, to some extent, functioning again. It was only when I looked into Max's eyes that I became so enamored I couldn't think of anything but him. Concentrating on anything else was hard, but without his eyes on mine, I could focus on more than just how much I wanted to please him.

We were going to Royce's main home here in the city. I

hadn't known he had more than one until John mentioned it in passing. Max was planning on taking charge of each location, one by one, and assimilating or destroying all of Royce's existing servants. With Royce tied up at the police station, now was the perfect time to destroy the heart of his network of vampires here in New York City. Royce might be able to throw enough money and lawyer-speak at the cops for them to let him go later tonight, but by then it would be too late. Even if he found out about Max's plan, he'd never be able to pool the resources he'd need to fend off what would be waiting for him when he got home.

The only one of Royce's friends who knew about John's betrayal was me. Royce wouldn't be expecting to be met by a whole crapload of bad guys when he came home to hide or sleep for the day. Or whatever it was vamps did while daylight still shone. He'd be off his guard and out-numbered.

I was only half listening while Max and John discussed some details about divvying up Royce's empire between them. John's reward for his treachery was to take Royce's place as master over the New York territories and to assume ownership of his holdings. As payment for putting him in charge, he would funnel money and other resources to Max in his hometown of Chicago.

Hatred for John was building up from a slow simmer to a boiling froth. That backstabbing little shit had to die.

Max's fingers tightened on my shoulder. Maybe he felt my tension building. I forced myself to relax and conceived soul-warming thoughts about using the stakes riding at my hip to destroy that cowardly flunky's withered husk of a heart.

After a while, those images worked their way into words, soft though they were. *'Don't look into his eyes again. I can't help you if you're under his influence.'*

My breath caught in my throat as I realized all those thoughts of violence weren't my own. It was the belt unhooking some of Max's claws so I could fight back. I hadn't meant to draw attention to myself, but Max shifted at the subtle change in my breathing, looking down at me. I fought the urge to look up and meet his eyes, instead keeping my head bowed and leaning into his arm. By resting my cheek against his chest, I had a great excuse not to look up and destroy this tenuous thread to sanity the belt was helping me build upon.

Max's voice cut through the silence, making my breath catch. It took a great deal of effort to fight off the urge to tell him everything I'd been thinking and beg forgiveness.

"What is it, pet?"

I tried to think of something, anything, to tell him. I fumbled for a second before stuttering out something that might sound like a plausible lie.

"You're planning on killing Royce. I don't want him to die."

There. That was laced with enough truth that he might believe me. If Royce died, Max wouldn't have any use for me anymore and my butt would be toast.

I felt the rumble of laughter in his chest more than heard it. I suppressed a shudder.

"It's unavoidable. Don't worry about it."

Once more, I forced myself to let the tension drain out of my muscles as he brushed his fingers through my hair. As much as I didn't want it to be, his touch was soothing, comforting. If not for the gravity of the situation, I might very well have fallen asleep like that, curled in the protection of a psychotic elder vampire's arms. The only thing that kept me awake was my recollection of what he'd told me about his plans, not just for Royce but for me as well. He wanted Royce to suffer the same pain as he'd made Max endure so many years ago. My role was to play their surrogate Helen of Volos.

That meant Max planned on killing me.

Even knowing that, I was drawn to him, had the urge to be near and to touch him. Felt safe in his arms.

'Stop believing that bull and remember what he's done to you. What he'll do again when we get to Royce's hide-away. You want to die like that?'

My thoughts briefly skittered to the time when Max had thrown me to Peter—how it felt to have the life sucked out of me a few drops at a time while I lay pinned and helpless, unable to do a damned thing about it—and when Max had bitten me just so Royce could hear all the terror and panic lacing my screams.

It had hurt when Peter first bit down, but it didn't take long for it to start feeling like I might simply die from the pleasure of it. Never mind the blood loss. Never mind that he and Max both had taken it from me by force. The intensity of something racing through my body, following the path of every vein and artery to its end, leaving behind a vicious desire and blissful longing for more, had done plenty to reinforce my belief that vampires lived up to their reputation as the most dangerous of the Others.

If Max had kept going, I might not have minded dying in his arms after all.

Trembling, I closed my eyes tight and projected my thoughts as hard as I could at the belt.

No, I don't want to die like that. I don't want to die at all.

That familiar laughter grated in my skull, stronger this time. *'Good. You won't. You're a survivor, that's what I like about you.'*

Yeah, a survivor. That explained why I always got into these life-threatening messes.

Max's voice disrupted my internal dialogue, though he wasn't speaking to me this time. "How much longer?"

"Another fifteen minutes or so," John replied. "I arranged it so that the security team and most of the elders are out of the house. There's only a couple of them I couldn't get to leave without raising suspicion. Mouse is

the only one who might give you trouble. She won't be
happy to see you."

I felt that low rumble of laughter in Max's chest again.
My fingers tightened on his suit lapel, wrinkling the expensive material.

"That won't be a problem. I can handle her."

"Okay. The others should be much easier to deal with."

I tried concentrating on the belt, ignoring the two vampires' conversation as best I could. I questioned the most
obviously burning issue first. *Is there any way to get out of
this alive? Any bright ideas?*

'We'll have to roll with the punches,' it responded. *'Max
will use his hold on you to keep you in line. The only way
of avoiding that is if you do not look into his eyes and keep
any physical contact with him to a minimum. If you can
keep away from him, between me and the charm, you may
be able to escape.'*

That was comforting. I contented myself with letting the
belt feed me images of what I would do to John as soon as
I managed a minute alone with him.

A few minutes later, John interrupted my violent train
of thoughts.

"We're here."

When I looked up, straightening from resting against
Max, we were in a part of Midtown I wasn't familiar with.
I could see an entrance to Central Park down the street
from where we'd parked, but I didn't recognize the area.

Royce's property was a tidy, good-sized apartment
building that looked more like a home for families with 2.5
kids and a dog than a vampire den. There were shade trees
lining the street, and the building had an intricate black iron
fence lined with roses and creepers. The brick façade was
offset by white shutters and a large lobby extending from
the front of the building. Oh, and the huge gathering of
Max's minions loitering in front of it.

I never would've figured Royce as the type to live in

such a domestic place. The location was spectacular; it was the building itself which didn't fit my mental image of him. Maybe it was meant to be camouflage. I would've pegged him for a mansion on City Island, or maybe one of those Uptown high-rise penthouses with a view. Then again, considering his nature, too many windows could be dangerous.

We were the last to arrive. One of Max's underlings got the door for us. As we stepped out of the car, Max took my hand and led me to the front door. His other vampires and human flunkies were milling around on the sidewalk and in front of the house, some of them smoking, others leaning against nearby cars or trees. If there had only been a handful of them, they might have gone unnoticed, but with sixty or seventy people lounging around, it was impossible to call them inconspicuous.

As one, they straightened up, falling into step behind us as Max and John led the way. My muscles seized up at the proximity of so many bad guys. Max had to tug on my hand a bit to keep me moving. He looked back at me, but I quickly turned my head to the side, sweeping my gaze over the crowd so I wouldn't focus on him. The amusement in his voice grated on the few nerves I had left.

"Don't worry about them. You'll be fine. Stay behind me when we get inside."

I nodded, doing my best not to show my uncertainty and keeping an eye on the people surrounding me. Despite my better sense, I found his words reassuring. Peter was in that mess somewhere. Nicolas was right behind me, looking grumpy and hurt. The bandage forced him to squint one eye, making his face seem lopsided. I didn't have an ounce of sympathy for him.

John unlocked the front door. We stepped into an enormous foyer with hardwood floors and no windows. A small end table by the door held wire baskets, each one labeled with a name, some with envelopes or papers in them. I spotted John's name, then Royce's. The sheer number of what I now recognized as mail baskets made my skin crawl. That was an awful lot of vampires for one building.

Beyond the foyer was a hallway leading deeper into the building. There were a number of doors—apartments, I assumed—and a stairwell at the far end. It was all illuminated by lamplight, with no windows to let in the sun or fresh air. The musty odor of vampire was strong, but not as overwhelming as I'd expected. Someone had been baking cookies; the sweet scent nearly succeeded in drowning out the smell of vampire.

Max held up a staying hand as we filed inside, waiting just inside the hall. Before long, a short woman with curves like an hourglass and intense dark brown eyes stepped out of the apartment across from the stairwell.

When she bared her teeth in silent warning, I pegged her as a vampire. She didn't match my idea of what one should look like. With her long brown hair threaded with a few streaks of white and her diminutive stature, she looked more like a gracefully aging soccer mom than a bloodsucking creature of the night. She should've been leading a Girl Scout troop or something, not baring dainty little fangs and twisting those beatific features into something bestial. Hell, maybe the smell of cookies *was* her doing—the scent wafting from her apartment made me wonder.

Anyway, she didn't look surprised to see us. Just really, really pissed off.

"Ah, Mouse. It's been a long time since I've had the pleasure of your company," Max said, releasing my hand as he approached her. "You didn't think Alec would be able to protect you from me forever, did you?"

The woman glared at him with eyes shifting to the eerie red of agitation, but said nothing. The one-fingered salute she gave him made me like her more. She ducked back into the room in a swirl of skirts, and Max gave chase. I hesitated before trailing after John, Nicolas, and the handful of vampires following in his wake.

The living room of the apartment was large and open, with minimal furniture and massive bookshelves covering the far wall from floor to ceiling. My jaw dropped when I saw the wall decorations nearer the door weren't more bookshelves or framed pictures or anything of the sort. There were swords and daggers of all kinds bracketed to the walls, hanging from every last inch of available wall space.

By the time I arrived, Max had lost the suit jacket and snagged a longsword off the wall. He was facing off against the petite female vamp. She'd picked up a slender blade that looked something like a bigger, meaner version of Zorro's rapier, with a smaller, thicker blade in her other hand. There were so many weapons on the wall that I couldn't even see where the missing ones had come from.

There was some shouting and a couple of gunshots coming from the hall, but I couldn't go back to check it out with so many people blocking the way. I resigned myself to being a bystander in Max's fight, drawn into it despite myself.

The difference in their styles was immediately apparent. Both vampires were excellent sword fighters, but they were using weapons from different periods and geographic locations. Max was confident with his greater reach, sure in his blows, driving the woman back and working to disarm her. His tactics made it obvious that he didn't want her dead.

I watched in slack-jawed amazement as she countered him, strike for strike, getting past his guard a couple times to nick his arms. Her methods made it abundantly clear she wasn't content with disarming him. She would kill him if she could.

"You remember what it was like, don't you? We had such fun, you and I." Max's voice was smooth, taunting, and sounded way too much like Royce for my peace of mind. He was deliberately goading her. "We can play again. Just stop fighting, and it will all go so much easier for you."

She bared fangs at him, reddened eyes narrowing to dangerous slivers. It looked terribly wrong to see a monster peering out of that sweet face. Her blows rained faster as his mocking laughter urged her into a fit of rage. Even with the assistance of the belt, I could tell I would never, ever survive a swordfight with either one of these vampires. They were moving so fast, I couldn't follow it; all I saw was a blur of flashing steel. Somehow they were countering each other, blow for blow, sparks flaring up as their swords connected.

All of a sudden, Max dove forward. Furniture was shoved unceremoniously out of the way as they collided and tumbled across the room, still moving at hyperspeed. They ended up by the kitchen with Max's sword buried deep in the woman's stomach, ruining her khaki-colored riding blouse as he pinned her to the ground.

The sword she'd been using skittered harmlessly across the floor when he kicked it out of her hand. At the same time, she drove the dagger upward until it was buried in his thigh. Max howled in rage and pain, staggering back.

Only then did I notice that, though her mouth opened and closed, no sound escaped except the wheezing of air in and out of her lungs. Mouse was a mute vampire? Interesting. Her name suddenly made sense. Quiet as a mouse.

I felt like I should do something, not just stand around watching on the sidelines. John must have figured out I was considering doing something stupid. He put a restraining hand on my shoulder, tugging me closer to the door. He flinched at my hateful glare, but didn't let go. A low sound quickly drew my attention back to Max and Mouse.

There was blood running down Mouse's face as Max held his wrist up to her mouth, the other hand forcing her jaw open. There were pink-stained tears streaking from her eyes, staining her pale cheeks, and I didn't think it was from the pain of being impaled by the sword. She was trying hard to pull his bleeding wrist away from her mouth, but not succeeding. She didn't need to breathe like a human, wouldn't choke from what he was doing, but some habits die hard. Once she swallowed reflexively, a grim, satisfied smile curved Max's lips.

"There, that wasn't so bad, was it?" he mocked, taking a low, singsong tone as he stood up. He yanked the sword out of her in the same, fluid motion.

Once free, Mouse twisted on her side, one hand pressed to the wound on her stomach while the other kept her balanced as she spat out his blood. Her expression was pained, as if she'd swallowed something foul. Maybe she had.

Everyone in the door, including me, skittered out of Max's way when he approached. He didn't pay any mind as he brushed past us, heading for the next room down the hall. Everyone else followed him to either play audience or play backup.

If she was the oldest vampire here—the only one, per John, who could potentially give Max trouble—I doubted he needed his minions for anything other than moral support. I stood awkwardly in the door, watching Mouse gather herself. She was taking deep, shuddering breaths as the wound on her stomach visibly closed, torn flesh knitting together seamlessly. The only remaining signs of her injury were the bloodstains and holes torn in her clothes. Judging by her expression, though, something was still hurting.

I was scared of vampires, but it didn't feel right to watch her suffer. I knelt down, holding out my hand.

"Do you need help to get up?"

She opened dark brown eyes, surprised and wary. Though she hesitated, she soon slid her tiny hand into mine and I helped her to her feet. The strength in her grip was enormous. Despite the care she took to be gentle, my fingers felt slightly numb once she let go.

She staggered once she was on her feet, chest heaving with unnecessary breaths. God, she was tiny. The top of her head barely came up to my shoulder. It must have hurt, but she straightened her back and squared her shoulders. She used a bloodstained hand to push her hair out of her face, tension gradually easing out of her as she looked me over.

"Your name is Mouse?" I asked. At her nod, I held out my hand in introduction. "I'm Shiarra. I'm sorry I couldn't help you before. Will you be okay?"

She smiled and took my hand, shaking it. Then she proceeded to go into a rapid bout of sign language, her hands fluttering like graceful birds.

"Sorry, I don't understand."

Judging by her expression, she wasn't surprised, just disappointed. Looking around, she found a pad and pen on one of the tables that hadn't been knocked aside. She proceeded to scratch out a quick note, which she tore off and handed to me. Her penmanship was an impeccably neat script. What was it with vampires and neat handwriting?

Don't feel bad. It doesn't take me long to heal. I think Alec is probably the only one who could stop him effectively. Are you one of Max's servants?

I shook my head—then stopped with a frown, spreading my hands in a helpless, frustrated gesture. "He bound me to him. I don't want to serve him, but I don't have a choice."

She gave me a sympathetic look and went back to her feverishly fast writing.

Chapter 29

I was not pleased when Peter turned up; apparently Max had sent him to fetch me. He stood in the doorway staring suspiciously at Mouse, radiating nervous fear.

She looked back at him with a cool, dispassionate gaze, not giving away anything. Somehow she managed to stay regal and composed despite her skirt and simple blouse, torn and stained crimson with blood. I crumpled the notes she'd handed me and stepped back so I was at her side, putting the paper in my jacket pockets as inconspicuously as possible.

"Max wants you both. Come on," he demanded, gesturing for us to follow him.

Mouse and I exchanged a look before falling into step behind Peter. Out in the hallway and on the stairs, more of Royce's people were being herded along. One or two were thrown over the shoulders of Max's cronies, others stumbling along like they were drugged or hurt. A couple of vampires being shoved forward by the intruders had blood staining their lips and the same shocked, glassy stare as Mouse. People clutched fresh bite marks on their throats or arms, cringing away from the leers of those who'd fed on them. Many of the humans were crying.

One guy slipped out of the grip of the vamp holding his arm and made a dash for the front door. I winced in sympathy as the escapee was casually backhanded by Peter. The man collapsed to the ground, not moving. One of the vamps hefted him up on his shoulder and carried him along with the others.

We joined the procession leading up to the third floor. The door at the top of the stairs was open. Max and most of the others were hanging around what must have been Royce's living space.

The entire upper floor was almost entirely taken up by one huge, open room. Terraced windows with shutters inside as well as out lined the walls, though the inside shutters looked more secure at keeping out sunlight. Tiny spotlights focused on pieces of large marble and bronze statuary set on pedestals between each of the windows. It was practically bare of furniture, only a couple of chaise-like lounge chairs and padded benches scattered here and there. Thick carpets and plush pillows in a few strategic places were somehow made more intimate by the rest of the place being so open and exposed.

At the far end were two doors. One was off to the side; I spotted some computers and a phone with the message light blinking. The other door was closed, and I guessed it was the entrance to Royce's bedroom.

Max looked paler than usual when I spotted him lounging on a chaise. The other vampires in the room were positively rosy-cheeked in comparison. His chin and white shirt were spotted with blood. I figured very little of it was his.

Royce's people were being shoved to the back of the room, save for a handful. There was a human woman I didn't know huddled shivering on the floor not very far from Max. She had her fingers pressed to her throat and her features obscured by the blond hair that fell about her shoulders. Had they taken her from the club?

One of the other vampires disabused me of that idea, hauling her up to her feet and pulling her out of the way. She was in nothing but panties and an oversized silk shirt that could pass for a nightie. For some reason, that pissed me off more than anything. For her to be here, dressed like that—not that it should matter to me. Royce's love life was none of my business. Honestly.

Without meaning to, I met Max's eyes when he held out his hand. I followed the unspoken command without hesitation, basking in the warmth of his gaze. He pulled me down to the cushions with him, bringing my wrist up close to his mouth and inhaling deeply. His gaze stayed focused on mine, making it hard to concentrate on anything other than the feel of his fingers on my skin and the depths of those gray pools, sucking me in. I reached out to touch his cheek as that velvet smooth voice rolled over my senses, reveling in it.

He drew me closer, pulling me into his lap. I didn't resist, though my heart rate revved up as the memory of having been bitten teased along the edge of my consciousness, helped along by being much closer than was healthy to a hungry vampire. Even caught in his eyes, I couldn't banish the remembered terror of it.

"You're afraid," he said, puzzled and curious. "Why?"

"I don't know." I wasn't sure why I lied about not knowing. It made me even more nervous when he bought my answer.

"Why did you help Mouse?"

That question threw me through a loop or two for a second. I knew I had a deer-in-the-headlights stare, but the muted anger underlying the question frightened me more than the not-so-subtle threat of being bitten again.

"She—I don't like—" I started to twist around to look at her, but his hand came up to turn my face back so I was forced to look at him again. Those sly, gray eyes demanded answers. I couldn't hem and haw around it anymore. "She was hurt. I had to help her."

He stared at me for a moment longer, the anger fading into something bordering on melancholy. "Your tender-heartedness is endearing. She could've killed you. Easily."

Mouse made a low hissing sound, distracting me. He didn't keep me from looking this time. She was pissed, her hands curled into claws as she took up pacing a few yards away. The rest of Royce's people, even the vampires, had drawn back from her. A couple of Max's vampires sidled closer, showing their fangs in warning. I was afraid of what might happen if she started a brawl. She was one scary fighter.

Max stared her down until she subsided, fists clenching and unclenching at her sides after she looked away. He then picked me up and deposited me on the couch beside him. I struggled to sit up straight as he rose and approached Mouse.

He stalked around her, predatory, circling her like a shark. I watched with wide eyes as she stood frozen in place with her lip lifted in a silent snarl. Only her eyes followed his movements. As he came up behind her, he settled his hands on her shoulders. He stared at me as he pulled her back against his chest, stooping down to rest his chin on top of her head. What I didn't get is why she didn't fight back.

"Mouse is bound to me now, maybe not in the same way you are, but well enough. Isn't that right, lovely?"

Her only answer was the flicker of hot red embers in her eyes.

"That injury must've taken quite a bit of blood to heal." I could see his fingers tightening on her shoulders, digging in deep. She didn't move, her expression curiously blank save for those hellishly burning eyes. "Are you hungry, my little Mouse?"

A fine trembling threaded through her. It might have

been my imagination, but Max's smile made me think—fear—it wasn't.

"She's just your type, isn't she? The pale skin, the red hair. You always had a taste for the Irish."

Oh, fuck me sideways.

She closed her eyes, and he yanked on her hair until she made a faint hiss of sound, air forcefully expelled between her teeth. Her hands came up to clutch at his arms as he pulled her off balance, holding her so her spine bowed and she was forced up on tiptoe. His eyes stayed on me while he spoke, ringing out for everyone to hear.

"That's just too bad. If you lay a hand on her without my say-so beforehand, I will gut you and leave you for the sun and the crows. Do you understand me?"

There was no way for her to answer him. The others in the room nodded quickly, too quickly, looking away as he threw Mouse down to the floor at his feet. He kicked her aside when she got up on hands and knees, sending her sliding across the floor. She slammed into one of those heavy pedestals, knocking down a marble statue of a woman in flowing robes, which broke in half when it crashed to the floor. I found myself pressed back into the cushions of the chaise as Max approached, remembering at the last second to focus on his lips instead of his eyes.

"There, now. Nothing to worry about, you see?"

I wasn't sure if he expected an answer, but I found myself nodding like the others had—anything to keep him from touching me in anger. Even with the augmented strength and stamina of the belt, I doubted I'd survive if he turned the full force of that anger on me. At my silent nod, he continued across the room, and for a brief moment I had the clarity to think, *This is it—I'm going to die.*

He reached out for the blond girl held by one of his flunkies and yanked her to his side. She made a faint, terrified sound as he hauled her up against his chest and jerked her head back by the hair.

For a second—just a second—I was glad it wasn't me.

I quickly found myself ashamed for being grateful he was visiting his punishments on someone else. Yet I didn't have it in me to do anything to help her. She whimpered, but didn't fight, didn't do anything but cry as he savagely tore into her throat.

No one moved while he killed the woman, sucking the life out of her.

After what felt like an eternity of agonized indecision and guilt, any chance to help her was lost. Max pulled away from his meal and simply dropped her. She landed with a graceless thump, eyes closed and skin waxen against that royal blue shirt. Max now had a rosy blush of health to his cheeks. I couldn't keep myself from staring blankly at the vicious wound he'd torn to get to her jugular, just like the marks on the dead girl from the dance floor at Twisted Temptations. Her heart had stopped, only a few meager trickles of blood working their way to drip, drip, drip to the floor.

Max was all business, snapping his fingers, then pointing to a couple of his men. "Clean that up."

The guys he'd pointed to jumped to the work, gathering the limp body and carrying her out of sight down the stairs. I felt sick as I stared at the tiny crimson puddle on the floor, the only sign that someone had just died in this room.

I should have done something. I should have moved, should have fought, should have pulled him off her, but I was paralyzed by something more than fear. The savagery in his actions was breathtaking, a brand of casual violence like nothing I'd ever seen. There were other humans in the room—not just me, but a bunch of his lackeys. He could have fed on one of us. She didn't have to die, not like that.

His methods were clearer to me, if no more understandable. Dealing with him was not the same thing as fighting with Royce or Rohrik Donovan. It wasn't even like fighting David Borowsky or Anastasia Alderov. This was monstrous, unnecessary brutality. This was waste, killing for the sake of killing, rather than by necessity. Killing to make a point.

When I dragged my gaze up from the floor to look at him, he smiled down at me. Soft. Polite. Even with the woman's lifeblood on his lips, staining his fangs, that smile was endearing and subtly appealing. A deep-seated fear the binding couldn't suppress washed through me as I met those empty, glittering eyes.

This was what a real monster looked like—a thing, a body with intelligence, but no conscience to guide it.

Chapter 30

Max took most of his people with him as he swept out of the room, heading downstairs. He left a couple of his men to watch over me, Mouse, and what was left of Royce's entourage. There were enough of us to overwhelm the guards if we rushed them, but, aside from me, Max's people were the only ones in the room with guns. Nobody had frisked me, so I wasn't sure if anyone knew I had weapons yet. Though I'd probably have the element of surprise, most of Royce's people were in shock or too hurt to fight. I wasn't feeling brave enough to take on two armed guards by myself.

Royce's people didn't seem to be holding up too well. There were only two other women in the room, both human, each one huddling and weeping in the protective arms of a lover or friend among the vampires left behind. There were bite marks and bruises on a lot of the humans cringing behind the vamps.

I have to admit, I stared when I saw a couple of the men fall into each other's arms. It's not that I'm homophobic so much as it wasn't the sort of thing you see every day. The poor guy who'd made a run for it downstairs was being cradled by a sobbing, dark-skinned man who had better taste in clothes than most women. Another was crouched beside them, rubbing the guy's back and whispering sympathies, his pale skin and ashy hair a stark contrast against the bloodstains around his mouth. By the angle of his neck and the limpness to the limbs, it looked like Peter had killed the crying man's donor.

Mouse was pacing, back and forth, back and forth, like a caged tiger considering means of escape. The look in her eyes was positively predatory. I was very glad that she was on my side. Even though Max had kicked her ass, I had the feeling he was the only vampire around with the age, strength, and speed to have done so. I'd bet good money John would've been creamed if he'd tried besting her in a physical fight.

I got up, too, feeling way too jittery to sit still, especially with the way Mouse was stalking around. When her gaze shot to me, drawn by my sudden movements, I ignored the spark of hunger in her eyes. The two guards on the door, vamps I didn't know, watched with deceptive boredom. I was sure they'd be on us quick enough if we tried anything funny.

Mouse stopped moving, staring at me. It was creepy as anything, what with the ruby gleam flashing from dilated pupils. What was her problem?

Before I could blink, she was on me. One of her hands was at my waist, bruisingly tight as she yanked me close, the other pulling my wrist to her mouth, fingers working at the edge of my armored clothing. Her fangs raked over my skin. As I inhaled to scream, Max's men started shouting and pulling at her, tearing her off me.

She twisted away from them without a sound, staying down when one of them shoved her to the floor. He held a gun on her, the other one taking my arm and pulling me close. I lifted my shaking hand to see what she'd done, shivering in reaction as the guy holding me grabbed my wrist to examine the tiny scratches her fangs had left on my skin. Holy Mother of God, she was *fast*.

"Max isn't going to like that," he observed, a brief glimmer of hunger making his eyes turn red. "Bad move."

"Shit, did she bite her?"

"No. Just a nick."

The guy holding the gun grimaced, gesturing to the room in the back. "Just have her wash it up, Bill. I don't want the boss thinking we fucked up again."

"Is there a bathroom?" Bill demanded of Mouse. When she nodded, gesturing weakly to the back of the room, he shoved me toward the closed door. "Move it. Go rinse the blood off, and hurry the fuck up. Don't keep us waiting."

After stumbling to catch my balance, I skittered around Mouse, who was staring up at me with an expression I couldn't read. Her guard waved his gun at me, and I moved faster, ducking into Royce's bedroom.

He slept on, of all things, a futon. A big futon, true, but a futon nonetheless. The sheets were rumpled, and it made me wonder if he'd left it that way when he got up, or if it was from the vampires dragging that girl in the blue shirt out of it. Before they dragged her out, what would she have been doing there? Waiting for Royce to come home and slide into bed with him maybe? I hadn't given much thought about whether all of a male vampire's "equipment" worked after they were turned, but—

No. That was quite enough of that train of thought.

Any other time, I might have been more interested in examining this most private part of his home to see if I could get more insight into the man. Instead, I hurried into the ridiculously large bathroom. The floor was slick marble and there was a shower and tub that looked big enough to host a party.

I pulled my jacket aside to examine where Mouse had clutched at me, grimacing at the feel of a forming bruise at my waist. To my surprise, she'd tucked a cell phone into the belt. In all the confusion, I hadn't noticed.

Why would a mute vampire have a cell phone? Whatever the reason, I wasn't going to question this fortunate turn of events. Mouse was unbelievably sly to have thought of pulling that stunt right in front of Max's men. I wouldn't waste the opportunity she'd given me.

First, I turned the water on to cover my actions. Next, I opened the phone and put it on silent mode. Scrolling through a long list of contacts, I found Royce's name and tapped out a quick message.

THIS IS SHIA. I'M AT YOUR HOUSE BY CENTRAL PARK. JOHN BETRAYED US— MAX HAS THE HOUSE AND YOUR PEOPLE. PLANS TO KILL US BOTH. BE CAREFUL.

Hopefully, this would give him enough time to round up the cavalry. It didn't take long before a reply message popped up.

ALMOST DONE WITH THE POLICE. THEY KNOW IT WAS MAX AND HIS PEOPLE. I'LL BE THERE AS SOON AS I CAN.

I never thought I'd say this, but thank God Royce was coming to the rescue.

Tears of relief stung my eyes. I couldn't let them fall, though. To keep the guards from catching on, I shoved the phone in my pocket and buttoned up the jacket so they couldn't see any telltale lumps. Next, I rinsed my hands and face. In addition to the shallow scratches on my wrist, there was blood on my fingers from touching the dance floor earlier to wash off. Gross.

When I walked back out, I headed quietly to the

chaise, settling down on the cushion. Mouse was back to pacing, the guards had resumed their bored expressions and posts at the door, and most of Royce's people had retreated to the far corners of the room. One of them stumbled closer to sit by me, his expression dull and shocked. There was some dried blood at the corner of his mouth. Max must have bound him, too.

"Are you okay?" I asked, unnerved he'd come so close but didn't bother to say anything. He turned to look at me, his eyes a pale seawater green, peering out from behind a few stray tendrils of shoulder-length brown hair. He was barefoot in jeans and an unbuttoned white shirt, leaving a good portion of his chest and stomach bare to view. He was lean, his skin littered with scars, and I tried not to stare.

"Yeah. Yeah, I'll be okay. Are you with that . . . that guy?" His voice didn't match his appearance. It was deep, rumbling, like Tiny's or Chaz's. It seemed out of place on that slender, wiry frame.

"I'm unwillingly along for the ride." I turned away to watch Mouse pace instead of staring into those dull, injured eyes.

"Did he kill Alec?"

I started at that, not badly, but enough to make him really *look* at me instead of stare through me. "No. He wants to, but no, he hasn't killed him."

Hope lit his features, at odds with the blaze of red in his irises and flicker of fangs visible when he whispered, "He'll save us. He'll kill them all."

I suppressed a shudder and nodded, looking away again.

After a little while, some of the other vamps and their toys came to join us, gingerly settling down on the cushions like a flock of nervous birds ready to take flight at any moment. Most of them kept their distance from me. It was weird to see the vampires protectively holding people against them. It was even weirder to see the people clinging to them in return.

The only one who never sat down was Mouse. All she did was pace, endlessly following a circuit, back and forth, back and forth. The most unnerving thing about it was that she was utterly silent. Those leather boots she was wearing didn't make a single sound against the polished hardwood.

After a while, I shut my eyes so I wouldn't have to watch Mouse or see all the helpless tears or the agonized expressions of the vampires.

I must have drifted off. It startled the hell out of me when I felt a hand close on my upper arm and drag me roughly to my feet. I started reaching for one of the stakes or a gun, but my jacket was buttoned closed, hiding and blocking easy access to my weaponry. Peter shook me a little until I straightened up. That had me more pissed off than afraid. Like John, I would make sure he paid in spades for all he had done.

Peter didn't pay me any mind, dragging me behind him toward the door. Mouse rushed forward, but when the guards trained their guns on her, she halted. He shot her a warning glare and a few terse words.

"Max told you to stay put."

She looked like she would've screamed if she could have. Her hands moved in abrupt, angry gestures. Though I didn't understand sign language, it wasn't hard to figure out that she was venting her frustration. I tried to give her as encouraging a look as I could, to let her know as covertly as possible that I'd found the phone and contacted Royce. I'm not sure if she got it, as she kept gesticulating at us.

The guy with the seawater green eyes rose up to put his arm around her. He whispered something to her until she relaxed, sagging against him.

I had more pressing concerns. Namely, Peter dragging me out of the room. I contemplated using my new strength to break his fangs and pound his face into pulp, but until Royce got here, I shouldn't tip my hand too soon. Whatever it was that kept me from thinking bad thoughts about Max didn't do a damned thing to make me feel less vindictive toward Peter or John.

"You know, if you asked nicely, I might just follow you," I snarled at him.

He grunted in response, not bothering to look at me. I almost tripped on the stairs, finding it awkward to follow him this way. He ignored my blunt curses all the way down to a fastidiously clean cellar where Max, John, and a couple of other vampires were waiting.

Peter yanked me around and shoved me forward. I braced myself, catching my balance, and whirled with a snarl to punch him.

The hit never connected. Max caught my arm midswing, and it stopped me so abruptly I nearly ended up on my knees. It was like having a band of iron wrapped around my wrist. Peter looked as surprised as I felt.

"That's enough," Max said, the harsh command in the words unmistakable.

I gathered my balance with as much dignity as I could muster, slowly straightening my back and loosening my muscles, letting my fingers uncurl out of the fist. Max didn't release my wrist until the tension left me. I rubbed the place where he'd grabbed as surreptitiously as possible. No doubt there would be a bruise there come morning.

Putting a hand on my shoulder, Max guided me to the others, continuing the thread of whatever conversation we'd interrupted.

"In your estimation, would it be better to leave her here as bait or bring her in as a distraction later?" Ah, I just love it when people talk about me like I'm not even there.

John shrugged, eyeing me thoughtfully. "Probably better to use her as a distraction than as bait. If you rough her up, it might make him angry. If he gets angry, he'll make mistakes."

I pointedly mouthed *you are so dead* at him, knowing Max would miss the murderous look. John's eyes widened and I felt Max tense, sensing I'd done something I shouldn't have. Maybe I should've been more lovey-dovey distracted by Max, but, for some reason, watching him murder an innocent girl right in front of me took the sparkle out of the relationship. His touch felt as warm and inviting as before, but I no longer felt the desperate urge to lean into it or please him. Maybe I was getting used to the bond.

Yeah, and next maybe winged monkeys would fly out of my butt.

John backed up a pace, putting some distance between us. "She's a tough-willed little bitch. Maybe you should lock her up, away from the others. Mouse or somebody else up there might be trying to help her somehow."

Max's fingers tightened on my shoulder. I leaned into his touch. Not so much because I wanted to, but because I thought it might help the illusion that I was deeply under his power. All I needed to do was keep in mind that looking into his eyes was a bad, bad idea, and I should be fine. The belt dimly concurred with me.

"You may be right. Have you fed tonight, John?"

What was with the sudden shift in topic? John shook his head, looking just as confused by the question as I felt.

"Let's test the theory then." Uh-oh. That didn't sound good. "Shiarra, pull up one of your sleeves and let John get a taste of you."

For the love of all that's holy, would nothing go my way tonight? I could either do as he commanded and keep up the ruse, or I could refuse him and end up forced into it anyway. I couldn't think of the right words to say to deflect the command while still making him think I was thoroughly, hopelessly under his influence.

My phobia of being bitten made me hesitate too long. Max laughed, though whether it was my indecision or the others' astonishment he found funny wasn't quite clear. His hands slid down to hold my upper arms, pinning them tightly at my side.

"Well, that answers that question. You're just full of surprises, aren't you?"

"Damn, you got me." I fell back on sarcasm, as I am wont to do when stressed, pissed, tired, and generally in fear of my life. Call it my form of denial. "Does this mean I don't get the award for best actress?"

His grip tightened, squeezing until I voiced an involuntary gasp. "No, you won't be getting any awards. Peter . . ." His attention shifted, though he didn't come anywhere close to loosening his grip. "Peter, hold on to her for me, will you?"

I was abruptly stumbling forward, shoved into Peter's arms. I didn't bother fighting since I knew Max had the speed and strength to catch me even if I got away from Peter. Instead, I went limp, figuring if I played it up like I was defeated for the time being, it might make them more careless of me later.

"How long ago did Alec leave the police station?"

I stiffened. That news concerned me intimately. John answered, glancing down at the watch on his wrist.

"I got a call twenty minutes ago. He should arrive within the next half hour or so."

"Excellent. Everyone is in place?"

"Yes. I'll lead him down here when he arrives."

Max nodded, a grim smile on his lips. I didn't like that look at all. Especially when he moved to the table and ran his fingers along the same sword he'd used against Mouse, still coated with her blood. I hadn't noticed it until then, mostly because I was more interested in glaring daggers at John and Peter than paying attention to the details about the room.

I made it a point to examine the place now. The basement ran the length of the house and was nothing but wide open space, with a little furniture and some boxes scattered here and there. The floor was plain cement, giving it a cold, damp feel. There were a couple of paint cans and a tool box on a low shelf, some gardening tools off in a corner, and a washer and dryer tucked away in a niche under the stairs. The walls were a featureless, whitewashed expanse, save for the doors set at each point of the compass in the four walls. I imagined they must lead to the tunnel systems Royce used to make his way around the city to his businesses.

All in all, it looked like a good, empty space for the elders to duke it out. I wondered where the rest of Max's men were hiding, because I had no doubt he was willing to play dirty and would use them to overrun the place as soon as he had Royce trapped down here.

I prayed it wouldn't be much longer. I wasn't sure my nerves would survive the next half hour alone with these people.

Chapter 31

An hour and fifteen minutes later, Royce still hadn't showed up. Max was glaring daggers at John. Made me wonder if any revenge I later visited on Royce's turncoat flunky would be moot.

To keep from worrying about Max turning his attentions on me, I stayed still and quiet, pretending like I was on a really weird surveillance job. Stay still, stay quiet, don't let the mark know you're watching and listening. Entertaining thoughts of pounding whatever was left of John into the dust helped pass the time.

"Why would he not be answering his phone?"

John shrugged uncomfortably, not meeting Max's eyes. "He could be caught in traffic. Or in a no-service zone."

Max growled something under his breath. I had the sinking feeling he thought he'd been had. There was no telling what he would do to any of us (meaning me) if he thought someone had tipped him off to his rival.

"John? Where is everyone?" Royce called from somewhere upstairs.

I didn't realize how tense I'd been until I heard his voice. As much as I wanted to relax and let relief wash over me,

I couldn't give him away. His puzzlement sounded natural, a better act than I'd ever been able to put on.

One of Peter's hands slapped over my mouth before I could call out a warning, his arm tightening around my waist as he pulled me back to the far side of the room. He hadn't pinned my arms, so I might be able to go for a weapon once the fight started. I doubted he thought of me as much of a threat. Understandable, considering the only other times he'd seen me, I hadn't had the hunter's belt on. I had put up a pretty pathetic fight in those handcuffs.

The other vamps, save for John and Max, came with us, moving with that eerie silence I attributed to nothing other than the undead.

"Downstairs, Alec!" John called, the vampires beside us leaning forward, readying their weapons.

Max picked up the sword and silently drifted behind the stairs to lie in wait. I squirmed in Peter's grip, not too hard yet, just enough to be believable. When the time came, I planned on reaching for one of my guns. If I could, I would pull Peter's hand off my mouth in time to warn Royce. That is, if he needed it. After the text message I sent him, he was no doubt wary of an ambush.

Royce didn't come all the way down the stairs, leaning over the rail to peer at John. If he looked the other way, he would spot me and the other vamps. Peter's grip tightened painfully, a warning to be still.

Royce would have to come all the way down to see Max. By then it would be too late. I struggled in earnest and felt Peter hiss an almost silent breath of warning in my ear.

"Where is everybody? What are you doing down here?"

John gestured at one of the boxes behind him so nonchalantly, I might have believed his act had I not been here to see all his plotting earlier. "I was looking for the Talisman of Artemis. Since you're on the hunt, I thought it might be of use. Could you come down here and help me find it?"

I couldn't see his face, but the amusement in Royce's voice

was clearly evident. "You know I returned the Talisman to Athena. You always were a bad liar, John."

That's when all hell broke loose.

I didn't see him move from the stairs, but suddenly Royce was there, tearing Peter off me and hurling him bodily into Max. It scared the hell out of me when I saw that Max was only a few feet away when Peter slammed into him. He thrust aside the heavily built vampire like a piece of stray newspaper blown his way by an errant wind. Royce met Max mid-stride. He deflected Max's sword and went for his throat with a hand curled into claws. All of this happened while I was still catching my balance from being torn out of Peter's grasp.

There were more people rushing down the stairs and moving to grapple with or shoot at the other vampires in the room. I had time to see a fur-sprouting Chaz bounding in my direction, Tiny and Devon, too, while a few of the vampires who had been with us at the club headed for John. All four doors in the room slammed open, more of Royce's vampires pouring in with fangs bared and eyes aglow.

Not a bad way to stage a coup. If I hadn't been so preoccupied, I would have applauded Royce's tactics.

The rest of Max's men must have heard the commotion. The room was soon packed with vamps from both sides, screaming, biting, and clawing at each other. Every now and then I could hear gunshots or the explosions of spells, drowning out the other sounds of battle in brief spurts.

The creepiest opponent of all was Dawn. I watched with some astonishment as she flowed gracefully through the viciously clashing bodies around her toward Max's people on the stairs, her eyes glowing with an eerie greenish radiance. I watched how some of the vampires simply stopped in their tracks when they spotted her, struck deaf, dumb, and blind as she became their universe. With a touch she made them into her guards. I watched in amazement as they turned on those who had a moment ago been their allies, tearing with fangs and claws into any of Max's vampires who attempted to hurt her.

Well, seeing as everyone else was having so much fun, I decided I might as well join the fray. I unbuttoned my jacket, drawing a stake and gun in one fluid motion. The belt was positively cackling with glee. The warmth of rage swelled up inside me, aching for release.

I gladly let it take me.

My world narrowed down to one target. John was engaged, but Peter's unmistakable, bulky form was working on escape up the stairs, bodily throwing other vampires out of his way. I noted a huge, furred body tearing apart one of the vampires who had been standing near me, knew it was Chaz, and was further warmed by the chorus of triumphant howls echoing deafeningly across the basement. The pack was here, and it was pissed. Max and Royce were still fighting, looking like nothing so much as solid blurs of force. Max had the advantage of a sword while Royce had none.

I was not concerned. My eyes were all for Peter.

A few vampires got between me and my prize but I barely noticed them, throwing any obstacles out of my way. Later, I came to realize I wasn't being too particular whose side they were on either. All that mattered was that there were obstacles in my way and I needed them gone.

I followed Peter up the stairs, giving chase, tightening my fingers around the stake as I closed the distance between us. He was fast, but I was lighter on my feet.

When we reached the landing of the second floor, he unexpectedly turned and stiff-armed me. My own momentum sent me crashing down on my back, breath knocked painfully out of my chest. I held on to the gun, but the stake was so slick with blood, despite the leather grip, it slid out of my fingers.

He caught my arms and straddled my waist, pinning my

wrists to the floor. His fingers dug in until I dropped the gun, too.

Grinning down at me, he bared his fangs in triumph. "You are one tough little bitch. Not tough enough for me, though. Didn't you learn that last time?"

"Fuck you," I spat up at him, trying to twist free of his grasp. He laughed at my efforts.

"This seems familiar somehow. What do you think, would Max have a problem with me having another taste?"

I faltered, an involuntary shudder threading through me. Even knowing I was stronger now, armored against that brand of attack, it didn't prevent a sudden, phobic reaction. We might as well have been back in that strange house in the woods. When he leaned in, I panicked, a hoarse scream passing my lips. I twisted and struggled, screeching denial as I fought his grip.

This couldn't happen to me, not again!

I could *hear* the tips of his fangs raking against the slick material of the turtleneck, preventing him from piercing anything vital, but I felt like my heart might just explode from straining against the steel bands of terror wrapped so tightly around it.

He laughed, low and pleased with my reaction, trailing his way up to my lips. He swallowed any further screams, covering my mouth with his own. His fingers tightened on my wrists as he slanted his mouth over mine. Then his fangs pierced my lower lip, drawing a few drops of blood.

I bucked against his hold. I wasn't handcuffed or hindered by frail human muscle this time. Now I had what it took, including the power and the engrained knowledge of how to leverage my body to flip him off me and reverse our positions. In the process, one of his fangs caught on my lip, not just pulling but tearing it.

The metallic taste of blood filled my mouth, more of it running down my chin. This wasn't the electrifying

experience of Friday night. This was just painful, plain
and simple. It fucking *hurt*.

"Thon of a bith!" I cried, digging my nails into his
wrists hard enough to startle a yowl of pain out of him.
"You ath-hole!"

It didn't take long for him to recover from the bite of my
nails. He had the sheer gall to laugh at me, amused by the
lisp caused by my split lip.

With a howl of fury, I surged back to sock him across
the jaw with everything I had. As soon as I let go of his
arm, his fingers shot up to encircle my throat, squeezing chokingly tight. His grip faltered when I hit him, his
head rocking back so hard the wooden floor cracked and
splintered.

That blind rage was back, consuming me. How *dare* he
frighten me? How *dare* he touch me?

How *dare* he fight back?

I don't know how many times I hit him. At one point, I
let go of his other arm to pound with both fists, alternating
as smoothly as a metronome. If he'd been human, one blow
would have shattered his skull. As it was, I'd bruised and
bloodied his face, split his lips on his own fangs, and
broken his nose.

My knuckles were red and raw when I stopped, my
chest heaving. Only then did I realize his fingers had fallen
from my throat. There was something innately satisfying
about having him lying there so limply, maybe not even
what passed among vampires as alive anymore. I took a
few seconds to admire my handiwork, pleased rather than
disgusted with the mess I'd made of him. Some part of me
was rejoicing at the blood, the violence, but not satisfied
with the damage. It wanted more.

It drowned out the little part of me that wanted to have
hysterics and run screaming from the room.

As I gathered my legs under me to rise, one of Peter's ham-
fisted hands reached up and tangled in my hair. He yanked

me back down as he screamed in wordless rage and pain right into my face, brown eyes gone feral with bloodlust.

My next move wasn't particularly thought out. I snagged another stake from my belt and drove it deep into his chest. He continued screaming, his fingers tightening even more on my hair. I must have missed the heart.

Peter's rage called to my own, leaving me warring between terror, fury, and exultation. I pulled the stake out and struck him with it again, then a third time. On the fourth and last time, I shoved it into his chest, up between the ribs, gritting my teeth as tears rolled down my cheeks. He clawed at my back, gasping for air as I straddled him, pushing the metal spike as deep as it would go.

"Die, you thon of a bith! Juth die already!"

With a last, fading cry, he obliged me.

Chapter 32

I remained draped on top of the body long after Peter stopped struggling beneath me, the hellish light having faded from his eyes one final time. It felt like an eternity, but was probably only a few minutes of me leaning as hard as I could into the stake, fighting against the resistance of the wooden floor beneath him.

The sounds of battle penetrated my stupor. There was more I had to do up here. I slowly staggered up to my feet. Not because I was hurt or tired, but because I was shocked at what I had just done.

If someone had tried to tell me before tonight I was capable of this level of violence, I never would have believed it. When I saw the gaping holes left in Peter's chest, the handle of the stake protruding between his ribs and the pulpy mess I'd made of his face, I realized that I—not Royce, not Chaz, but me, Shiarra Waynest, human being and private investigator—had viciously murdered an (un)living being just a few moments ago. I had to force myself to twist away so I'd throw up on the floor instead of the body.

I came shakily back to myself a few minutes later, rubbing the back of my hand along my mouth. The taste of bile was strong in my throat as I cautiously avoided looking at the corpse and the spreading pool of blood on the floor. I hurried back to the stairs, stopping along the way to pick up the gun I'd dropped. At this juncture, I wasn't interested in retrieving the stake. It would take a hell of a lot more than a desire to keep a matching set of stakes on my belt to make me touch that body again.

I didn't want to go back downstairs without backup. Maybe I could free Mouse and the others. The captives were safer up here than in the basement, but I was sure they'd appreciate the help. There was no telling what Max's flunkies would do to them if they thought Royce was winning the battle in the basement.

With each step I took up to the next floor, more confidence returned. The fine trembling in my hands tapered off surprisingly quickly considering the physical reaction I'd had to what I'd done. I was admirably succeeding at not thinking about Peter's remains lying strewn on the floor behind me.

'You'll have plenty of time to beat yourself up over it later. Enjoy the afterglow of success. You're alive, he's not,' the belt said. I found myself hating it very much just then because I realized it was the reason I wasn't wallowing in guilt or shock anymore. *'Besides, there's more to do tonight. Finish this fight before the sun rises. After that I can't help you anymore. There isn't much time.'*

Damn the thing three ways to Sunday, it was right. It had been hours since we'd been to the club. I didn't know how much time was left until sunrise. Rather than think on it too heavily, I moved faster, keeping as quiet as I could. If I hurried and was lucky, maybe I'd pull off this rescue with time to take a crack at John.

I paused in my tracks at that last thought. That wasn't me. It was the belt, insinuating I could do more awful things I didn't want to think about. I'd have to reassess using this thing in the future if it was going to make me so bloody-minded.

The pleasant haze to my thoughts concerning violence made me distinctly worried about how I'd feel once the sun rose and the belt's influence faded.

The door at the top of the stairs was closed. I'd be at a severe disadvantage this way, but I didn't want to leave the others trapped up here. I had to do something to save them. Something to atone for the god-awful thing I had just done.

I stood there for a long moment, indecisive, when a ridiculous idea occurred to me. If I wasn't so worried about being found out, I might have laughed. The idea was so stupid, it had to work.

I knocked on the door, making it light, tentative.

"Yeah?" came the muffled voice of one of the guards. Bill.

"Macth athked me to come get you," I said, affecting a frightened quaver to hide the lisp. I aimed my guns square at the middle of the door. "He needth everyone down-thtairth."

"What?" the vamp said, opening the door. "Why the fuck would Max send—"

That was as far as he got. One bullet took him in the heart, the other in the right eye. He soundlessly staggered backward, the other vampire barely having time to get past his shock and lift his gun before I did the same to him. I peripherally noticed everyone else in the room surging to their feet, calling out questions, but I didn't want to chance that the bullets were enough to keep the henchmen down.

I swiftly tucked the guns away and pulled out a stake. I was startled when my fingers brushed three handles, and frowned in puzzlement. All of the stakes were there. Frowning hurt, so I grimaced instead. That hurt even more. Ignoring the pain, spitting out some of the new blood trickling into my mouth from the tear in my lip, I knelt down by the first body as the belt explained.

'We are all parts of a cohesive whole. Once used, a stake will remain embedded in flesh either for a couple of minutes

after the Other is truly dead, or once it has gone beyond a certain range of its housing,' it said while I methodically staked the two vampires lying on the floor at my feet. One of them twitched slightly, but otherwise they didn't move as I did my dirty work. *'You can count on always having a weapon on you when wearing me as long as you remember those limitations.'*

Listening to the belt made it easier to go through the motions of staking the downed vamps without going into a jitter fit. When I looked up, the others in the room were watching me with wide, frightened eyes. All except for Mouse; I couldn't read her expression.

"All right," I said, slowly rising to my feet. A couple of the vamps sidled back, and one of the women hid her face against the chest of one of the guys. Were they that scared of me? "Royth ith here. I need your help downththairth. Thtay here if you can't fight. Everyone elth wif me."

Mouse quickly moved to join me, but no one else came to my side until she gestured impatiently at the others. I was disappointed to see only two more were willing to back me up, the guy with the seawater eyes and another man who was tall and rail thin, but had a determined look in his eye at odds with the wariness with which he regarded me. I stepped over the body of the guard who'd opened the door and quickly took the stairs, keeping a hand on the stakes in case we met with another bad guy on the way down.

Mouse put a restraining hand on my shoulder when we got to the first floor, pointing to the room where she'd fought with Max. We stopped in the apartment so she could grab two swords. I wasn't totally sure how she planned on using both at the same time. Fancy work like that was for the movies, not a real battle.

The other two vamps also selected blades from the walls, lifting them from their brackets with such practiced ease I had to wonder how often they used those things. The weapons were obviously more than eccentric decorations.

I'd figured that much out as soon as Mouse battled Max. Were they here specifically for the purpose of driving off intruders in a less-than-conventional way?

Whatever. I didn't ponder it too long, once more taking the lead as we rushed to the stairwell. There were still sounds of fighting coming from below, but not as loud or as frantic as they had been before. I couldn't see more than flickering shadows and a splash of blood on the floor at the bottom of the stairs.

"Wait here a few thecondth before following me, okay? Come down one at a time."

"Sure," the guy with the seawater eyes agreed, regarding me thoughtfully. "Don't worry too much about us, we'll be okay. I'm more worried about you. Are you sure you want to go first?"

"Yeth, I'm thure," I replied, grinning ruefully. Ugh, smiling hurt. "I'm tougher than I look, and I'm thure I'll draw attention off the thtairth long enough for you guyth to make it down thafely."

The others nodded and stepped back as I drew my weapons. Taking a stake in one hand and a gun in the other, I rushed straight down. Rather than risk being shot or tackled as soon as I came into view, I employed some of the unearthly speed granted by the belt. I took in as much of the scene as I could at a glance while I made for the open door on the far wall.

There were dead and injured people sprawled everywhere. Some were moaning, clutching at their injuries, or clawing their way to the far corners of the room to get out of the fray. Most were obviously dead, sightless eyes staring, accusing. The grossest things in sight were the corpses clearly savaged by Weres. Some were missing limbs. Others had their guts spilled out on the cement. None of it bore too much scrutiny. My stomach was already queasy from the attack on Peter. The unspeakable reek in the room from spilled innards wasn't helping.

One of the first bodies I spotted on the ground was the crazy mage, Nicolas. Well, half of him. I didn't want to know where his legs and the lower portion of his torso went.

I was alarmed to see one of the Weres down on the ground, savage bite wounds visible through his thick brown pelt. He lay panting by the stairs, bleeding heavily. It wasn't Chaz, but I couldn't tell whether it was Dillon, Simon, or Vincent. I hadn't seen them shifted too often, so I didn't know one from the other in their full-Were forms. Even as I watched, the uneven, heaving breaths slowed to a halt, furred chest not rising again.

I didn't have time to grieve. There were too many combatants on their feet to wade my way to safety or concealment. A yelp was startled out of me as a bullet whined by my head. Ducking, I rushed to take cover in the nearest tunnel, but not before I saw John taking aim at me again and Chaz bowling right into him, knocking him off his feet.

Since there wasn't much I could do to help Chaz, I tried to spot my other friends, hoping everyone else was okay. Tiny was wrestling with a vampire who was snarling into his face, snapping fangs at him like a rabid dog. I didn't envy the vampire. Tiny dwarfed him, so I wasn't too worried the vamp would win, even with the benefit of his supernatural strength.

Devon was crumpled on the floor across the room. I was afraid he might be dead, but there were too many bad guys between us for me to risk going to check. Dawn was nowhere in sight.

Max and Royce were still fighting. They weren't moving too fast for me to follow their actions anymore, though each time they exchanged blows it was a blur. Royce had picked up a metal pipe from somewhere, using that to counter Max's sword. He was covered in shallow wounds, his clothes torn in too many places for me to count. That he was still bleeding, not healing the wounds, was a bad sign. To Royce's credit, Max was also bleeding in a couple of places and looked far more battered. However, more of Max's men were still fighting than ours. I was getting a bad feeling about our odds of winning this fight without more losses.

I need not have worried because just then Mouse flew down the stairs with astonishing speed. She waded into the fight like a pro, her moves fluid, graceful, dancing with the blades between one group of enemies and the next. They slashed and whirled, her bloodstained skirt swirling around her ankles as she thrust and parried and cut down anyone in her path. It was dizzyingly fast, and once again, I found myself grateful she was on our side.

She was cutting a path to Royce, tossing him one of the two swords without faltering in her own fighting, shifting smoothly from two swords to one. It was like watching Zorro, if Zorro wore a skirt and didn't mind slicing his opponents to bits instead of slashing his trademark on their clothes.

When he caught the sword, a new, predatory grin curved Royce's lips. Max went on the defensive, falling back, and I was alarmed to notice they were coming right toward my hiding place. Rather than get drawn into their fight, I ran out to find an enemy to engage.

More gunshots were followed by a high-pitched *yark*-type sound. John was shakily standing up, shoving Chaz off him. My baby collapsed on his side and was panting around the wounds in his chest; no silver, or the shots would've killed him. Instead, it would take him a few very painful minutes to recover. John would pay for that.

The vamp didn't have time to get his balance. This time *I* tackled him to the floor, snarling deeply enough to do a Were proud.

"Ath-hole!" I shouted, reaching for a stake.

Startled, he gaped up at me, having the good sense to drop his gun to grab my wrist to keep me from impaling his heart. His strength was sufficient to slow me down, though I had the advantage of leverage over his bad angle.

My efforts were winning out. The stake was slowly plunging toward his chest.

"Damn you," he gasped up at me, hatred and frustration twisting his features while we warred over where the stake would land. "Everything would've worked if you'd just stayed out of this, you meddling trollop!"

I hissed down at him, some of my own blood trickling down my chin to splatter on his cheek as I put all my weight on the stake. "Jutht lay down and die already, you backthtabbing little thit!"

With a low grunt, he *shoved* at me, and it was more than just physical force. It was like a clap of air propelled me upwards, sending out a small shockwave from us, throwing me off him and to the side. I lost the stake as I slipped in some of the blood and whatever else was on the floor when I scrambled to my feet, only to lose my footing again when he swung at me. More blood spilled into my mouth from the blow as my teeth bit into my cheek.

He might have followed through with a kick, but Chaz had crept up behind him and grabbed hold of one of his ankles. He pulled the vampire off balance and sent him flat on his ass on the floor next to me. Though my ears were ringing and I was a bit stunned, I rolled to reach him again, ready with another stake.

I needn't have bothered. Chaz yanked John over and crawled on top of him, setting massive jaws against the vamp's windpipe, crushing his throat. John's eyes widened with terror and pain, his mouth opening and closing soundlessly as his hands clawed at the thick, steel grey fur above him. With a vicious twist, Chaz tore out John's throat.

While that might have killed a human, John was anything but. Not only was he a vampire, he was also an elder. His initial panic kept him from reacting properly at first, but he was soon pounding at Chaz's already injured chest. Having been on the receiving end of one of those blows, I knew it had to hurt.

Chaz snarled and clawed at him. I gaped from less than two feet away, getting splashed with gore as the gigantic Were tore into the vampire with gusto. What I did to Peter upstairs was a love tap compared to the mess Chaz made of John.

Once the bloody mess stopped heaving and twitching beneath him, Chaz stopped, backing away with a low growl. As soon as he moved out of the way, I was streaking forward with a stake.

Except it wasn't *me* directing the motion.

A final, gurgling sound came from his ravaged throat as the stake connected and John died for real. Even all the damage Chaz inflicted hadn't been enough to kill him. I stared down at my hand on the stake, chilled I hadn't been directing my own body.

'You need to be sure with an elder. There was no time to delay.'

I wasn't sure how to respond. *Had the belt taken possession of me?*

'Yes,' came the simple, snide reply to my unspoken thought. *'I act for you when necessary. That's part of how I work. Haven't you figured that out by now?'*

Fuck.

Shoving the worries and implications as far to the back of my mind as possible, I decided to have the screaming heebie-jeebies later. There was still too much going on around me to concentrate on the problem of my potential demonic possession by the belt right now.

Chapter 33

Chaz staggered to his feet, already bleeding less heavily from the bullets he'd taken. He lowered a clawed paw to help me up and I took it gratefully, being careful of the thick black talons.

I only had a moment to appreciate the strength in that paw-like hand, that tree-trunk arm thick with fur and muscle, before we were torn away from each other. He was being mobbed by some angry humans led by Logan, while I was pulled into a scuffle between some vampires. I vaguely recognized Mr. Seawater Eyes before the two of us were back to back, him with his sword and me with a stake. We fended off our attackers in an ever-widening circle, moving as though we'd done this a thousand times before.

What I could make out of the guy's skills beyond the haze of battle showed he was truly proficient with swords. I couldn't admire his handiwork much as three vamps were focused on me, doing everything they could to trip me up and take me down. The bad guys sporting cuts opposing him were more wary than my opponents, who mostly suffered bruises. If I wasn't careful, the guys with cuts might decide to abandon Mr. Seawater Eyes for weaker prey—me.

"Do this often?" he asked conversationally, the sword

flicking out to put a line of crimson on the arm of one of
the vamps reaching for him.

I barked out a short laugh as I ducked a punch. "No, not
really."

"Pity," he said, and I could hear the grin and the eagerness in his voice. He liked this battle stuff almost as much
as the belt. "You're good at it, especially for a human."
Slash, hack. Ew. "If we survive this, I'd love to know how
you got involved with Max and Alec."

"Later," I said, a little "oof" wheezing out of me as one
of the vamps connected with a kick to my ribs, making me
stagger.

That separated us, and I was alone in my little island of
chaos, whirling and punching and kicking and stabbing at
the grasping hands trying to drag me down. No matter how
many I put out of commission, there were always more. Fatigue was starting to set in.

'The sun is close to rising. Not much time left,' the belt
said, the voice in my head only a faint whisper.

"Crap," I cried as I landed a hurried roundhouse into the
head of a vamp going low for a tackle. There were more
ready to take his place, and from the looks of things, the
rising of the sun would not make these guys back off.

I'd be helpless, back to normal human strength, speed,
and stamina once that happened.

Surrounded by hungry vampires.

Fuck.

'See if you can make the stairs.'

The stairs were an awfully long distance away and between me and a lot more bad guys than I was willing to
take on. There weren't any other openings I could see. In
fact, there were so many vamps circling around us, there
wasn't *any* opening or escape. The first touch of despair
crept into my thoughts as I realized I couldn't see any of
my friends. Not even the huge, unmistakable presence of
Chaz or either of the other wolves.

The only reason I didn't see Mouse until she was next to me was because she was so short. She cut a swath through some of the vamps to my left, and I took advantage of the opening as the others converged on her.

With a last burst of fading speed and energy, I tumbled to a halt, panting behind a line of Royce's vampires that were still standing. They were protectively keeping their backs to the wall as they made a row between the remaining bad guys and a few of those on our side alive, but too injured to keep fighting. I was pleased to see Devon was there and sitting up against the wall, ashen-faced, but alive and aware. Dawn was using part of her blouse to tear off makeshift bandages for the claw marks on his chest and shoulder. I knelt on the floor, trying to catch my breath, a thousand aches and pains dulled by the protection of the belt flaring to life as the sun rose outside and banished the spirit.

At the same time, almost every vampire still standing staggered as if hit by a physical blow. Exhaustion took most of them, a few tumbling to their knees or coming to a halt no matter where they were or what they were in the middle of. Some passed out where they were, tumbling to the floor in ungainly heaps. That's when I spotted Chaz, taking advantage to rise up off the floor and bodily heave the three vampires that had been pinning him to the ground across the room.

The only ones unaffected were Max and Royce. As the other vampires wearily shuffled to the sidelines, too sluggish to continue fighting, the elders were black and crimson blurs. Their blades showered sparks as they clashed time and again. I watched from behind the protective wall of vampires, mesmerized by the fluid violence of their fight. It took me a minute to realize that, in addition to their swords, they were both using the same type of force on each other as John used to thrust me away.

It made me uneasy to see this dance of death bringing

them so close to the defensive line of our people, now peppered with holes from the vampires who had collapsed from exhaustion or whatever at sunrise.

It became frighteningly apparent why this was when Max took an unexpected tactic, pressing the advantage so he could close the distance between himself and Royce. He used his swordplay as a distraction, joining their weapons so he could grab the remains of Royce's ragged shirt collar and use a combination of strength and that weird force to hurl him halfway across the room.

That's when Max turned to me, holding out his free hand with his eyes blazing that terrifying crimson hue. "Come to me."

That melodic chime called to me like the beckoning of a siren. I had to answer.

I didn't realize the depth of my error until I was already wrapped in his arms. He had to break eye contact with me to focus on Royce. That's when I came back to myself—not that it did me any good. My strength paled against his. I was trapped firmly up against his chest, my arms pinned, quelling my struggling.

As Royce levered himself to his feet, he didn't raise his sword. His black eyes narrowed dangerously as Max raised his blade up to my throat. The bite of steel and welling of blood had me hissing in pain, tilting my head up as far as I could to avoid the edge.

"We needn't continue this petty squabble, Alec," Max chided, sounding all too pleased. "I have something you want, you have something I want. Up for a trade?"

Royce growled, the sound rumbling over my skin like a physical blow. Max's grip on me tightened painfully as I shivered against him.

"I don't trust your word, old friend," Royce said. "You were supposed to stay in Chicago until negotiations were over. Athena will not be pleased."

The spine-unhinging fear Royce had thrown at me,

Chaz, and Devon back at his office was now radiating from Max. Terror wrapped cold claws around my heart, making me scream and twist and writhe. Blood ran in a hot trail as the sword bit deeper into my skin. The screams of other people in the room were soon added to my own, formless dread driving everyone, including the vampires who hadn't passed out, to react in instinctive response.

Royce took advantage of the uproar. Fear warped my perceptions of him into some bestial, savage creature coming to destroy me. He used more of that unreal speed to close the distance between us, leaving Max no choice but to bring up his sword to counter at the very last second.

It wasn't enough. They impaled each other on the swords, neither hitting anything vital. Both weapons were unsettlingly close and kept me pinned tightly between them.

Yes, I screamed like a girl. I *am* one. You try getting caught between two elder vampires at each others' throats and see how you deal with it.

I probably hurt myself more than they ever intended to when I tried to escape being pinned between them. Max snarled a harsh *"Quiet!"* in my ear to get me to shut up. Much as I didn't want to obey, I had to, the pathetic screaming I was doing abruptly cutting off into a tight squeak of fear and protest. The two elders glared at each other, fangs bared, eyes all for each other. I might as well not have been there for all the notice they were paying me.

"Go back to Chicago. Leave this place and never return," Royce demanded, twisting his wrist for emphasis. I was pressed tight enough against Max's chest to feel his muscles flinch as the sword dug deeper into his shoulder.

I couldn't see his face, but the tone of his voice made me think Max must be grinning behind me. If he was feeling any pain from being impaled, you couldn't tell from the way he sounded or acted.

"I'll do as you ask with one concession."

Royce's eyes narrowed dangerously, trickles of crimson light flowing into them. It was scary as hell, particularly with my bleeding throat being only a few inches away from his bared fangs.

"There will be no compromise. You've broken our laws of homestead, secrecy, and negotiation. By rights, I should be killing you, not letting you walk. Don't make me do it, Euphron."

"Taking that route, are you, Rhathos?"

Royce flinched at the name. The light died out of his eyes, and when he spoke again, it was quiet, reserved, any hint of anger or pain carefully suppressed. "What do you want?"

Max's hand caught in my hair, forcing my head back and to the side. I tried not to fight, to scream and flail and panic, but it was a losing battle. His tongue drifted along the shallow cut on the underside of my jaw. Visions of Peter holding me down, preparing to bite, danced in my head. A faint cry died in my throat when he pulled away.

"Let her go. Give your little Helen to me without a fight, and I will call all between us even. Athena would be so pleased," he whispered, taking on a sibilant hiss. No one could miss the vicious undertones, the lilting way in which he said Helen's name. "Centuries of conflict resolved in an instant, and all it will take is just one . . . little . . . concession." He punctuated each word with slight jerks on his sword, driving it a bit deeper into Royce's shoulder each time.

Royce shook his head, maintaining the pleasantly blank expression, though I could see his skin had gone pasty. The black blood running out of all the cuts littering his skin moved more sluggishly than before. Even so, I wanted to weep with relief. He wouldn't let Max use me for his revenge.

"Something else. You can't take any of my people as a

concession; they can only come to you of their own will. You know that."

"Free passage in and out of the city, then. With no need for formalities or forewarning."

Royce's expression hardened. "At least two days advance notice, and no more deaths or harm to my people. That includes unclaimed humans on my territory."

"Done."

With that, Max was suddenly just *gone.* I'd seen Royce do it before, utilizing his speed to make it seem like he'd disappeared. Max's sword clattered to the floor before I was even totally aware that he'd moved. He must have run off down one of the tunnels, because the other vampires who came here with him trundled off toward them, some of them dragging the wounded or unconscious behind. Royce dropped his sword and caught me as I sagged, the sudden relief of being released unharmed almost making me swoon.

"Are you all right?"

I lifted a shaky hand to my throat, gingerly touching the cut. I couldn't look at him.

"Shiarra?"

"I'll be okay." His skin was almost as pale as mine, some of his wounds still trickling blood. It made me more nervous than I already was. I regained my footing as best I could, struggling to stand on my own. He let me go once I got my balance back, and I rapidly put some distance between us. "What about you?"

He looked down at himself, picking with disgust at the tattered remains of what had once been a designer button-down. It would have been lovely without the bloodstains. A sickened little voice reminded me it was the color of the shirt the girl upstairs was wearing while Max drained the life out of her.

"Well," Royce said, "I could use a meal, a shower, and a change of clothes, but that will have to wait."

I didn't want to think about his mention of a meal.
Someone was going to have to open up a vein for him. I'd
done enough bleeding for one night, thank you very much.
Before he could get any ideas, I nodded and rushed to
Chaz's side.

He'd reverted to human form, kneeling naked and bleeding among the mess of remains by the stairs. Tears trickled down his cheeks as he cradled a still, limp body to his
chest. It was Vincent, the guy I'd barely known, who once
in a while came out with us to the movies. He'd reverted
to human in death but still had all the injuries he'd suffered
when shifted. Innumerable fang marks and ragged tears littered his frame. Simon hung back awkwardly, not making
an effort to conceal his nakedness, though he was using a
hand to put some pressure on a seeping wound on one arm.
Dillon hadn't shifted back yet. He was hunched over Chaz
and Vincent, making a low, mournful sound in his throat.

I wasn't part of the pack, and I didn't think now would
be the right time to intrude on their grief. Instead, I sur-
veyed the rest of the room.

Devon was talking quietly with Dawn as she helped him
to the stairs. One of the vamps had come up on the other side
of him, giving him a hand despite his protests. Mouse was
busy collecting fallen weaponry off the floor. The guy with
the seawater eyes was helping somebody else to the stairs.

I couldn't see Tiny anywhere. Frowning, I looked at the
bodies on the floor, searching for his unmistakable figure.

Almost lost in the shadows at the far corner of the room,
he was using the remains of a tool shelf for support while
he lit up a cigarette. He gave me a smile, showing teeth in
a savage grin of victory. He couldn't be too badly hurt if he
was looking that pleased with himself. I found myself smiling back.

Even as the first threads of relief seeped through me,
something strange happened. Between one blink and the
next, I found myself halfway from the stairs to one of the

doors. The same one Max and his people fled through. I didn't remember moving.

"What the fuck?" I mumbled, putting a hand to my forehead. My head was hurting, just a little, though it hadn't been a second ago. What was going on?

Another blink, and I was at the door itself. I braced my hands against the frame, widening my eyes. No one noticed anything was up with me yet.

"Um, guyth?"

Everyone was too busy helping the injured or seeing to the dead to notice me. The querulous note to my voice warbled into a thread of panic as I found myself inside the passage, not remembering how I got there. I was blacking out for a few seconds every time I closed my eyes.

This time, I screamed. Max was calling me to his side.

"Help!"

Chapter 34

Strong arms wrapped around my waist from behind, hauling me back toward Royce's basement. I struggled and screamed, not sure why, only knowing the overwhelming need to rush headlong down that tunnel.

"Stop fighting, I'm trying to help you!" a voice I didn't recognize growled in my ear, grunting when my elbow connected with his sternum.

I felt an overpowering need to break free and run, to meet the silent call's source. The hands holding me back were nothing more than a distraction. I twisted and squirmed to get away, the desire to run drowning out all other thoughts.

Royce's pale hands were suddenly cradling my face, forcing me to look up into his eyes. The longing to run was still there, but it was dim now. Fading under the intensity of those depthless black pools, sucking me down to a quieter place. Despite the fierce need to escape, I soon settled in the arms of the man who held me, spellbound by Royce's gaze.

"Why didn't you tell me you were bound?" he hissed, sounding deeply disappointed. "Damn it thrice, no wonder he gave you up without a fight."

I couldn't find my voice to answer him.

"I don't know of any way but one to break his hold on you," he whispered, that sweet, smooth voice almost as tantalizing as Max's to my confused and way too overworked senses. "I'll have to bind you as well. I need you to agree, Shiarra. I won't do it against your will."

A trickle of fear penetrated my consciousness. I blinked, rousing from the false calm he had me under. My voice came out weak and thready as panic returned. "No. I can't."

Distantly, as if in a dream, I heard Chaz's voice from somewhere far away. "What the hell are you doing to her? Don't touch her!"

"Don't do it! Don't listen to him, Shia!" Devon shouted. I could hear a scuffle, but Royce wouldn't let me look away.

"Don't be fools. Do you people want her running back to Max? I'm doing what I can to protect her from him, so save the righteous indignation for another time."

Slender, delicate fingertips traced along my temples and jaw, keeping me focused on him throughout their little spat. Despite the thunderous, warning growl from Chaz, I couldn't help relaxing. Royce's voice took on a sweet, surreal quality, pleading, cajoling in a way I'd never heard, drowning out the harsh demands from Max.

"You want to stay with your friends, don't you? Let me do this, Shiarra. Let me help you."

Like an angel on his knees, begging to show me a slice of heaven. Royce was anything but an angel, and I had no doubt his "help" would come with a price I wouldn't want to pay. Only the deeply ingrained terror of knowing what being bound by blood as well as contract to him meant made me hesitate. I wasn't sure I'd be able to stand up against this brand of assault much longer.

"Please, Roythe," I pleaded with him, clinging to that little bit of sanity screaming about what a terribly bad idea it would be to agree to this. Chaz gathered up one of my limp hands in his, though I was still far too focused on

Royce's eyes to look at him. It was impossible to turn away. "I can't. There'th got to be another way."

"You know there are no other options here," Royce said. "You need to choose now, between Max and your friends, people who love you. If you don't do this, you know Max will call you back to him. Even if we manage to keep you safe for tonight, he'll be back, and I can promise you he won't be nearly as lenient and understanding as I am."

Jack's mocking voice played back in my mind. *There's a new player in the game. It'll be down to him or Royce. Or us.* I hated that the smarmy bastard was right. He'd warned me I'd get tied up with forces above and beyond my ability to cope with; I just hadn't wanted to listen at the time.

Honestly, I might have laughed if I'd been more myself. The idea of Royce being "lenient and understanding" would've been hysterical under other circumstances. I tried to rationally consider what he was saying, to think it through, but it was incredibly difficult to concentrate. Would it be so bad being bound to him? Oh, yes. Yes, it would. Still, was there anything else I could do that wouldn't result in my being summoned by Max?

I wanted to close my eyes so I wouldn't be forced to stare up at him while I weighed my options. It was unbelievably distracting. He pressed on, not giving me the time to think it through, that impossibly alluring tone begging to allow him the chance. The serpent in the Garden of Eden had nothing on that soft, surreal voice.

"Please, Shiarra. Say it. Say yes . . ."

There is a point where a person can only take so much. I'd done my best to keep my head despite everything that had happened to and around me the past couple days. As much as the idea frightened me, I was lulled into passivity by whatever he was doing. The charm around my neck should have prevented any mind games of this sort, but it hadn't been doing me much good lately.

I swallowed hard and stared up into the mesmerizing

gaze that quieted Max's siren call, silently praying I was
making the right choice. My voice came out as little more
than a strained whisper once I found the breath to answer.

"Yeth."

The curve of his thin lips was more mischievous than reassuring. Terror assailed me at the thought I'd just made a
horrible mistake. Chaz squeezed my hand reassuringly. It
helped. He was here, he wouldn't let Royce or anyone else
hurt me. It couldn't go that badly if he was by my side,
could it?

Don't answer that.

"Just keep your eyes on me," Royce instructed, pulling
back half a step. He lowered his head just a bit. His eyes
stayed focused on mine as he withdrew one of his hands
and brought his wrist up to his mouth. The few drops of
crimson on his lips and trickling down his arm shattered
my false calm. I jerked back from his offering, knowing
Jack was right about this, too.

The guy who had his arms wrapped around me whispered in my ear, holding me tighter against a still, cold
chest. Vampire. "Just relax, it'll all be over soon."

I wished I could believe that.

I wanted to tell Royce to stop, to wait, to give me a
minute to wrap my wits around needing to swallow his
blood. There wasn't any time for it. Before I could get the
words out, he was pressing his arm to my lips. The taste of
that bitter, metallic liquid coated my tongue as I twisted
away. Royce's other hand tightened slightly on my jaw,
holding me in place.

However, he'd kept me calm before, it wasn't working
now. I closed my burning eyes, too sick and tired for tears.

If I didn't do this, Max could call me back to him. There
was no guarantee he wouldn't flat out kill me this time
around, if for no other reason than to piss off Royce. I
didn't want to die like that. I could do this. I could drink

Royce's blood if it would keep me alive and sane, out of the hands of that psycho, Max.

It tasted awful, but I drank a few drops, feeling it burn a chill path down my throat. As soon as I swallowed, Royce pulled his arm away and the vampire who had been holding me let go.

I thought I might be too weak to stand. That I'd have hysterics, panic, or do something equally stupid. Instead, I felt . . . fine. The taste lingering in my mouth wasn't anything to write home about, that's for sure. It felt like something was tickling the back of my throat, but otherwise, I was fine. I stood where I was, probably looking sort of stupid to the others as I sought an appropriate reaction. What does Ms. Manners say you do after drinking a vampire's blood? Thank him? Curse him? Run screaming from the room? I didn't know, and none of those options sounded that great.

Chaz wrapped his arms around me, blocking my view of the rest of the room. I blinked woozily up at him. His features were twisted with concern and fear; I wished I knew a way to persuade him I was all right. First I'd have to figure out how to convince myself.

"Are you okay, love?"

I cleared my throat but my voice still came out hoarse and raspy. "I think I'll be all right."

Wonder of wonders, it didn't hurt to speak. I touched a hand gingerly to my lip, and was surprised to feel . . . nothing. No pain. There was a small ragged bump like a scar, but I wasn't lisping anymore, and the cut from Peter's fangs had vanished. Did vampire blood do that?

"Shiarra."

The call of my name was like the dulcet chiming of a bell, ringing out with command. I pulled away from Chaz and stared at Royce. He was watching mè, his eyes narrowed to thin slivers. Had he always sounded that way, or was I hearing him differently with his blood inside me, changing me?

"Do you still hear Max's call?"

"No." I shook my head, but realized after only a few seconds it was a lie. He was there, whispering in my mind; it just wasn't as strong as it had been. The instant I focused on it, the call was louder, more insistent, demanding. My eyes widened and I took a step back, putting a hand to my forehead. "Wait, why is he still there? I thought you fixed this!"

Royce sighed and advanced on me, his easy, boneless grace more attractive than it had ever been. I'd once admired his walk, that predatory mien, but the draw I felt now was magnetic. Not like before. I wanted to get closer to him, to meet him halfway, but didn't quite dare. Was I seeing Royce through rose-colored glasses now that we were bound by blood?

Hadn't I always felt this way?

One chill finger tilted my chin up so I was once more staring into those depthless black eyes. "I have the advantage of proximity. For the moment, my tie to you is stronger than his. He won't be able to reach you while you're with me."

Chaz was suddenly there, slamming Royce by the throat up against the wall and sending me stumbling back. Chaz's eyes were positively wild as he hissed through his teeth, muscles straining as he fought the rage putting him on the verge of change.

"You lying son of a bitch! You never said any of that! You didn't tell her she'd be bound to *both* of you leech fucks!"

"Chaz, no!" I cried.

Though I felt sick at Royce's revelation and the implications of what he had done, I still had an intense desire to be near him. I didn't want to see him dead.

Chaz's hand spasmed around Royce's throat until

rivulets of blood trickled down his fingers. His hand shifted into claws, biting into the vampire's skin.

Royce didn't look fazed. He calmly met Chaz's narrowed blue eyes as though staring at him from across the expanse of his fancy desk in his office, laying out the terms for a business contract. Not like he was being held bleeding against the wall of his corpse-ridden basement.

"Take your hands off me. You heard her; she agreed to this."

Chaz slammed him against the wall again. The first hints of red bled into Royce's eyes. His fingers clenched at his sides, but he didn't fight back.

"You told her you were breaking Max's hold on her, not leaving it there!" Chaz accused him.

"I'll ask one more time. Take. Your. Hands. Off. Me." Each word was enunciated slowly and clearly, making me nervous. Almost as much as the unnatural swelling of muscles under Chaz's skin. He was going to shift, and it wouldn't be pretty when he did.

Rather than do what Royce asked, he howled an angry challenge into his face, and I could see the upper and lower fangs sprouting in his mouth. I couldn't remember ever seeing Chaz get this mad before, so angry he was losing control over his ability to keep his beast in check. It scared the hell out of me.

Royce's actions scared me more. He no longer hesitated to shove Chaz away. With a thrust of that odd force, he sent Chaz flying across the room until he crashed into the opposite wall, plaster and dust raining down on impact. Chaz groaned and lay where he'd fallen, a hand slowly moving up to the back of his head where he'd struck. Even from where I stood, I could see the fresh blood on his fingertips when he pulled his hand away.

Gaping in shock, I slowly turned to look back at Royce, somehow more terrified by this show of force than by the implications of what he had done to me. Everyone else in the room had gone dead silent, holding their collective breath to see what would happen next. The vampire brushed himself off as though he were wearing a clean, tailored suit, not the ragged remains of a ripped shirt displaying more of his chest than it hid. He met my eyes once more, wordlessly extending his hand to me.

I didn't want to go to him. I really didn't. Right then I would've much preferred running screaming from the room so I could go hide under a bed somewhere.

Instead, I stiffly approached him, lightly taking his outstretched hand in my own. Once our skin made contact, more false calm stole over me, making the drama playing itself out before my eyes less frightening, less real. My tense muscles started to unknot themselves, and I found myself longing for the sound of his voice.

"Shiarra, I need you to listen closely and pay attention to what I'm about to tell you," Royce said, waiting for my nod of acknowledgment before he continued. "When our blood works its way out of your system, you won't be drawn to us anymore. However, you'll find yourself craving it in the next few days. You can come to me and reinforce the addiction—and the bond—or you can ignore it and suffer withdrawal. The symptoms will be very painful, but you'll be free of us both if you are strong enough to withstand the need for our blood. Do you understand?"

I considered it, my hazy thoughts focusing on what he said only because he'd ordered me to listen carefully. Between the unbelievably seductive draw of his voice and the faint but insistent calls from Max, I was surprised I could concentrate on anything at all. Still, he was asking for something amounting to a decision here, though I wanted to beg for him to keep this bond as strong as it was now. It felt so *good*, so *right* to hold his hand in mine, to feel his voice like a caress, teasing at my senses. I didn't want that taken away.

"I understand," I squeaked out, though I hoped I understood as well as he wanted me to. Maybe he hadn't been as conniving and vicious about this as Chaz had thought.

It was so odd to feel so calm and composed with his hand in mine. There was no lingering sense of terror, no sickening feel of coming off an adrenaline rush, no wash of self-disgust at the atrocious things I'd done tonight. If staying with him meant feeling like this all the time, I'd take it, and gladly.

"Good." He smiled at me, and even the glimpse of his fangs didn't scare me. Instead, I felt that same, soul-warming contentment as when Max had been pleased with me. I basked in the heady glow, barely hearing his words.

"Until it wears off, you need to stay here with me."

Chapter 35

"Get your hands off her," came a low, angry voice from somewhere in the shadows. It sounded weak, worn, but familiar somehow. "Right now."

Royce turned a winsome smile in the direction of the voice. "That isn't necessary. Put down the gun, Devon."

The hunter limped closer, looking almost as pale and drawn as one of the vampires. He had a gun leveled at Royce's head. That was worrisome. He was a good shot. Even with me in the way, he could make it.

"Devon, don't," I started, moving to interpose myself between them. Royce hushed me, and I obeyed.

"I'll let her go in a few days, as soon as the bond fades."

"Yeah, right," Devon sneered. "She's so taken with you, she won't want to say no when you offer her another drink. She'll be safer far away from you and Max both."

I was getting tired of people talking about me like I wasn't there. I cut in this time, bristling at Devon's tone. "So what if I say yes? What's it matter to you?"

He pointed sharply toward the far wall, and guilt ate at me at the sight of Tiny helping Chaz stagger up to his feet. Blood was trickling from his scalp. With a Were's metabolism, that must have been quite an impact for it to still be bleeding.

"That's what matters to me. You barely even looked at him. I know how much you care about him, Were or no. You want to abandon all of your friends for that monster whose arm you're hanging on? The same one who did that to Chaz?"

I tightened my fingers around Royce's, and he mirrored my motions, coming to settle beside me as we stared at Devon. Though I hadn't paid much attention to Chaz, I certainly hadn't forgotten who hurt him—or why.

"I'm not abandoning anyone. Chaz was asking for it when he picked a fight with Royce."

"Oh really? And how do you feel about the idea of drinking a vamp's blood? Him drinking yours? Do you remember how you felt about those things even just a couple of hours ago?"

I frowned, thinking. The idea of either didn't bother me nearly so much as it used to, true. Come to think of it, the idea of being bitten was intriguing now, knowing what it felt like. Royce wouldn't be trying to scare the life out of me in the process like Peter and Max had.

That's what clued me in to how right Devon was.

It took a monstrous effort to pull my hand out of Royce's, to step away.

"Shiarra?" Royce's tone was soft, concerned. My heart ached for that note in his voice.

"No." I took another couple of steps away, feeling like I was tearing off something vital in the process. It was painful, which only helped strengthen my resolve. Covering my eyes with a hand, I kept backing away. "Don't, Royce. Don't do this right now."

I felt the first stirrings of anger radiating off him. I shivered in reaction, fighting the urge to return to his side and apologize.

"Your hunter friend is dividing us. If you truly want to

be free of us both, then I need you to realize how unwise that is. My will is all that protects you from Max's call right now. The fact that I'm giving you a choice should tell you my intentions are pure."

Yeah, the choice that wasn't a choice that showed he was about as pure as the slushy snow you'll find in the gutters at Christmas.

I hated that he could use something so little to back me into a corner, hated more that I couldn't risk his being wrong about this. I stayed where I was, silent, trembling, and wanting more than anything to be somewhere far away from this dark, smelly basement with all of the dead bodies, regrets, and divided loyalties it held.

"Shiarra," said Devon, his voice low and radiating fear, "please come with us. It's daylight outside; we can go somewhere they'll never find you until this blows over."

I ignored him as best I could. It sounded like such a great idea, to run and hide for the time being. After feeling Max calling me to his side, I knew that would be suicide. There was no way I could take the risk.

"Royce," I said, hating the waver in my own voice. "Can they stay here until it's safe for me to leave again?"

"Of course."

I don't think anyone in the room missed the note of triumph under those smooth tones. Not even me.

Tiny helped Chaz come closer to me, and I moved to meet them halfway. I don't think Chaz would've made it if he hadn't had the big man to help support his weight. This time, it didn't hurt to leave Royce's side. I decided not to think too hard about what that meant. Instead, I wrapped my arms around Chaz's waist and buried my head against his chest, trying very hard not to cry.

Chaz rested his chin on top of my head, the arm not clinging to Tiny circling my shoulder. He stank of blood and sweat, with the underlying musk of Were underneath. I was too upset to care about his decided lack of clothes. I pressed tighter against him, savoring his warmth and the imagined protection of his arms. Though he'd done an admirable job of helping keep the bad guys at bay, he hadn't been able to save me from being bound. That kind of metaphysical tie wasn't something he could fix.

That made me wonder. Chaz couldn't fix it—but maybe Arnold could.

Infused with new excitement at the idea, I twisted a little in Chaz's arms so I could look at Royce. That almost blasted every notion right out of my head. Somehow I managed to cling to my one, tiny ray of hope. "Where are Sara and Arnold? Weren't they with you?"

Royce shook his head, folding his arms across his chest. "Your mage friend was quite incensed the police would not believe that you were in danger, and so he caused something of a scene. I could stop them from pressing charges, but since he did some damage to the office of the interviewing officer, he's being held overnight. Sara did not want to abandon him, so she stayed at the station. He should be released after the paperwork is sorted out."

Uh-oh. That wasn't good. Still, maybe once he got out he'd be able to help do something about this unnatural tie I had to the two vampires.

Royce continued, "If you don't mind, I think we should all clean ourselves up. I'm sure someone here will have some extra clothing you can borrow. I also need to take my rest for the day, so perhaps we can continue any discussion this evening."

A shower sounded absolutely fantastic. I nodded wearily and we all started for the stairs. I had to release my grip on Chaz's waist so Tiny could help him up the stairs. A couple of the vampires stayed behind and started cleaning up the unbelievable amount of gore. I had no idea what they intended to do with the bodies. Honestly, I didn't want to know.

Mouse urged Dawn and me to come to her apartment.

Chaz, Devon, Tiny, and some of the vampires all followed Royce farther up the stairs. I noted we were all leaving bloody tracks behind us. Gross. This was all just too much, and I surely would've disgraced myself in front of everyone if I hadn't already tossed my cookies earlier.

Dawn and Mouse let me clean up first. Once I saw myself in the mirror, it was no wonder why. With all the crud clinging to me, the blood on my face and neck, I would've told me to shower first, too.

Shuddering at the nightmarish vision reflected in the mirror, I quickly divested myself of my gore-encrusted weapons and clothes. Though it hadn't been doing me much good lately, I kept the necklace on.

I didn't have as many bruises as I was expecting. The worst wound I'd suffered was the one where Max's sword had nicked my throat; a shallow line that stung like a mother when I rubbed a bit of soap around it. Like the cut on my lower lip, it had closed unnaturally fast, leaving a fresh and painfully tender scar behind.

When I stepped out of the shower, someone had left a change of clothes and taken my armor, weapons, and trench coat with them. There was a note with the new clothes. I recognized Mouse's handwriting telling me she had taken my stuff to be washed. I felt curiously naked without them when I emerged from the bathroom a few minutes later, dressed in someone else's loose-fitting cotton shirt and a pair of draw-string pajama pants. They were a bit too long for me, but nicely comfortable.

Dawn slipped silently past me, barely acknowledging my presence when she hurried into the bathroom. I couldn't blame her. Even the ethereal beauty of an elf can only stand up to so much wear and tear. She was reaching her limit.

Mouse was in the living room using an oilcloth to rub down the swords. She'd righted most of the furniture. In front of the couch was a low table with a steaming pot of tea and some crackers arranged on a tray. One of the cups had a few drops of tea left in it. Dawn must have had at the food and drink before hurrying into the shower.

I fixed myself a cup with a bit of honey and lemon and settled down next to Mouse on the couch, closing my eyes as I inhaled the sweet scent. The warmth seeping into my palms from the delicate china cup was more than welcome.

Mouse didn't say anything, of course. She did smile at me, though she was looking a little transparent around the edges, too. Every vamp in the building would need to feed soon. The thought would've unsettled me more if I wasn't so tired and relaxed from the mix of the warm shower, fresh clothes, and hot tea.

Though it normally would have, Royce's voice breaking the silence didn't startle me.

"Shiarra, would you please come with me? I'd like to discuss a couple of things with you before I rest for the day."

I had an extraordinarily difficult time opening my eyes, fighting back exhaustion so I could get up to join him. He looked a lot better now, his hair slicked back from his face, wet from the shower. He'd put on silk pajama bottoms, but hadn't bothered with a shirt, thus leaving his scarred chest and arms bare to view. His color was better, and there were no open cuts on him anymore. However, there were too many scars to account for the damage done to him tonight. I wondered if he'd gotten them while still alive. I was also grateful to see he must have fed on someone else.

Taking the tea with me, I carefully cradled it to my chest while Royce led the way. Upstairs, the shutters on the windows were all tightly closed and latched, the only light coming from the tiny spotlights illuminating the statuary. The hostages I'd freed and the bodies of Max's guards were gone; only a few scarlet stains on the hardwood remained to show where they'd been. Chaz and the other two were-wolves were showered and clean, sprawled snoring on some of the decorative pillows on the floor. Tiny was seated on the chaise, plucking at some bandages on his leg and not paying much attention to us when we walked in. Devon wasn't in sight, but I could hear the shower running. Bitch and moan about Royce as he might, he was still taking advantage of the vampire's hospitality. Hypocrite.

Royce led me into his bedroom, holding the door for me before shutting it behind us to ensure some privacy from Tiny and Chaz. He moved more fluidly than he had earlier, but I was too tired to be concerned about the implications or repercussions of being led to the vampire's bed. I stayed where I was by the door while he settled down on his futon, making such a simple, mundane action look effortlessly graceful and sexy. I was too exhausted to care overmuch, though I still needed some answers. Before I lost my train of thought again, I asked the question that had been eating at me for the last couple of days.

"Arnold gave me a charm before I fought you the first time. It was supposed to keep vampires from toying with my thoughts and emotions. I can sort of understand how Max got around it, seeing how I was bound to him. What I don't get is how you got to me. How did you do it before the bond?"

He gave me a pleasant, all too innocent smile. "I'm an ancient, elder vampire, Shiarra. I think that speaks for itself."

"No," I replied, dissatisfied with his answer. "It doesn't make sense. How could you defeat mage-work like this? I could shrug off Dawn's glamour like it was nothing, and yet I watched her turn vampires into slaves to fight for her. What you did was . . . different. I don't understand it."

His response was unexpected. He looked sheepish, rubbing at his eyes with his fingertips as he tried to hide something that looked suspiciously like embarrassment. His apologetic manner was cute. I'd never thought I'd refer to the vampire as cute, not even in my head, but his awkward attempt at collecting his thoughts was strangely endearing. Even if the next words to come out of his mouth were anything but.

"I'm sure you've figured out by now my specialty is in using my abilities to cloud the minds of others, to manipulate emotions, and to use it as a form of control over people when I need to. Most vampires don't have the edge I do over wards against mind magic. Even Max does not have my ability to break down walls of will."

My alarm must have been obvious, since he opened his eyes to study me when I whispered my next question. "Have you been doing that to me all along? Does being bound by blood make it easier for you to get past my defenses?"

"If you weren't wearing that charm, you wouldn't be able to come up with such a lucid question. It does make it more difficult for me to, as you put it, 'get past your defenses,' but it wasn't impossible before you were bound."

"Why was I able to think straight until Max called me, then? Shouldn't I have been drawn to him all the time? Or to you?"

"No. With practice, most of us can expend effort to dampen or strengthen the attraction inherent in a blood bond. We can fine-tune it to suit whatever serves our purposes at the time. Max and I have had a long time to perfect that skill."

I didn't say anything, just stared down at the cup in my hands and watched the surface of the liquid tremble.

"Theoretically," he continued, "if you were not wearing the charm, our hold on you would have a greater effect on your thought process. The bond may have temporarily displaced any trace of your own thoughts, your personality would be gone, making you only what we wanted you to be. The change would last for the first few weeks while the bond set in, augmented by additional doses of your host's blood. Not that it matters at this point." He sighed deeply, then continued. "Aside from all of that, the bond isn't why I asked you to come here. It may be an unnecessary worry, but I have the feeling Athena may attempt to contact you. If she does, I would strongly suggest you run as far and fast away from her as possible."

Right now wasn't the best time to think about what might happen if Royce changed his mind about leaving me alone. If he offered to prolong the bond with his vampiric charm up on full, there was little chance I'd deny him. Grasping at any opportunity to change the subject, I quickly asked the first question that came to mind.

"Who the hell is Athena?"

Royce smiled, though there wasn't any humor in it. "Athena is the vampire who made Max and me what we are."

"Your sire."

"Yes."

I mulled over his words, thinking about some of the things Max had said earlier. Suddenly, I wasn't quite so tired anymore. Royce was in the mood to answer questions, and I was going to take advantage of it.

"Who is Helen of Volos? Why did Max keep talking about her?"

Royce's expression abruptly darkened, and he no longer met my gaze. "She was something of a bone of contention between us at one time. We were both relatively newly turned vampires. Our passions ran stronger, less controlled, and it was nearly the death of us both."

"Tell me about her," I demanded, though I softened it with a "please" when I saw him tense up.

"First, try to understand what it is for vampires to be as we are. The one who makes us holds us in a bond stronger than the one you feel for me right now."

That was a scary thought. I shivered before gesturing for him to continue. "I think I get the idea. Go on."

"Max and I loved our sire with great passion. Even men who were not bound or made into vampires by her desired her. Some went to great feats of skill or strength, greater than was normal even during that age of heroism and magic, just to win a smile from her lips or the favorable brush of her hand. Wars have been fought in her name, and she reveled in that adoration and devotion. Thus, you can imagine her fury when she discovered Max felt love for another woman."

I crept forward, settling cautiously on the edge of the futon. It was so low to the ground, I felt awkward sitting there with my knees practically up under my chin. What a vampire who was impervious to the cold needed with a down comforter was beyond me, but it was plenty comfy to sit on.

Considering his words, I hazarded a guess, intrigued by this glimpse into ancient history. "Are you saying she got pissed when she found out, and sent you to go do something about it? Get Helen out of the way?"

Royce closed his eyes and nodded, his expression remaining carefully neutral. The barely detectable edge to his voice clued me in that he was not happy telling this story. "I was to seduce her away from Max, then destroy her as his punishment. After a time, I found I did not want to kill her. Like Max, I soon fell in love with her, too.

"She was easy to like—pretty, and a very warm soul on the surface. While she did not have the classic, statuesque beauty of Athena, there was much more to her than simple looks. However, Helen had a very shrewd mind. I almost did not discover that fact in time. Max did not believe me when I told him she knew what we were. She told one of the local warriors of the blood-drinking monsters in the people's midst, and promised him she'd lure us someplace where we could be cornered and destroyed. That way, she'd be rid of us both while opening herself up as an offering to her champion."

The slight sneer on his lips did not hide Royce's pain at this betrayal, even after all these years. I placed a hand lightly on his knee, as I was sitting too far down on the bed to reach his arm or shoulder. I kept my voice as low and neutral as possible since I didn't think he'd take pity or sorrow well from me.

"I'm sorry."

"Don't be," he muttered, not opening his eyes. It was probably the only reason I could think straight just then. "Max did not believe me when I told him. He didn't want to believe Helen was capable of such deception. I brought him with me to the place where she was to meet the man she'd arranged to have kill us. We were too late; a division of the local town guard was already searching for us, and I reacted badly to her betrayal. Even with the evidence right in front of him, Max still thought I was only acting out of jealous rage. We fought until I managed to pin him to a tree with my sword—I didn't want him dead. I was sorely wounded from the battle and Helen was the closest human. Though I should have held my rage in check, I fed too deeply and killed her, fleeing before Max could free himself."

I listened in spellbound fascination, finding a few things Max said suddenly making sense. "So Athena was pleased by what you did and rewarded you, and then cast Max away, didn't she?"

"Yes," he replied, voice faint. "Max was not allowed to come back to her side for over a century. He was lucky to have survived so young without the benefit of a mentor and the protection afforded by an elder. By the time he returned to her, I had been set loose to expand our sire's holdings and influence in other countries. We have rarely crossed paths since then. I never really bore Max any true animosity, but he has viewed me as a threat or an adversary ever since."

"He thought if you loved me, he could use me to take out his revenge by making you feel the same loss he did when Helen died."

"Exactly."

"Wow," I said, though that seemed pretty inadequate under the circumstances.

"Wow, indeed." Royce smirked, opening those glittering black eyes to regard me. It took an effort to concentrate on what he was saying instead of drowning in the depths of his gaze. "We vampires tend to hold grudges. We do have the luxury of time in order to plot our vengeance in ways no other creature on heaven or earth can conceive. He set himself up so, if he succeeded tonight, he had many things to gain by my death. Accomplishing that would have been made easier if I'd been incapacitated with grief as he was by Helen's murder. He's been planning my downfall for a long, long time."

I decided to ask the one thing that bothered me most about this story. It wasn't the right question to be asking and probably didn't matter, but I had to know.

"Would his plan have worked if he killed me? Do I mean that much to you?"

Royce arched an eyebrow at me, a hint of a grin tugging at his lips. "You can't tell as much for yourself?"

The slightly playful turn of the conversation threw me. "Uh, no. Not really."

He closed his eyes and settled into the pillows, his roguish grin growing wider. For once, the sight of his fangs didn't inspire any fear in me.

"Go back to your boyfriend's side and get some rest. I'll answer that question another time."

I felt the compulsion behind the words, the touch of his will making it an order instead of a simple brush-off. It pissed me off, but I had to obey, rising unsteadily to my feet.

"Asshole," I muttered, and made sure it was loud enough so he could hear it.

His soft laughter followed me out of the room.

Chapter 36

I woke up in a dark, unfamiliar place, the smell of vampire and Were overwhelmingly thick on and around me. For a second, I felt a rush of panic, but only for as long as it took me to remember I wasn't at home in my own bed.

I was sprawled across someone's chest—Chaz. He was awake, but unmoving, lying quietly beneath me. The others were awake, but seemed happy enough to lounge on the cushions. We were in an open space, the only illumination coming from a computer monitor halfway across the room from where we lay. With the windows shuttered up tight, I couldn't tell if it was day or night.

When a dark figure cut across the meager illumination given off by the computer monitor, I started. Chaz's arm tightened around my waist in response.

Royce turned back to the desk and tapped a few keys. He made a vaguely dissatisfied sound under his breath before turning away from the computer, walking past us. He glanced our way as he moved toward the stairs.

"Finally awake, hmm? Mouse arranged some food and clothing for you both. I'd suggest taking some time to call your office, perhaps your family. The newshounds seem to have gotten quite out of control regarding your disappearance."

"Good morning to you, too," I muttered. My ribs and joints ached enough to merit a groan as I sat up, fixing Royce with a mild glare as I lay on the sarcasm. It came more easily than it had yesterday, even though I still felt the desire to get up and wrap my arms around him, to press as close to his body as I was to Chaz right now. "Did you sleep well? Oh, sure, I did, too."

His lips twitched as he suppressed a smile, turning away to head down the stairs without another word.

Chaz levered himself up on his elbows, chuckling. "Ease up, sleepyhead. Much as I hate admitting it, he did save your life." He reached out to brush a hand over my cheek, tucking some stray curls behind my ear. "Don't be too hard on him yet. We still have to put up with him for a few days. You can give him hell after the bond wears off and you don't have to stay here anymore. Sound good?"

"Yeah, I guess," I muttered, chastised but unrepentant.

We went downstairs and enjoyed some of the best food I'd ever had. Someone had done a run to *La Petite Boisson*, the exclusive French restaurant Royce owned, and picked up something special from their kitchen. The cream sauce on the sautéed chicken tasted divine. Devon, Tiny, Chaz, and the other two werewolves ate with gusto. If they felt any tension for having Mouse hovering over them, watching them eat, none of them acted like it.

I was glad to get my own clothes back, now nicely washed and neatly folded with the belt and guns arranged on top of the pile. Even my trench coat had been cleaned, smelling again like fresh leather instead of the charnel reek of blood. Someone had done a reasonably good job of figuring out my size, and a pair of designer jeans and a light sweater had been set aside for me in case I didn't want to wander around looking like I'd walked off the set of the latest *Terminator* movie.

Royce's people had been busy elsewhere, too. There was no sign of my battle with Peter anywhere in the hallway on the second floor. The body and all the blood had been cleaned up, leaving the place smelling of some strong cleaner and a fresh coat of floor wax. If the eggshell white walls had been spattered with gore during the fight, you couldn't tell it anymore.

I didn't want to think too hard on Peter's death. I also wasn't brave enough to go see if they'd done the same cleanup job in the basement.

You might not have ever known the Showdown from Hell had taken place here last night. Of all things, it looked *normal*. The only sign of a cleanup job was the lingering scent of ammonia. The few people puttering around the halls barely took notice of us, giving polite nods or smiles, for the most part ignoring the interlopers in their midst. Their lack of concern was downright eerie.

The only ones who paid us any mind were Royce and Mouse. Royce showed up before we'd finished our meal. The two vampires watched us eat with an odd sort of fascination. Maybe they missed eating solid foods. Admittedly, it might have bothered me more if I hadn't been so intent on watching Royce in return. It took actual, physical exertion on my part not to get up from the table and move closer to him, to touch or please him somehow, to do something to make him turn a warm smile on me just one more time.

It took more effort than I wanted to think about to excuse myself to flee to another room so I wouldn't act on those urges. I borrowed Chaz's cell phone and a pad and pen from Mouse, grimacing when I saw it was past seven o'clock on Monday night. Jen was probably wondering what the hell happened to me and Sara. I doubted my partner had gone in to the office either, what with Arnold being in jail and all.

Though I did want to find out how Sara and Arnold

were doing, the first thing I did was call my own cell phone to collect any messages. The cheap piece of plastic crap was probably long dead and gone. I only hoped Max hadn't thought to copy down any of the contact info stored in the phone before he destroyed it.

When I called, it went straight to voice mail, which was completely full. I resigned myself to listening to all the messages, taking brief notes. Half the messages were from some obnoxious reporter who had somehow gotten my private number. Two were from Officer Lerian. I had a bad feeling he wouldn't take any excuses about why Chaz and I hadn't shown up to give our statements. One message from Sara, another from Arnold, both wondering where I was. Two from Jen: one about a client calling to follow up on her case, and another asking where Sara and I were since it was well past ten on Monday morning and should she rebook my appointments for later in the week.

Worst of all, three messages were from my parents. Two from my mom, falling into hysterics both times. First, because of something in the news about me being attacked by Peter and looking like I was being all kissy-face with Royce, and another because the cops swung by and said I was reported missing.

The worst one was from Dad, who sounded nice and level—the deceptive calm before the storm. He told me to call back and explain what I was doing messing with the Others again and mentioned how my mother was worried sick. He wanted to know exactly why I hadn't said anything about being contracted to Royce for the last six months or so and expected to get answers as soon as I got his message.

That was a phone call I was *not* looking forward to making.

So first I called Sara. She'd used her best lawyer-speak and still hadn't been able to get Arnold out of the slammer. Apparently, Royce's description of Arnold "causing a bit of a scene" was an understatement.

Sara said they weren't letting him go until he agreed to release the detective who had been questioning him. He'd used some metaphysical superglue to keep the officer's butt adhered to his chair while Arnold went to find someone who would listen to him. The other officers didn't take it very well. Since he hadn't technically hurt the guy, they couldn't do much more than keep him locked up until he agreed to release the spell. Arnold was sticking to his guns and demanding the officer apologize for calling him a spark, a no-talent Copperfield rip-off, and a few other more creative epithets, before he'd let him go.

So far it was still a stalemate, though Sara said when she went to grab some coffee, she saw the odds on the betting pool was on the officer cracking in the next two to three hours. Rumor had it the chief was getting pissed and putting the pressure on him to apologize, particularly after Sara started hinting that a discrimination suit would be forthcoming after the officer used those delightful little expletives against someone who'd come to him for help, not as a suspect.

We laughed about it together and I told her where she could find me. I didn't give her the dirty details about what happened last night. This morning. Whatever. That could wait until we were face to face.

I didn't have a number to reach Jen and tell her I was okay, but Sara reassured me she'd told Jen we'd both be out for a couple of days, and to rearrange our schedules. That was nothing new in our line of business. Hopefully Jen didn't find it too alarming.

I did want to work out swinging by the office tomorrow so I could wrap up the Pryce investigation and ship the invoice off to the agent, Cheryl Benedict. As long as the insurance company paid on time, which they mostly did, the check would cover next month's rent. Officer Lerian would have to wait until I found out from Royce exactly how much was safe to tell the police about what Max had done.

Obviously he didn't want them involved or he would have called them in while Max was entrenched in his home.

No way was I calling the reporter back. That left my parents.

It was cowardly of me, but I was relieved to get the answering machine instead of the panicky voice of my mother or, worse, the cold, iron-hard tones of my dad. I left a message, figuring that was better than leaving them completely in the dark.

"Hi, it's me. I'm sorry I haven't called back for a couple days, but I'm fine. Everything is okay now. My cell phone is missing, but I'll call you when I get back home in a few days. I love you both."

I ended the call, feeling immeasurably relieved at not having to explain myself any further. Maybe staying here with Royce for a few days was a blessing in disguise. It would give my parents time to blow off some steam.

It would also give me time to come up with a suitably PG version of what my life had turned into these last few months so my parents wouldn't go into an apoplectic fit when I explained why I'd legally bound myself to a vampire. Somehow, I'd also have to figure out how to keep them in the dark about Chaz being a Were and Arnold being a mage. My parents are very Catholic, and while I wouldn't say they go to every Sunday Mass, they still think of anything Other as an abomination against God. Not that I could blame them. I'd felt that way, too, right up until I'd gotten close enough to see beyond the furry or fanged exterior.

When I was done with my calls, I wandered back to Mouse's living room, noting before anything else that Royce had gone. The rest of the guys were talking to each other in hushed tones. They quieted the instant I walked into the room, silencing their obvious plotting.

"What's happening?" I asked, tossing Chaz his cell phone. He fumbled it—which solidified my notion they were up to some no-good, down and dirty scheming without me. A Were, graced with some of the most uncanny speed, strength, agility, and heightened senses of all the Others, having a tough time catching a cell phone? Please.

"Nothing to worry about," he reassured me, a little too cheerfully, a little too quickly. I frowned at him. "I have to go to work. I've already missed a few appointments with my regulars, and I can't miss one of my new leads tonight."

Chaz was a personal trainer. Lifting weights was a tad redundant considering his nature, but hey, it did fabulous things to that already fabulous body. I could hardly complain.

"All right," I said after a noticeable pause, still wondering what exactly they had been talking about. "What time will you be back?"

A shamefaced expression crossed his features as he floundered a bit attempting to come up with a reply. It dawned on me he'd been plotting with the other guys to find a way out of here. I narrowed my eyes at him and folded my arms. This better be good.

"I'm not sure. I've got some stuff to get done tonight. Some pack business to attend to, that sort of thing. It may keep me pretty late."

Hmph. He was probably trying to get out of here because he didn't want to be hanging around a vampire's den. I knew the feeling. If I wasn't coasting on the bond, I'd have been clawing at the walls trying to figure out how the hell to get out of here, too. After all, I was one of a handful of humans in a building full of vampires. I had more to worry about than he did. However, I did have *some* compassion, and relaxed my stance as I gestured to the door.

"If you guys are antsy being cooped up in here, you don't have to hang around on my account."

Devon frowned severely at me. "We all have things to do. We were just trying to decide who should stay here with

you. At least one of us is going to be at your side at all
times until the bond is gone."

I rolled my eyes and settled down on the couch next to
Chaz. All he did was give me a quick hug before standing
up. Knits between my brows deepened as he gestured to
Tiny and Devon, sounding defensive even though I hadn't
tried to argue.

"When one of them can't be here, I'll send someone
from the pack."

Only when one of "them" couldn't be with me?

"What about you? Aren't you going to be around, too?"

He stiffened, barely noticeable. If I hadn't been watching him so closely, I would have missed it. "No. Just call
me when you're back home, and I'll come over."

"What? Why?"

"I can't." He looked away from me, not meeting my
eyes. "Don't ask me to stay here and watch you stare at
Royce like he's the love of your life. You have no idea how
much it hurts to see that, knowing you've never looked at
me that way."

He glanced up at me, blue eyes meeting mine before
flashing away. Not so quickly that I couldn't see the pain
reflected there. He must have seen how much I was struggling while we were eating. How I'd been watching Royce
so closely despite all my better intentions.

"I'll be there when you need me, but don't ask me to
stay around for this."

That stunned me. The other guys had gone terribly still
and quiet, trying not to be noticed. My voice was strange
to my own ears, strangled sounding.

"Are you breaking up with me?"

He glanced at me again quickly, too quickly, then
looked away.

"No. No, I'm not doing that. I love you, but I just can't
stay here right now. It hurts too much for me to stand around
and watch you watch him." Those crystalline irises were

hidden behind fallen lids, a pained expression crossing his features as he clenched his hands into tight fists at his side. By the time he met my eyes, he'd schooled his features into a passably blank expression. I knew enough now to realize he was hurt.

"Good-bye, Shia."

I could only watch, hot tears trickling down my cheeks while Chaz silently turned on his heel and walked out of the room.

Chapter 37

The next few days were a dull, gray haze in my mind. I felt like the biggest shit in history for not having noticed how much my infatuation with Royce was hurting Chaz, for not hiding it better.

Chaz had been good as his word. Tiny and Devon left the same night, right after one of Chaz's wolves showed up to take their place to keep an eye on me. My "guards" came in shifts, sticking around for a few hours until being relieved by the next Sunstriker. Not one of them was happy with the duty, but they weren't content to leave me alone with vampires for any length of time either.

Royce didn't seem to mind having me tailing him when he worked at one of his offices. (God, how many offices does a guy need?) He left me to my own devices for the most part while he concentrated on whatever he was doing.

There were a few times he went somewhere without me and my watchdogs in tow. Usually that meant leaving me with Mouse, who tried to keep me busy and cheer me up. It was a bit of a silly thing for a vamp to be doing, and I probably didn't take enough notice save for when she and/or the Weres had to forcibly keep me from answering Max's call. He made attempts to draw me to him at random intervals, hoping to catch Royce or his people off guard.

It creeped me out when it happened, but also gave me a new appreciation for everything Royce and the Sunstrikers were doing.

When I was with Royce, Max's call had no effect on me. The dull ache of Chaz being gone was alleviated and replaced by a temporary haze of adoration and euphoria by Royce's presence, but it didn't take long for me to crash back into a funk. By the third day, even being close to the vampire wasn't always doing the trick to lift my spirits. Some part of me was recognizing how artificial that momentary joy was. The only solace I had was in knowing I could call Chaz once I was home and could do something to make it up to him. Somehow.

Arnold got the apology he wanted from the pissy detective. He and Sara showed up late on the same night Chaz and the others left. Arnold told me regretfully there was nothing to be done except let the bond and the desire for blood run their course. Sara had been pretty white-faced while Arnold explained to her exactly what Royce and Max's blood had done to me. I think my expression must have mirrored hers, because he gave us both some insight and details neither vampire had made me privy to.

Even through my haze of adoration for Royce, I knew I needed to get the hell out of Dodge the minute the stuff was out of my system. I made Sara promise to stay as far away from me as possible until the blood worked its course. She blessedly didn't argue, though that in and of itself was frightening.

It took me a couple days to recall Mouse's offer to help break Max's hold on me. When I asked her about it, she explained to me that she would have done exactly as Royce had—bound me to her, kept me close, and waited for it to

wear off. She may or may not have let me go once the bond
wore off, depending on whether I showed signs of being
too dependent on her to handle the separation.

My ability to trust a vampire's statement at face value,
already low, has since plummeted to new depths of paranoia and distrust.

I remained down and bitter right up to the twelfth day
following the battle. That was when the withdrawal pangs
hit. The pain dragged me out of my funk and had me wishing, just for a little while, that somebody would kill me already and get it over with.

My insides felt like they were on fire. My stomach
cramped painfully and I desperately craved something to
drink no matter how much coffee or water or soda I con-
sumed. Royce was there, but did nothing other than hold
me while I alternated between shivers so hard my teeth rat-
tled, and flashes of fever so hot I wondered why there
wasn't steam coming off me in scalding waves.

My head ached abominably. Though I begged and
pleaded and cried for him to give me a taste, only a few
drops of blood, just enough to make the pain stop, Royce
never said a thing. When it got so bad I tore at my throat
to reach that burning pain, dig it out, and make it end, he
held my wrists and kept me pinned in his lap. I alternated
between cursing him eternally for being such a heartless
bastard, to pleading with any tiny shreds of humanity he
might have to help make it stop.

That was not one of my better moments.

It was like that most of the night. Maybe an hour before
dawn, the worst of it tapered off and I was able to finally,
blessedly, sleep. When I woke up, I was on Mouse's couch
and none of the vampires were in sight. Dillon, the Were
left behind to keep an eye on me, had his head tilted back
against the headrest of the chair and was snoring away.

When I stood up, I almost fell right back on my ass.
My legs felt weak, rubbery, and a ghost of the headache

remained. Once I regained some of my balance, I rapidly crept away from Dillon, not looking back as I rushed into the hall. Panic made me forget everything—socks, shoes, trench coat. I didn't have any money or a phone to call my friends for help, but I wasn't thinking that clearly.

The guy seated by the table in the foyer dropped the paperback he was reading, standing up and making a grab for me. He shouted something, probably to stop, but I ignored it. Ducking around him, I rushed out the front door. Summoning every last ounce of strength I had, I escaped into the cheerful autumn sunlight, welcoming the cold wind on my skin. It helped clear my head as I put as much distance between myself and the vampire den as possible.

God, oh God, what had I *done*?

I don't know why I felt so much panic. Why I was blind and uncaring as to where I was going. Why I needed to get as far away from this place as fast as my legs would carry me. After all, if Royce or any of his people had meant to hurt or use me, they'd had plenty of chances these last few days while I was so star-struck and enamored, I couldn't see straight. Even in my blind hysteria, I knew I wasn't running because of the Others. It wasn't Royce or Dillon or Mouse who frightened me.

It was *me* I was running from.

See, the funny thing about that is you can't escape yourself. Even as I tried to forget what I'd done, tried to forget Peter's blood on my hands, Royce's blood in my mouth, Max's fangs in my flesh, the pain in Chaz's eyes when he looked at me, I knew I couldn't get away from it. Self-loathing washed over me in a sickening wave, and I ignored the startled looks of the people around me, the crush of traffic, the looming buildings. All I wanted was for the sunlight to warm my skin, to wash away this taint on my soul, to put as much distance between myself and Royce's home as possible so I could forget all I had done there.

I veered into the park, losing myself in the trees. Barely noticing my feet were bleeding and lacerated from going barefoot.

I'd begged, not just asked, but *begged* for Royce to give me more of his blood.

I stopped, my stomach heaving as I gasped in air and swallowed back the urge to throw up. I was alone in a copse of trees, thick maple leaves providing shade and privacy. A few dappled streaks of sunlight between the trees illuminated the dust motes dancing in the light breeze. I crept to one of those beams of sunlight, using both hands to wipe tears away as I closed my burning eyes and turned my face up to the pure, unsullied warmth, breathing it in like my life depended on it. Even the heat of the sun couldn't banish the soul-deep chill I was feeling.

The one thing I feared most in life was being bound to a vampire. That fear had been realized when Max took me. So deep under their influence was I that by the time Royce had done it, too, it hadn't seemed like such a tremendously bad idea. I had willingly put myself under his power. I had wanted, *needed* to stay there, happily fixed to his will and jumping to do his bidding like a puppet on a string.

And he *let me go*.

Royce always had a million and one reasons he didn't reveal behind the things he did. Everything was calculated, designed to win him some manner of advantage or influence, to put you more under his thumb. So why hadn't he reinforced the bond when I was literally begging him to do it? Why hadn't he taken advantage of it, when he'd so obviously tried to influence me in so many ways before? Why hadn't he used the bond to the hilt and ordered me to give him my blood and my body the way he'd clearly wanted me to before all of this had happened?

It didn't make any sense. It also didn't make me less afraid. In fact, his actions made me even more terrified.

His actions, or lack thereof, meant he was manipulating me in some other fashion—somehow I hadn't thought of yet.

Lowering to my knees, I put my face in my hands, and wept until there were no more tears left to cry. I'd come so close to losing my life, my will, my freedom, and my soul, I would have completely lost it if I weren't already so numb from my emotional breakdown.

When the tears stopped, I thought it mightily unfair the sky should be such a flawless, cloudless blue, and the sun shining so cheerfully in that sky. There was even a bird singing in one of the nearby trees—a raucous, joyful song. It was more irritating than comforting. Especially since my feet had really started to sting, and now I was going to have to either walk back to Royce's place and explain myself, or figure out some magic means of getting home.

I raced a hand through my hair, brushing the unruly red curls out of my eyes while I cursed and limped my way back toward the street. I hadn't been paying a lot of attention to where I was coming from or where I was going while I was running, so I took a little time to see if anything around me looked familiar.

Surprisingly, it was a face rather than a place that caught my eye.

"Fancy seeing you here!" came a cheerful, gravelly voice. "Don't tell me you're still in trouble with vampires?"

I dredged up a smile for the Were cab driver who had taken me from Royce's office back to my car a long time ago. Ironic that the last time he'd seen me, I'd also been crying my eyes out. That time, it was over Royce backing me into a corner and making me agree to sign contractual papers, leaving me without any legal protection from him. Now I was crying my eyes out because, in a twisted sense, he hadn't taken advantage of the benefits those papers gave him.

"Unfortunately, yeah, that's the kind of trouble I am in," I said, using the sleeve of my sweater to wipe away some of the tear tracks from my cheeks. I don't know if it did much good, but the cabbie was still gratingly jovial and wasn't making it a point of rubbing in that I looked like a slice of hell warmed over.

He took a bite out of the hotdog he was holding, leaning against his cab parked at the curb. The restrained power radiating off him was as I remembered, along with the ridiculous amount of thick black hair visible on his arms and peeking out in tufts at the neck of his shirt. Weres are usually pretty furry, even as humans; he was no exception.

"She break up with you or something?"

"What?" Confusion took me. Then I remembered how last time he'd thought I'd gotten in a fight with my vampire lover. My female vampire lover. Who didn't exist. I sighed and rubbed my hand over my face, trying to think of a tactful way to explain to him that I was not a lesbian, nor was I sleeping with vampires.

His free hand reached up to rub at the salt-and-pepper stubble on his jaw as he eyed me, gauging my hesitation before he spoke again.

"Well, either way, you look like you could use some help. Do you need a ride to a hospital?"

He pointedly glanced down at my feet and I blushed a bit, feeling stupid for having reacted so poorly when I woke up. Running away didn't solve anything.

"Actually, I could use a lift home. I don't have any cash on me," I admitted.

"Don't worry about it. You can always pay me later."

I felt myself sag with relief. That small kindness was almost more than I could bear.

His cab reeked of stale cigarettes and old fast food mingled with Were-musk, just like last time. The cabbie kept up a pleasant, unobtrusive chatter the whole ride back to my place. I think he intuitively knew how stressed out I was, and how very much I needed to be kept focused on something other than the thoughts rampaging through my head.

It was only after he dropped me off in front of my building, waving as he screeched into an illegal U-turn, that I realized I had never learned his name.

Chapter 38

The next few weeks were centered on me trying to pick up the shattered pieces of my life.

The bullet holes in the walls of my apartment were plastered and painted over. The pissed-off clients whose appointments I had missed ended up with discounts sufficient to make them happy and me grit my teeth.

I bought a new cell phone and wasted three hours digging up all the phone numbers I needed to add into the replacement. With the bond gone, Sara lost some of her edgy nervousness around me. Officer Lerian forgave Chaz and I for blowing off making our statements once I gave him everything I knew about Max Carlyle. Funny how handing him the keys to unlock the mystery behind one of the biggest slaughters this city has ever seen, along with information to track down the bastard who did it, might make the police forgive me.

I dug up the number to Jim Pradiz, the reporter who'd written the article that had me spazzing out in the grocery store. I gave him a statement to chew over so people could know the real story behind my disappearance, Max Carlyle's plan, and how all those people died in Twisted Temptations. I kept the White Hats, Dawn, Arnold,

Sara, and Chaz out of it. J.P. stayed true to form and added embellishments, but none of them included anything to do with me being a vampire's toy or Royce having any hand in the deaths of the revelers at the club.

Officer Lerian wasn't too happy I went to the press, but the police backed me up and concurred with my story.

Devon and Tiny disappeared to parts unknown. Neither one of them returned to Royce's or tried to contact me after the night Chaz told me what a shit I was being. I could have gotten in touch with them via Jack, but that wasn't an avenue of possibility I wanted to explore. Jack has not tried contacting me either. I'd like to keep it that way.

As soon as I got my car out of the impound, I went to see Mom and Dad. I omitted a few details, like how my boyfriend was a Were and my friend Arnold was a mage, but otherwise told them pretty much everything. I explained about the contract that tied me to Royce and what led up to him showing up at my apartment. I even showed them the teeny, tiny scars left behind from Max and Peter biting me. Mom nearly fainted. Dad got this dark look like he was ready to start whittling up some stakes and go hunt down Max himself.

After my explanation, my parents decided they weren't speaking to me while they got a handle on the fact that their only daughter was consorting with Others. We all agreed we'd take some time to cool off and just have a nice, sane, normal family dinner once Thanksgiving rolled around. No need to tell my brothers, Mikey and Damien, about any of it either. Not unless they saw the news and came around asking questions.

That was just fine with me. My parents had to find out sometime about the wacky turn my life was taking. Frankly, they took it better than I expected.

I haven't been able to sleep well since the bond broke. Without it, I can't stop thinking about all the things I've done and experienced thanks to my ties with the Others.

What Peter looked like after I smashed his face in. How it felt to drive the stake into John's chest. The whispered encouragement to kill and hurt things I gave in to when the belt was around my waist. The unnatural attraction I'd felt to both Max and Royce.

Sometimes I wake up in cold sweats, my hands rubbing at the place where Peter and Max bit me. I wish I could forget what it felt like, what they had done.

What I had done.

One of the things I've learned from all of this is that, even though the visible scars might fade, some emotional ones take a lot longer to heal.

Things between Chaz and I are settling down. He's distant with me now in a way he's never been before. I wish I knew how to fix it and make things right between us. Somehow I get the feeling I broke what we had into too many pieces to put our relationship back together again. Still, I'm trying. The dinner we had a few nights ago was like it used to be, a pleasant escape where we talked about what was going on in our lives, not about Max Carlyle, Alec Royce, or anything related to me fighting with or being bound to vampires. It's better, if not exactly the same.

Royce hasn't made any attempt to call or see me since the day I freaked out and ran off. All he did was send a package to my office a few days after I left. He'd sent my clothes, weapons, and boots, along with a little note. It took a few days for me to screw up enough courage to open the plain white envelope it was sealed in and read what it said.

I'm sorry for the pain you had to endure while you were with me. I know those words are inadequate, but please believe they are sincere. If you need help, or a friend, don't hesitate to call on me.

—Alec

* * *

So that's my story of how I (kind of) became a White Hat, and (temporarily) became blood-bonded by Royce, and (no, really) learned that he wasn't such a bad guy after all.

Please read on for an exciting sneak peek
of the next Shiarra Waynest novel,
DECEIVED BY THE OTHERS,
coming in July 2011!

My hands shook as I put my pen to the contract laid out before me. The *Notice of Mutual Consent to Human/Other Citizen Relationship and Contractual Binding Agreement* that would permanently cement my relationship with Chaz.

If he'd sign it too, that is.

"Shia?"

The pen left a streak behind when my hand jerked. I looked up, quickly shuffling some other papers over the contract to hide it amidst the clutter on my desk.

"Yes?"

Jen, our receptionist and bookkeeper, peered into my office over the rims of her glasses. She eyed the papers like she knew I was hiding something, but was too tactful to say anything about it.

"What was the name of that crazy guy who was here a month or so ago? The one you didn't want to take calls or appointments from?"

I wrinkled my nose. "You're talking about that tall blond guy, right? His name is Jack."

She nodded and disappeared around the corner. Curiosity piqued and the contract momentarily forgotten, I rose from my squeaky office chair to lean against the door frame. Jen was on the phone, her feet propped up on her desk while she wrapped up a game of solitaire on the computer.

"No, sir, I just checked and she's in with a client. I'm sorry, but I'm not about to interrupt her meeting. Like I said, you can leave her a voicemail or I can take a message."

I frowned, folding my arms as I watched her multi-task her game and the phone call. Jack calling wasn't a good sign. The man was a White Hat, one of those crazy vigilante groups that go around destroying any supernatural critters that cross their paths. The first time I'd met him, he'd threatened me at knifepoint to join his cause. The second time around, he walked into my office in broad daylight and held a gun on me because he thought I was working for vampires. Aside from being a few beers short of a six-pack, he was bad news, pure and simple.

"Like I said, *sir*, she is not available." Jen's tone had turned professionally icy, and I strongly considered giving her a raise. She was doing an excellent job of getting rid of the pushy creep. "You're free to leave a message with me or call back another time." She paused, listened to his reply. Shortly she was nodding along to whatever he was saying with a sly, triumphant smile. "Yes, I'll see she gets it right away. What's the message?"

Swinging her feet off the desk, she opened up an e-mail and clattered out Jack's message. She saw me out of the corner of her eye and made a face, though she kept her voice cool and polite on the phone.

"Yes, I'll get this to her as soon as she's free. Thanks for calling Halloway and Waynest Investigations."

"Thanks for getting rid of him," I said as soon as she plunked the phone down. "That guy is nothing but trouble."

"No kidding. I'll forward the message since he left a phone number, but I don't know if it'll mean anything to you. All he said was 'tell her this time it isn't us.' Any idea what he means?"

I frowned, brows furrowing. "That's all he had to say? 'It isn't us'?"

"Yeah."

"I have no idea what that's supposed to mean."

Shaking her head, she turned back to her computer and sent me the e-mail, my preferred form of message. Sara was much more organized than I was when it came to keeping track of Post-it memos. My desk was a rattrap clutter of dust bunnies, chewed up pens, and scattered business cards that should've been filed away or organized somehow long ago.

"If he shows up here looking for me while I'm out of town, call the police. He's a nuisance."

"Okay," she agreed, not bothering to turn away from her game. Shrugging off my uneasiness, I turned back to my office, but she stopped me with another word. "Oh, Shia?"

"Yes?"

"I almost forgot. Some guy named Alex or something left a message on the main voicemail for you last night. I forwarded it to your phone."

I'd ignored my calls earlier so I could avoid any new emergencies getting piled on me before going out of town. Which Alex might have attempted to reach me before I left? Alex Mills, the insurance agent? No, he was out of town on vacation. Alex Temps, the client I tracked down a stolen antique for a couple weeks ago? No, no, he had bitched about my rates from start to finish and hadn't been in the least grateful when I completed the job. He'd already paid, shortchanging me by $150, the stingy bastard. I doubted I'd ever hear from him again. Who could it be?

Wait a minute. "Alex" calling me right around the same time as Jack the White Hat?

Oh, no. No, no, no. That could only mean one thing.

Stifling a shudder, I made sure to keep my expression calm and blank. I didn't want to upset Jen. If she'd listened to the message more closely or caught me looking upset, she'd realize who it was, too. Her wounded, disapproving looks were the last thing I wanted to deal with right now.

"Thanks, Jen. I'll check it out."

"No prob."

I closed the door, stepping back around my desk and moving the files aside so I could review the contract one more time. My concentration was shot, my good mood and anticipation for my vacation soured in the uncertainty that came with having a White Hat and Alec Royce both trying to get in touch with me again.

The clock on my computer read 3:15 PM, which meant I still had a little over two hours left before my boyfriend Chaz would swing by to pick me up for my first real vacation in months.

Being stuck recuperating in a hospital or taking time off from work to wait for the effects of a vampire's blood bond to wear off does *not* count as a vacation, by the way.

Sara was supposed to keep an eye on my apartment and my messages while I was gone. It was only for a few days, but that was more (voluntary) time off than I'd taken in quite a while. Her boyfriend was letting me borrow one of his laptops so I could keep an eye on my e-mail and stay in touch. He'd threatened to sic his familiar, a tiny black mouse named Bob, on me every night for a week if anything happened to his coveted Fragware 5000. I'd sworn up and down I'd treat it like my own. Seriously, who wants a *mouse* crawling on them in their sleep? Ugh.

Anyway, things should've been winding down. My current clients were given the message that I would be out and Jen was supposed to refer everything to Sara until I got back. Jack and Royce surfacing again changed all of that.

I frowned down at the blinking message light on my phone, strongly considering waiting until I returned to town to listen to it. Alec Royce, like Jack the White Hat, was straight up bad news. He was a wealthy, good-looking man who had made a couple of half-hearted attempts to seduce me away from my boyfriend Chaz. We should've been able to go our separate ways since I'd saved his life, and he'd returned the favor by saving mine.

However, the guy was a vampire, and I should've known better than to think that he'd forgotten about me over the last month. He'd used threats and coercion to get me to sign a contract that bound me to him by letter of the law, and then later bound me to him in a much more tangible way—by blood—in order to save my life. While I was grateful for being saved, the method he used to get me out of the clutches of Max Carlyle still gave me nightmares. The remembered taste of his blood on my lips made me shiver, and not entirely in a bad way. Disgusted and horrified as I was, it had been an electrifying experience to feel so needed, so safe, so complete, while under his sway.

As you might imagine, I'd done everything possible to keep the hell away from him since then.

I thought changing my cell phone number might have helped my efforts to keep him and some of the other undesirable elements of my past from contacting me, but the number to my office was plastered all over the Yellow Pages and the Internet. I wasn't thrilled to know he wanted to talk to me again, but having him call me was marginally better than having him show up here at my office or, worse yet, at my apartment.

Grumbling under my breath, I lifted the receiver and punched in the password to listen to the messages. There were a couple others I had to wade through before Royce's smooth, cultured voice came on the line.

"This is Alec, and I'm leaving a message for Ms. Waynest. Shiarra, I just wanted to make sure you know that whatever happens while you are out of town is not my doing. If someone tries to make it appear otherwise, I'd appreciate being informed so that I can take action. I hope all is well with you, and enjoy your vacation."

Well that was confusing. Both Jack and Royce were telling me they weren't responsible for whatever was going to happen while I was out of town. First and foremost, how the hell did either of them find out I was travelling? I don't post my itinerary on the ten o'clock news. Second, what was it they were so worried about?

It wasn't unusual for Royce to cover his bases. Though he hadn't tried contacting me since I'd run away from his home after the blood bond wore off, it wasn't entirely out of character for him to make efforts to keep his name out of anything potentially nefarious. If he was worried that something might upset some plans of his or make him look bad, he'd take action.

Jack covering his ass didn't make any sense to me. We hadn't parted on the best of terms. Actually, the last time I'd seen him, I was walking out of the White Hat Super Secret Ninja Hideout after announcing that I felt safer with the monsters than I did with the hunters.

Yeah, I do need to brush up on my people skills a bit.

Regardless, it didn't matter. Whatever it was they were worried about couldn't possibly be any worse than what I'd already been through. Fighting mad sorcerers and psychotic vampires was not on the to-do list while I was on vacation. I was anticipating a few awkward moments since this trip was geared around me getting to know Chaz's unofficial family better, but that shouldn't have been enough to make either Royce or Jack stir themselves into giving me some kind of warning.

Chaz and I had been discussing doing something like this for a while. The biggest problem with our relationship is that Chaz is a werewolf. He's the leader of the Sunstriker tribe, one of a few packs that live in and around New York City. The Moonwalkers have the biggest pack in town and they'd laid claim to Central Park, along with a bunch of the parks and reserves all up and down Long Island. That meant the Sunstrikers and many of the other smaller packs had to head out to places like Caumsett State Park, the Blue Mountain Reservation, or even as far as the Catskill Mountains when getting together as a group to run as a pack or to hunt. All that travel just to avoid difficulties with the Moonwalkers.

It was pretty inconvenient for the smaller packs. Not everyone can explain away needing to take three or four days off from work every month around the full moon without people getting suspicious about what they're doing in their time off or why they keep going out of town.

So, as you might imagine, the parks and preserves not claimed by the Moonwalkers were always coveted and fiercely protected. Sometimes the smaller packs get into skirmishes with each other when they end up vying for the same hunting grounds on the full moon. It generally didn't get so out of hand that humans, like me, got caught up in their problems. However, if Chaz and I ended up staying close together during the height of the moon cycle, I would need to be prepared to have lots and lots of furry critters around. There was also the possibility that he might take pack problems home with him now and again, and neither one of us were too keen to have me get involved in that sort of thing.

This vacation was our "trial run" to see how I might handle having a whole crapload of shifted Weres around me during the full moon. We'd drive up there tonight, and the daylight hours would be devoted to getting to know the people that made up his tribe. Friday, Saturday, and Sunday night, the moon would be full, and I would get to see them together as a pack. I'd have to be careful, though. Tempers would be short and some of them might change before the full moon.

No doubt, this would be one weird four-day weekend. I was reasonably certain I could handle it. As long as Chaz was with me, I would be fine.

To be honest, I was more excited about the prospect of

staying in a cabin out in the woods with Chaz than seeing a bunch of furry people running around in the dark but, hey, I could handle it.

Though I was awfully nervous about the contract I'd been in the process of signing when Jack called. While we'd resumed dating, Chaz and I hadn't slept together since he revealed what he was. Legally, he couldn't touch me. Even sleeping in the same cabin would be pushing it—but I was tired of how careful we had to be, how distant he was with me after both Royce and that psycho vampire, Max Carlyle, had temporarily bound me to them by blood. By offering to sign a *Notice of Mutual Consent to Human/Other Citizen Relationship and Contractual Binding Agreement* with him, it should make him sit up and take notice that I wasn't going anywhere, that I truly wanted to be with him, and prove that I trusted him again.

My worry was whether or not he trusted *me* enough to sign it, too.

This little camping trip seemed like the perfect opportunity to make things right between us. We'd gotten a good group discount at a small resort up in the Catskills. It was too early for snow, and it would be too cold to tempt many vacationers. Plus, now that school was back in session, tourist season was officially over. Chaz had assured me that the guy who owned the property wouldn't have any problem with the Sunstrikers—he was also Were. One well known among the supernatural community for having bought a bunch of forestland out in the mountains and cordoning off his borders to keep out hunters and tourists while letting any packs staying with him know exactly how far out they could safely range on the hunt.

It was hard to picture anything going wrong. After all, I'd been introduced to Chaz's pack before. We'd even gone out to dinner or the movies with a few of them. The only other time I'd seen the entire pack in one place was when we showed up to fight David Borowsky, the crazed sorcerer who meant to enslave all of the Weres and vampires in New York using a weird magic artifact. Sure, they were dangerous, but since I was the pack leader's girlfriend and had helped save their furry butts, as long as I didn't do anything too stupid, they should be able to hold their hungers and tempers in check.

What could go wrong?

I pondered these things while I stared at the contract. Screw it. I tucked the papers away in my bag and followed Jen's example, amusing myself with a card game while I waited for the clock to tick by and Chaz to come pick me up.

Thrilling Suspense from
Beverly Barton

Available Wherever Books Are Sold!

Visit our website at **www.kensingtonbooks.com**

Romantic Suspense from
Lisa Jackson

Title	ISBN	Price
See How She Dies	0-8217-7605-3	$6.99US/$9.99CAN
Final Scream	0-8217-7712-2	$7.99US/$10.99CAN
Wishes	0-8217-6309-1	$5.99US/$7.99CAN
Whispers	0-8217-7603-7	$6.99US/$9.99CAN
Twice Kissed	0-8217-6038-6	$5.99US/$7.99CAN
Unspoken	0-8217-6402-0	$6.50US/$8.50CAN
If She Only Knew	0-8217-6708-9	$6.50US/$8.50CAN
Hot Blooded	0-8217-6841-7	$6.99US/$9.99CAN
Cold Blooded	0-8217-6934-0	$6.99US/$9.99CAN
The Night Before	0-8217-6936-7	$6.99US/$9.99CAN
The Morning After	0-8217-7295-3	$6.99US/$9.99CAN
Deep Freeze	0-8217-7296-1	$7.99US/$10.99CAN
Fatal Burn	0-8217-7577-4	$7.99US/$10.99CAN
Shiver	0-8217-7578-2	$7.99US/$10.99CAN
Most Likely to Die	0-8217-7576-6	$7.99US/$10.99CAN
Absolute Fear	0-8217-7936-2	$7.99US/$9.49CAN
Almost Dead	0-8217-7579-0	$7.99US/$10.99CAN
Lost Souls	0-8217-7938-9	$7.99US/$10.99CAN
Left to Die	1-4201-0276-1	$7.99US/$10.99CAN
Wicked Game	1-4201-0338-5	$7.99US/$9.99CAN
Malice	0-8217-7940-0	$7.99US/$9.49CAN

Available Wherever Books Are Sold!
Visit our website at **www.kensingtonbooks.com**